The Curie Conundrum

Donald and Jackie Rosenblatt

First Edition Trade Paperback
April 1992

Seabar
PUBLISHING

Salt Lake City, UT

Seabar Publishing, Inc.
P.O. Box 25726, Salt Lake City, UT 84125
(SAN 297-6102)

This first edition trade paperback first published in 1992 by Seabar Publishing.

Printed and manufactured in the United States of America.

ISBN 1-56672-001-x

The Curie Conundrum

Donald and Jackie Rosenblatt

CREDITS

Special thanks to Princeton University Press, University of California Press, and Warner/Chappell Music, Inc. for allowing us to reprint selected passages of the following copyrighted material.

Copyright information for reprinted works:

This story is a work of fiction and all of its characters are imaginary. Many of the places described are real, but many are not. The scientific information about superconductivity is factual; some of the authors quoted are real, some are not. While the temperature of superconductivity is rising each year, a material superconductive at room temperature has yet to be discovered.

Any reference to the Curies and the Institut du Radium is purely fictional, although the building does exist in Paris and was the inspiration for this book.

PROLOGUE

April, 1906

The weary man rose at last from his seat at the work bench. The copper cauldron before him finally contained a cluster of shiny black crystals, the result of his tedious efforts to extract the barium impurities from uranium ore. As he stretched to ease his tired muscles, his arm dislodged the contents of the shelf above.

From the jumble of pots and bits of glassware, a sintered powdered core magnet tumbled toward the copper pot, hit the rim, and broke into tiny fragments. A piece of magnet about the size of a pea floated merrily a few centimeters above the black crystals, suspended in mid-air.

Rubbing his eyes in disbelief, the man fumbled for his pencil in the pocket of his leather apron. Hallucination or not, he carefully documented the phenomenon in his laboratory journal. He trembled with excitement as he poured the shiny crystals into a sample jar and twisted firm its glass stopper. He then labeled the jar and placed it in his secured storage cabinet.

Anxious to discuss the event with his wife, Marie, he rushed into the darkened street. Turning towards Pont Neuf, his mind racing with possibilities, he failed to see the horse drawn coach bearing down on him.

Dust slowly settled over the lifeless body as the heavy coach disappeared into the night.

CHAPTER 1

FRIDAY, JUNE 5

The shrill alarm of the telephone jolted Charles Holden out of his sleep. His long limbs unfolded from the tangle of white sheets like the blades of a Swiss army knife. Spikes of brown hair rose like a corkscrew as his head poked through the covers, his long arm reaching, searching for a way to end the unwelcome intrusion. A spear of light stabbed through a tiny slit in the blackout drapes, causing his eyes to wince in sudden pain, the more sensitive green eye closing in self defense.

"Why the hell didn't you return my call?" The abrasive voice was just as unpleasant as the telephone's ring. Herman Butler, the hard-driving CEO of Consolidated Electronics Company demanded. "It's almost nine, and we have to talk."

Rolling over, Charles was surprised to see that his digital clock-radio agreed.

"What's so urgent, Herman? It was too late to call you last night when I checked my answering machine. Besides, I still haven't seen a check for the Thornton job. Before we talk, what about my money?"

"I told accounting to pay you, but one of our new scorekeepers wants to know why a corporate investigator commands ten thousand dollars just to go down to Thornton to do a little snooping . . ."

Charles cut him short. "Herman, you know how I work and what I charge. No surprises. And, I did find that guy you were after, the one selling rejected hearing aids in Mexico."

"Yes, and I promise you'll get your check. I'll bring it when we meet with Griman."

"Griman who?"

"Get over here as fast as you can, and I'll tell you all about it. You have some learning to do before we meet this guy." Herman hung up before Charles could answer.

* * *

The shiny chrome and glass entrance to Translators International, its beckoning silver arrow pointing "UP," gleamed in contrast to the dull, inconspicuous and shabby travel related businesses crowding the area where Avenue of the Americas leads into Greenwich Village near 11th and 12th Streets in Manhattan.

It had been over a year since Karen Bright had marched boldly past the faded and outdated travel posters pasted askew in the windows, grimy and streaked, and stepped into the polished private elevator leading to the TI offices on the third floor, hoping she was traveling to a new career.

When Karen began work as a technical translator with Translators International, her ease in handling scientific terminology surfaced rapidly. Her upcoming assignment as a translator in Berlin at a conference on superconductivity was a real plum, and by adding some vacation time, she could spend a few days in Paris after the meetings. Afterwards, the company would pay her passage home on a new French luxury liner.

Karen, comfortable in her private office, was carefully examining a *Royale* brochure, feet propped on her desk with a goodly amount of shapely thigh exposed, when an out-of-shape body in shiny polyester pushed through the doorway without knocking. The sun-wrinkled face was topped by a drooping forehead and scalp sparsely sprinkled with rusty hair. She felt the leering stare even before she saw the unannounced visitor.

"I know," she said, retrieving her skirt and hastily shifting to a sitting position, "the door was ajar, so you just came in."

"Well, they told me to go right to your office down the hall. I'm Frank Griman . . ." he paused as the phone buzzed.

"Karen," said the conniving voice of TI's director, J. Lawrence Johnson, speaking low to keep from being overheard, "some fellow named Griman is on his way down. The guy may be some kinda kook, claims he has a letter written by Marie Curie in December 1933. The thing looks real to me, but watch yourself. I told him our rates per page for technical French, and he's given me a check. I'll call the bank while you're working on it." He clicked off abruptly.

Chafing at the way her boss got her into jobs without consulting her first, Karen hung up and watched the paunchy man in the rumpled brown suit settle into the chair as he placed two worn yellowish sheets of paper on her desk.

"This letter is from Marie Curie to a Dr. Georges Colbert." Griman watched for Karen's expression of disbelief, but she showed no reaction. "I bought a desk at a secondhand sale last week," Griman continued. "It came from the chemistry department at Columbia University. This Professor Colbert was, I've heard, quite a famous scientist at Columbia back in the thirties. Anyhow, this letter was stuck behind the front drawer. I never would have found it if I hadn't needed to practically dismantle the desk in order to get it into my den."

Karen continued to be politely attentive. She was damned if she was going to display any excitement to this lecherous looking character, even though what he was saying certainly piqued her interest. She wasn't quite sure just what it was about this guy that had triggered her distaste so rapidly.

"Well, my high school French is pretty rusty, so when I saw the 1933 date and Marie Curie's signature, and the French postmark on the envelope, I figured it's time to get an accurate translation. But your outfit is certainly pricey." Griman again awaited some kind of response.

"I'm sure you've done the right thing, Mr. Griman. A letter like this could be a valuable museum article at Columbia." Karen wondered as she spoke if this were really true.

"Yeah, that's what I thought, but there's more to it than that. Madame Curie is asking for certain scientific verification of some chemical experiments, I think. But, as I said, my French just isn't good enough. At least she typed the letter; that makes it easier."

Griman felt he was in control of the interview, and this girl must be smart enough to help, and she certainly was good to look at, even though she was all business.

"I can't do it for you right now." Karen looked at her watch. "It's close to five. I'll take it home tonight. Why don't you come in around ten tomorrow? I should be able to have a typed translation for you by then."

"Miss Bright, if this letter is valuable, and your company has both my check and the letter, that leaves me a little disadvantaged."

"Actually, it's Dr. Bright. I hold a Ph.D. in modern languages. Your letter is in responsible hands."

Griman didn't really smell a rat, but he was curious as to how she would handle this objection. He had already decided the letter was worth a fortune. "Nothing personal, it just doesn't seem right to . . ."

"If you feel that way, why don't you just keep the letter tonight and bring it in tomorrow? Then you can sit right here and wait while I try to get the job done for you."

"Well, Miss Bright — Ms. Bright — the way you put it, I guess you're pretty dedicated to doing a good job. You just go ahead and take the letter. I'm sure I can trust you. You won't show it to anyone or make copies or talk about it, will you?"

Griman had leaned forward out of his chair. Karen couldn't tell if he was trying to make threatening eye contact or if he was just trying to look down the front of her dress.

"You have my word." Karen smiled for the first time. "Our work is always confidential; we're very much aware of such problems. That's why we're all bonded." She rose and ushered Griman to the door.

"See you at 10:15. Is it Karen?" he ventured.

"Karen is fine; Dr. Bright's a bit formal." She was glad to know the next meeting would not be prolonged.

* * *

It was midafternoon when Charles Holden returned to his bachelor apartment just off Central Park, shaking his head in disbelief as he dumped an armload of books on the table next to his friendly red leather chair. Automatically returning the sunglasses he always wore outdoors—to protect the lighter of his two-colored eyes—to their protective case, he reviewed his discussion with Butler. Never know where this business will take me, he thought. I haven't been to Europe in four years, and now I'm gallivanting off to Paris on a job that sounds like some nutty movie script. Evidently Griman has been hard to persuade that the services of a professional investigator are necessary, but Butler is convinced it will mean a fortune for his company if the stuff can be found. Now if I can figure out just what I'm supposed to be looking for . . . I'm sure glad Joe is available.

He had just discarded his go-to-meeting necktie and shrugged into a soft old tennis shirt when the door buzzer sounded.

"Joe, come on up," he said, pushing the door release button by the small speaker in the wall.

"Hope you've got something cold to drink up there, it's just like a blast furnace today." Joe Saunders sounded hopeful.

Looking like a wilted department store clerk just escaped from a bargain basement sale, instead of the distinguished Columbia professor he was, Joe threw his sweat-stained jacket on the couch and tugged open his rumpled collar.

"What's all this crap you told me on the phone about giving you a quick one hour education on electronics?" Joe managed a smile as Charles handed him a frosty bottle of Strohs.

Seeing the slouched figure before him, the wide-set blue eyes over a childlike pug nose, Charles thought, sorry, old buddy, I just can't level with you this time. Charles didn't want to discuss the fact that his new job had to do with the relationship of a former Columbia professor with Marie Curie. Joe probably knew enough about Professor Colbert that such knowledge would provoke a stream of unwanted questions. Deep in his role as hired investigator, the younger man studied Joe now in an appreciative way. He was the best friend Charles had in New York, and he was so damned smart.

"Good of you to come over, Joe," said Charles, giving him a bit of the magnetic smile that had earned him the nickname, 'Dear Sweet Charlie,' from all the girls at school. "I always knew my tennis buddy was a real egghead, but I didn't ever expect I'd need to pick his brains."

"Actually, I don't want an education on electronics, I just want you to explain enough about superconductivity so I can follow what my client wants me to do. This fellow I have to meet tomorrow has one of those keep-your-mouth-shut jobs for me, and he's in a hurry. Joe, what the hell is a superconductor anyway? You're a physicist, so you ought to know."

"Even you must have heard what's going on in the world of science. Your superconductor is probably the hottest item of the last fifty years. Tell me more about this job you're getting." Joe settled into Charles' red leather chair, all ears.

"I'll have to fill you in later, Joe. I'm the one asking the questions. You're supposed to be the answer man." Charles pushed aside the books and found an empty pad and pencil in the drawer of the side table.

Joe Saunders looked thoughtfully at a Mondrian print on the wall and tried to assume a non-professorial approach to explaining superconductivity to his tennis buddy. He knew Charles was no dummy, but he feared boredom would overtake him if the conversation got too technical. However, a simplistic overview probably would not be sufficient for Charles' apparent needs.

"When certain materials get really cold," he began, "I mean really cold, around 450 degrees below zero, they have no resistance to electric currents; they achieve a super conductive state in which they display extraordinary electrical and magnetic properties." He took a healthy swig from the Strohs. "Currents in circular wires at this temperature could flow for longer than the age of the universe." He paused for breath, looking at his now empty beer bottle. Charles took the hint, and went to the refrigerator for a replacement.

"Go on, Joe, I can hear you."

"Well the practical applications for superconductivity are endless. Trains could float from levitating superconductors while traveling in a frictionless state at 300 miles per hour. Smaller, more powerful computers using heat-free, resistance-free superconductors would perform hundreds of times better than present day computers."

"People could afford the medical services of MRI units, you know, those fancy new magnetic resonance imagers that are like 3-D x-rays—they cost about $700 a picture now—because superconductors would, by making them vastly more simple, also make them affordable. Non-loss storage batteries would make electric cars practical—think what that would do for the pollution problem—very high horsepower motors could be made smaller, and on and on."

"You're getting carried away, Joe. I get the idea. I take it none of this has happened because there's no way to get anything cold enough. So, what's the new wrinkle?" Charles wanted more meat and less potatoes.

"When a man named Onnes managed to liquify helium in 1908, working at the University of Leiden in Holland, the investigation of superconductivity became possible because he could achieve a temperature of minus 450 Fahrenheit, or four degrees Kelvin. By the way, since it's such a rare gas, helium costs about six dollars per liter. The use of helium in a cooling system would therefore be extremely expensive and totally impractical. So, even though superconductivity was proven a valid discovery by 1911, it took years for anything valuable to evolve." Joe paused, rendered a sumptuous burp, and again lifted the beer bottle.

Taking a breath, Joe continued, "Then a real breakthrough came in January of 1987 when Paul Chu, a Houston University superconductivity researcher, found a material that is superconductive at the liquid nitrogen temperature of 95 Kelvin or 288 degrees below zero Fahrenheit. Now, liquid nitrogen can be much more easily handled than liquid helium and only costs about 19 cents a liter."

"So what kind of material did Chu come up with?" Charles was trying to relate Chu's discovery to the work of Curie. "Was it a uranium alloy?"

"What made you think of uranium, Charles? Sometimes you surprise me." Joe did not wait for an answer. "Not uranium. Actually, Chu wasn't using what you might expect, like a platinum alloy. High temperature superconductors aren't really metals at all. They are in the family of superconductors from a crystal structure known as perovskites. Chu's material turned out to be a ferro-electric yttrium-barium-copper oxide called YIBCO, having a chemical formula of YBa2Cu3O7."

Joe paused for another swig.

"Shit, man, you're losing me now," Charles interrupted.

"Okay, well anyhow, now all the big guns like Westinghouse, Bell Labs, IBM, Los Alamos, not to mention Nippon Telegraph and Telephone, are all working desperately on similar materials, all in the effort to continue raising that temperature threshold. The first one to find a material that's superconductive at room temperature will really hit the jackpot. Are you following me, Charles?"

"A little bit. But how can those non-metals be used like wires?" Another perceptive query from Charles that surprised Saunders.

"You've got a good question there. Processing useful forms of those ceramic superconductors is certainly tricky, but not insurmountable. The problem is being aggressively pursued on many fronts, such as expansive forming, plasma plating, and magnetic encapsulation." Joe finished his Strohs and shifted forward in the red leather chair. "I see you've got a lot of articles here on the subject. I think you ought to do some reading. From here on it gets a little heavy. I mean, I don't think I can go into the theory of twinned perovskites and keep you awake long enough to count."

Joe looked at watch. "You ready for that tennis game tomorrow?" He seemed to be signing off on his lesson about superconductivity.

"No, this seems to be a hurry-up job; I guess I have to stay here and do my homework. I was really looking forward to a good game after that long sit on the plane home from the Orient. But you've given me a lot to digest in a short time." He swung an imaginary tennis racket with a swoop of his long arms. "Just one more thing before you leave, Joe. If you had a superconductor at room temperature, how would you know it? I mean, is there a simple test?"

"As a matter of fact there is. Could I have another beer?" Joe settled back in his chair.

CHAPTER 2

The entire staff of Translators International was expected to show up on Saturday morning, since much of their work was done for people who could not leave their own jobs during the week. Frank Griman's request for a quick overnight translation had not been a hardship for Karen because she had to be in the office anyway.

Looking perky and much younger than her almost thirty years, Karen was satisfied with her translation of the Marie Curie letter now. She was sure it was accurate and literate as well. A couple of those technical terms had eluded her last night, so she had waited to consult the *Technical French to English Dictionary* before finishing the job here at the office.

As she carefully proofread her work, she was still overwhelmed with the significance of the words written so simply on December 18, 1933, on those four flimsy pieces of paper. Madame Curie knew her husband's discovery should be pursued and had asked her dear friend, Dr. Georges Colbert, for help. What had happened, Karen wondered, that the plea for help should have been disregarded? Surely, Colbert would not have ignored the request. Perhaps the letter was misplaced before it could reach his eyes.

Unusually pensive, her smooth forehead narrowed in a frown. Could the letter possibly be a fake?. If it is, it couldn't be the work of that little weasel Griman. He wouldn't have the imagination, even if he might not be the world's most honest man. No, the letter had to be authentic.

Karen thought about her coming trip to Berlin and the superconductivity conference. "I could enjoy the lifestyles of the rich and famous," she laughed, then, quickly sobering, she told herself, "Now who's less than honest? You have a code of ethics to live by, little girl, and you promised complete secrecy."

She stood up, all businesslike and efficient now, but she answered herself, "Wouldn't hurt to find out what that man intends to do with his knowledge; you don't want it to get into the wrong hands."

She retrieved the pages from the printer and set them on her desk blotter with the pages neatly aligned. The original letter she now sealed in a brown envelope. Then she shredded her handwritten translation and glanced at her watch. Forty minutes before Griman was scheduled to arrive. Time for a trip to the ladies' lounge and the coffee pot in the back hallway.

Across the hall from Karen's office sat T.I.'s newest staff member, Philip Brown, his brawn stuffed into a tight pink shirt with seams strained by bulging biceps. His vapid blue eyes studied the ceiling as he searched for a word. It wouldn't come. He hated the language of patents, and this one, a French patent on Beechnut packaging, was one of T.I.'s more tedious jobs. After examining the library shelf, he stepped into the hall and, with a voice surprisingly high-pitched for a man of his physical stature, shouted, "Anyone seen the French-tech dictionary?"

A female voice from an open door responded, "I think Karen had it this morning."

When Philip Brown entered Karen's office, he glanced quickly around the room, saw the French-tech volume on her credenza, and let his eyes wander to the typed sheets on her desk. The 1933 date on the translation was curious. The inquisitive man said to himself, "Johnson seems to give her the jobs with the most side benefits. Wonder what it is this time? Maybe I can grab a piece of this action."

He picked up the four typed pages, slipped into the Xerox room across the hall, and had the papers back on Karen's desk in less than five minutes. Taking the dictionary he had gone for in the first place, he returned to his office with four new folded pages of manuscript in his inside breast pocket.

* * *

Herman Butler phoned to tell Charles that the Saturday afternoon meeting had been called off.

"I talked to Griman. He said that he's decided to get a better English version of the Curie letter and it won't be ready until Saturday." Butler changed his tone of voice. "I think it's a stall. I think the son-of-a-bitch is getting a lawyer to review the proposed contract we gave him. Anyhow, he's coming to my office late Saturday morning. Why don't you come in early Monday morning. By then I should have had enough time to work out the details. Have you done any homework on our new subject yet?"

"I've learned more than you would believe me capable of, Herman. I might keep at it and miss my Saturday tennis game." Charles wondered why he had admitted that to Herman.

"Good boy. See you Monday." Butler hung up, as he often did, without saying good-bye.

Might as well get started reading, thought Charles as he loaded his tape player with one of the early Brubeck-Desmond recordings, and he sat down to concentrate on the work Joe had referred to about the Meissner effect, the so-called 'simple test' for superconductivity.

Saturday, June 6

Frank Griman pulled his six-year-old Chevy wagon into the garage entrance on the side street off Park Avenue, clumsily turning down the steep driveway into the dim opening.

"Don't you feel self conscious bringing such an old piece of dreck into the General Motors building, Frank?" questioned his passenger, a skinny, chinless fellow who peered sullenly from under heavy but colorless eyebrows.

"This wagon's great, Bill. It suits my hobby. With it I can haul all the stuff I find at those garage sales and auctions. Do you know what delivery costs are these days?" As he got out of the car, Frank wondered why this pimply cousin was always so disagreeable. He knew he'd had a rough time in the Marine Corps, but he was doing very well these days with his law practice; he could at least afford a smile.

"No, and I don't give a rat's ass about delivery, or your hobby for that matter."

"Well, I only asked for your legal help because Ma always wanted me to give my business to family members. Besides, the job is interesting enough to lure you away from your sacred Saturday golf, and there wouldn't have been any job without my hobby." As he spoke, Frank huffed to keep up with Bill's long legs.

"Knock it off, Frank, and take a look at those new cars in that display room over there," said Bill as he pointed to the high ceilinged showroom on the Fifth Avenue side of the lobby. "Now those are wheels!"

"Maybe I'll be able to look at 'wheels' like that if this deal turns out like I hope, and you do a good job protecting my interests in the contract." Frank refused to be intimidated by someone ten years his junior.

"How do we get to this guy's office? There doesn't seem to be any building directory here." Bill stood before the shiny black marble walls at the double bank of elevators.

"They don't use directories anymore," Frank explained, trying not to sound overly smug. "See, you use these push-buttons by this screen, and you get a readout index." He punched in the letters for Consolidated Electronics. Instantly, a long list of names, each with a corresponding office number, appeared on the lighted panel on the wall before them. "There it is, Bill: H.E. Butler, 3514. Let's go up." He led the younger man to the elevators.

Upstairs at the front desk, the receptionist with the frozen smile consulted her appointment book, going through the formal motions even though she'd been called to work Saturday just for this one appointment. She studied the unlikely pair, the unattractive tall man in the ill-fitting suit, and the scruffy little guy who looked like a used car salesman. This must be some weird deal, she told herself. I get time-and-a-half for Saturdays, and Mr. Butler doesn't throw money away.

"Will you please tell Mr. Butler that Mr. Griman and Mr. Higginbotham are here?" Frank gave the long legged girl his up and down inspection, relishing the view.

Inside Butler's office the message came through the intercom. His barrel chest and ample belly thinly disguised by his carefully tailored vested suit, the ruddy faced, brusk CEO waited with Jim Collins, Consolidated's in-house counsel. Collins, looking like a typical New York Yuppie, minus the vest but wearing a neatly knotted silk tie, sat across the room on the white leather couch.

"Who the hell is Higginbotham?" asked the attorney.

"The guy probably brought his own lawyer," Herman answered. "I thought he used the translation bit as a stall. He seemed to have a pretty good grasp of French when he showed me the letter."

He pushed the red lever connecting him with the outer office. "Show them in, Louise." Herman moved three chairs to face his rosewood desk.

At their first meeting Butler had been so fascinated by the Curie letter he had paid little attention to the man who brought it in. Now, as Griman stood before him, Butler looked at the man's shoes to see if they were, like his, tastefully expensive, and then at his shirt to locate, also like his own, a suitable hand-stitched monogram. Finding neither, Herman congratulated himself on lowering his first thought of paying a million down to a half million. He was proud of his ability to save Consolidated those important costs. As for the so-called lawyer, he was something else again. Judging from the suit and case of acne, he was probably fresh out of some podunk law school.

Introductions finished, Herman opened the meeting with his most businesslike tone, saying, "Mr. Griman, let's get right down to work here. None of us likes working on Saturday, but this business has a high priority. I see you've brought the contract with you. Let's just go over the basics here and make sure we all understand each other." He extracted his copy of the contract from the desk drawer.

Bill Higginbotham cleared his throat and interjected, "I'm here to see that my client's confidences thus far offered are duly protected."

"Nothing to worry about there, Higginbottom," Butler soothed, purposely mispronouncing the name, "I have a check for ten thousand dollars all ready for your client." Herman continued quickly to forestall any objections.

"Collins, why don't you just give us the nuts and bolts of the contract so we can have Frank sign it. I've already hired Charles Holden to do the searching, and I want him to leave for Paris next week, if possible. So the sooner we get this contract out of the way the better." He addressed himself to

Higginbotham, explaining, "Holden doesn't come cheap, but he's absolutely tops in his line of work. If anyone can find what we're looking for, Holden can."

Clearing his throat, Collins faced Higginbotham and began, "Now, according to the letter under discussion, Marie Curie wrote to Professor Colbert in 1933, telling him that she was in possession of a certain compound discovered by her husband . . ."

"I'm aware of all this, Collins. I have read the letter." Bill Higginbotham was impatient with the tone of condescension.

"Now, see here, Griman," Butler spoke as his face flushed with sudden anger, "just how the hell many people have read the Curie letter?"

"Just the four of us here, and I suppose Professor Colbert, who's been dead for decades. And, of course, the girl at Translators International who put it into this English version." Frank decided he would throw the ball back into Butler's court. "How about your man Holden? Have you shown it to him?"

Butler ignored the question and said, "About that translation, Griman, why did you go to Translators International? We could have had the job done without risk of exposure to strangers."

"The firm was highly recommended by the Better Business Bureau, and the girl didn't know a superconductor from a spastic squirrel. She thought the letter might be valuable to Columbia University, or maybe a museum. I didn't arouse her suspicions that the letter could have some other value. I just let her take it home to work on." Frank realized his reassurances were weak.

"What's done is done," Butler conceded. "You'd better give me the girl's name. I'll have her checked out. Let's get on with the contract terms, Collins."

Jim Collins shuffled his papers and coughed. Bill Higginbotham watched with disdain, wondering how a lawyer with any talent at all could confine his work to dealing with pompous jerks like this.

"Number one," Collins began, "Consolidated will pay ten thousand up front, with the balance of $490,000 in an escrow account. The escrow funds will be released to Mr. Griman after delivery of the Curie material and proof, probably by the Meissner Effect test, that the material is a high temperature superconductor. The front money, however, can be retained by Mr. Griman, regardless of Consolidated's securing the Curie compound, provided that:

"A: Consolidated's investigator is the sole party attempting to obtain the Curie material from France.

"B: Mr. Griman and his counsel (whom I have just now included) do not make any disclosure, written or oral, of the Curie document to any person—that will, of course exclude those now present and the girl, Karen Bright did you say her name is?

"C: Mr. Griman will forfeit all monies paid to him by Consolidated Electronics, and will pay an additional sum of ten thousand dollars to them, if the aforementioned Curie letter is proven to be a forgery or otherwise intentionally falsified or misleading document."

Jim Collins paused to see how Bill and Frank were reacting to the contract terms then added, "D: If Consolidated's agent has not been successful in the search for the Curie material within thirty days, all rights are returned to Mr. Griman, and the escrow will be dissolved. Any question?"

"Yes," Frank said, "Just what is this 'Meissner Effect test' you mentioned? Is it complicated, would I be able to witness and understand it?"

Herman Butler jumped in before Collins could start a tedious explanation. "It's really very simple, Frank. It's just an office procedure done with a magnet, and, yes, you can be present to observe. You will not have any doubt about the results. If the material is really a superconductor, you'll be able to see for yourself immediately."

"I advise my client to go ahead and sign the contract, Mr. Butler," said Bill, taking a pen from his inside jacket pocket. "Now, where's his check?"

* * *

Most of the staff had fled the office at noon, chattering and laughing as they hurried to whatever plans they had for the shortened weekend. Karen lingered to double check her briefcase, make sure she had everything necessary for her trip to Berlin and the assignment at the conference on superconductors.

She was scheduled to leave Monday night on the TWA red eye. She would stop in Hamburg, then fly on to Berlin. The conference did not start until Thursday, but TI did not want its promised translators showing up late because of airline delays. That's fine with me, thought Karen, I'm happy for the extra time; it'll give me a chance to do a bit of tourist exploring.

"What other flights do you have?" somebody said from another office.

Surprised by the sound of a man's voice, Karen strained to listen, then heard, "I said, what other flights do you have to get me to Paris on Monday?" Then came the sound of an eraser drumming on a desk. Karen relaxed. Philip hadn't been on staff that long, but everyone in the office could recognize his pencil drumming habit. She went back to her organizing.

Analyzing all the materials from the International Conference of Electronics Materials Society, she decided each presentation would last about twenty minutes. She would have four papers to translate orally for the general session in the main auditorium, and another three on Friday morning. Only three of the eight papers had been pre-printed in English. She noted that she would be going from English to German on Thursday's papers, and from either French or English to Russian on Friday's. Thank God they're not in Japanese, she thought as she read the title of the first scheduled paper Friday morning: *Tests on Thallium Perovskites* by Shiraka Hidek. She could speak a little Japanese, but—read it? Forget it!

Looking at the various titles in the program, Karen could not keep her mind from wandering to the Curie letter. She wondered if Frank Griman had any idea of the sensation that letter would cause at this Berlin conference. When she had asked what he intended to do with the letter, he'd said he would probably sell it to a museum, but he hadn't reached any decision. Karen resolved to stick to her promise of confidentiality, yet she suspected Frank Griman already had ulterior plans for profit. He had danced her around a little too casually, feigning ignorance of anything to do with superconductivity.

Concentrating on the electronics conference was difficult. Besides Griman and his letter, Karen was distracted by ideas for making the most of her very few days in Paris. She would definitely go to Galleries Lafayette for some French lingerie; for years she had yearned for replacement of a gift from there. Who's going to see me in such finery anyway, her inner mind questioned. I am, she answered herself, I guess that's enough reason.

Philip Brown knocked on her door.

"Karen, why are you still here? Don't you have anything better to do on this beautiful day?" He entered uninvited. Looking at him lounging against the wall, his skin too smooth and his lips too pouty, Karen decided that Philip would be the last man this side of Alpha Centauri to see her in her new French lingerie.

"I might ask you the same thing, Philip. You never spend an extra minute around this place. What's keeping you here?"

Philip contemplated Karen's figure, thinking she certainly did good things to that red sweater. "Well, Johnson wants that Beechnut patent finished, and I'm going to Paris Monday. I hear you're off, to Berlin, isn't it?" He wondered if she wore a bra under that sweater.

"I'm leaving Monday night, doing a technical conference in Berlin." She decided to pretend she hadn't heard his call. "What's taking you to Paris?"

"Just made up my mind I needed a week or so off. I talked to Johnson this morning, and he gave his okay if I could wind up the patent translation. You aren't going by way of Paris perchance, are you, Karen?"

"I'm going to stop there on my way back. I haven't arranged exactly when or where I'll be staying," she lied smoothly. She had confirmed reservations at the Intercontinental in Paris, but damned if she'd pass this information on to Philip Brown.

If there was one thing she definitely did not need in her life right now, it was some ego-tripping jock. Besides, after her divorce she had become wary of most men. Walter Bright had been a mistake of youth, a mistake she would never make again. As Walter had been, Philip was tall, smooth and sensuous. However, Karen knew from watching him at the office, Philip was certainly no one to trust. It seemed to her he was an opportunist and most interested in one Philip Brown, putting him in what she considered to be very shallow company.

"Why don't you have dinner with me at the Riviera Cafe tonight?" Philip suddenly ventured. "We can talk over our forthcoming trips abroad."

She heard herself saying, "That sounds okay to me, but it had better be on the early side. I've left a lot of homework for tomorrow." The Riviera Cafe suddenly seemed a welcome substitute for grocery shopping and cooking, or settling for a TV dinner. Besides, she worked with the creep anyway.

"Great. I'll meet you there at seven." Philip turned around and marched back toward his office.

Dates nowadays are too New Yorkish, Karen thought. Nobody ever says, "I'll pick you up and take you to dine." Just as well; I don't want him to come near my place!

* * *

Charles balanced a large box of crackers, a knife, and a jar of peanut butter, and headed for the kitchen table where books and papers were strewn. The phone rang. He detoured to the phone by the red chair and dumped his load on the little table.

"Charles, it's Herman Butler. Are you there?" Without waiting for an answer, he continued, "We had another meeting with Griman today. He brought his half-assed attorney with him, probably some relative. Anyhow, I did get a signed contract delivered, and I don't think we should wait until Monday to get cooking on this Curie Business."

"Oh, yeah?" Charles fumbled with the cracker box, phone cradled between shoulder and ear.

"It turns out Griman has already given the letter some exposure that worries me. Some outfit down in the Village did a translation. A girl, Karen Bright, who works for this Translators International, has read the whole thing."

"Herman, you're always in a big rush. I have a tennis game tomorrow morning, and I'm sure as hell not going to meet you tonight. Besides, my price goes up for working on Sunday. You know this technical reading you have me doing comes slower to a guy who's been out of college a few years." Charles got the lid off the peanut butter jar and stuck his finger in for a taste test.

"Forget the homework, Charles. You can do that on the plane to Paris. I've got your reservations. But I'm concerned about Griman and this French translator. You know if the French government finds out what we're doing, I'll never get that superconductor into our Jersey lab, and that's what we have to be sure to do." Herman was throwing out flak faster than Charles could catch it.

"Okay, Herman, as I've told you before, I'm only in this for the money. I'll meet you at the Gotham Tennis Club lunchroom at 1:30 tomorrow. You know how to get there? In the meantime, I know a guy I can put on this Translators International gal right away, but Griman will have to be your problem. Oh, by the way, can you bring the famous letter with you? By now I'd really like to study it."

"Charles, you ain't privy to that letter, but I'll bring you everything you need to get the job done. I have that Thornton check for you, so you can buy me lunch at your club. See you there at 1:30." Click. Dial tone.

* * *

The Riviera Cafe, situated all alone on a small, triangular block just north of Sheridan Square, hummed with activity this warm June evening. Close to the longest day of the year, the sky was still light, but hurricane candles burned on the tables outside on the patio where groups of diners were happily enjoying the rare mellow atmosphere.

Even though Karen and Philip, arriving almost simultaneously, were early by New York standards, no more outdoor tables were available, so they took a tiny window table just inside the busy entrance.

"I've been hoping we could get together ever since I came to TI," Philip said, unfolding an oversized napkin after admiring Karen's cool linen summer dress and seating her ceremoniously.

"Oh?" Karen feigned surprise. You're about as subtle as a wrecking ball, she thought.

"Being in the same business, so to speak, we could help each other by sharing know-how. This conference in Germany you're working, for instance, sounds great. Was it your idea or a Johnson assignment?" Philip tried to put the pieces together; answers could affect his actions. Did the Curie letter come before the jaunt to Europe was planned? How long has she known about it?

Karen took a sip of her white wine, the house brand, which turned out to be French and damned expensive. The first course arrived, a steaming lobster bisque, truly an achievement par excellence, Karen thought, returning to Philip's questions about the conference.

"It's just the usual stuff, Philip, the company's assignment. I'm going to Berlin to do some oral translations of technical papers. Four English-to-German the first morning. The second morning's a little tougher, French-to-Russian. You've done that kind, haven't you?" Karen studied Philip more closely. He's a lot like Walter, she thought. Couldn't pick out the right tie if his life depended on it.

"You give me more credit than I deserve, Karen. I can't speak Russian well enough for a Russian to understand me, so I gave that one up a long time ago. What's the subject of your conference, another one of those medical ones on AIDS?" Philip watched her alluring brown eyes scan his tie, proudly convinced he was making some points on this silk number. He had known that it would pay off someday.

"I'm supposed to do an AIDS seminar next month in Chicago." She gently inserted her spoon into the delicate bisque. "This one's on superconductivity," she continued, "if you know what that is."

Philip's lips almost formed "no shit!" as he dropped his napkin on the floor. He bent to pick it up, getting a good look at Karen's magnificent legs as he reached. Great as they were, the impact of her last words dulled their turn-on value. It couldn't be just a coincidence, could it? Superconductivity, the Curie letter, her stopping in Paris on the way home. What the hell was going on here?

"Sorry about that," Philip managed to voice. "I'm sure getting sloppy in my old age." The waiter's busy changing of plates gave him time to collect himself. "How are you getting back to New York, and when will you be in the office?"

"Not sure yet, Philip. I'm thinking of maybe catching the new ship, *Royale*, home, but I haven't worked it out just yet. At least it would be a welcome change from the boredom of those trans-Atlantic flights." Karen evaded this query with the same skill she had used regarding the subject of her Paris hotel. She had been assigned an outside single stateroom on the *Royale's* fourth deck and could hardly wait to occupy it.

"Do you know anything about superconductivity, Philip? I've looked at the pre-printed papers they sent for the conference. I gather this is THE most exciting new frontier of science if you read between the lines. It seems they're all researching like mad for a material that has a practical application." Karen chattered easily, thinking Philip might have some background from his own technical translations, and hoping to divert him from talk about her plans.

"I know a little about it," Philip dodged, very careful not to give the slightest clue that he had read the Curie translation. "I translated a Swiss paper from the IBM lab in Zurich for a professor at the University of California a few months ago, although I didn't pay much attention to the details. There was one other occasion, a federal conference on the commercial applications of superconductivity last March. The President appointed a commission then to establish our national program, and I translated a news story about that into Japanese for our Mr. Johnson—I can't remember where he sent it. But I do remember a funny description of all these high government mucky-mucks sitting around watching a little magnet suspended over some really cold stuff."

The arrival of the salad course gave Philip a chance to study her reaction to his words. "Have you translated anything about superconductivity around here lately?" He tried to make his question sound like a natural follow-up.

"This German thing is the first I've heard about it." Karen leaned to one side while the waiter replaced her soup bowl with salad plate. This conversation was bringing the Curie letter into sharp focus. The letter graphically described Pierre Curie watching as a tiny magnet hung over a petri dish full of some strange compound. Karen was off in another world. She jumped back to attention when Philip spoke.

"I believe they call it the Meissner Effect," Philip said.

"What?" Karen now wondered if Philip was reading her thoughts.

"You know, the floating magnet bit. Kinda cute, don't you think? One of those IBM papers I translated made the point that the measuring of superconductivity with an electrical apparatus was a very big, expensive laboratory setup. Now this Meissner Effect, a ten-year old kid could run that test, even though he wouldn't understand that he was watching, quote, 'the expulsion of a magnetic field from within a material,' unquote, as the paper said."

"Let's get back to your trip to Paris, Philip. Do you have a girlfriend meeting you?" Karen wanted to stop thinking about Marie Curie's letter. It wasn't her business to get involved, yet the temptation was a constant threat. She wished that she had never heard of Mr. Griman and his damned letter.

"I'm just a lonesome old bachelor, Karen. I'm going alone. That's why I thought you might meet me in Paris." His lame attempt at enticement couldn't be much more obvious.

"I doubt if you'll be lonesome for long. But I thought you were a divorcee, not a bachelor. At any rate, I don't think you can qualify yet for senior discounts." Karen loved her French salad, so full of endive with a touch of fennel. The mustard dressing heightened it perfectly.

"Interesting that you know I'm a divorcee. I guess in a place like TI there are no secrets in any language. It was really a rather brief adventure. Incompatibility, as the old saying goes. I didn't have enough in-come, and she didn't have enough pat-a-bility. Maybe I'll find a wealthy French lady, you never know." Philip wished the French salad had more lettuce; this thing tasted like wilted licorice.

"So you're going to Paris on a lady hunt?" She thought the odds were not good. A lady wrestler, perhaps, might be attracted to Philip. Personally, she thought there was something sinister about him, something she couldn't define.

"Actually, I'm going there to brush up on my French. I don't hear enough of it spoken in New York to be a good translator. Helps to get over there every couple of years. I'd go more often if I didn't hate flying so much."

At least he's candid about a weakness, Karen thought. "Good point, I agree. Where did you say you were staying?"

"A hotel near the Sorbonne. It's the Grand Hotel de Lima on Boulevard St. Germain. I want to be near the Sorbonne. I could get help there with my technical French. It's my bugaboo." He wanted to work up a little sympathy in his dinner companion. Might help him extract a bit more information about the connection of the Superconductivity Conference in Berlin with her trip to Paris.

At the mention of the Sorbonne, Karen had another mental flash of Marie Curie's letter. The paragraph about the laboratory at the great university jumped into her thoughts.

Two kilos of black barium compound were moved from the shed to our PCN laboratory of the Sorbonne on Rue Cuvier. Laboratory sample flacon No. 16 then accompanied my later move to the Radium Institute on Rue Pierre Curie. All the old apparatus and materials were kept intact, remarkably, throughout our three laboratory relocations. I'm sorry to report, Georges, that in removing the old jar from storage, I found the aged vessel had cracked and much of the compound was lost. Fortunately, I managed to save about 300 grams, which I have now carefully hidden. Georges, when (or if) you come, my journal for December has the information you'll need. I give you this in the event my physician's indications are correct and before you arrive my battle with my beloved radium, which is eating me away with each tick of the clock, may be final.

"Are you okay, Karen?" Philip reached across the table and grasped her shoulder. "You look a million miles away and kinda pale."

"I'm fine, Philip. Watch your sleeve, the jus."

Karen was surprised at the thought suddenly replacing Madame Curie's words. Could Philip know about the Curie letter? No, just a ridiculous coincidence.

They finished the meal with small talk, and Philip's suggestion came as expected soon after leaving the Riviera Cafe. They were strolling across Sheridan Square when he unabashedly assumed they would spend the night together.

"No, thanks. I'm not into that, Philip. It was a great dinner, but, as I told you this afternoon, I've got homework tonight. Besides, I think you should save yourself for Paris. That wealthy French lady would appreciate your being a little randy when you find her," Karen teased.

"If I find her, I'll let you know when you call me in Paris—and I hope you will."

She could feel his eyes following her as she walked away without giving him an answer.

CHAPTER 3

Sunday, June 7

"How's your superconductor study coming, Charles? It certainly hasn't hurt your tennis." Joe Saunders still smarted from another defeat. He had expected a big advantage because of Charles' jet lag after his trip to the Orient last week.

"Gaining on it, Joe. Sorry we can't have lunch. I've got a date upstairs with my employer." Charles noted that he was already late. His Tokyo-purchased fake Rolex showed 1:35. He vaulted up the outside steps from the locker room to the club's cafe.

The Gotham Tennis club on Long Island was not the posh sort of club Herman Butler usually frequented, but by following Charles' directions he'd had no trouble finding it. When the old club revealed itself, not far from the Metropole hotel, Herman idly considered someday taking up tennis again, if his knee got better, but he would sure have to find a better club than this. Even Charles must find the place too common, he thought as he waited in the pale green Cafe Lounge. Although some of the scenery is good, he decided, watching two young girls in short skirts on the court beneath his window table.

"You're late, Charles. Why don't you join a decent club downtown?"

"Maybe if you guys would pay your bills I could afford to," Charles snapped back as he took a seat at the table by the window.

"Here's your check. Two, actually — one for the Thornton job, and another for $2,000 to cover expenses . . ." Herman thought this would more than mollify Charles.

"I don't know if that will cover things. I've already advanced $500 to my friend Albert Winch," returned Charles, still aggressive.

"Who's Albert Winch, for hell's sake?" Butler was honestly puzzled.

"He's the tail I put on Karen Bright. Remember, the girl at Translator's International? He'll report directly to you after I leave for France, so you'd better recognize the name. He wanted his money up front." Charles picked up the stained menu. "Let's eat before we go into details, Herman, I'm starved."

"Good idea. Is there anything edible in this place, or should I just have a martini?" Butler was only half joking.

"They frown on martinis here, Herman. You'd better have a V8. Actually, they make a very good chef's salad. With that food blister you're developing, I think a salad would be a wise choice." Charles wondered if he had overstepped. Usually he saved his sarcasm for an exit line.

After lunch with audible munching of crisp salad greens competing with the conversation, Herman Butler moved aside his empty plate to check the memo pad he removed from his inside pocket. "I think that about covers it, Mr. Investigator. Any questions?"

"Just the travel details, Herman," Charles answered.

"We're working on your papers. You can pick them up Tuesday. We'll have your Pan Am ticket to Paris, a copy of our contract with Griman, and a letter of introduction to M. Remy, the director of the Radium Institute of Paris. We're giving you some phony business cards. Your cover name will be Cecil Harmon of *World Science* magazine. You are supposed to be writing a story on heavy elements. Also, we've fixed up a letter of introduction to the building manager at 36 Quai de Bethune on Ile Saint Louis. That's the last residence of Marie Curie, you know. You may need to go there. And a reservation confirmation at the Intercontinental Hotel. Just use your credit card, we'll take care of the costs." Herman put his pad back, satisfied that he had covered everything.

"How about the return trip?"

"We have to talk about that. When you get the Curie material it must be handled carefully. It can't go through any x-ray or any metal detector at airline security. That would tip off the French government, who would love to confiscate the stuff. Once you have your hands on it, call me, and we'll talk about getting you and it home."

"And if I don't get the stuff?" Charles asked.

"You'll stay until you do, but don't forget, we have a time clause in that contract. If you don't do the job, I don't care how you get home!" Breathing heavily and flush-faced, Butler was through with the conversation.

* * *

The bright neon bikini on Lisa Griman was a startling contrast to the dim room with its tiny windows and heavy dark furniture. She and Frank were invited to a Sunday brunch at the Holmes' swimming pool, and she was already dressed for action. Maybe she would take a change for later, in case she got too much static from the other gals at the party. Why bother to dress twice? Meanwhile, the suit was not getting much of a response from Frank. He slouched in his chair in the den, reading his contract with Consolidated Electronics for the fourth time.

Lisa came into the den, her red hair sweeping to one shoulder. That, and the very brief swimsuit on her slender figure and her demanding brown eyes should have been sufficient to move Frank's eyes from the absorbing contract. This failing, Lisa said, "Frank, you're about as much fun as a good case of the measles!"

She walked behind Frank to peer over his shoulder. "What the hell have you been studying all morning?"

"We, my dear, are about to become very rich," Frank said, without looking up.

"So you're having another one of those fantasies." Lisa said, "What is it this time? Gawd, that desk you bought last week is just plain ugly!" Lisa eyed the dark wood, badly stained and scratched.

Frank pulled the check from Consolidated out of the large brown envelope on his lap and handed it to Lisa. "You can thank the ugly desk for this, and $10,000 is only the beginning!" he said proudly.

"I'm starting to listen." Lisa was suddenly very solicitous. The quick breathing activating her breasts at last caught Frank's attention.

When Frank had finished explaining the happenings of the past few days, Lisa walked over to Dr. Georges Colbert's desk now in the Griman den.

"From this ugly piece of junk, my gawd! It's so out of place here, Frank, and it's so dammed beautiful!" Lisa patted the desk. "Gotta give you credit, Frank. You finally slipped into a bit of luck. What did your dear cousin Higginrumps think our next move should be?" Lisa reached rearward and pulled down the elasticized bottom of her skimpy suit.

"No next move. We just wait a week or two while Consolidated's man Holden fetches the Curie Compound. Then we go get our half million and maybe take a little jaunt to Hawaii. You'll finally get to wear that suit in the right circumstances. It really wasn't made for the Holmes' cruddy old pool." Frank looked at Lisa critically. With ample funds she might be as nice as she was when they were married five years ago. Lately she'd been nothing but a pain in the ass. He was fairly certain she'd been cheating on him, and strangely, it hadn't bothered him.

"You know, Frank, I've read about this superconductor business very recently—yesterday's paper, I think." Lisa hurried out to the kitchen trash can, and grabbing the science section of the *Times*, returned to the den.

Frank was surprised. He thought Lisa never looked at any part of the paper except the fashion ads.

"There it is. The International Conference of Electronics Materials Society is meeting in Berlin June 10-13 to discuss the world's progress in high temperature superconductivity. That's next week, Frank. I'll have to change my hair appointment. It's a good thing our passports are up to date. I'll call my travel agent friend Helen, she can get us the reservations in a hurry." She gave another tug on the suit.

"What the hell are you talking about?" Frank scowled.

"You ass, Frank. That letter's worth a helluva lot more than your paltry half a million bucks," Lisa continued as Frank scowled, "World wide! Big bucks, Frank—Achtung! We head for Berlin day after tomorrow!" Lisa grew more exited with each breath.

* * *

Karen was up early Sunday morning, facing the challenge of packing. She was determined to get by with only one large canvas bag and a carry-on. She was pretty sure she could manage with her new Andiamo soft sided luggage. That piece is fabulous, she remembered. If I put it on the bed, I can just keep piling stuff in. This is one time when being short is a big advantage, she noted, I don't have to fold everything double.

Her tiny bedroom in the third floor walk-up was a mess, clothes on hangers draped across the bed, boxes of shoes stacked on the floor, and an array of lingerie, purses and books piled on the only chair in the small room. If Mom were suddenly to show up from Iowa, there would be hell to pay!

Taking one of the dresses from the heap on the bed, she went to the window to widen the curtains. Never enough light to check for any spots on her clothes, she thought. Karen was at once aware of the man on the corner peering steadily at her window. He was nondescript but strangely out of place. Definitely not one of the neighborhood regulars.

Albert Winch didn't move fast enough. She caught his stare before he nonchalantly put a few quarters in the corner newspaper dispenser.

Your imagination's working overtime, Karen chided herself, he's probably just a guy looking around while he waits for his bus. Why don't you grow up and finish your job? She went back to calculating the number of days she would be gone, versus the clothes that she would need. Berlin and Paris were not problems, mostly work clothes, and a couple of casual outfits for sight-seeing, and don't forget the comfortable shoes. But the *Royale*—well, on a beautiful cruise ship like that you wanted to look right, or why bother to go at all?

* * *

Monday, June 8

Charles Holden received a telephone call from Albert Winch just before noon on Monday.

"She may have made me, Charles, but I don't think it matters . . ."

"What do you mean, Al? Of course it matters." Charles did not try to conceal his annoyance. "You're supposed to be the infallible tracker who can be invisible while he keeps Houdini himself in sight."

"Yeah, well she happened to open her drapes at the very moment I was trying to locate her digs, one of those dumb things. Anyhow, I've followed her to work and I've done a little checking with Translators International. She's not available for any appointments this week because she's on an overseas assignment. The girl at the front desk was very helpful, thought I was an insurance salesman." Albert thought he was vindicated.

"Where overseas, Albert, and what assignment? Was she perchance going to Paris, France?" Charles became impatient.

"Naw, West Berlin. She's going to some conference as an interpreter." Albert wondered what Charles was so worried about. "She's leaving tonight on the 8:25 flight from Kennedy," he answered, "but I'm on to something else, Charles. There's another guy that seems to be tailing her. I'll try to find out more about him if he follows her to the airport tonight when she leaves for Berlin. Want me to report back?"

"That's a weird one, Al, but stick with it. I may be hard to reach tonight, but you can leave a message on my machine, or call me first thing tomorrow morning."

Charles hung up and turned another page of the technical journal he had copied in the library. He was reading a paper by Frohlich and Bohm, published in 1950, that told how lattice vibrations enable electron pairs to create a superconductive state. Every paper he read led him to more reading. From here on, though, he was into the heavy, really technical, material. He thought of calling Joe Saunders again, but he reconsidered and decided he knew enough for the task he was hired to do.

Charles turned on his newly purchased study tape, *Simple French for Travelers,* and then decided that he'd had enough of that, too. He replaced the instruction tape with an Oscar Peterson album, then headed for the kitchen and a beer.

Packing was always a problem. He studied the small revolver in his dresser drawer and wondered if it could be tucked in his luggage. He had done it before on domestic flights, but never overseas. Although he had a permit to carry a gun, and it wouldn't be in his carry-on bag, he decided that it had better stay home. The little weapon was comfortable when out on a job, but it wasn't necessary. As an investigator he had only needed to draw it twice, and he had only fired it on the practice range.

Charles hated to pack, especially for a trip of indeterminate length. One bag and a briefcase was his rule. But that took a bit of planning. Don't forget to stick in a formal bow tie, he reminded himself, you never know when you'll need it.

* * *

Karen arrived at Kennedy airport grateful to have missed any heavy traffic tie-up. Her TWA 747 was posted on time, for departure at 8:25. She was happy to be going ambassador class, at least, even if the first class ticket was out of her employer's price range. She was scheduled for a stop-over in Hamburg at 11:45 a.m. and should arrive in Berlin by 1:00 p.m. Tuesday afternoon, so she was in for a long trip. If everything went smoothly, she could check into her hotel, the Kempinski, and have until Thursday morning to herself before she would have to report for work at the conference.

Hopefully her new pink knit was wrinkle proof, and she'd arrive looking as sharp as she felt now, but looking around the waiting area in the terminal, she was struck with how casual, really almost unkempt, most of her fellow passengers looked. T-shirts, jeans and warm-up suits were the order of the day. A few business-men were in suits. But most of them had open collars, no ties. Oh well, better to be over dressed now than embarrassed when checking in to the hotel, she thought, it's reputed to be very plush.

The trip would probably be dull, Karen decided when they were out over the Atlantic. If the card in the seat pocket was accurate, she'd already seen the movie, her paperback kept putting her to sleep, and she didn't really want to concentrate on the sheaf of technical papers in the slim briefcase under her feet.

Karen unobtrusively studied the young man next to her in the aisle seat. He was attractive enough, slender, clear skin, medium blond hair and sharply defined dark eyebrows. But he had been curt when they introduced themselves, only saying in as few words as possible that he was an engineer from Los Angeles, also heading for the Berlin conference.

Karen turned off her overhead light and closed her eyes.

The stewardess roused them from their half slumbering state with offers of wake-up coffee and face cloths. Karen's seat mate must have been tired before, because he initiated conversation now in a friendly, easygoing manner. Juggling their trays and drinks, opening wrapped utensils and dispensing with the usual commentaries about food quality and service, they settled into a brief discussion about the difficulties of business travel in changing time zones. His company, a high-tech branch of an old privately held copper wire business, wanted him to pay particular attention to the Japanese papers at the Berlin electronics conference, he said. When Karen told him she was translating several of the papers at the same conference, the young engineer looked at her with total disbelief.

"I thought you were probably in the fashion business, like a buyer or something," he ventured. "I guess you're just too attractive to look like a translator," he added, blushing slightly.

"Well, thanks for the thought," Karen said, "I've been up to my derriere in French superconductors for the last few days." She noted that the young man's blush reappeared. "I did see a few Japanese papers on the schedule, but I think they were submitted in French. Why the emphasis on the Japanese papers?"

"I guess my boss thinks they're moving faster than the rest of the world. He thinks they'll have a superconductor in dry ice in a matter of weeks. They've already reported a 125K compound. That's about minus 225 degrees Fahrenheit. Trouble is, it's a thallium compound which is too toxic to play with. Sorry, I guess I'm getting a bit too technical."

"Not at all," Karen said. "I seem to remember something about a paper on thallium perovskites."

"I'm impressed, you really do know what it's all about, don't you? My wife would never believe it, a pretty girl like you speaking my language."

"Yea, well lot's of us silly girls get into the act these days," Karen countered. "Why didn't you bring your wife along?"

"Well, young William, he's only three, kinda needs mom at home. He gets along without 'Old William', that's me by the way, but mom he needs."

The conversation was interrupted by the announcement that the aircraft would soon be arriving in Hamburg. Old William straightened his shirt and pulled his loose tie together. Now that's a good looking tie, Karen thought, as she fumbled mirror and lipstick from her purse.

Karen decided the thirty minute stop was worth a stretch of the legs, and a trip to the ladies' room in the Hamburg terminal was better than the cramped quarters of the 747. It cost fifty cents to tip the attendant, but that, she felt, was indeed a bargain. She returned to her seat looking and smelling fresh and gorgeous and was a little disappointed to find Old William sound asleep with a technical journal in his lap.

The short hop from Hamburg to Berlin was uneventful, and William was enthusiastic enough to share space at the window with Karen to watch their arrival and see the area over which the U.S. planes had flown their famous "airlift" all those years ago.

Karen was not sorry she was dressed like a competent career woman when the taxi drew up to the Bristol Hotel Kempinski. The doorman tipped his pill box hat and briskly escorted her through the gleaming brass and glass doors with a courtly old world flourish. Inside, reminiscent of the thirties, the figured carpets, soft lights and warm woods spoke of graciousness and comfort.

Upstairs, she was pleased to see her room had a charming desk with a good lamp in case she had to do any extra translating to do. The usual tourist brochures displayed on the double dresser proclaimed Berlin's dedication to art and culture, but the lure of the down filled comforter and beautiful big square embroidered linen pillows was even greater. Quickly stripping and wrapping herself in the white terry robe from the bathroom hook, Karen surrendered to the squishy embrace of the carved wooden bed.

* * *

"Karen Bright is in Berlin. She left New York City last night. My man didn't find any reason to suspect she would be going to Paris to snoop out the Curie Connection." Charles Holden was talking to Herman Butler from a wall telephone at the Gotham Tennis Club. "But Winch thinks something else is going on. You haven't put another bird dog on the girl's tail, have you?"

"Of course not, checking her out was your chore." Butler sounded firm.

"It's probably nothing, but Winch is supposed to give me an up-to-date report today. I'll let you know."

"How much did you tell your little Albert about the Curie letter?" Herman, suspicious as always, asked hastily.

"Nothing at all, Herman. However, he is paid up for two more days. Do you want him to check on Griman?"

"No, we've found out Griman is also going to Berlin tonight. What do you think they're up to, Charles? You know there's a superconductor conference there at the end of this week. Could be they're all over there to sell the Curie letter to a higher bidder." Herman waited for Charles' reaction.

"I suppose that's possible. I doubt that the Bright girl is doing anything except her translating job at the conference. Now Griman, that's a real interesting coincidence. How did you size the man up, Herman?" Charles balanced the phone on his shoulder as he dried his hair with a towel.

"He wasn't the type to go looking for more money. He was going to be perfectly happy to sit on his fat backside, take no risk, and collect a half-million. Of course, someone else could have changed his mind. Well, never mind, that conference doesn't start until Thursday. Charles, you have to get going. I'll see if we can change your flight to tonight. Go home, get ready. I'll call you in an hour. If you find that compound by Friday, it won't matter who they sell the letter to." Herman concluded his verbal directive.

"Well, it could matter to my fat backside, as you so explicitly put it. Whoever Griman sells that letter to, if indeed he sells it, will sure as hell be after my ass. Griman knows who your messenger boy is, remember?" Charles threw the towel onto the floor.

"That's why we pay those ridiculous fees you demand. Don't screw up, Charles, you hear?" Herman Butler hung up.

Charles had to hustle to buck the traffic. Too bad he had to return to his apartment for his travel gear. As he opened his apartment door, his phone was ringing.

"You're all set, Charles, Pan Am 8:05 tonight instead of tomorrow. Had to change your seat from business class to first, so you can thank Consolidated for the luxuries bestowed upon you. I figure you should be able to get to the Radium Institute Wednesday morning. Your contact man and cover story are in the instruction letter. Call me Thursday night." Herman added, "I gotta meet with our board, so I hope you don't have any questions, I'm already late."

"No questions, Herman. Roger, over and out, wish me luck." Charles cradled the phone, noting from his wrist watch that the count-down was getting short. He'd have to be at Kennedy in about two hours.

Wednesday, June 10

It was close to noon Wednesday when the Grimans arrived at Berlin's International Congress Center in the Westend district. They had come, at Lisa's insistence, directly after checking in at the Hotel Schweizerhof and finding that their room would not be ready for them until after 1:00 p.m. Lisa had correctly guessed that a list of participants would be available at the registration desk at the Congress Center, even though the superconductor conference wouldn't officially begin until the next morning.

"Why do you think that list will do you any good?" Frank asked his wife, looking around at the bewildering maze of escalators, hallways, and stairways leading to shops, restaurants, translating booths that resembled broadcasting stations, all as far-out modern as a space age city and all marked with signs in too many languages for him.

"Hell, there are too many Japanese names," Lisa muttered. She had told the lady at the desk she was a reporter and needed to look at the list to confirm the VIP's at the conference.

"So what are the Japanese names going to tell you?" Frank was speaking softly as Lisa was standing where anyone at the registration could overhear her.

"Ah, this is the gentleman. Dr. Chernov H. Dromensky, the U.S.S.R. Ministry of Electronic Sciences, Moscow." Lisa examined the list carefully. "Which hotel has Dr. C. H. Dromensky booked?" Lisa leaned over the desk, breaking into her most charming smile, and asked, "Can you please tell me which one is hotel number two?"

The lady at the desk spoke English with a heavy German accent. "Hotel number two is the Bristol Hotel Kempinski," she offered. "It is on Strasse Kurferstendamm. Do you want the exact address?" She inquired politely.

"I'm sure we can find it. You've been most helpful, danke schoen." Lisa turned to Frank, "Let's see if we can get a cab to the Bristol Kempinski."

"What about stopping at our hotel? I'd like to unpack and change shoes. It's been a long time since we left New York," Frank complained.

"Later, Frank. We've got to find out if Dr. Dromensky has checked in. He's our man, I'm sure of it. The Russians will pay through the nose to see that Curie letter. The sooner we sell it to them, the less chance for Consolidated to beat us to the punch." Lisa was taking over, and Frank decided to let her.

After two false tries, they finally found the way to gain access to the motor entrance, down a corridor on the first floor, hidden off to the side. Funny how the escalators only started to move when you stood on them, Frank thought, they can catch you off balance if you're not careful. He hoped that he would get another chance to explore some of the huge complex they were leaving. He had only seen a very small part of its 24,000 square meters of space. He had to hurry to catch up with Lisa, who was already getting into a waiting taxi.

As Lisa and Frank entered the Kempinski, Karen Bright stepped from the elevator into the lobby. She was headed directly for the front entrance when she suddenly spotted Old William sitting on a tapestry covered chair with a map spread out before him on the coffee table. She turned abruptly to say hello just as Frank, leading his wife, almost crossed her path.

Frank was sure his heart actually stopped when he saw the girl. She hadn't looked his way, and he instantly pivoted, shoving Lisa back out the hotel entrance.

"Don't ask now, just move!" Frank pushed her around he corner.

"What the hell is going on?" Lisa's patience had expired.

"Karen Bright, the girl who did the translation for me, she's here in Berlin. I saw her just now in the lobby." Frank was wet from sudden perspiration. He took out a handkerchief to mop frantically around his collar.

Visiting briefly with William about making the most of the few hours available for sight-seeing, Karen noted from his map that if she were to vary her schedule, she could take in the Museumsgebaude Berlin-Dahlem on the way to the Congress Center.

Yesterday afternoon, she told the young engineer, she had enjoyed walking down Kurfurstendam Strasse past the surprisingly modern shops that displayed many varieties of the celebrated German china and porcelain. She told him about the boutiques with high fashion styles, a multi-storied department store with windows full of ultra-streamlined kitchen appliances and some colorful outdoor furniture that she would have given her eye-teeth to have been able to send to her folks.

Naturally the shops are new, they agreed, nearly everything in the city needed to be rebuilt after World War II.

Farther down the street she had been awed by the Kaiser Wilhelm Memorial Church dominating the scene with a huge gaping hole in its ruined tower—black and devastating. She had explored the ruins of the old cathedral, cleaned up and preserved, standing adjacent to the new church, a haven of tranquility created by walls of stained glass windows. Tears had rested on her cheeks as the setting recalled so well the terrible days of history.

She had been delighted to find the world famous Berlin Zoo so near at hand after her deep plunge into intense emotion. Happily, she joined the crowds strolling the gravel paths. People were everywhere, some singles, couples arm-in-arm, mostly extended families of parents, grandparents, aunts and uncles, and children darting in and out, all viewing the animals at eye level across strategically designed invisible barriers.

Karen told William how she had laughed at the bears enjoying the crowd, licking their noses with pink tongues and waving at the people with giant paws, but she warned him she thought it was a bit too far to walk, she'd asked too much of her feet for one day, next time she'd take a cab!

William escorted Karen to the front entrance and watched as the doorman helped her into a waiting taxi.

Frank Griman, watching from the street corner as Karen entered her cab, said, "We can go in now Lisa. That was too close. I certainly don't want that woman to see us."

"Don't worry about her, Frank, she probably has an interpreting job at the conference. If she's here to sell the Curie letter, we're too late anyhow. Let's give our Russian VIP a shot at making us a cool million." Lisa arched past the front desk to the house phone. She knew the clerk would never give her a guest's room number, but he'd be glad to call the room.

"Dromensky," the voice in the receiver said, nothing else.

"Do you speak English, Dr. Dromensky?" Lisa asked.

"Of course, who is calling please?" The voice did not sound very affable.

CHAPTER 4

New York City

Tuesday Night, June 9

In spite of two traffic jams, Charles was deposited at the Pan Am terminal at Kennedy at 7:20 p.m., thankful that Herman had up-graded him to first class—sure made the checking in easier. He arrived at the boarding gate a full five minutes before final call, and settled into his seat in the 747 with a grateful sigh. The attendant did not offer him the usual choice of drinks before take-off, but she did offer him a choice of newspapers, from which he selected a late edition.

As the plane taxied to the runway, his eyes hit a small headline on the bottom of the first page:

MAN FOUND DEAD IN TAXI AT KENNEDY

NEW YORK: police are seeking the person responsible for the murder last night of a man identified as Albert Winch, 47, of New York City, who was found on the floor of a taxicab parked at Kennedy Airport. The driver, John Conway, said he had left his vehicle in the regular line-up to talk to the taxicab authority. When he returned to his cab to move up for a fare, he noticed blood running under his feet from the rear floor. Investigation revealed Winch crumpled on the floor of the cab with his throat cut from ear to ear. The driver could not identify the body and was at a loss to explain its presence in his vehicle. Police are continuing investigations . . .

Charles looked so white that the flight attendant, having recited her routine greetings and instructions, went immediately to ask if he needed help.

"I'm fine, thanks. Please bring me a Beefeater on the rocks as soon as you can serve." Charles suddenly wished that he had packed his small friendly revolver. The shock from the story was accompanied by the realization that he was now into something quite messy. Poor Albert. Of course, neither he nor Albert had suspected they were playing in rough company. This explained why the reliable Albert hadn't checked back with him, since he usually did exactly as he promised.

After Charles had downed two Beefeater martinis, he was suddenly exhausted and his whirling brain gave way to a sleep that lasted most of the Atlantic crossing.

Wednesday, June 10

By the time the 747 arrived at Orly, Charles felt surprisingly refreshed and in good shape, even after the long ride to the Intercontinental Hotel at 3 Rue de Castiglione. As expected, his room would not be ready until noon, so Charles left his luggage with the porter and treated himself to the comfort of a shave in the hotel barber shop.

"Now, to proceed with the job I came to do," he said to himself as he asked the doorman to get him a cab. "Let's see what we can find at the Radium Institute on Rue Pierre Curie."

Once in the taxi, he pulled Herman's instruction sheet from his briefcase for a quick review. He was confident he could pull off the ruse Butler had outlined, but he fervently hoped he wouldn't need to try out his French.

* * *

Berlin

Wednesday Afternoon

The waiter had deftly delivered three vodkas to the three people sitting on the couches in the far back corner of the room near the side entrance at the Kempinski Hotel. The big man with the bulbous nose, black beard and graying hair sat impassively as the man beside him in the rumpled brown suit fumbled with the unfamiliar coins. The woman sat with her skirt pulled almost above her knees, crossed leg swinging impatiently, flipping her long fingernails through her mane of flaming red hair.

As the waiter retreated, the big man turned to the woman.

"Now, Mrs. Griman," Dromensky had sensed that he would be dealing with her, not the insignificant husband. "I trust you are not wasting my time. You know there is no such thing as a room temperature superconductor. If there were such a thing, yes, it would be worth a great deal of money. A great, great, great deal, yes."

Dromensky stroked his ample beard. His eyes were catlike in the subdued light. A mean, spooky son-of-a-bitch, Frank thought. Frank was very nervous about dealing with this man who now pontificated as if giving a scientific lecture.

"It would be a great discovery, a Russian Soviet? discovery. Your American scientists could never equal such an advance. The tilted perovskites Dr. Chu worked with at the University of Houston were originally named for the great Russian mineralogist Count Lev Aleksevich von Perovski. Dr.

Chu's superconductor must be held at 100 degrees Kelvin; that is equal to 300 degrees Fahrenheit below zero. Now, Mrs. Griman, you tell me there is a material that would be a superconductor right in this room. Yes, this would be a magnificent Soviet achievement." Dromensky paused to stare at Frank, who was raising his hand in a halting gesture.

"Dr. Dromensky, how much is a great, great deal of money, sir?" Griman interjected, "Are we talking here about one million American dollars?"

"First, Mr. Griman, I must know more, much more, but yes, as you Americans say, that would be a reasonable baseball field amount." Dromensky again looked at Lisa and queried, "Show me, please, something you have, why we should continue this meeting."

Paris

Wednesday Morning

Charles tried to picture the Radium Institute before him as it must have looked to Marie Curie on the day of its completion in July of 1914. He had dutifully studied the Madame Curie biography written by her daughter Eve as part of his "homework." Now he was surprised to see the building looking very much like the picture in the book, which had been published in 1937. A handsome three-story building of brick, with alternate square and round windows on the third floor subtly interconnected by delicate stone arcs and figures.

Conceived by Dr. Roux, director of the Pasteur Institut in 1909, and designed by the great French architect, Nenot, the Institut du Radium, Pavilion Curie, (the words cut into stone above the entrance) was built at a cost of 800,000 gold francs. Pretty reasonable by today's standards, Charles thought. The old laboratory building was separated from the Curie Biological Research Therapy Center by a garden and trees planted under Marie Curie's supervision. She had planted the rambler roses herself, and roses were blooming in the garden, but Charles could not tell if any of them were the originals.

As he entered the building, he was ready with the letter of introduction Butler had given him. With his half-dimpled smile he offered it to the matronly woman in the black skirt and white blouse who looked at him expectantly.

She accepted his offering, peering over the tops of her reading glasses, little half glasses secured by a black ribbon about her throat. "Do you have an appointment with Dr. Remy?" she asked in perfect English.

"No, I have just come from New York, and since I arrived sooner than I expected, I have taken the chance that your director could spare me a few moments." Charles projected his most sincere, earnest attitude, looking her directly in the eye. He smiled to himself when her forehead wrinkled in a frown as she noticed his different colored eyes. Diverts them every time, he chuckled to himself.

"Yes, well, please be seated. I will check with Dr. Remy."

The helpful woman peered at the card Charles had given her and picked up the telephone. Charles heard her recite from his invented business card the false name he was using.

"Monsieur Harmon, oui, HARMON, CECIL, oui, *World Science Magazine*, oui American." Her voice continued in a rapid French that Charles did not attempt to follow.

"Please come with me, Mr. Harmon," she announced, returning the handset to its holder and rising from the small reception desk, "Dr. Remy will see you." She led the way down a high ceilinged hallway whose walls were covered with photographs of Madame and Pierre Curie at various locations and periods of their colorful lives. Other portraits of distinguished gentlemen, rotogravures faded and brown, bearded scientific figures of the thirties, as best Charles could tell, were sprinkled in with the Curie photos.

The director, a scholarly man in his early 60's with a firm handshake and cordial smile, also spoke very good English. He greeted Charles, offered him a chair, and then patiently studied the letter of introduction.

"So, Mr. Harmon, you are doing an article which will provide us with some international publicity." Dr. Remy spoke hesitantly while he considered the possible consequences of giving Cecil Harmon access to the Curie archives. Dr. Remy continued as he re-examined Butler's creative letter, "We have not been very active in soliciting world support for some of our projects. A little publicity might be good for us."

Maybe Butler has been too inventive, Charles thought, as he tried to read the facial movements Dr. Remy displayed on a second reading of the letter.

"You think, perhaps, that Madame Curie's search for heavy transuranium elements is actually having a strong rebirth in various laboratories around the world?" Dr. Remy didn't seem to expect an answer as he added, "I have wondered myself why the quest to discover new elements has not been more aggressively pursued. It was, you know, Marie Curie's most enthusiastic mission in her later years."

"My editor is very much dedicated to such a theme for our December issue. He felt that a brief review of Madame Curie's work would provide a fitting climate for several articles about Americium, Nobelium and the several other new elements that have received less than their share of deserved attention." Charles tried to sound authoritative, but wanted to end this conversation before Dr. Remy's inevitable recognition of his ignorance surfaced.

"Well, Mr. Harmon, as I told that Mr. Black yesterday, we must be very careful in handling any of Madame Curie's laboratory journals. My most important assignment at the

Institute is to preserve these original documents with great care and respect for the sake of all posterity. Your letter says you would like to examine and take notes on Madame Curie's journals for the year 1933. That was the last year she was able to conduct any meaningful work here. She died, you know, the following year." Remy looked contemplative. "It's strange that your visit should follow so closely that of Mr. Black," Remy concluded.

"Excuse me, Doctor, may I ask, who is Mr. Black?" Charles did not like what was now becoming obvious, someone else had been here on the same mission.

"I thought, perhaps, you might be working with him," Remy speculated. "He was also an American writer. He came early yesterday explaining the new Curie biography he was writing. He must be doing it in depth because he also wanted to examine the Curie historic laboratory journals. The man was interesting, and we had a most pleasant visit."

"I am at a disadvantage, Dr. Remy. I'm afraid that neither do I know Mr. Black, nor did I know of a new biography in the works." Charles said.

"Never mind, Mr. Harmon, I will have Mademoiselle Fournier escort you to the library where we keep the Curie journals."

"Is there someone I can hire to help translate the material written in French?" Charles asked Dr. Remy.

"Mlle. Fournier is able to translate any text you wish to take notes on. I must ask you to wear these when you handle the journals." Dr. Remy reached in his desk drawer and handed Charles a pair of white gloves, enveloped in a plastic bag. "Mlle. Fournier would have to be with you at any rate, whether or not you employ her interpretive skills. May I suggest that you offer her some gratuity when your task is completed? It may take some hours for you to absorb the material you are seeking, and, since Mlle. Fournier is only a student doing part-time work at the Institute . . ." Remy paused.

"Of course, Doctor, you are more than kind," Charles responded quickly.

'Cecil Harmon' left Dr. Remy's office shortly after Christine Fournier arrived on the scene. As he walked down the steps to the archives, admiring the shapely legs and smooth hips he followed more than the historic atmosphere, Charles casually queried the shapely young student, "Did you, perchance, accompany an American to the archives yesterday, a Mr. Black?"

"No, Monsieur, sorry, I was not at work yesterday."

Berlin

Late Afternoon

When Karen returned to her hotel, twilight was approaching, and she certainly knew she had done enough walking for one day. After marching gallantly through the picture galleries of the Dahlem museum, viewing each of the 26 Rembrandts there, she had continued to the sculpture collection, the Museum of Ethnography and the collection of engravings, she had gotten confused and lost in the back stairways, and finally decided she was a candidate for cultural indigestion.

Then she'd taken a cab to the Westend district of Charlottenburg to the massive Congress Center. She was astounded at the enormity of the place, but she had no trouble locating the registration desk. The uniformed girls working there were very happy to direct her to the third floor where offices, lounges, and snack bars were available to all the technical personnel. She would be sitting in a glass booth directly west of the speaker's rostrum when she was actually translating, a set-up similar to a radio station control booth.

Karen picked up a conference schedule and located the assignment desk. Enough was enough. She'd be too tired for dinner if she didn't make herself rest first.

It was pleasant to look forward to a companion for dinner tonight. 'Old William' had suggested they join forces in the Grill. Since they were both staying in the hotel, why eat alone? He had insisted that his wife didn't object to such business associations, so why should she?

* * *

On the fifth floor of the same hotel, two men were huddled together in one corner of the large suite, deeply engrossed in a conversation in Russian, when the telephone interrupted. Dr. Dromensky picked up the phone, and with his hand over the mouth piece, said to his companion, "It is the call from our people in New York."

Certain that he had been shown a professional translation by the Grimans, Dromensky had wasted no time enlisting the help of his cohorts in New York. Why should they pay the Grimans? They are not the only ones who know the contents of the letter. He'd meet the Grimans, as planned, but meantime . . .

"We are in luck, Ivan Ilych." Dromensky even sounded excited as he shared information with his constant companion, a GRU officer posing as a fellow scientist. "They identified the translator, and she is working this very conference. You won't believe it, she's staying at this hotel. Name's Karen Bright."

"Why not just eliminate the Grimans? I can go to their hotel." Ivan was ready to move.

"No, the Griman woman said they have taken precautions to protect the document, and we may be premature. Later, perhaps, in Paris. We don't have time for games here. No, the next move will be to find K. Bright. She probably knows which American company has sent a courier to Paris, and if she is working with them, she will probably lead us right to the Curie superconductor. I will arrange a meeting with her, then you can follow her like a shadow. Meantime, you get us reservations for Paris. We should leave tomorrow."

"Very well . . .," Colonel Denkov seemed unusually accommodating.

"Wait, you had better stay here with K. Bright. I'll go to Paris and meet the Grimans as planned. I'll notify Moscow of our change of plans." Dromensky poured two small glasses of vodka.

* * *

Standing in the hot water in the deep bathtub, with the water of the shower massaging the kinks in her neck and shoulders, had almost, but not quite, eased Karen's fatigue. Still an hour or so before dinner, she thought, as she switched on the TV and headed for the bed. The shrill ring of the phone jerked her out of her pleasant state of relaxation. "Who could that be?" she worried.

She groped for the phone amidst her stack of papers on the little desk and used its long cord to carry it to the bed as she answered.

"Is this Karen Bright, please?" To Karen's trained ear the voice sounded Slavic, probably eastern European.

"Yes, who is speaking?"

"I am sorry to disturb you, Ms. Bright, but I understand you are a very capable translator. I am Dr. Chernov H. Dromensky. I have brought with me to Berlin a Russian paper. I now find it must be put into German. In checking with the International Congress Center, they suggested I call upon you for help.

Could we possibly meet briefly in the lobby? I bring the paper, perhaps you have a look?"

"Well, Doctor, I really don't have much time for an extra job." Karen glanced at the television as the sound came on suddenly.

"It is not a very long paper. It would be worth quite a bit to me if you could spare an hour or two, Ms. Bright."

As Karen watched the TV screen she suddenly blurted out "My god!" in stunned shock. She was looking at a picture of an absolutely nude man sporting an enormous erection.

"Excuse me, Dr. Dromensky," she recovered. "Well, I might look at the paper." The picture had now proceeded to a very graphic sex act with a surprisingly attractive woman added to the scene. All those prostitutes working on the street could have tipped me off, but I really wasn't prepared for that, thought Karen as she stretched to shut off the TV, phone still in hand.

"May I invite you to dine tonight and give you a chance to examine the paper? It describes some recent work on high temperature superconductors. You must be very familiar with the terminology of superconductors since you are a translator at the conference tomorrow . . ." Dromensky was fishing for some confirmation of his feeling that Karen was aware of the value of the Curie letter.

"I'm sorry, Dr. Debenski, I have an engagement for dinner." Karen was still thinking about the TV picture. What a place! I'd better be cautious, stick with Old William.

"It is Dromensky, Ms. Bright, D-R-O-M-E-N-S-K-Y. How about a cocktail in the lounge, in a half-hour. You can refuse me if you do not want to do the job, and I will still have time to search for someone else tomorrow. Fair enough?"

"Okay, Doctor, fair enough. How will I know you?"

"A blue jacket, gray trousers. I have a beard. I think you will have no trouble. I am very grateful. I meet you soon then." He hung up before she could reply further.

Karen turned on the TV again. They were still going at it. Shutting off the offending machine, she turned to the closet to find appropriate attire for meetings with two different men.

CHAPTER 5

Paris

Wednesday Afternoon June 10

Charles returned to the Intercontinental Hotel, surprised to find it was only shortly after noon, although he had spent almost two hours at the Institute du Radium. He had filled a small notebook, much to the joy of Christine Fournier, who turned out to be a fountain of information and talent, well worth the very generous tip. Experience had proved a large gratuity became a key to otherwise sealed doors. His employers might object to the expense record submitted at the end of a successful investigation, but Charles was used to that.

Much of this morning's translation was unnecessary, but Charles had diligently pursued the task, hoping that when Christine reported to Dr. Remy, as she was sure to do, the director would not suspect that Charles was interested only in one brief entry in the December 1933 laboratory records of Madame Curie:

Today we have continued our work on the precipitation of Actinium X. We must build a better centrifuge. I have written to Georges Colbert asking him to help with a project I have in mind for Flacon 216 brought from the old shed. If Colbert comes, he may also help me redesign the centrifuge.

I will take Flacon 216 to Ile Saint Louis. I am reminded of my poet friend Paul Valery, and his *Canticle of the Columns.* I feel these experiments were, as he put it, "heavier than the world bearing our own loves, we journey across the days as over a stone the waves." But my favorite is stanza six. Enough for now. Tomorrow another carboy of acid will be needed. The new ores from Spain are coming in next week.

Charles had asked Christine about Paul Valery.

"He was a French symbolist poet much admired by Marie Curie, although she had little time for such things." Christine sensed his interest, and asked, "Would you like to read the piece Madame Curie mentioned?"

"Of course," Charles said, "it would be very interesting, but has it been translated into English?"

"Oh, I forgot. No, I don't know that it has. I don't think we even have a French copy here, at least I've never seen one. You might check the bookstores."

Now, reviewing what he had learned this afternoon, and studying his notes, Charles realized he must find a copy of *Canticle of the Columns.* He wouldn't have time to rummage around in strange bookstores, either. Butler's instruction sheet had definitely read: "You will find the hiding place, according to Madame Curie's letter, mentioned in her journal. Look for any entry about Georges Colbert and/or Flacon 216 on or around December 18, 1933."

The clue had to be in stanza six of Valery's poem. Looking at his watch, he figured it must be about 6:00 a.m. in New York. What a good time to call Butler at home!

In New York a machine answered Charles, "You have reached 219-4832. Please leave your message after you hear the tone and we'll return your call when we return."

"Herman, this is Charles Holden calling from Paris. Call me at the Intercontinental . . ."

Butler's voice cut in. "Damn it Charles, can't you figure out the time difference? It's six-o-fucking-clock in the morning here, for crissakes. I hope to hell it's good news." Herman was calmer than Charles had expected.

"The old story, Herman. The good news is I've been to the Institute and have a handle on how to find the stuff. The bad news is someone else was there yesterday. I think it was somebody working with Griman, or maybe it was the guy Albert was following when he got his throat slit." Charles paused, "I guess you did hear about Albert Winch, didn't you?"

"Yeah, but I haven't been able to get any details. I don't want the NYPD to think we have any interest in Albert Winch. Wrong kind of publicity. Can't help the poor devil now anyway."

"Well, I think we owe something to his family. After all, he was working our job when he got it." Charles knew this was a frail appeal to Butler, no matter how impassioned.

"You mean, working your job," Herman countered, predictably. "Let's talk about that later, Charles. The important question right now is, can you get to the superconductor ahead of the other guy, or are you going after him first?"

"I'd like to try to beat him to it, and I have a clue, but it's a bit oblique. Have you ever heard of a French poet named Valery?"

"No, why should I have?" What the hell does a poet have to do with anything?" Herman was getting impatient now.

"Well, find a book of his poems, and find a poem called *The Canticle of the Columns.* Get somebody to translate the sixth stanza into English, and then call me back here and read it to me. Then I should know where to look for the stuff. Think you can handle that?" Charles hoped the urgency of the request was obvious.

"Give me a couple of hours. I'll get someone on it right away, but we'll probably have to wait for the library to open.

I should be able to get back to you about 5:00 p.m. Paris time. You be in your room there and I'll let you know. Anything else?"

"Yes, see if one of your people can find out if Frank Griman has a friend named Black. His cousin the lawyer might know. Also, check that translator outfit and see if anyone there ever heard of a Mr. Black, or if anyone knows if he's a friend of that Karen Bright. Meanwhile, I'll try to do some checking on him from this end."

"Right, is that it? I think my night's over anyway, so I'll get right on this." Butler stifled a yawn.

"Oui, c'est complet," Charles hung up. He knew he should get right back into action, keep moving, or the effects of the night flight would catch up with him. With Butler doing his research on the New York end, Charles figured he could use his time to pursue a little inquiry about the mysterious Mr. Black.

When he had asked Dr. Remy if he knew how to locate Mr. Black so they could perhaps compare notes, the director had said he only knew the fellow had mentioned walking from his hotel to the Institute, and had said he would walk back. Dr. Remy had suggested the nearest hotel likely to book an American tourist would be the Grand Hotel de Lima, on Boulevard St. Germain. Charles decided that the hotel was as good a place as any to start his search.

Berlin

Wednesday Evening

Karen crossed from the elevator into the lounge area, her timidity eased by the reassuring murmurs of voices and the clinking of glasses coming from the clusters of couches and chairs scattered throughout the gracious room. Cocktail hour is the same the world over, she thought.

Chernov Dromensky, with his catlike eyes, spotted the pretty blonde immediately. Rising to meet her, he signaled to his so-called scientific companion, Ivan Denkov, to slip away to the big lounge chair in the corner where he could be unobserved while studying Karen in great detail.

"It is Ms. Bright, yes?" Dromensky offered his hand. "Will you join me at this table here?" He gestured to the one table under a bit of light as he introduced himself.

Correct blue blazer, gray trousers, and neatly trimmed black beard. Must be the one. "That would be a good idea," said Karen, "I'll need some light if I'm to look at a manuscript."

The lounge attendant, linen napkin on arm, appeared from nowhere. Karen ordered a scotch and soda. He's buying, she thought, might as well stick him. Sure can't buy it myself with this dollar exchange. With only a quick flick of a frown, Dromensky spread a thick sheaf of pages across the smooth leather table top.

"I can tell without looking, Dr. Dromensky, that I won't possibly have time to tackle anything of that size." Karen accepted her drink from the silent waiter and wondered how much money she could have earned moonlighting.

"Well, Ms. Bright, if you could just do the first three pages — the synopsis and introduction — that would be all I would need for the meeting tomorrow, and then perhaps you could take the copy with you and find time for it later. Are you staying in Berlin after the conference?" Dromensky looked hopeful.

"No, I am leaving for Paris Friday afternoon. I'll stay there for a few days and then I'm returning to New York by ship." Karen wondered why she was giving this stranger so much information.

"Ah, that would be perfect. You could take your time with nothing much to do at sea. Then you could mail the translation to me from New York," said Dromensky smoothly. So, she was going to Paris. With Ivan Ilych on the job it should not be too difficult to procure the Curie superconductor. "I will pay you $200 now and then you can bill me for the balance when you finish the job. Does that meet your rates?"

Karen sipped her drink. Why, she wondered, was that first taste of scotch so wonderful. Why does he want only three pages done for the conference and then later the entire translation? How can I bill him in Russia? It doesn't make much sense. What's with this guy? Maybe he's just a Russian scientist, maybe not.

"I think I can handle that for you, Dr. Dromensky. It will have to be in long hand, but I'll try to write distinctly." Karen looked at the title page as she spoke: *U.S.S.R. Experiments Using Several Rare Earth Elements to Produce High Temperature Superconductors.*

Karen's mind went right back to the Curie letter. Had Pierre Curie used rare earth elements? She couldn't remember any mention of it. In a sudden surge of patriotism, Karen hoped the Russians were on the wrong track.

"Did you use the Meissner Effect to evaluate the experiments?" Karen blurted out, realizing immediately she shouldn't have asked anything.

"You seem to know a great deal about superconductivity, Ms. Bright. I am impressed by such a beautiful American woman knowing any of such things," Dromensky commented.

"Our test procedures are described in the paper." He handed her two $100 bills.

Of course you'd be impressed, you smug communist, Karen thought. American women are supposed to be dumb and decadent. "I'll leave the translation in an envelope with the desk clerk before eight tomorrow morning. So, if you'll excuse me doctor, I'd better run. Thank you for the drink." Karen glanced at her watch as she took a final swallow and rose to leave.

As she made her way across the now busy room, she searched for Old William, not noticing Ivan Ilych Denkov moving silently behind her.

* * *

At Budapester Strasse 21, near Tiergarten and Kurfurstendamm in Berlin's Schweizerhof Hotel, the Grimans were busily preparing for a quick trip to Paris. Lisa was fussing with their luggage as Frank watched from the room's one easy chair.

"I think you've got us into a mess with that Russian, Lisa. He looks more like a terrorist than a scientist to me. I don't see how we can make a cash deal out of it." Frank had his shoes off, and was massaging his toes. "The problems is, he won't give us the money until we give him the letter and the dope on that guy from Consolidated, but when he gets that he'll have no reason to pay us anything. You can't sue the son-of-a-bitch, he's a Russian VIP. Really, we were better off with Butler's deal."

"Butler's deal was too chintzy, Frank. This thing with Dromensky will work. A million dollars is nothing to them. After all, he's the government. He said he'd have a way to make a smooth trade—his consulate in Paris will have the million bucks for us, all nicely unmarked cash money, Frank."

Lisa's greenish eyes seemed to actually dilate, and the corners or her mouth moistened as she mentioned the money.

"Yeah, he teased you with that thousand dollar down payment, but that's probably all we'll get. I don't mean to be hard-nosed, but what about my contract with Consolidated? There's a penalty, you know, for what we're doing," Frank persisted.

"Oh, screw that contract, Frank! Think about one million in cash. We'll put it into a Swiss bank account, and Consolidated won't be able to prove a thing. Even if they could, we'd only have to forfeit the ten thousand. Wake up and live, Frank, we're moving to the Big Time!"

"Okay, Lisa, but we may be putting Butler's man Holden into a lot of danger. He could wake up and die before this is over, and so could we, come to think of it. Your Dr. Dromensky scares the hell out of me." Frank looked at his watch. "We have a couple of hours before we have to leave for the airport. Can we at least try some of that famous knackwurst and a couple of steins of German suds?"

"In the old days, you would have said, we have a couple of hours, let's try the bed and have room service send something up . . ." Lisa looked at the untouched big bed all nicely covered with an inviting down comforter.

"Well my dear, this ain't the old days, and at least one of us is out of practice. Maybe next week when things calm down we can make like the old days, but for now there are just too damn many distractions." Frank was surprised by the extent of his honest disinterest in Lisa.

Paris

Later Wednesday

Charles wanted a drink and some sleep. Jet lag was finally catching up with him. Might feel better if he could get out and walk a bit, he decided. He remembered some of Paris from his visit there four years ago, but now he wasn't even sure if the Left bank was north or south. Better ask the concierge. That's what those dressed up guys pushing pencils and moving papers behind those impressive desks are there for, right?

"Can you tell me how I might walk from here to the Grand Hotel de Lima?" Charles smiled. Even the fatigue lines around his eyes couldn't dim their different colors, and the contagious appeal of his broad grin and youthful face brought the usual quick response to his request.

"Do you know Paris at all?" the concierge responded politely, at the same time handing Charles a small city map, opening it with a practiced flourish.

"I don't know much. I guess we are right about here?" Charles was pointing to the spot on the map where Rue de Rivoli met Rue de Castiglione.

"Yes, that is close, sir. However, you see way over here across the river," he explained while using a pencil point, "this is the Jardin du Luxembourg and next to that park area you see the Boulevard St. Michel. Now along here, you see, is your Grand Hotel de Lima. A very long walk from here, monsieur." The concierge paused, looking at Charles' expression of disappointment. "If you would like to enjoy a pleasant walk, sir, why not take a taxi from her to the Jardin du Luxembourg and do your strolling there. It is lovely this time of year. Then you are only a short distance from the hotel you wish to find."

"I suppose that's a good suggestion. I was in that area earlier today. I just thought I might see something of Paris if I walked over there. I do appreciate your help." Charles noticed that there were now three Americans anxiously wishing he would get out of the way.

"Please keep the map," the concierge offered as a parting courtesy.

Charles had the doorman hail a taxi and found himself fifteen minutes later at the Jardin du Luxembourg, once again near the University, at Rue de Vaugirard. Two doors down the street he spied the display windows of a rather large bookstore, probably the one used by most of the Sorbonne students. He delayed his notion of a brisk walk as he entered and found himself surrounded by aisles full of volumes that could hold all the world's knowledge, if only one knew the language.

"Parlez vous Anglais?" Charles asked a lady who, with pencil screwed into a knob of gray hair and shoulders weighed down by a heavy gray wool sweater, looked as though she must have been there forever.

"Yes, may I help you?" she inquired politely.

"I'm looking for a book of poetry."

Heavy gray sweater looked puzzled. "Ah, yes, la poesie," she smiled. "We have many volumes, monsieur, not so many in English, however."

"I'm looking for a book of poems containing the works of Valery." Charles looked hopeful.

"I think we may have something, monsieur. Another American yesterday asked for a book like that yesterday." She was gone before he could reply. Can that bastard really be so far ahead of me? Charles asked himself.

"We have a book, but we only have it in French, I know, because the other man also spoke no French, and I searched for a translation for him." She smiled at Charles as she handed him a slim green volume. "Perhaps at the library?"

"That's okay, I mean c'est combien." Charles wanted to show he was at least making some effort.

"The price is 35 francs if you still want it."

"Could you translate one part of one poem for me?" Charles ventured. "I'll be glad to pay you for any inconvenience."

"I'm sorry, my English is not so good. I do better than the other clerks here, but poetry, no, I cannot do that for you." She accepted his money with no further encouragement or suggestion.

Clutching his purchase, Charles settled for a ten minute tour of the famed gardens, footsteps crunching on the graveled paths as he admired the purple blossoms of whatever kind of flower they might be. He found a stone bench overlooking a charming pond facing the Palais du Luxembourg, and accepted its invitation. He opened his new treasure, thumbed through its pages until there, on page 108, he found "Le Cantique des Colonnes."

Si froides et dorees
Nous fumes de not lits
Par le ciseau tirees
Pour devenir ces lys

Charles folded the top corner of the page, put the book in his pocket and headed for the Grand Hotel du Lima.

The regular desk clerk was off duty, but a slender teenager hurried from a back room, wiping her hands on a towel. She tried to be helpful—actually her English was very adequate—but after a thorough search of the big book before her, she assured him no American writer named Black was registered there, and Charles had to admit he was not too surprised. If he could call himself Cecil Harmon, then anyone could be Mr. Black. Chances are the name would start with a "B", but that was much too thin a clue to work with. He would have to find a different approach.

Berlin

Wednesday Evening

Old William didn't look old at all, waiting for Karen at the doorway of the Restaurant Kempinski. His clean shaven face, conservative suit and fresh white shirt was a reassuring contrast to the Russian she'd just left. As they were ushered to their table with its gleaming crystal and napkins carefully folded to resemble giant sea shells, Karen felt herself settle into pleasurable comfort, pleased that modern iridescent glitz had not taken over this room's understated elegance. Certainly a far cry from the typical convention dining rooms she'd so often seen.

"Gosh, am I glad to see you," William exclaimed with boyish enthusiasm, "I've spent the whole afternoon with Mr. Osototo. We were speaking English, but my ears are very tired of hearing about the *incledible* new Japan Rail superconductor high speed trains now being designed in Tokyo."

The gray bearded man, broad shoulders stretching the narrow confines of his ill fitting suit, stepped briefly to the door of the dining room. He could see the pretty young lady seated with a handsome American who should be able to keep her attention riveted long enough. He headed for the elevators. Ivan Ilych, he told himself as the elevator rose, you will have plenty of time to do a complete search of the room of Miss Karen Bright!

The Soviet operative headed quickly for Karen's room. He had no trouble finding a good place for his bugs, and he was skillful enough to leave no sign of entry. Problem was, where in the hell was the Curie letter? Nowhere he could find, and he didn't miss a corner or a crack. His professional fingers examined the seams of the coat and jacket pockets, riffled the papers in her briefcase, searched the drawers of the desk and even probed the empty suitcase.

* * *

"I've had enough Russian for a while," Karen told her escort after the waiter had given them time to peruse their menus. "I've contracted to do some translating for one of the Russians attending the conference, and I find them hard to take. So maybe we should enjoy being Yankees together, savoring a wonderful German dinner." She looked up at him and added, "For starters, you can fill me in on some basic data, like I don't even know your last name."

"It's Foester, and what's yours?" William, focusing on her for the first time directly, realized how really beautiful Karen was. On the plane and in the hotel lobby she'd been merely a friendly and attractive fellow traveler. Now she seemed to exude a glow of charm and affection that could make married Old William a bit nervous.

"Bright," Karen responded, without any explanation.

"Not married, are you, Karen Bright?"

"Not any more, William. Have you ever tried German fruit soup? Sounds intriguing, doesn't it?" Karen did not wish to start a discussion of her background in general and Walter Bright in particular.

Not until the fruit soup had made its debut and been rated a C+ did the conversation turn serious again, and Karen suddenly asked, "William, do you think a room temperature superconductor will ever be found? Who do you think is close to perfecting it? The Russians act as if they are, the Japanese seem confident they're on the right track, and, as near as I can tell, the Americans don't seem to think anyone is close at all. At least, that's what I gather from the technical papers I've been translating for this conference." Karen took a tentative taste of the veal and was happy with the result. No C+ this, more like an A, she thought.

"Its been a fascinating subject, Karen. Unlike most engineering problems, superconductors do not respect conventional rationality. What I mean is, even the most erudite engineers who call themselves solid state physicists usually start solving a problem intuitively. When things start coming together, they are able to create a mathematical framework to clothe their phenomenological observations. If their intuition has been correct, then the formulas and theories enable them to predict and implement new phenomena. Now in the subatomic world where the state of superconductivity is born, all of the predictions based on intuition have been wrong." Old William paused to evaluate Karen's reactions to all this.

"You're implying that the progress made in raising the temperature where a material will superconduct has not been progress at all, only luck. Could it be that someone sixty years ago found a superconductor and didn't know what to do about it because it couldn't be scientifically explained?" Karen changed course suddenly when she realized she'd said too much, next thing she knew the Curie secret would be out. Watch yourself, girl. So she said, "Could you be more specific, William? What about the progress they're talking about so far, has it been all luck?"

"Historically, nothing much happened for fifty years after Onnes discovered superconductivity in 1911. For years scientists believed that electrons flowed through crystals in the outer reaches of the force fields that hold atoms together. They would flow freely until they were impeded by foreign atoms, or by the vibrations of atoms in and out of their proper positions. Electrons colliding with misplaced atoms would make the lattice vibrate even more, heating the wires and slowing the flow of current. Thus, these lattice vibrations, or phonons as they are called, slow down as the temperature is lowered, until, near absolute zero, the lattice vibrations cease and a superconductive state exists. Well, that wasn't the right answer. After about fifty years, a new theory was born."

"Do you mean that our best brains, these great scientists, for half a century believed in the wrong theory? With the progress of technology in recent years, that's pretty hard to believe . . ." Karen was truly shocked.

"Not exactly, Karen. The theory was correct of normal conductors like copper, silver, platinum and so forth. But even Kamerlingh Onnes, using mercury wires, found that resistance did not always diminish gradually with lowering temperature. He found that with mercury, resistance to conductivity disappeared altogether quite suddenly at four degrees Kelvin above absolute zero," William paused to take a breath as the waiter hovered to remove his plate.

"As I started to say," he continued, "fifty years later three scientists came up with a new theory to explain the difference between normal conductors and superconductors. Bardeen, Cooper and Schrieffer won the Nobel prize for this new theory which postulated, strangely, that it was the phenoms, or lattice vibrations, that actually make superconductivity happen. This theory proposed that the lattice vibrations create pairs of electrons (christened Cooper pairs) that would act as single particles and these particles would travel lock-step with other Cooper pairs in a military-like formation that would keep a superconducting current flowing forever. The obstacles that interfere with single electrons become powerless when the Cooper pairs condense into a superconducting current." William was slightly embarrassed. He realized he had almost presented a classroom lecture on physics to this lovely lady who must be bored to tears by now. Still, she seemed to have a flicker of curiosity in those alluring brown eyes.

"I agree with you, William, it certainly is a fascinating story." Karen sensed his reluctance to go on, and she wanted to encourage him.

"I am being a bit simplistic, you know. The quantum mechanical explanation is considerably more complex. Well, to continue, this concept of Cooper pairs has now bumped up against new complications."

"In what way?"

"It seems," William went on, "that we still don't know how high temperature superconductivity works. Now the new copper oxide sandwich materials, the sandwiched perovskites, are superconductors above the temperature of 150 degrees Kelvin, but the enigma is that above 33K the lattice can't vibrate quickly enough to create Cooper pairs. So the scientific laws that allowed the discovery of hundreds of superconductors below 33K just won't work at the higher temperatures."

"I gather that much of this conference we're involved with is speculation about the next new set of laws that will explain why these newer materials superconduct at high temperatures." Karen looked at William for agreement.

"You've got it right, Karen. But there's more to it than that. One of the chief concerns of both the scientists and their governments is that the future consequences are so important that there must be a real sharing of information." Then he added, "And in my opinion, that's just wishful thinking. Fierce competition and secrecy are going to be a strong undercurrent during this conference."

"So when or how will a breakthrough come?"

"I don't know the answer. Of course, Dr. Chu's announcement in 1987 opens a large can of worms. From here on, things could get very rough. But sometime, soon I think, someone will find the right stuff. Probably an isotope of some kind, I think. When they do, it's going to be very interesting to see how the news is released."

"William, suppose there already is a material which is superconductive at room temperature. If someone knew of it, what do you think they should do?"

"I'd say they'd better be damned careful. They'd be like the guy clutching the razor blade—couldn't let go of it or he'd bleed to death. Dozens of companies, even governments, would kill for it." William signed the check and rose to help her with her chair. "But I wouldn't put it at the head of my worry list, if I were you. Enough business. Would you go for a nightcap in the lounge?"

"Thanks, but I still have a bit of work before the conference tomorrow. You've made it easier, though. Helps to know something about the subject and what the speakers are trying to get across. The slogan 'ask Mr. Foster,' was never more true." And little do you know you've scared the wits out of me, Karen thought.

As they left the dining room and headed for the elevator together, Ivan Denkov, watching from the lobby, wondered idly if it would stop on one floor or two.

CHAPTER 6

Paris,

Wednesday, Later

Charles entered the lobby of the Intercontinental at precisely 5:00 p.m. The taxi ride back to Ruc Castiglione in heavy traffic was something a person only did once if he could help it, he thought. The driver had at least tried to smile, but detouring around a truck by driving up onto the sidewalk was a bit much, even for an investigator who was supposed to be in a dangerous line of work. From now on he'd join the throngs in the Metro. Shouldn't be too hard to figure out—a few stairways and escalators and a little study of the color-coded system maps and he'd go with the best of them.

Finally up in his hotel room, he made his way to the soft easy chair, and had the first shoe off his grateful foot when the phone rang. Grabbing his book of poetry, and opening it to "The Canticle of the Columns," he reached across the heavy brocaded bedspread to answer expectantly.

"Hi Charles."

Butler sounded as if he were speaking from next door. Satellites certainly had improved the quality of overseas phone calls. What could superconductors do for the world's communication systems, Charles wondered.

"What have you found?"

"Nothing on your Mr. Black, I'm afraid. I did find out that another translator from T.I. named Philip Brown has gone overseas somewhere. Could Brown be Black?"

"Could be anything, Herman," Charles responded. "Can you get a line on where Brown was going, and where he might be now?"

"We're trying. We sent our guy down to nose around T.I. and the boss, a Mr. Johnson, said an employee named Philip Brown was off somewhere for a week's vacation and no one seems to know just where. Could be Winch was chasing him. We did find out that Griman is in Berlin. Checked into the Schweizerhof Hotel there with his wife, and Karen Bright is also there, at the Kempinski. I don't know what that damned Griman is up to, Charles, but if you just go after that Curie stuff and get it home quick—" Butler was winding up for his "little general act" as Charles cut in.

"Okay, Herman, I got it. Now what about "The Canticle of the Columns;" Valery's poem? It's the sixth stanza I need." Charles had his copy open as he asked.

"Yea, I got that for you," Herman began.
"'Si froides at dorees
Nous fumes de nos lits'"
"Par le ciseau tirees", Charles interrupted,
"Pour devenir ces lys'!"

"Damn it, Charles. We had to do a lot of work to get this. Why did we bother if you already had it?"

"The translation, Herman. Remember, I ain't Maurice Chevalier." His impatience raised his voice.

"Sorry, Charles," Butler actually apologized. Speaking slowly, he read:

"'Out of our stone beds,
Gilded and so chilly,
We were freed by the chisel
To become these lilies'."

"Now what hell does all that mean?"

"I don't know yet, Herman, but I'll work on it and give you a call tomorrow. Let me know if you get any more dope on Black, Brown, Griman, Bright or whatever. Au revoir from Paris." Charles hung up before Butler could get in any more orders.

Looking at the translation, he compared it with his notes from the Institute. The key had to be in there somewhere. Maybe a drink would help. He picked up the phone again and called Room Service.

Berlin

Late Wednesday Night

Ivan Denkov was proud of the job he'd done in bugging Karen's room. Upstairs in the hotel suite, he sat confidently, watching a sophisticated VCR receiving set. He'd carried his new space age equipment in a normal sized briefcase, and had been able to plant tiny TV cameras. Each had its own transmitter and rechargeable batteries good for 48 hours of continuous operation. The tiny cameras fit nicely into the room's lighting fixtures, and four of them provided a full view of the entire room, the signals synchronized, blended, and recorded.

"So, Ivan Ilych," said Dromensky, who was busy gathering his personal effects from where he had scattered them all over the room. "I will leave late tonight for Paris. You stay with the Bright woman until she goes to Paris on Friday. There is a chance she is going to meet with someone." He spoke while beginning to assemble his traveling gear." Do you have anything worth watching yet?"

"That depends on your point of view, comrade. It is interesting, but I think we are wasting our time." Having recorded the entire sequence of Karen's activities until she was asleep in bed, Ivan was now reviewing the video tape on the monitor. What he saw on the screen was Karen, completely nude, stroking her golden cap of curls with a shiny silver brush, while she held part of Dromensky's Russian paper in the other hand. She paused to put down the brush and write a brief note on the pad of paper on the small telephone table. As she swung around, her breasts came in full view of the camera, full focus on the lovely uptilting curves.

Brutality went with Ivan's job, but he was not a voyeur, and he found himself blushing and looking away. He thought of his wife and two children in Leningrad, and decided not to call this tape to Dromensky's attention. He knew Dromensky was a lascivious old dog who should not be aroused. In fact, his distrust of Dromensky had festered during this trip. He resented the manner in which he was being ordered around, and he was beginning to really dislike this so-called comrade.

"The girl is not going to help us solve this mystery." Ivan thought further surveillance would be a waste of time. "You have lined up the necessary assistance from our French embassy. Perhaps I should travel with you to assist with the Grimans."

"No, Ivan Ilych, I will meet you Friday in the suite at the Bristol in Paris. I have a 'bait bag' which will finish the Griman problem. This girl here is our only other source of information. If we need her, that will be your department." Dromensky waved off further conversation. Ivan rewound the tape and remained silent.

Paris

Pan Am brought the Grimans to Paris two hours earlier than Dromensky's midnight Aeroflot flight, and Lisa pranced to the reception desk at the Bristol Hotel still quivering with anticipation. From the level where they stood, Lisa could look down a short flight of steps to the formal lobby, where women in fine woolen suits with handsome silk blouses, accompanied by dignified gentlemen in three-piece suits, graciously accepted after dinner liqueurs. Through the glass doors in the background, musicians played soft music amidst a bower of flowers and fountains. Paris and wealth, two of her most consuming fantasies, were transforming into reality.

As Lisa urged Frank to hurry after the bellboy, he fervently wished he could be anywhere else, the Hawaii he'd longed to see, maybe, or better yet, back home. The meeting tomorrow morning with Dromensky couldn't be anything but a big mistake. Oh hell, he thought, better go along with it; Lisa's supposed to be the smart one of the family. He followed behind as the bell boy led the way to their room.

* * *

I just know that's the answer, thought Charles, as he snapped the book closed and rose to reward himself with a refill of his glass from the room service tray. A review of Marie Curie's life story had confirmed the fact that her apartment at 36 Quai de Bethune contained interior columns, gilded and decorated with carved lilies. It just has to be that one of them will be on an outside wall, nice and cool, and one of those lilies will have an opening somewhere. Wait 'til Herman Butler hears about this!

Berlin

Thursday, June 11

Karen stopped at the front desk at 7:45 Thursday morning to leave the envelope containing her neatly penned pages of translation for Dr. Dromensky.

"I'm sorry, miss, but the doctor checked out last evening at about 11:00 p.m. I believe the other gentleman is still in the room, however." He turned to examine the cubbyholes behind him, "Are you by any chance Miss Karen Bright?" he questioned.

"Yes, I am," said Karen, astonished by the news of Dromensky's departure.

"Well, Fraulein, the doctor has left this for you." The clerk pushed forward a large brown envelope as he looked past her to help a waiting guest.

Still holding her own envelope, Karen moved to the door, tearing open this new offering. Out fluttered a $50 bill and a note written on a hotel memo pad. She read, "Miss Bright, I am so sorry. A sudden change of plans now makes your work unnecessary. Please forgive the inconvenience. You may keep or destroy the manuscript copy I gave you, and I have enclosed some added funds for your valuable time. Sincerely, signed Chernov H. Dromensky, Ph.D., Director, U.S.S.R. Ministry of Electronic Sciences."

Karen picked up the money and put both envelopes in her briefcase. Then she continued to the front entrance and got into a waiting cab to take her to the conference hall. She'd find the hospitality room and get some rolls and coffee there, she decided. And maybe a friendly smile, too, from someone. This Dromensky business was strange, and she'd had a wild nightmare last night about Marie Curie's warning her to watch out for "those Russians." This is one of those times it would be helpful to share a bizarre experience with a companion. Not Walter Bright, though, that's for sure! Her thoughts kept her engrossed until she entered the orange-tiled underground entrance to the congress hall. As she made her way to the escalators, the cab carrying Ivan Ilych Denkov pulled up to the entrance.

Paris

Thursday, June 11

Finally ensconced in his hotel room, Philip kissed the packet of papers and carefully placed them in his briefcase. It had taken a day and a half, a good bit of persuading the officials in the Euro-American lines office, not to mention a bundle of money, but at last he had his precious tickets for the trip back to New York on the new ship, *Royale*. There had been some heavy explaining to do, because his charge cards were in the name Philip Brown while his passport read Gerard P. Brown, same as his birth certificate. Bless you, Mother dear, he thought, for at least giving me the option of a middle initial. Philip, like that TV private eye, Philip Marlow, was at least bearable.

The flight across the Atlantic had been a seemingly interminable nightmare. The airline couldn't give him the aisle seat he'd requested, and he'd been by the window in a seat over the wing, unable to keep his eyes from the movement of one small rivet turning itself round and round, surely the beginning of total disintegration of that inadequate piece of aluminum skin between him and the endless black ocean forty thousand feet below. Wringing wet and icy cold, he'd promised himself if this airplane ever landed safely in France, he'd kiss the ground.

Fortunately, now he could return to the States by ship. Too bad he couldn't finish all the arrangements before he left New York, but he'd damned well got those *Royale* tickets, even if it had cost six months' salary. He could even endure being seasick if he knew there was good solid steel between himself and the deep blue. Philip wondered idly if he'd ever be able to conquer that terrible fear of flying. Probably be killed in a crash first.

* * *

Charles took the Metro from the Palais Royal Station. When he walked from the hotel, the little Metro sign showed up just where the doorman had predicted, and by studying the map by the ticket booth just inside the tunnel entrance, he'd been able to follow the destination lines until he found that the purple one, Marie d'Ivry route, would take him directly to Pont Marie and he wouldn't have to go through all the connections at Chatelet. Now emerging, he climbed the stairs and could see that the bridge itself, Pont Marie, was just across the wide street by the river. It would lead him to Ile St. Louis, and 36 Quai de Bethune should be on the other side of the island, facing the left bank.

Across the wide stone bridge, he made his way on the worn gray cobblestone street, admiring the beauty of the carefully polished and arranged fruits and vegetables offered by the produce vendor, the almost sinful allure of the freshly baked goodies displayed in the windows of the patisserie, and even the charm of the cat peeking through the lace curtains of the window of the neighborhood restaurant. He came to the end where the next bridge would take him across the River Seine again, and he quickly located his street, if that narrow space bordered by a sidewalk barely wide enough for two people could be called a street.

The massive carved wooden doors were at least nine feet high. They formed an imposing wall hiding all signs of any human occupancy. The number plates were even above that, so Charles found himself leaning back and craning his neck to read them.

As he approached number 36, however, the little street was suddenly closed in by two vehicles parked half on the sidewalk, one with a rotating light flashing blue. A uniformed gendarme, stiff billed hat pulled firmly down over his brows, stood guard before an opening tied with a thick yellow cloth sign that even Charles could guess meant Keep Out.

"Parlez vous Anglais?" Charles said to one of the men standing at the edge of the gathering crowd.

"Yes, monsieur." The man turned to study Charles.

"May I ask what is happening here?" Charles asked, wondering just how bold he dared be.

"Do you have business here, monsieur?" The question was firm, the look severe.

"Yes, sir, I am an American writer. I have a letter of introduction to the building manager requesting that I be allowed to visit Madame Curie's original quarters in this building."

"Then I must ask you some questions. I am with the police conducting this investigation." The policeman had taken a small note-pad from his pocket. He opened the cover, extracted a pencil, and said to Charles, "Your name, sir."

"It's Cecil Harmon. I'm with *World Science magazine,* doing a story on some of the later work of Madame Curie." Charles answered glibly. You idiot, he told himself, of all the people to ask, you had to pick the cop!

"You will not be able to see the concierge. It seems he was murdered sometime last night. He was found in the Curie apartment early this morning, his throat slit with a razor. Messy business. May I see your American passport?"

Charles very quietly said, "Oh shit!"

"Pardon,"

"I'm afraid I have left it at my hotel," said Charles as he turned to leave.

"One moment, please, Mr. Harmon." The policeman pointed to a spot on the sidewalk. "Wait right here." He stepped over to one of the small police cars. A very large man in civilian clothes emerged, rising slowly as if he'd been released by the air pressure of the opening door. After a brief exchange with the other officer, he stepped forward and, fixing Charles' attention firmly with eye contact that put him in command, said, "I am Chief Inspector Bodine, Mr. Herman."

"Harmon," Charles said, wishing to hell Herman was here in his place.

"Sorry, Mr. Harmon. Would you mind coming with me to the headquarters of the Criminal Division? It is not far from here. You won't be detained very long." Bodine opened the rear door of the police car and waved Charles in, staring persistently at his eyes.

These French dicks are just like the Irish cops in New York City, Charles thought, polite and very, very deadly. He'd have to smooth talk his way through this passport problem. If these cops discover he was lying, this short detention might get very long. Damn that asshole Herman Butler. The optimistic enthusiasm of the morning vanished, and depression was setting in. The Curie compound was probably gone with Mr. Throat-slitter, whoever the hell he was.

* * *

Lisa Griman had ordered breakfast in their room at the Bristol and Frank, marmalade-smeared croissant in hand, had just settled into a "come what may" attitude of full enjoyment, when the phone rang.

"Chernov Dromensky here, Mr. Griman. I should be pleased if we meet in my suite, 501, in, say thirty minutes. Would this be suitable to you?"

"Okay, Doctor," said Frank, with a catch in his voice that signified a sudden return to the seriousness of the present. "Ten o'clock, yes, we'll be there, suite 501, thank you."

As Frank hung up the phone, Lisa sat at the dressing table, topless, brushing her hair and viewing herself in the mirror with satisfaction.

"Did the old fart say he had the money?" Lisa asked as she reached for a lace bra and started fussing with the straps.

"He didn't say. Are you sure we want to go through with this, Lisa? Maybe it's not too late to back out." Frank felt the same surge of nervousness that had plagued him in Berlin.

"Of course it's too late. Besides, I'm not going to let us walk away from a cool million."

"Cool is right," Frank said. "It will be a cold day when we get anything from that Cossack creep . . . We better get moving if we're going to be on time."

Entering through the door of suite 501, both Frank and Lisa were startled at the grandeur of the rooms. Before them was a huge damask covered couch flanked by two generous armchairs, windows open to the sun with expansive views of the famous mansard roofs of Paris, and against the wall a large leather topped table on which rested an expensive looking medium sized suitcase, gray suede and strapped with leather.

"Ah, good morning, Mr. and Mrs. Griman. Welcome, my friends, to Paris, a most beautiful city, don't you think?" Dromensky waved them to the sofa. Frank found his cordiality as phony as before. Lisa seemed comfortable, if not impressed.

"Shall we get right down to business so you can enjoy your Paris vacation?" Dromensky seemed cool and nonchalant as he moved to open the suitcase. "This contains your money, one million American dollars. Would you like to count it? We have here hundred dollar notes put together by my embassy into one hundred packets. You see?" Dromensky lifted a green bundle. "So we have one hundred packets of one hundred notes, each note worth one hundred. One hundred little stacks, each stack worth ten thousand American dollars. That is a million dollars—a fortune, indeed, in my country, if not in yours."

Lisa got up and headed for the suitcase. She was suddenly afraid she might wet her pants, but she paused, caught her breath, and managed to say calmly, "Yes, I think we'll do a spot check count, Dr. Dromensky. Are the bills marked in any way?" She reached in and pulled out a packet, fanning it with an almost professional flourish.

"Mrs. Griman, please. My people have gone to a great deal of trouble to get this money together in such a hurry." Dromensky looked at Frank and continued. "There would be no reason for us to mark these notes. What you are giving us in return is well worth this money. We have no interest in your government's agency, what is it, the I.S.R.?"

"The I.R.S.," Frank corrected. "How do we proceed from here?"

"Very simple. Now, Mr. Griman, you have the original Curie letter with you. Also, the English translation and a copy of your contract with that electronics company and the name of the courier they have sent here to pick up the Curie compound." The way Dromensky said this, Frank wasn't sure whether he was making a statement or asking a question.

"And if we do?" Frank countered.

"So, the three of us will take this valise with your money in it to a nearby railroad station where we will find coin operated storage lockers. You will select a locker to hold the case and then give me the key. I will hold the key until you give me the documents, the name of the courier, and when I am satisfied that this will lead me to the superconductor material, I will return the key to you. The rest, of course, will be up to you." Dromensky paused, "Do you follow?"

"I'm not sure what you mean by satisfied," questioned Frank.

"Nothing for you to worry about, Mr. Griman. If the documents are accurate and your courier cooperates, you will have your key long before I have the superconductor material. If for some reason something does go wrong, although I can't imagine what that might be, I will simply keep the key and return home, and you may proceed with your previous arrangements, no one the wiser. Fair?" He now looked to Lisa for affirmation.

"That sounds good enough for me, Dr. Dromensky," Lisa responded without hesitation.

"Shall we now go to the railway station? Gare St. Lazare, I think, is the most convenient." He picked up the case with its neatly stowed packets and headed for the door.

* * *

As Charles rode in the back seat behind the uniformed driver and Inspector Bodine, the little police car threaded its way over the St. Louis bridge past a cluster of mothers with impatient children in front of a glaciere, waiting to buy ice cream cones. Charles barely noticed them, or the line of tourist busses packed together behind the massive buttresses of Notre Dame, or the throngs of walkers, most of them laden with guide books and maps, heading down the graveled walks for their tour of the magnificent cathedral. Instead, his mind whirled with questions. Was Frank Griman capable of two murders, and had he tried to beat everyone to the stuff? Not likely. Must be that mysterious Mr. Black. The same technique that did in poor Albert Winch seemed to have been used on the concierge, probably no coincidence. But according to Butler, only Griman and that translator, Karen Bright, knew about the Curie connection. So, had Karen Bright worked with, or maybe hired, Black, who might turn out to be Translator International's Mr. Brown? Again, not likely, too dumb a move for a bright girl, no pun intended.

Passing around the front of the cathedral, the car wheeled through the gold and wrought iron gates off Quai des Orfevres and parked by the Palais de Justice. As Charles was led past more lines of tourists awaiting admission to Sainte Chappelle, he wished fervently he were heading for a view of those medieval stained glass windows instead of where he was being taken. His escorts led him to a back door and up a narrow stairway to an office that apparently was part of the Criminal Division.

"Please have a seat, Mr. Harmon, I will be with you shortly." Bodine spoke English effortlessly, and obviously was accustomed to being understood. Leaving Charles in the bare reception area, he disappeared down a hall of many doors, each having a neatly painted name and number on a glass panel. He returned abruptly with a manila folder and a drab, no-nonsense woman carrying a hard backed note pad.

"Follow me, please." Bodine showed Charles into a small conference room. The woman put on a pair of businesslike glasses. The three of them sat at a small table, and as Charles put his briefcase before him, the thought occurred that, if he didn't know better, he could easily have been at a corporate business meeting. The establishment really didn't have anything left of the palace it once was, but neither did it have the trappings one might expect of a police station, and certainly not of a Criminal Division.

"Now then, Mr. Harmon. You say you are an American writer for a science magazine and you just happened to arrive at 36 Quai de Bethune with a letter of introduction to the gentleman who was murdered last night. Do you know this man's name, and what reason did you have for wishing to meet him?" Bodine was patiently prodding, waiting for Charles to volunteer information. The woman sat poised, ready to write.

Might as well try to stick with the cover story, thought Charles. He dug out the letter of introduction from his inside jacket pocket, and stalled a bit fishing for the phony business card from his wallet.

Bodine read the letter slowly. When he finally came to the end and the signature of the French counsel from New York, there was a noticeable change in his treatment of Charles. He now appeared almost affable.

"So. I am sorry, Mr. Harmon, for this unfortunate affair. Which hotel are you staying in? I can have one of my men take you there." Bodine gestured to the woman to close her notebook.

"I am at the Intercontinental." Charles hoped that Bodine was not going to ask for further verification. The passport of Charles Holden would certainly create a major problem for Cecil Harmon.

"Why was the poor guy murdered?" Charles asked the Inspector, trying to display a casual curiosity.

"The killer was obviously deranged, Mr. Harmon." As he spoke, Bodine pulled an official photograph from the manila folder he'd carried into the conference room. "The crime lab picture shows it. Look here." He pointed to a very ugly corpse surrounded by debris everywhere, broken chair and table legs piled in heaps with chunks of plaster piled on top, and plaster dust added to the rubble on what must be intricately patterned parquet floors.

"There is no logic here, Mr. Harmon. The maniac, as you can see, has taken an axe and smashed the furniture, and broken these magnificent columns. The manager, who lived below, probably heard the commotion and came to investigate. The intruder had a large razor or a very sharp knife as well as his axe. Look at all this blood. It will be very difficult to restore this room. It is, after all, an historical monument." Charles was surprised to see Bodine reveal so much emotion.

Charles reached for the picture, and now that he could study it closely he could see that the famous rooms had been supported by columns embellished with sculptured garlands of leaves starting from the floor and entwining themselves around as if growing to the extreme height of the ceiling. The column closest to the window had a broad slash across its base, but the column next to the body had also been attacked, and seemed to have a hollow spot behind one of the plaster leaves. Naturally. A damned lily leaf, and the son-of-a-bitch had found Marie Curie's flacon 216 and the secret to super-conductivity. Mr. Black, whoever he is, has himself a real prize.

CHAPTER 7

Berlin,

Thursday, June 11

Up in the glassed-in interpreter's booth which overlooked the auditorium with its plush seats and automatic language earphones, Karen stretched and rubbed her head where the headset pressed. The four papers she'd just translated from English to German had been highly technical. Ironically, the last speaker, from Los Alamos Laboratories in the United States, had spoken with a heavy German accent. That's when the written text proved necessary.

The question and answer period was a real challenge. The questions came in all languages. The last one, from a Frenchman, about superconductors changing automobiles from fossil fuel to electricity, with no-loss rechargeable batteries, gave her the giggles as he gestured and spoke of "leak-wood hair in the shit-ro-hen."

Then her conscience pricked again. Professional ethics demanded confidentiality, but the world needed what she knew: that a for-real room temperature superconductor actually did exist. That French guy, silly as he seemed, wasn't being the least bit stupid. He had obviously become well aware that commercial applications would control the development of the high temperature superconductor.

The moderator closed the morning session with a clearly relevant admonition: "This morning we have heard some important reports on the research progress being made in high temperature superconductor materials. We are grateful to these gentlemen and to the firms they represent for sharing data at the generic level. While there are certain perils in collaboration, we are on the edge of such a major new scientific era that only freely exchanged information can turn dreams into reality. The major problem now is not how rapidly superconductors will enter the marketplace, but how to avoid the dangerous secrecy which plagues the honest competition needed to drive technological development."

Right on, thought Karen, but right now I need a break from the whole thing. Maybe after I'm in Paris I'll try to check it out and find someone to tell. After all, Madame Curie's stuff really belongs to France. Frank Griman might be doing something about flacon 216 this very minute.

She gathered her papers and was heading for the translator's lounge when a tight purple skirt, doughnut size hoop earrings and masses of blonde swirling hair planted themselves in her way. The vision spoke.

"Karen, saw you across from Booth Three. Are you through for the day? How about sharing a cab downtown?"

"Well, if it isn't Edie Harris, freelancer-at-large. I knew this convention needed a lot of language people, but aren't you a bit far from home base?" Karen tried to show some congeniality, but Edie's fat fees for independent work, along with that flashy style, always put her on the defensive.

Edie quickly confirmed the opinion by saying, "Karen, dearie, I don't mind telling you I'm sick of this superconductivity shit! According to the schedule, we don't have to be back until tomorrow morning. Why don't we go in search of some of the good stuff they talk about in Berlin? I'll bet it wouldn't be too hard to find a couple of nice big German boys and brush up on our sex lives. A poor working girl ought to have a little fun, whaddaya say?"

Edie tried to come on strong, as she always had, but Karen knew the routine. The idea was, if you don't like what you hear, you can pretend you know she's kidding. Karen, however, had known her long enough to realize she meant exactly what she said.

"Where are you staying, Edie? I'd like to share a cab, but I want to go back to my hotel and drop off all this junk I'm carrying. Maybe we could have dinner, but you'll have to handle the sex search on your own. This town is raunchy enough, that's for sure. Have you checked the hookers on every corner of Kurferstendamm? I can't even handle the TV programs in my room! We'd better get going; that lineup for cabs gets fierce in a hurry. I tried going out the front entrance yesterday, and it's no better there."

Carrying their briefcases and books, the two translators headed for the escalator and motor entrance.

Paris

Later Thursday

Frank and Lisa were back in the Bristol with Dromensky. The domineering Russian kept them under control all during their trip to the train station, directing the way to the lockers and subtly indicating which one they should choose. At the hotel's front desk he stood aside, smoothly nonchalant, but carefully close to the young woman, while Frank retrieved his documents from the hotel safe. Now they were upstairs in Suite 501, and Dromensky took charge.

"Mr. Griman," he began as he dropped the storage locker key in a glass ashtray on the same table used earlier to display the valise filled with money, "you will allow me to examine the papers."

Frank tried hard to maintain some self control, even though Lisa demonstrated her impatience with her stocking arranging and hair patting. She's a fool if she believes she's going to distract this bird with her sexy legs, Frank thought. Still clutching the long white envelope, he asked, "Dr. Dromensky, I'm still not clear about your terms for returning the key to us. You said you needed the documents and also the identity of Consolidated's courier? We don't really know anything definite about him. All we know is what our contract with Consolidated spells out. They have a time limit for getting the Curie material, and supposedly their guy is an expert searcher."

"Patience, Mr. Griman. Why don't you pour yourself and Mrs. Griman some of that fine wine on the table there while I read." He extended his hand for the envelope and settled steel rimmed reading glasses on his prominent nose. "I shall answer your questions when I am through."

"Help yourself, Lisa. I'm heading for the bathroom." Frank stumbled toward the little room just off the entry hall, suddenly weak in the knees.

Lisa rose to help herself from the linen wrapped bottle and took a healthy gulp of the sparkling red Cabernet. Different from the bar white wine she sometimes had with the girls, but good. She studied the label, Bouvet-Ladubay Rubis. Maybe I'll order it again when I get the million, she thought.

Dromensky stroked his beard slowly as he read, the careful rhythm obscuring his quickening pulse as he gently handled the delicate pages of the original letter. This is better than I'd hoped, he thought. Definitely looks authentic, and the translation simple, but accurate. He moved on to the technical pages of Griman's contract with Consolidated Electronics. Carefully refolding the papers and returning them to their places in the envelope, then to his inner breast pocket, he removed his glasses and joined Lisa at the wine table.

"You should not regret ending your dealings with those Consolidated people, Mrs. Griman," he said. "Shall we drink a toast to the end of their, do you say, red tape?" He filled the two remaining glasses on the tray and moved to refill hers, "And also to our victory?"

"You make it sound like we just won a battle, Dr. Dromensky. Does that mean you have what you want, and we can take our key and au revoir?" She drained her glass, toast or no toast.

"Not quite yet." He looked to Frank who had quietly moved to Lisa's side. "Now we must have the name and address of this man Consolidated sent to find the material. We must be sure he has not removed from its location that which we are seeking."

"Shit, that's easy," Lisa chirped. "Didn't you say he was named Holden, like that famous movie star, only Charles? And staying at the Intercontinental?"

* * *

It was shortly after two o'clock when the little white car with the blue light on top pulled up in front of the Intercontinental Hotel.

"Merci," said Charles as the uniformed officer saluted and drove off. "And I hope I never see you again," he breathed, as he pushed through the revolving doors and headed left, straight to the Tuileries Bar. A martini couldn't hurt, and it might help, he thought, as he entered the surprisingly crowded room. Guess it's lunch time, may as well eat.

An hour later, much more comfortable after his martini, a memorable bowl of onion soup and whatever that chicken special had been, Charles had the time to contemplate his predicament. He was sure the infamous Mr. Black now had Marie Curie's superconductor. But what would be his next move?

Herman Butler had made quite a point that day at the Tennis Club about the probable instability of the material and its vulnerability to metal detectors or x-rays. If this guy Black knew enough to decode Valery's poem, he was probably intelligent enough to know what he was dealing with and how to get it out of the country. If he was working alone.

Today's overseas airline flights, especially after all those recent hijackings, subjected all luggage to security inspection, not just the carry-ons. So, if Black wanted to get the stuff back to the States . . . Ship maybe? They also had walk-on detectors, but the ones leaving port at New York at least, let the stevedores haul the baggage around as fast as they could. Worth investigating, anyway.

"Good afternoon, monsieur. Were you able to find the Grand Hotel de Lima yesterday?" The concierge's helpful tone did not conceal his curiosity as he looked again at Charles' eyes.

"Oui, your suggestion was perfect," Charles replied, "but now I have another question. If I wanted to return to New York by ship within a day or two, would it be possible?"

"Would you wish to sail from France? The *QE*2 sails almost weekly from Southampton, but that is England. You realize there are very few so-called 'transatlantic crossings' these days."

"Anything at all from France," Charles persisted, "a freighter perhaps?"

The concierge shuffled through stacks of papers he'd piled under the desk. His face lit up as he extracted a colorful brochure.

"Voila! You are in luck! The luxury liner *Royale* is so new I almost forgot her. She will make her last crossing of the season to New York, leaving Le Havre Sunday night, to arrive the following Friday." His round face split with a big grin, as if he were emerging victorious from battle. "Shall I see if I can book passage for you, Mr. . . ." He paused, realizing Charles had never given him a name.

"Holden, Charles Holden. Thank you, but first I have to see if I can arrange my affairs for that time. What is the steamship line, and do they have offices here?"

"Euro-American lines. Their offices are near all those travel agencies and airline companies just off the Place de l'Opera, 26 Rue de Auber."

Handing him a ten franc note, Charles turned to go, saying, "Many thanks. I'll get back to you." Next stop, the desk for his key.

The room clerk handed him a telephone message form with his key. Probably Herman nagging, thought Charles. Well, I have to get his help anyway, see if he can pull some strings and figure out how I can check the *Royale* passenger list. Of course, I don't know what name Black might use, but Griman or that Karen Bright might be listed, and it's just possible they may be working together (stranger things have happened), or traveling together to protect their take.

The elevator took him to his floor. Making his way along the wide carpeted hallway, rounding three corners enroute, he finally arrived at his room.

The red message light on the telephone blinked in the darkness. He flicked on the light, tossed his jacket on the bed and kicked off his shoes. Before he went to the phone he read the message in his hand. Written in English, it said, "Norman

Teal of Consolidated Electronics Co. would like you to call local number 266.91.45, ext. 501, for an urgent message from Mr. Butler." The note was stamped in purple ink, indicating it had been received at 14:46 hr.

"What the hell?" Charles said aloud.

* * *

In the Dromensky suite Lisa was on her fourth glass of wine. Frank fidgeted with his room key as Dromensky picked up the jangling telephone. Placing his hand over the mouthpiece, he told the Grimans, "See, that did not take long at all." Then he moved his hand and answered, "Extension 501."

"Charles Holden calling. Is there a Mr. Norman Teal there, please?"

"This is Norman Teal, Mr. Holden. Thank you for calling promptly." Dromensky pulled up a small chair, settled himself and continued, speaking in muted tones to disguise his Slavic accent. "I've just arrived in Paris. Have you spoken with Herman Butler today?"

"No, I got this message a few minutes ago and thought I'd better respond right away. I talked to Butler yesterday. May I ask about your connection to Consolidated, Mr. Teal?"

"Herman asked that I make a rush trip here to assist you with arrangements for getting the—ahem—" Dromensky paused, changing the tone of his voice, "Curie material back to the States. You do have what you were sent for, do you not, Mr. Holden?"

"Mr. Teal," Charles answered after a long silence, "I don't think this matter should be discussed on the telephone. I have a few matters to take care of at the moment, so why don't you come to my hotel at five. I'll meet you in the lobby." Charles glanced at his watch: 3:40.

"Very well," Dromensky said, "I will meet you in the lobby at five. Perhaps we can have a cocktail and discuss our plans. How will I know you?"

"I'll be wearing a brown suede jacket, blue shirt and tan trousers. You should find me near the entrance. See you then, Mr. Teal." Charles hung up, wiping the beads of moisture from his brow as he looked at his gray wool jacket on the bed.

Dromensky smiled broadly as he replaced the handset and turned to Lisa. "I see no reason to detain you two any longer." He plucked the locker key from the ashtray.

"Has Holden got the stuff?" Frank held out his hand to accept the key.

"I'm not so sure about that, Mr. Griman. You must not concern yourself further with my problems. I will handle Mr. Holden. Just go. Retrieve your money and enjoy from now on a good life. I wish you well. Now I must make some arrangements, so good afternoon." Dromensky ushered them to the door without additional ceremony.

"Thank you, Dr. Dromensky, it's been a ball. Be sure to look us up if you ever get to New York." Lisa tried to look coy as she waved her handbag in farewell. Frank grasped her arm tightly as he steered her to the elevator.

The burly man stood watching, his sharp, feline eyes squinting in concentration until the American pair disappeared behind the closing doors. After checking to be sure his door was tightly closed and locked, he refilled his glass with the last of the wine. He tossed the empty bottle into the wastebasket and rubbed his hands together in a gesture of finality.

CHAPTER 8

Paris

Sometime Thursday, June 11

In a small Paris hotel room, a solitary man carefully examined the aged brown glass jar. It was a little larger than a fifth of whiskey, and reminded him of the apothecary jars still seen occasionally in windows of older drug stores. About midway between the ground glass stopper and the slightly flared base was a yellowing label, on which had been hand printed in green ink "Flacon 216, 2-8-33," followed by the initials in script, "M.C." There was not a hint as to the nature of the contents on the worn, discolored label.

He had done his homework. He'd purchased a test kit put out by the Colorado Superconductor Co. of, strangely enough, Fort Collins, Colorado. The kit didn't consist of much, but it did have explicit instructions which he had memorized, and a few simple tools. It all boiled down to the fact that, if the stuff could really superconduct at room temperature, the tiny magnetic disc included in the kit would float in the air, or levitate, when it was suspended above the superconductor material, something they called the "Meissner Effect" having to do with its "diamagnetic properties." The more stuff under the magnetic disc, the higher it would float, but the magnet was special too, made of some "rare earth material" that created a very strong and very lightweight magnet.

So here goes, he thought. He read from a tiny thermometer on his key chain, 71 degrees F. A clean ashtray was ready and waiting on the clean towel, and the kit's furnished plastic tongs ready at hand. He carefully tapped the glass stopper, and after a bit of persistent, repetitous twisting it moved freely. He poured a thin stream of the shiny black powder until it formed a layer about a quarter of an inch thick in the ash tray. Now, picking up the tongs, he maneuvered until he had the tiny disk held securely.

"Millions if it floats," he murmured softly, "if not, no regrets." No thoughts of two slit throats.

He placed the magnet gently into the black stuff, and watched it instantly rise and hang in mid-air about two inches above the ashtray, seeming to stare at him obscenely as if it were on an invisible thread, trying to make up its mind where to point.

"Holy shit, I'll be damned, I got it, I really got it!"

Berlin

Thursday, late afternoon

Karen left Edie ordering a drink in the lounge as she returned to her room to drop off all her papers and, above all, change her shoes. Why do your feet always swell when you're in a strange place, she thought, as she fitted the key with its heavy tag into her now familiar door.

A small white envelope lay on the rug just over the threshold, obviously shoved under the door. She stooped to pick it up, and, moving to the desk by the window, read "Karen, please call me, room 606, after 5:00 p.m. There's something you should know." It was signed, "Fondly, William Foester."

Funny, wonder what that's all about, she mused. Looking at her watch, Karen realized it was still too early to call. Just seemed later because she'd been on duty so early this morning. Might as well join Edie for awhile.

Karen, with freshened lipstick, soft curls once again framing her face and her favorite doeskin pumps on her feet, entered the lounge at the far end of the Kempinski's lobby, and was not surprised to find that Edie had wasted no time. Three people were now seated at the cocktail table. At first glance, Edie seemed to have done fairly well.

"Karen, meet Karl Vough," she indicated the pink cheeked, very Teutonic young men next to her, as both of them stood for Edie's introduction.

"Karl is with the Max Planck Institute in Stuttgart. I translated his paper this morning . . ." Edie made no attempt to explain the other man, a slender, olive skinned fellow with a crooked front tooth.

"George Castle," he said softly, extending his hand.

Karen had to give Edie credit, she seemed to have done better than usual with her male call.

"I ordered for you, Karen," Edie said, and indicated the drink on the coaster next to George. Taking her cue, Karen sat down and gave him her get-acquainted smile. Turned out George was from the States, from the Argonne National Laboratory in Illinois, and worked for the U.S. Department of Energy pilot center for superconductivity research. Can't get away from it, sighed Karen.

As the drinking and conversation progressed, Karen had the feeling that her new American friend was trying hard to pump the German scientist, but Karl was having no trouble staying with the small talk and avoiding any direct questions about his technical field. In fact, both Edie and Karl were arriving at the alcohol level that raises the decibels, and Karen was just as glad to cooperate when Karl suggested they find somewhere else to go.

"I know a place we should check on," said Karl as he pulled Edie to a standing position.

"What would be open so early in the day?" protested Edie, struggling to pull down the piece of purple fabric serving as a skirt.

"Something different, one of Berlin's specialties, open from noon to seven a.m. Let's go get a cab."

"I want to be back here around five," said Karen, relieved that Karl had not suggested doing any driving himself.

"No problem. You won't be far away," said Karl, already on his way to the revolving doors.

A gentle wave of contentment settled over the room as dignity once again prevailed. Behind the table of Japanese tourists in the corner, Ivan Denkov took a final swallow of beer and placed some coins in the waiting saucer on the table. He was happy to be off duty until five o'clock.

* * *

Twelve minutes after leaving the Hotel Bristol Kempinski (Karen kept track as unobtrusively as she could), the quartet arrived at the Club Ludwigstrasse. Even though it was still afternoon and bright daylight outside, once through the heavy doors, the black ceiling and walls and dim lights common to nightclubs all over the world set the mood as soon as their eyes adjusted to the contrast.

They were shown to a small table next to a tiny stage occupied by a musical trio consisting of guitar, electronic bass, and drums, playing soothing mellow jazz. The sticky smell of pot assailed nostrils over the smell of stale cigarette smoke, and Karen wrinkled her nose in distress.

"This joint smells like joints," said George, joining in Karen's recognition. His words sailed meaningless over Karl's head, and Edie chose to ignore them.

Their round of drinks was served quickly, and was accompanied by a generous bowl of German pretzels. The blue spotlight turned to the guitarist, who eased into his solo, dark hair falling over his pale cheeks in concentration as his fingers, emerging from the rhinestone studded sleeves of his denim jacket, seemed to have a life of their own.

Karen, relaxing in genuine pleasure, was jerked out of her reverie when a tall, sinewy blonde with heavy blue eye make-up and sultry lips stepped into the spotlight, and the guitarist changed his beat to a rapid, heavy rhythm. Any expectations that the blonde's voice would match the skill of the guitarist came to an immediate end as the vocalist, with a scratchy, raspy voice, started a German ditty whose words Karen could not translate, but obviously were smutty and suggestive.

Karl, of course, knew what was going on, and surprisingly, Edie also seemed to. They had their heads together, grinning, as the blonde now slowed her tempo and started to strip. When two bouncing bare breasts loomed directly above the tiny table, Karen had had enough. She fumbled in her purse for some German bills, placed the notes on a saucer in front of her, and whispered, "Sorry kids, I've got to leave you. Don't worry, I'll get a cab. See you tomorrow at Congress Hall, Edie. Have fun . . ." Ducking to be sure she wouldn't be caught in the spotlight, she headed for the door.

George's arm reached across her to hold the heavy door open. "Let me take you back to your hotel," he said softly, "A little of that goes a long way for me, too."

"You know, George, I'm really not a prude," said Karen, once they were settled in a cab, "but I'm actually not that comfortable here in Berlin, with its undercurrent of espionage, intrigue, and pornography blatant everywhere. My grandfather had a nasty encounter during World War II with a German officer who pretended to be friendly, and I guess I feel I must protect myself." Karen broke off. She was saying too much to a stranger. The evils of too much booze.

"I feel it too, Karen. I wanted to get close enough to Karl to wring some trade secrets from him, but I'd hate to have to explain some dumb incident in a place like that! How about your friend, will she be okay?"

"Don't worry about Edie. She can handle Karl, the stripper, and the whole crew without half trying! But tell me about Karl, and the information you were trying to get from him. Do the Germans really have something we in the United Stated need to know about superconductors?"

Suddenly serious now, heavy eyebrows pulling forward in a concerned frown, George said, "Look at it this way, Karen. We in the United States are spending about 25 million a year on the superconductor project, but that money is going for research and development, and for fundamental research at that. The Japanese are more canny, they don't see room temperature superconductors arriving on the scene until the year 2010. By then you can be sure, they'll be ready technologically. Meanwhile, the Germans are figuring out the consumer end of the business, like how to make superconducting cables for generators, and transformers and motors. What I'm getting at is: when we finally get this high temperature material, we won't know how to use it, and the Germans will."

George paused long enough to see if he still had an audience. Seeing Karen's obvious interest, he explained, "Basically, my job with the U.S. Department of Energy is to look for ways to close that gap."

Here we are, back to that damned Curie letter again, and my pet albatross, moaned Karen to herself. What am I going to do about it, or am I? Would George be able to help because of his job with the U.S. Government? I'd almost decided to bare all to the Curie Institute people when I get to Paris, but the more I learn about the whole picture, the more patriotic I become. Damn! My time schedule puts pressure on, too! It will just have to wait, can't get involved here in Berlin and still keep my reservations for Paris tomorrow, she decided.

"I wish you good luck, George, for your sake and ours, too. Look, here we are back on Kurfurstendamm. It looks like such a normal commercial city street I find it hard to realize this is where the gang of Nazi hoodlums started the devastation of Jewish stores and businesses that finally culminated in the holocaust. Theoretically, the conflict is over, but we're still talking about fierce national competition, and that ugly wall wasn't far from here!"

"Well, it's not all bad, Karen. This convention has given us some good exchange of information." As he spoke they rounded the corner of the hotel, past crowded tables on the sidewalk under an EIS sign, where millions of ice cream calories were being consumed with enthusiasm by the afternoon tea time customers. As the taxi drove up to the Kempinski entrance, he said, "I've thoroughly enjoyed your company—I know you said you have an appointment now, but will I see you at Congress Hall tomorrow?"

"For a short time. I have three papers to do, then I'm leaving directly to catch a flight to Paris. Thanks for your help—" She left with a wave and a warm smile. Why didn't I encourage him, she asked herself. Maybe because he was a bit too smooth?

Up in her room, her watch read a few minutes after five when she picked up the phone and asked for room 606.

"Karen, I'm glad you called. I was afraid you'd be out for the rest of the evening with your girlfriend."

"How did you know about her?"

"I tried to flag you down at the convention hall when you left with her, but I got stopped by someone and couldn't get away."

"She's just a fellow translator I've known. Sorry I didn't see you."

"That's why I needed to get in touch, Karen. There's someone else you didn't see. I'm pretty sure some guy is following you. I saw him concentrating on you after dinner last night as we left the dining room, then he was sticking pretty close behind you today. You and your friend left the hall, and he was in a big rush to get out the door and into a cab behind you. Could be a coincidence, but it looked suspicious to me. I wanted to warn you . . ."

"I can't imagine why anyone would want to follow me," Karen started to protest, and with a sudden chill she remembered that man watching outside her apartment as she was packing to leave New York. A shudder went through her body from the tired spot between her shoulder blades to the tender bottoms of her feet.

"Let me take you to dinner, Karen, I don't like the idea of your being alone."

"I'd be grateful for your company, William. But let's make it simple and early." Reminds me of saying almost the same thing to Philip Brown, Karen thought.

Paris

Late Thursday Afternoon

Without leaving the telephone, Charles placed a call to Butler at Consolidated Electronics in New York. He listened to the ringing sound and mentally willed it to answer. Be there when I need you, he thought as Butler's gruff voice replied.

"Charles, I was hoping to hear from you before I left for lunch. Were you able to put the poetry in motion?"

"The poetry led me to the trough, but I couldn't drink." I might as well ease him into it, Charles thought, "Some horse, or I might say horse's ass, got there before I did. A poetic injustice that landed me in the police station." He could imagine the color rising from Herman's double chin to his bulbous nose and forehead frown lines.

"What the hell are you trying to tell me? I didn't send you over there to perform like some idiot amateur!"

"Calm down, Herman. First, I need to know, does the name Norman Teal mean anything to you?"

"Never heard of him, why?"

"Didn't think it would. Who else knows I'm in Paris?"

"Far as I know, only Griman and the attorneys. I've done my best to say nothing about the whole venture in the office here." Of course, thought Charles, he's going to cash in for himself as much as he can.

"Okay, here's the story." As he gave Butler a modified version of the day's events, calculated to ease the effect of total loss, his mind was already racing ahead to his next moves. "We're still in the game, but we have some catching up to do. What I need from you now is some information. and I think you'll have to pull some strings."

"Name it."

"What I need is the complete passenger list of the *Royale*, scheduled to sail from Le Havre on Sunday, the twentieth. Can you arrange for me to get it at the Euro-American office here in Paris at 26 Rue de Auber? They'll be closed by the time you could arrange it for today, so I'll check with them first thing tomorrow morning."

"I think I see what you're getting at, Charles. If they knew enough to find it, they must also know they shouldn't try to fly it —"

"Something like that. I'll check back with you to get the name to use at Euro-American tomorrow. You won't be able to reach me here, I'm changing addresses. Is there anything else I should know?"

"We learned that the Grimans checked out of their Berlin Hotel and left no forwarding address. Keep your eye out for them, maybe they're selling out, but I didn't think they had the know-how or the guts. We also found out that Karen Bright plans to go to Paris tomorrow after the wind up of the conference in Berlin. Her office says she's planning to be at the Intercontinental for a couple of days. I'll get that list. Remember, I'm still counting on you, Charles!" Butler hung up abruptly, as usual.

The unruly cowlick at the back of his head now waving like a misplaced antenna, Charles searched frantically through the pockets of his gray jacket. I know I wrote that number somewhere, he muttered. Success, finding it deep in the recesses of the inside breast pocket, and unfolding the crumpled note, he headed back to the phone once more.

"Institut du Radium," in response to the ring.

"I'm trying to reach Christine Fournier," he said, trusting they'd understand his English.

"She's just leaving. I'll see if I can catch her."

This had better work, as he balanced the phone between his ear and shoulder, and sat down to put his shoes back on.

"This is Christine," came the tentative feminine voice.

"This is Cecil Harmon, do you remember, you were so helpful to me with the journals of Marie Curie?"

"Oh yes, did you find the book of poetry that you wanted to read?"

"Yes, thank you, at that big bookstore near the University. But that is not why I called. I find I need some more help, and you're the only native I know to call on. Could I possibly see you now?" He wondered if it would insult her to offer payment.

"Could you tell me the nature of your problem, Mr. Harmon? I have some plans after I leave here."

"My reservation in this hotel got fouled up and I need a place to stay for a few more days. This whole city seems to be overbooked, something about a fashion market, and I thought you might have some suggestions." I'd leave a trail a mile wide if I went to the Concierge for help, Charles thought, and I can't go fumbling from place to place looking for somewhere to hide. Even if I found a room in some flea bag hotel, they'd have to register my passport, and Mr. Teal, whoever he is, might have the right connections to trace it.

"I may be able to help monsieur. I'm on my way home, and I live in the Marais district. Often there are places available there. Would you like to meet me at my apartment and we could search for a room then?"

That's one for our side, thought Charles as he stuffed her address into the jacket now settled on his shoulders. He swept the contents of the bathroom shelf into his tote bag, grabbed his coat from the closet, picked up his suitcase and was out the door.

At the Institut du Radium Christine was assailed by Dr. Remy as she went out the front door. There had been much distress in those staid halls today, and Dr. Remy seemed eager to talk to her even though she was in a hurry to leave.

Charles' watch read 4:40 when he asked the doorman for a cab to the airport. Checking out is always a wait-in-line affair, but the people at the desk didn't give him any trouble about leaving early. He left no forwarding address.

Once in the taxi, he told the driver he'd changed his mind, and could they please go to Rue St. Cloud in the Marais District instead? He had to actually hold up extra bills to stop the driver's outraged objections, not only over the loss of the extra airport fare, but also the need to plunge into rush hour traffic on Rue Rivoli. At least he'd avoided Norman Teal, whoever he might be. For the second time Charles was sorry he'd left his friendly little gun back in old New York City.

* * *

Frank Griman was not ecstatic. The lure of one million dollars close at hand could not mitigate the mantle of guilt that had dropped on him the minute Lisa blurted out Charles Holden's name to Dromensky.

"You know, Lisa, we've practically signed that poor Holden's death warrant." Frank was surprised at Lisa's total indifference. "I think I'm going to see if I can warn him." Looking at his watch he added, "It's nearly five, I'm going to call the Intercontinental and see if I can catch him."

"Do what you want, Frank, but make it snappy. Time's wasting."

"Hotel Intercontinental, please," he said to the operator.

He watched Lisa struggle with her suitcase as he waited for the call to go through. "Intercontinental? May I speak with Mr. Charles Holden, please?"

"I'm sorry, sir. Monsieur Holden has checked out."

Defeated, he slowly replaced the phone. Then suddenly to Lisa, "Holden's gone, and what's that going to do to Dromensky? He'll be sore as hell at us, that's what! You're right, we better get a move on. We'd better get to that locker before the Russky changes his mind!"

"What the hell do you think I've been doing? I'm ready now, Frank, and while you've been wasting time with the phone, I've worked out our schedule." She folded the last garment, snapped the lock on her case, and continued, "You get your stuff packed and check us out of here. While you're doing that, I'll go to Gare St. Lazare and pick up that nice little gray suitcase. We can meet at the airline shuttle terminal on the Champs Elysees."

"You can wait five minutes, for crissake!"

"No, 'cause you'll have to stop at the front desk for our passports, and also go to the travel desk and get us seats on the next flight to Zurich. I looked it up. There are flights from both Orly and Charles de Gaul, depending on when we leave. It's possible to take a shuttle to either airport, they leave every hour on the half hour from the Tourist Information Center right there on Champs-Elysees. If we have waiting to do, we can do it at the airport. We sure as hell don't want to hang around here!" She looked at her wristwatch. "Shuttle leaves on the half hour, so let's aim for the 6:30." Without waiting for an argument, she slung her purse over her shoulder and was out the door.

"Be careful," Frank said to her retreating back.

* * *

Christine Fournier found Charles sitting on his suitcase on the broad expanse of grass in front of the arcades at Place des Vosges, whose passages framed the monumental residences of the 16th and 17th century, now restored to their original architectural excellence with life renewed.

Charles had been trying to think of a logical story to tell Christine as he surveyed the busy scene. For a brief moment, he considered telling her the truth. "A killer is after me, and he knows my real name, so I don't want to use my passport to register at a hotel. But you only know me by a fake name anyway." Shit. Cecil Harmon is what she knows me by, so that's what it will have to be. I'll wing it somehow, and stick with the truth where possible.

"Sorry to keep you waiting." said the pert, slender and self confident girl who interrupted his concentration. She was wearing the current uniform of the French working girl, a slim dark skirt with a marvelous jacket, an outrageous wild hairdo and giant gold earrings. Charles was only pushing 40, but the glow of youth on this radiant thing, at the end of a very long day, suddenly reminded him he'd been around this investigating game a helluva long time.

"Hello, Christine," he said, with his always effective boyish grin, pushing his sunglasses to the top of his head.

"We had a perfectly horrible day at the Institute. Poor Dr. Remy was so upset! The police have been there, and they've told us about a terrible break-in at Madame Curie's apartment on the Ile St. Louis." Christine's smile vanished as she prepared to give Charles the whole story.

"That's too bad," he sympathized, "what was taken?"

"Not much, if anything, but the dreadful thing was, they killed the building manager. Dr. Remy told us it must have been the work of a madman, or someone on drugs. The manager's throat was cut, and the apartment trashed and damaged badly. Why would anyone want to do that to a museum place? That apartment was almost sacred to me, my grandfather worked with Madame Curie, you know." Distress put a tremble in her voice.

"I didn't know. Maybe this is a very bad time to impose on your kindness . . ."

"No, please, monsieur. I have told my boyfriend of your problem, and he will meet us in my apartment in just a little while. Together we will see if we can find a solution for you. Let us go on up." She waited for him to gather his things, and led the way around the corner to an obscure door which opened to a stairway to the rooms above.

They had been upstairs in the tiny, but adequate apartment only long enough for Christine to open a bottle of wine and fill two glasses, when a knock signalled the arrival of her boyfriend.

She opened the door to a lean, casually dressed, far more mature fellow than Charles had expected. He had been thinking of this helpful girl as a teenager, but Leon's arrival quickly added a dimension of sophistication to the scene.

"I have done some searching in this neighborhood on my way here," Leon explained, after introductions were made and he, too, had a glass in his hand. "I met with no success. When Paris fills for market week, as you are finding out, the whole city is booked. This district, by now, has acquired mostly permanent residents, and there do not seem to be rooms available for a short time." He seemed to be giving Charles a thorough inspection, and nodding to himself as if coming to a decision, he said, "Do you suppose, Mr. Harmon, you could put up with the sofa in that little alcove?"

"I'd gladly pay, and I promise I will not be any trouble," Charles said gratefully, "That is, if it's satisfactory with Christine?"

"I think we can manage, if you do not require more than a simple bed?" Her question seemed calculated to keep formality the theme.

"That's settled then. Now, how about you two letting me take you out to dinner, and maybe we could even find some music afterwards? I understand the French are really hearing some great jazz these days."

Christine's face lit up. "Oh, we could go to one of those brasseries near Chatelet, where the people are usually having such fun, and then maybe go to hear some music down in the cave at Le Petite Opportune?" Her voice rose in question as she looked to Leon for approval.

"Sounds like a good idea, Christine. I happened to hear on the radio last night that Tommy Flannagan would be broadcasting live from there tonight."

CHAPTER 9

Paris

Lisa Griman had no trouble finding the locker at Gare St. Lazare, although the throngs of people hurrying through the railroad station changed its entire appearance drastically. The locker area, however, looked the same as this morning when they had placed their precious bag in "cold storage." Was that only this morning? Seems like another century, Lisa thought.

After a few false tries, she discovered she was turning the key the wrong direction. The locker opened, and she had the bag in hand. She couldn't resist a quick peek, to be sure there hadn't been a switch, but a partial lift of the lid revealed those lovely bills winking at her, same as before.

Lisa moved as swiftly as the crowds would allow. The pleats of her green skirt flipped around her knees, and her red hair bounced to the rhythm of her quick steps. She snaked her way clutching the suitcase, the answer to all her dreams, as close to her body as its rigid shape would allow. She had almost reached the entrance near the taxi ranks when a sharp pain in her hip puzzled her. It felt like a bee sting, but she resisted the impulse to rub the offending spot. As her vision suddenly clouded and she fell to the hard worn floor, the gray case lay beside her as she gasped for breath.

The commuters, wary of involvement and hurrying to make connections, moved around the fallen form, stepping high and brushing against each other in their efforts to push forward. By the time the security guards finally arrived on the scene, the crumpled green form was still. Examination revealed her purse, still slung from her shoulder, its strap tangled in the strands of dyed red hair. It contained credit cards and a key to the Bristol Hotel, which might help with identification. She had no other luggage.

Berlin

Thursday Night

Karen and William decided to walk from the Kempinski around the corner to a restaurant on Kurfurstendamm that William had spotted earlier in the day. The line of patient customers waiting for lunch seemed to promise good food inside, and the sign on the window said it would be open for their early dinner.

They entered a glass foyer from the street and were shown to a small corner table near the mirrored back wall which reflected a flurry of waiters busily serving only a few customers.

"Couldn't have been better if we'd planned it," said Karen, her eyes reflecting the shimmer of the candle on the table. A soft blue silk collar framed her face and highlighted the smooth texture of her skin. "You can see the whole room, and we'll know if my 'tail' shows up." Serious now, she added, "I hope I'm not taking advantage, or trying to be a habit, William. I know you have a wife at home, but honestly, I'm scared enough to be very thankful TWA assigned us seats together on the flight coming over!"

"I'm the lucky one, Karen. These conventions are usually so dull after five, the only thing I have to look forward to is the call I always make to my wife." He suddenly reddened under his shock of blond hair, and he quickly added, "Don't take it the wrong way, but I guess I'm really a chauvinist. I thought my wife was the only lady I could talk to who was both beautiful and intelligent, and I can take only so many of those nights out with the boys."

"That's flattering, William, and I think I'd very much enjoy knowing your wife. I've been a working girl so long I've become quite a cynic myself."

When the waiter arrived for their orders Karen was surprised to discover that she was hungry, and that a glass of wine sounded appealing, even after all that drinking this afternoon. William chose a stein of beer, but one of those huge frosty glasses commonly served in this country would be overwhelming to her by now, she feared.

"Do you have any idea who might be following you?" William asked as the waiter retreated. "He looked very foreign to me."

"William, there's something very important I want your advice about. I know I can trust you—this business about superconductors . . ."

"More shop talk, Karen? What about the nut who's following you?"

"I'm coming to that. I do have sort of an idea, not who, but maybe why. It's kind of far-fetched, but this letter I translated . . ."

William stopped her suddenly with a hand gesture as he whispered, "Your foreign friend, whoever he is, just surfaced from behind a newspaper at that table up in front. Don't look up, and I'll see if I can get close."

He left her, napkin in hand, and headed in the direction of the glass entryway. When Denkov saw the young American slide his chair back, he rose and with a few quick steps was out the door.

William seemed determined to play the hero as his long legs closed the gap, and he too, hurtled out of Karen's view.

Thoroughly frightened now, Karen searched her mind. Have I seen him before? She tried to recall the brief glimpse of that person standing outside her window on the New York street, but the image wouldn't blend, somehow, with this latest form. Something wrong with the set of the body, or maybe the shape of the clothes. This guy brought Dr. Dromensky to mind, although it certainly wasn't he. Maybe it's a case of mistaken identity, but I'm terribly sorry I got Old William involved.

As she worried about William, his words came back to her in an ominous echo, "If someone knows about a room temperature superconductor, he's in great jeopardy." She chilled as she recalled, "Clutching a razor blade you couldn't release." Shit! Someone knows you know something about Marie Curie and her damned letter!

Disheveled, as if he'd been in a fight, William was heading toward her. Before he could make his way back to the table, Karen decided she must keep her mouth shut, at least here in Berlin. William was too nice a guy to share an albatross, and that little boy at home needed him. With a little luck, I'll make it to Paris, she reasoned, maybe find some help there.

Looking like a ten-year-old coming into his schoolroom after a victorious entanglement with the class bully, William was holding his upper arm with his other hand. He indicated he was heading for the men's room. Seeing her alarm, he said, "Looks a lot worse than it is. I'll be fine."

Just a few heads turned in their direction. Karen tried to assume an indifferent pose, but her concern showed when William returned and she could see the big tear in his jacket.

"Son-of-a-bitch had a knife, and I guess he ruined my wife's favorite camel hair jacket."

"Oh, William, it's serious, I know. Are you sure you're not hurt? I can try to mend the jacket for you . . ."

"Honest, it's just a nick, and I think I scared the bastard off, but maybe we should call the police."

"If you scared him, that's probably the end of it. Let's just go. Suddenly I'm not hungry."

As he motioned to the waiter for the check, William said, "Now go on with what you were saying."

"What was that?"

"Something about translating a letter . . ."

"Oh, the letter. Just a dumb idea. Here's the waiter."

William Foester stubbornly refused to leave Karen's side, even when they were once more inside their hotel.

"William, please, you've done enough. I almost got you killed tonight. Your jacket is ruined, your shoulder is scratched, your pride is damaged, and your appreciative female business companion is grateful, but bushed."

"Nonsense. With all that excitement, you never even had a chance to eat your dinner. Are you sure you don't want to get some kind of snack? You really ought to eat something. But you're right about my pride. I think we should notify the police. Can't you tell me why you think that guy is following you?"

"Not really, William. I could make a wild guess, and then be awfully sorry if it were the wrong one. Why don't we just ignore the whole thing? And I honestly could not manage to eat one bite. I'm flying to Paris tomorrow immediately after the morning session. If I even suspect one tiny bit that I'm being followed, I'll for sure call for help there. Meantime, I think I'd better go to my room and get things together so I can head right to the airport from the Congress Hall." She stepped into the elevator.

"I'd better go with you to your room," William persisted, as they arrived at her floor. She moved forward, and he followed behind, almost lock-step.

"Really, I'm fine. I'll see you before I leave tomorrow, and thanks for everything you've done . . ." Karen turned towards her room as they both left the elevator.

"Hey, Karen Bright
It would be a delight
To use all my charm
And keep you from harm
So you'll have a safe night."

With a burst of giggles, Karen turned, hand on hip and catching a deep breath, replied:

"Hey, William Foester
This girl keeps the nice things tossed her
So for the sake of Mrs. Foester
You'd better get lost, sir."

She was still laughing as her key turned in the lock and the door closed behind her. But she remembered to put the chain on and turn the dead bolt.

She gathered an armful of underwear, scarves, stockings and sweaters from the various drawers in the big old armoire. She threw everything in a heap on the bed and dragged her suitcase out of the closet. I'm ready for a couple of fun days in Paris, she thought, and here's one little gal who doesn't plan to waste one precious minute. Enough of this serious stuff!

As she worked, trying to organize her things so she wouldn't have to unpack everything again in Paris, she realized the blues and greens were looking alike. Which belt went with what? Was the light always this dim? She checked the desk light, it was on as high as it would go, the bedside light only cast its glow on the pillows, and the overhead light probably had about a 20 watt bulb. Maybe without that fancy shade it would shine brighter, Karen thought.

Standing on the desk chair directly under the light fixture, she raised her arms and tried to get hold of a ruffle. Almost, not quite, able to touch. Those thick telephone books might help, she thought, and she carefully balanced them on the chair, then climbed up. Slowly, shoeless so she wouldn't slip, she eased herself up on her toes and hooked her index finger over the edge of the lampshade.

Dislodged by her pulling, a small gray box and a tiny TV camera fell to the floor with a soft thump. The chandelier shade followed.

I should be frightened, Karen thought. I'm too dog tired to be scared any more, and now I'm just damned mad. Her first impulse was to throw the offending junk out the window. Careful, you silly, don't forget you're still in someone else's country. Soberly now, she examined the box. Must be some kind of transmitter, she decided. Throwing one of her scarves over the eye of the TV camera, she examined the lamp shade. Yup, there it was, a tiny hole the lens must have been aimed through. Right at the bed, naturally.

Keeping the scarf tight, she moved to place the ugly burden on the desk. Does it have a companion? Moving close, she turned off the desk lamp in order to examine it. Sure enough, a tiny transmitter perched above the bulb. She wrenched it loose, put it under the scarf, and went to the bedside. Opposite the side she'd been sleeping on, there it was, another tiny camera above the bulb on the lamp, aimed to cover the entrance to the bathroom. I'll bet the sons-of-dirty-so-and-so's have one in there too, she thought, and, adding her third trophy to the collection, she headed for the bathroom. This one was harder to find, but she finally spotted it in the dark recess over the medicine chest, along with a handful of dust.

Shaking with anger now, she headed for that loathsome television set and jabbed at the buttons until the screen brightened and once more the porno film appeared on the screen. This time the stars seemed to be two females with naked breasts the size of watermelons who were working over an ugly bald headed old man.

She pulled the desk chair over to face the screen, went to her collection on the desk and carefully brought it over. She lined up the cameras and the little box on the chair seat, and removed the scarf with a flourish. Feast your eyes out, you bastards!

* * *

Ivan Denkov was in a foul mood. That tall meek looking American had caught him off guard, even after he'd heard the telephoned warning to the girl on his tape. He hoped the little episode with the knife would teach them a lesson, but Ivan chafed at having acted like such an amateur.

The girl had lulled him into boredom with her simple observance of routine, minding her own business. And he'd even mentally accused that ass, Dromensky, of handling the real action in Paris while he, Ivan, was stalling around here in Berlin. After all, wasn't Dromensky supposed to be only a scientist? Why had Moscow put one of their skilled GRU people, specially trained in surveillance, under the control of such a clumsy clod?

Now, possibly the picture had changed, and he must continue his work, no matter. Giving in to the powers over him with a submissive shrug, Ivan settled down to view the morning tape of the video camera in Karen's room, at the same time sorting through the briefcase full of the papers he had collected at the superconductor conference.

As he watched Karen go through her usual morning ritual, emerge from the shower and use the heavy towel to turn that thick tangle of gold once more into a shiny groomed cap of curls, he extracted the program listing all participants and paper presenters. Grunting with satisfaction, Ivan marked with his pudgy finger the name he recognized from a briefly glimpsed lapel badge. William Foester, listed as research engineer, Sullivan Electric Wire Products Co., Los Angeles, California, told him about as much as this video tape was telling him: nothing. However, his identity should be reported.

Sighing, Ivan conceded he'd better follow directions and report the day's knowledge to Dromensky. His decision made, he placed a call to Paris.

In suite 501, Dromensky sipped a glass of Stolichnaya while relaxing in his favorite silk robe, a bit of western finery he carefully concealed from his cohorts. As he reached for the phone, he sloshed vodka on the satin lapels. The resultant irritation was vented instantly in harsh tones when the caller identified himself as that dolt Ivan.

"Comrade, it is very late, and I have had a bad day. What do you want?"

Smoothly, Ivan answered, "Just to give my required report, Comrade. I thought perhaps you should know there has been a development here."

"Has the girl changed her plans? Will she not be in Paris as we determined?"

"She has not changed her reservations."

"Then what is the purpose of your call?"

"The girl has made contact with an American engineer who may be the man we seek."

"You are wrong, Ivan, the Grimans have named the man sent from New York to retrieve the superconductor, and he is here in Paris."

"Has he told you what you want to know?"

"I have not yet made contact." No point giving Ivan any details about Holden getting away today.

"Then, perhaps, he is not there, but here. The girl has had several meetings with this man, and they seem to have business talks, not lovers' conversations." Ivan decided to wait and see if he would need to reveal Foester's spotting him.

"Impossible, Colonel Denkov. His name is Charles Holden, and he was here in Paris earlier today. He's working for Consolidated Electronics Co. of New York."

"Could he have an accomplice here in Berlin? He could have your superconductor, and need help getting it back to New York. Maybe even plant it with the girl, hoping to divert attention. Didn't she plan to return by passenger liner, the *Royale*?" Ivan was proud of his on-the-spot reasoning.

"That may be, Ivan Ilych, but the contact will not be made in Berlin. My sources indicate the strong possibility that the travel will be by ship." Dromensky saw no reason to give details of his conversation with Intercontinental's concierge, who had happily given him details of the handsome American's inquiries about ship schedules, after the generous and not even subtle transfer of franc notes.

"Comrade Doctor, have you checked with Moscow after these new developments? Has there, perhaps, been a change of assignment?" Maybe I should check with Moscow myself, thought Ivan.

"Yes, Colonel, and your orders are to follow my direction. At the present time, that means, continue on to Paris with the girl. You see, I, as a scientist, know that, if Holden does have the superconductor, he cannot take it through airline security controls. The ship, as you surmised for the wrong reasons, is how he must transport the material. I intend to visit the offices of the *Royale* tomorrow and book passage. I will do my best to see the passenger list, and then we will know for certain if this Holden intends to join Miss Bright. Meanwhile, you must be sure you do not, for any reason, lose her. She can lead us to him, and we need not worry about trying to locate him until then."

Dromensky sounded so sure of himself that Ivan had to admit that this time the doctor was probably right.

"What about the Grimans? Are they still in Paris?"

"Our men here did a smooth job with that one. The borrowed funds are safely returned, and the new neurotoxin gun produced a perfect heart attack for the Griman woman. I suggest you use it on her husband as well, when we find him." said Dromensky, without one hint of emotion.

"Find him? Is he not in Paris?"

"Unfortunately, he gave us the slip. My guess is that you will also find him on the *Royale*. I'm certain he'll be trying to find Holden to warn him that we are after his treasure. That Consolidated outfit doesn't know he was breaking his contract, and he still stands to make a profit if Holden is successful." Dromensky wondered if he hadn't given Ivan too much information. "At any rate, he knows too much about us. We must find him and silence him."

"I started to tell you," Ivan was groping for the right explanation. "the American spotted me tonight, and possibly Miss Bright did also." He didn't have to mention the knife.

"That was very careless of you." After a pause, he continued, "You'd better catch the earlier flight to Paris and pick her up again here. We know the hotel she's booked, and you also know her flight schedule. I believe she'll keep following routine as she has so far."

"What about our surveillance gear?" Ivan realized he'd get no sleep tonight.

"Just check out. Leave the TV transmitters; they're not traceable to us. Take what you can, and get here as soon as possible. I'm in 501. Now I really must get some sleep, comrade." Dromensky hung up with an insulting click in Denkov's ear.

CHAPTER 10

Paris

Thursday Night, June 11

Frank Griman had been waiting at the airline shuttle terminal for over an hour. He'd watched the nervous shuffling of the passengers jockeying for seats and worrying about their luggage as the bus loaded for the 6:30 trip. Now the 7:30 bus was about to depart, and still no sign of Lisa. It wasn't like her to be late, and he was reasonably sure she hadn't run out on him—where could she go without a passport? He never had been good at waiting, but this business of being forced to sit patiently, guarding two suitcases like some trained watch dog, with no way to communicate, was sheer torture.

Finally, he could stand it no longer. He wrestled the two suitcases and Lisa's cosmetic bag over to the desk marked Consigne, which he'd figured must be a checkstand. Rid of his burden, he hurried back out to the street, and managed to pick up a cab that had deposited passengers, now lining up for the 8:30 shuttle. The driver looked confused when he finally understood that Frank really wanted to go to the train depot, but he was happy to comply when Frank showed him an American ten dollar bill.

Frank didn't even notice the bizarre sculptured stack of clocks guarding the station's entrance as he raced past them on his way into the station. He found the correct row of lockers after some searching. Finally, he reached his goal, and there, second row, third locker down, the door stood slightly ajar, key in the lock as it should be, awaiting the ten franc coin required to remove it. Frank swung the door open. Beads of perspiration fell from his unruly eyebrows, and his shirt collar was wringing wet. Nothing. Lisa had been a real bitch at times, but she didn't have the imagination to pull this kind of dodge on him, especially in a foreign country. Any kind of answer would be bad news, but Frank went to find a telephone.

Lisa, after all, had been the one who'd insisted they get far away from the hotel and Dromensky, but he had to start somewhere, reasoned Frank. He waited for the hotel operator to answer.

"Bristol Hotel," very calm and very French.

"Please, do you speak English? I'm trying to get in touch with Mrs. Griman. Did she leave a message, by any chance?"

"Are you Mr. Griman?" said the operator in welcome English.

"Yes, and I seem to have lost contact with Mrs. Griman after we checked out. Did she perhaps telephone you?"

"No, monsieur, but I have a message for you from the Hospital Saint Antoine. We told them you had checked out, but they wanted you to call them immediately if we should hear from you. I can give you that number."

Frank replaced the receiver on the pay phone. Numbly, knowing without a doubt that his worst fears were confirmed, he pulled more coins from his pocket, dialed, and identified himself to the official at the hospital, not daring to hope he'd ever get a chance to be impatient with Lisa again. He wasn't even aware of the teardrops blended with the perspiration on his cheeks as he said, "Yes, doctor, I'm afraid she did indeed have a very bad heart." Embarrassed at the rapidity with which the lie had been uttered, he agreed to come as quickly as possible to the hospital to identify the body.

He could feel his shirt sticking to his back as he began to absorb the whole picture. Lisa was gone, the money was gone, and those bastards were undoubtedly looking for him to finish their job.

Friday Morning, June 12

Discombobulated, that's what Dad would have said I am, thought Charles, for a minute I didn't even know which city I was in. Not a very smooth move for a would-be super sleuth. Awake in the little alcove on the couch that had served for a bed, he struggled to an upright position. Heavy dark fabric framed the opening of his little hideaway, and the air was musty. Christine had done her best to make the area private and comfortable when they came back from Le Petite Opportune last night, but she needn't have bothered.

His body had been on alert from the excitement of his so-far successful flight from his unknown pursuer, and the stimulation of Flannagan's jazz piano in that unlikely old cellar with its winding stone staircase and seating on stone benches against a cavern wall, still had his blood pulsing. And that didn't include the effects of the wine they'd consumed. His sleep, when he finally relaxed, had been heavy and deep. Yes, he was definitely somewhat disoriented! And he'd better shape up fast, he thought, because time was fleeting.

Charles shook himself free of the down quilt, peeked out of his little nest, and near as he could tell from there, he was alone. Nice of them to let me sleep, he thought. But, on reflection, he wasn't even sure Leon had spent the night here. Never mind, they've both gone to work by now. On to a toothbrush.

Brushed and washed, and dressed again in last night's clothes, his eyes took in the details of the apartment he'd missed last night. There, on the little counter that served for most of the kitchen, Christine had left him two croissants, carefully wrapped in a white napkin, and beside them a crock of butter and some of that wonderful French cherry jam. And bless her, a carafe of coffee on a little warmer. I'll live, he thought, as he hurried to fill the cup left invitingly beside the carafe.

Cup in hand, he put through a credit card call to Butler, and was relieved to hear the familiar harsh voice after the first ring.

"Hope you're ready to go, Charles. We've got you all set."

"Herman, stop jumping in backwards. Did you make arrangements for me to get that passenger list?"

"Didn't I say I would? Not only did I, but you're booked in a great outside room on deck five."

"What about the possibility that they went to Southampton to catch the *QE2*? Or maybe a freighter from Calais? I'll have to examine that list before we talk about my going."

"I don't think so, Charles, we've checked all the departure times. The *QE2* won't be in Southampton until next Thursday. Not likely our dude would be content with slow freight. Anyhow, you can always cancel if you don't like the list, but after all, your *Royale* leaves day after tomorrow. Your contact at Euro-American is a Monsieur Duvalier."

"Good enough, Herman, over and out." For once Charles got the jump on Butler and hung up first.

The privacy was welcome, but he could have used Christine's advice about which Metro to take to get to the offices at 26 Rue de Auber. Where have all the people gone, Charles wondered, as he looked in vain for signs of any taxi activity around the square at Place des Vosges. Quicker to figure out the Metro signs myself, he decided, as he ducked down the concrete steps, at least I know I'm heading for the Place de l'Opera.

Had Charles been able to take a taxi directly to his destination, instead of traveling by the circuitous metro route he'd devised, he might have seen Chernov H. Dromensky talking to M. Duvalier in the Euro-American Lines office. As it was, the wiry Frenchman working busily with a stack of papers at the front desk was a little confused by a second man asking for a passenger list. True, the first had not looked as American as the New York office had advised, but, for two hundred francs, a Xerox copy had seemed a fair exchange. Now, this second request made him uneasy. However, this man asked for him by name.

"Oui, Mr. Holden, I was instructed to give you the *Royale* passenger list. It came in by teletype this morning. I thought perhaps you had sent the other gentleman, but he did not pick up your ticket. I have that right here for you, sir."

"What other gentleman?" Charles asked the clerk, wondering to himself if this was just an employee giving an excuse for not doing a job, or was the ubiquitous Mr. Black once more ahead of him?

"C'est a mistake, M. Holden. Je regrette, I thought this gentleman was representing you, although he did look more Slavic than I had expected."

"But you do have a list for me, I hope, along with my ticket?"

"Of course, M. Holden. You see, when this man came in a few minutes ago, he asked me for a *Royale* passenger list. I was working on it just then, adding a few more names that have just booked. So I asked, are you the gentleman sent by the New York office? When he said yes, he was, I just ran off a copy for him. He took the list from my hand before I could verify his identification, and he left without asking for your ticket."

I'll bet he did, thought Charles, watching the giveaway evasive tremors of a practiced deceiver. And how many francs extra are now in your pocket, M. Duvalier?

"I see how you could have become confused, M. Duvalier, but did the man give you his name? Was he, perhaps, Mr. Black?" Charles was reaching now.

"Unfortunately, no. He was a large man with a trimmed beard and a jacket that seemed too heavy for this time of year. He spoke English, but with a bit of an accent. That is all I remember." He folded three copied sheets and placed them in the same envelope he'd used for the ticket. "Here is your list, your ticket, your luggage tags and your departure information. This will give you all you need to know for boarding. Will you require transportation to Le Havre?"

"Won't be necessary, thank you. You've been very helpful." Wishing that were true, Charles opened the door and joined the determined moving stream of pedestrians on the crowded sidewalk. What he needed now was a safe place to digest his information.

The safest thing was just to blend into the midday crowd, where he found himself shoved by the group's momentum, rounding the corner to the front of the massive opera house. When he reached the Place de l'Opera, he remembered from his other time in Paris, four years ago, a marvelous lunch at the famous Cafe de la Paix that borders the Place and Boulevard des Capucines. He'd even shared a sidewalk table with a better than average blonde. Why not give it a try?

As long as he was trying to resemble Mr. Average Tourist, Charles was glad he'd decided to leave his brief case with all its confidential information at Christine's apartment. He'd put it under his suitcase on the chair by the sofa bed, and now as he moved to take the tiny table just vacated in the glass-enclosed section on the sidewalk, he was glad he didn't have to cope with a bulky object. Space was at a premium, the chairs were spindly, and where do they expect you to put long legs?

Friday, Very Early Morning

Frank Griman had been in the hospital director's office for what seemed like years. His nose no longer rebelled at the pungent odors of medicines, anesthetics, sickness overlaid with the heavy fumes of disinfectants that permeated the air. But his body longed for relief from the effort of trying to stay alert. One compassionate intern on duty offered him a sleeping pill and a cot in the interns' lounge, and now he was sorry he'd had to refuse.

In spite of the language barrier, people tried to be helpful, and basically the painful process had been quite simple. The conversation with the U.S. Embassy "secretary on duty" had gone very well, and everyone at Hospital Saint Antoine had been extremely solicitous. He'd filled out a mountain of documents and forms, written a few checks, and that was it. No autopsy required. Lisa's body would go directly to her sister in Monmouth, New Jersey. The cost would be greatly reduced if Frank would accompany the coffin, which could go by ocean freight on the *Royale*, leaving from Le Havre Sunday night.

The man from the embassy had agreed to make all the arrangements, but Frank himself must deal with the freight office in Le Havre, and that would be closed by noon on Saturday. So Frank and the coffin would have to travel by train Friday morning. God, it's been Friday for a couple of hours. If he could just hold himself together long enough to get the job done, a small pension near the freight office was holding a room for him, and he could crash there until time to board the ship.

The embassy guy had also advised him to get some legal help in New York to deal with immigrations and customs red tape. Bill Higginbotham ought to be good for that, if he could find him away from the golf course on the weekend.

A curious mixture of emotions welled up within him as he sat planning. Lisa was always the arranger, and here he was, handling her mistakes. Damn her greed! The Curie letter had looked like a way to put some spark back in their life together, and now he was so shit-scared he couldn't even mourn her. Might be hard to convince the sister about the heart attack, but he sure as hell couldn't leave any door open to investigation. The Russkies have their money back, but would they leave him alone? A freight train to Le Havre and a sea voyage might be as good as any place to lay low for a while.

On the other hand, Butler at Consolidated didn't know he'd even thought about breaking his contract, so maybe he still had a deal, if Holden can do a better job than Lisa did. If not, he didn't want to know about it now anyway.

Paris

Later, Friday Morning

This could even be the same table he remembered, but too bad, no young lady here now, only a half consumed glass of wine and an ashtray with the ruby stained remnants of three sick-sweet smelling French cigarettes. The nimble footed waiter made his way through the barricade of wire chairs and deftly whisked the table free of its nostalgic reminders, jerking Charles back to coping with today's problems.

"Omelet du fromage, and vin blanc," would buy him some time, Charles hoped, and he spread his prized passenger list before him.

He was pleased to see that the computer had favored him with stateroom numbers neatly listed by each name on the alphabetized column. That would be a real help once on board. He ran his pencil down the row. The first name to pop out was Brown, Girard, P., in 32, Promenade Deck. He put a small pencil dot by the name, but he was sure Butler had said the Brown in the Translators International office was a Philip. Here was another one, Mr. and Mrs. Black, N 60, Normandy deck. Another pencil mark there.

The omelet arrived, and its compelling fragrance called for attention. Those croissants of the morning are long gone, he realized, as he picked up his fork. Mmmm, no wonder they speak of French cheese with reverence, and they must have used at least four eggs. Maybe the wine will dissolve some of the cholesterol, he lied to himself, I'm glad the waiter brought a carafe instead of the glass I expected.

Pushing the plate aside, feeling noble about the tiny bit left untouched, he refilled his glass and went back to the list. Still in the B row, there it emerged, loud and clear, just as if it had been printed in bold-faced type, Karen Bright, Cabin P-142. Now he had to fish out the ship's diagram and program the location into his mind. While he was at it, where had Herman put him?

Tracing the lines of the diagram, Provence deck became No. 4, and there was 142, one of the rare outside singles, close to the stairs. And his ticket said he belonged in V 109. That turns out to be Versailles deck, No. 5, looks like a large stateroom. Good for old Herman, had to pop for a couple of extra bucks. I'd sure as hell better find his Curie superconductor. That number doesn't put me on the same side of the ship as Ms. Bright. Too bad; it might have been handy, he thought.

Moving faster now, his pencil spotted his name, Holden, among the H's—glad he put me back to my own name, won't have passport trouble—and moved on. He looked in vain for any Norman Teal, or anything similar, but there at the end, in the last minute additions out of alphabetical order, appeared the name, Frank Griman, L813. Way down deck No. 8, but it looks like a single. What will Mrs. Griman do?

Those two names together were enough to justify his sailing on the *Royale*, Charles was convinced, but this is going to be a helluva cruise. Somehow there has to be a third person involved, because both Griman and Bright were in Berlin when the Curie apartment was ransacked. Will Black, or Teal, or whoever, be sailing with them, or will his job be done?

* * *

Dromensky opened the door of suite 501 and was dismayed by the sight of Ivan Denkov, on the sofa like a baby polar bear on a piece of ice, bundled in the hotel's white terry cloth robe and licking crumbs from his lips with his long tongue. Remnants on the room service tray indicated a generous breakfast had been consumed.

"You are quite a sight, comrade! I know you arrived late last night after a hurried trip, but do you realize what that kind of room service meal will cost?"

"Don't be so upset, Doctor. Moscow will pay. The cheese omelet was tolerable, but this French coffee takes some getting used to. You were out early. Have you accomplished anything?"

"Certainly. I have made the required standard report to the security officer at the embassy here for both of us. I have told him of these new developments. I work with Directorate T, the Scientific and Technical branch, and since we are responsible for obtaining strategic scientific data, I thought this Curie material fell into that category. However, the security officer has decided that your branch, Special Services II, the Counterintelligence Division, should handle the next part of this search, since you are responsible for penetrating foreign security.

"In order to determine how best to continue, I have managed to obtain a passenger list for the *Royale.* It looks as though you will be able to enjoy this soft Western life for another week because you will be sailing on that beautiful new ship. I hope you have not forgotten how to work for the State."

The domineering manner and menacing tone Dromensky adopted to hide his disappointment provoked a quick defensive response.

"Now just one minute, Comrade scientist, you are, after all, speaking to a loyal officer of the GRU. I want no more of your academic philosophy. Let's get on with our work. Who is on this list of yours?" Ivan decided offense worked best with this lout.

"They're all on it. Dr. K. Bright, Mr. C. Holden, and, as I suspected, Mr. F. Griman is a last-minute addition. One of them is sure to have the Curie material, and you must retrieve it at any cost. It must belong to the Motherland." Dromensky was waxing patriotic, but for whose benefit Ivan was not sure.

"Since you're being so efficient, did you book my stateroom and purchase my ticket?"

"That has been done, and the ticket will be delivered here to the concierge within the hour. I managed to book you into a room near that of Mr. Griman. That should give you a greater opportunity to get the job done correctly."

"If you want me to use the neuro-toxin method, I will need the tool."

"That also I have arranged."

"In that case, since we are just waiting, would you like to hear the audio tape of that American, William Foester, I told you about? And perhaps we can review the latest TV tape. I managed to bring those, in my rush, although I had no chance to retrieve our equipment."

"Very well," Dromensky decided he could afford to humor him a little, "What do you expect from these tapes? Miss Bright probably is of no further interest to us, unless she has been designated to meet with Holden on the ship."

"I think, Doctor, you may be missing a possibility," Ivan said as he unpacked his VCR and wired it to the TV set in the room. "Karen Bright has been very much involved with this Foester. They may be planning to carry out the search together for Madame Curie's treasure. We know she is arriving here in Paris today." Satisfied his connecting wires were secure, he pushed the "play" lever on his expensive little surveillance device.

The screen instantly displayed a state of confusion with flashes of light, close-ups of fingers, a whirl of patterned carpet and wallpaper, and finally, three nude women. Dromensky was totally fascinated with the sequence that followed.

"I have enjoyed our little show, Ivan Ilych, but I would not suggest that you turn these tapes over to our Security Officer. Never mind, you will still be a Hero of the Soviet Union if you can bring back the superconductor," Dromensky chuckled.

Squirming inwardly from embarrassment, Ivan admitted to himself that the girl had succeeded, more than she could have hoped, in making him look the complete incompetent fool, in front of the one least likely to forget his inefficiency. She'd pay of course.

CHAPTER 11

Berlin

Friday, June 12

As Karen waited one last time in the orange tiled loading area of the Internationales Congress Centrum, she realized she'd never had time to really explore the entire building. This morning, as she arrived for her final translating session, the advertising posters of coming attractions were being changed, and next to appear in the auditorium at the far end would be the Bolshoi Ballet, accompanied by the Moscow Orchestra. That would have been a real treat. In fact, she thought, Berlin might be worth another trip.

But, right now, she felt more than ready for Paris. Hopefully, the weight of the "Curie albatross" and the bizarre happenings of the last couple of days could be left behind. All except her new friendship with William Foester. When Karen finished that final translation this morning and stepped out of the booth into the waiting arms of "Old William," she'd actually had to fight back tears.

Helpful to the end, William had helped her gather her stuff from the checkstand and carried her suitcase down the elevator. He even checked for threatening faces in the jostling crowd, but she finally insisted he go back to hear the next lecture.

Maybe I'll visit him and his family some day, she thought, if I can come up with a good excuse for a trip to California.

After the wait, it was Karen's turn for a taxi. The driver was young and confident. Plenty of time to reach Templehof, even allowing the extra hour necessary for international flights, he assured her. Now, at the airport, as the long line of cabs disgorged its passengers, Karen was less optimistic than before. Good thing I had the hotel concierge reconfirm my reservation and get my seat assignment, she thought. Juggling her briefcase and purse, she paid the driver and gave her suitcase to the porter.

"Attention. Airfrance flight seventy-one. Your gate has been changed from B6 to A13. All passengers departing on Airfrance flight seventy-one, that flight is now boarding at Gate A13."

A quick glance at the indicator board above Passport Control told Karen the gate change meant extra distance, not less. Thankful she wore flat heels, Karen broke into a jog trot. She threaded her way through the crowds, down those interminable corridors, and arrived at the gate just as the boarding began.

"Bon jour," from the perky flight attendant reminded Karen this was to be the fun part of her trip. She smiled, even as she wedged herself into the center seat between two sets of broad shoulders bulging over the armrests, their owners' bulky briefcases taking up more than the allotted share of the small stowage space under the seats in front of them.

She noticed a program from the superconductor conference sticking out of the side pocket of the case of the man sitting by the window. The participants at that conference had come from everywhere, Karen thought.

After a delayed and jolting takeoff, Karen waited hopefully for the "Fasten Seatbelt" light to go off. That would mean drink service, maybe even lunch, could start. However, an announcement came from the overhead speaker in French, "We are expecting some turbulence for the next twenty-five minutes or so, and seatbelts must remain fastened. The message repeated in German and English. Then, almost as an afterthought, "Our flight attendants will begin their complimentary beverage service as soon as seatbelts may be unfastened. If there is anything we can do to make your flight more comfortable . . ."

"I can think of something," Karen mumbled, half aloud, as the occupant of the window seat now had his black briefcase parked awkwardly on his knees, half onto her lap. And wouldn't you know it, now the other jerk was starting to write! She closed her eyes.

Fifteen minutes later she was roused by a gentle touch on her shoulder and a softly murmured, "Pardon, would you care for some champagne?" The attractive blonde attendant was offering a long-stemmed glass, and, mercifully, some shifting had taken place so Karen's arm was free to reach for the ambrosia. Maybe it will be a good flight after all!

Evidently, during her brief nap, her seatmates had been discussing something. Now, as luncheon service began, they each put work aside and continued the conversation. They talked across her, in French, completely ignoring her. Why not? Why should they expect a pretty, young American girl to have any knowledge of their language?

As she eavesdropped, Karen decided that Window Seat was Parisian, possibly with the government in some scientific capacity. Aisle Seat seemed to be an historian from Geneva. They were sharing stories of distress and pleasures of business travel. The Parisian praised the Berlin convention facility and the scope of the meeting.

From the historian: "Did you find the usual dominance of Americans, Germans and Japanese at the conference?"

"Of course I did," Window responded. "France still seems unwilling to spend any money on purely scientific research. Everything must be instantly adaptable to the betterment of French society; otherwise, the funds are cleverly withheld."

"None of your French scientists has dedicated himself to pure research since the days of Marie Curie, or perhaps Louis Pasteur." The tones of an academician definitely prevailed.

"You are quite correct. I remember reading that in 1927 France spent less on higher education than on feeding cavalry horses. At least we've made some progress in the last few decades."

"Yes, no more cavalry horses."

Trays covered with linen clothes, each bearing its own little bottle of wine and tiny basket of aromatic French rolls, were handed to them by the still smiling stewardess, and Window Seat even offered to pour Karen's wine for her. It's a good thing he can't read my mind, thought Karen. If he knew what I know about Marie Curie and her "fundamental research," he could help France lead the world in pure science by being the first nation to discover room temperature superconductivity.

Suddenly the plane's atmosphere changed subtly, a slight change of direction she could feel through the pressure of the seat behind her, and the illuminated "Fasten Seat Belt" sign went dark. They were out of the turbulence and free to head for Paris. And I'm going to be free, Karen determined. I'll make one attempt to find out from the Institut du Radium if old Griman has been there. After all, it's his baby. But if he hasn't, I'll just go find somebody at the U.S. Embassy and dump this whole load on them. Paris, here I come!

Paris

Friday Afternoon

After leaving what he hoped was the appropriate amount of bills and coins in the little tray provided with the almost indecipherable hand written check, Charles decided it was time to have another go at finding the elusive Mr. Black. I really didn't push very hard at that little hotel, he told himself, as he left the Cafe de la Paix and headed for the taxi sign on the corner on Boulevard des Capucines.

Maybe I'm just getting used to their ways, but that driver was actually decent, thought Charles, as he paid and received a smile and "merci, monsieur," in exchange for a reasonable tip. He entered the Grand Hotel de Lima, determined to get more answers this time.

"Parlez vous Anglais?"

"Oui, how may I help you, monsieur?" The gray haired desk clerk, with his sweater and open collared shirt, looked different from any of the help at the Intercontinental. A little money may do some good here.

"I'm looking for a friend of mine who is supposed to be staying here."

"Oui, and his name?"

"His name, yes. Well, you see, that's the problem."

"Je ne comprendes pas. I'm afraid I don't understand, sir. Your friend, you do not know his name?"

"Of course, I know his name. But I do not know the name he may be using. He is, how can I put this," Charles smiled broadly, including a wink of his left eye, "he is trying to avoid his ex-wife, and is probably using a different name."

"That does not seem likely, sir. We check passports when our guests register."

"Well, I know it seems a strange request, but if I could look at your register for this past week, I think I may be able to recognize the name he is using. Since you are a fairly small hotel, there are probably not so many Americans checked in." Charles produced a U.S. ten dollar bill to accompany his smile.

"Quite a few this past week because of market, you know." The bill was accepted so quickly Charles thought surely he was dealing with a practiced magician. It seemed to disappear in mid air.

With knobby, arthritic hands, the clerk shoved the leather-bound register towards Charles. "If you please, apportez le moi immediatement, excuse me—Please sir, give it back to me as soon as you look, I don't want the manager to see, you understand?"

"Of course—" Charles took the book to the only chair he could find in the so-called lobby and placed it in his lap, unobtrusively, he hoped. Pulling the *Royale* passenger list from his pocket, he leafed back in the register to the listings for June 7, the date he figured was the earliest for Mr. Black's arrival. If the mystery man had beat him to the Radium Institute by a day, that would have been Monday, the 8th. If Director Remy had been right about the so-called Mr. Black walking to the Institute from Hotel du Lima, he had to be in that register somewhere.

Like the siren of a fire engine on its way to a three alarm inferno, the name alerted him, Gerard P. Brown, arrived 1:00 p.m. Monday, June 8. The *Royale* list matched with Gerard P. Brown, stateroom N32, Promenade deck.

Charles stuffed the passenger list in his breast pocket and hustled the big registration book back to the anxious clerk. Trouble was, Butler's report about the Translators International man named a Philip Brown, not Gerard. I could use a few more details, Charles thought.

"Do you remember this American who checked in on Monday, name of Gerard Brown?" He placed another ten dollar bill on the page to which he pointed.

"I'm sorry, sir, I don't think I have seen him. Wait, yes, a Mr. Brown in room 308. I have spoken with him a few times on the telephone. I can't tell you that I have seen him, however. I do know he speaks excellent French. Shall I ring him for you?"

"Yes, merci, s'il vous plait," Charles pronounced slowly and hopefully.

After ten rings, the clerk said regretfully, "No answer. Would you like to leave a message?"

"No, it would confuse him, I'll be hard to find. I'll have to call him later, but many thanks for your help. That was room 308?"

"My pleasure, Mr. . . ."

"Harmon, Cecil Harmon. Thanks again." Charles turned quickly towards the exit, remembering the fate of his good friend Albert Winch and the police description of the dead manager at 36 Quai de Bethune. Search for Mr. Harmon if you like, Mr. Black.

Moving purposefully, aware that the afternoon was rapidly disappearing, Charles headed for Rue de Vaugirard and found the bookstore once again, now quite proud of himself at his ease in tooling about Paris.

The gray wool sweater lady was in the rear of the shop and seemed to recognize Charles at once.

"Do you remember, I purchased the Valery book of poetry a couple of days ago?"

"Oui." A smile cracked the funny round face that looked like a balloon with a nose painted on it.

"At that time you mentioned that another American had purchased the same volume a short time before."

"Oui, monsieur, I remember."

"Could you possibly tell me about him, perhaps what he looked like?"

"Oh, monsieur, you know many people come and go here, and I am not so good at, how you say it, descriptions. But, let me think, he was rather tall, a bit gaunt, not so debonair as you, sir, not handsome."

"Thank you for those kind words, madame, you are most gracious. Remember anything about the eyes, or hair color?"

"No, I am sorry, about that I can not be sure, I was not paying much attention. I think he was about your age, and I do recall he had great difficulty with the French language."

"You mean he did not speak excellent French?"

"Not excellent, sir, he did not really try to speak it at all, and he had difficulty understanding me when I did. You must excuse me now, the manager is watching us, and I must get back to work."

"Of course, you have been most kind. Merci, madame." Might as well be playing the old pea and shell game, thought Charles as he left the bookstore. One speaks French, one can't. Brown, Black, maybe even Teal. How many of the sons-of-bitches are dodging through the streets of this beautiful city? And who's chasing who? Maybe, by now, Christine has talked with some of her fellow workers and has been able to learn something that will give me a clearer description of the Black who came to the Institute.

He ducked into the convenient Metro station on Boulevard St Michel, determined to make his way back to the Marais district and some conversation with his new friends.

* * *

Karen shook herself from the comforting depths of the green velour chair she'd dropped into in her room at the Paris Intercontinental Hotel after the bell boy finished his usual routine of drapery adjusting, thermostat changing and tip receiving. Why, she asked herself, does it always take twice as long as you anticipate to transfer from the airplane to the hotel? And I didn't even have a misplaced suitcase or a long wait for customs inspection. The taxi ride was simple, too, but now I really have to get a move on if I'm going to visit that Institute du Radium before it closes.

She rose reluctantly and moved to the bathroom door for a careful self-inspection in the full length mirror. The investment in that knit suit was certainly justified, she decided, as she peered over her shoulder to check for wrinkles on her skirt. Change my shoes and add that hand printed silk scarf, and no one will know I've been on the road all day.

Ten minutes later, the smile of approval and quick attention she received from the doorman as he ushered her into a cab proved her analysis had been correct.

The ride across the river to the institute on the Left Bank was tantalizing. The top of the Eiffel Tower beckoned as she viewed it from the bridge, the stalls of the booksellers along the river cried for leisurely perusal, and the merry churning of the engine of the *Bateau Mouche* urged her to join the happy tourists enjoying their exploration of Parisian highlights from the boat on the Seine. Instead I have to cope with this albatross burden of guilt and indecision, Karen lamented.

Once inside the historic old building tucked so inconspicuously into the quiet side street, Rue Pierre et Marie Curie, she was most cordially received by Director Remy, but confounded by his words. She expected a simple yes or no to her inquiry about Frank Griman, but the formal little Frenchman volunteered the information that not only did a Mr. Black recently examine the Marie Curie journals, but also a Mr. Harmon followed the next day for the same reason. Now what? Griman could be one or the other, but why two? Hello,

Albatross, damn you, can't shake you, can I? If I did go to the U.S. Embassy, would they believe any of this?

Thinking about the problem was Mr. Albatross' first name. Not doing anything about it was his last, and time schedules and closed offices meant putting off any action until tomorrow. Go sit in a corner, big bird, and leave me alone, at least long enough for me to enjoy the evening.

The plump, motherly looking woman at the institut's front desk was more than cooperative when Karen asked her to recommend a nearby restaurant. "Why not enjoy some music while you're dining? You are not too far from Le Petit Journal Restaurant and Jazz Club. It is on Boulevard St. Michel."

"That's really more than I dared hope for."

"The girl who just left, our young Christine, sometimes goes there, and she comes and tells us of the wonderful jazz music she had heard. It does not cost too much, I think."

"Sounds good to me, but can a single girl go alone?"

"A single lady can have an early dinner, and then, for an extra bottle of wine, remain at her table when the music begins, Christine tells me. I think a very popular pianist will be playing this week."

With the club's address carefully tucked into her pocket and the small map booklet from the hotel's desk clutched in her hand, Karen was delighted by the golden glow of the late June afternoon highlighting the rough stones of the old walls around her as she stepped into the street. At least it's not a cold, dark winter day, she thought, and I can explore a bit on my way. As she spread her map to orient herself, she let out a squeal of delight as she saw the Place du Pantheon would be in line with her destination. Could I be lucky enough to find it still open?

She stepped forward, immersed in thoughts of those giants of Western culture who had provided so much of her education in reading the French language: Voltaire, Victor Hugo, Emil

Zola—now housed in the Pantheon—had actually walked on these same paving stones!

* * *

"Bonjour, Monsieur Harmon," Christine greeted Charles as she opened the door to his buzz and waited for him to climb the long flight of stairs. "You found my note? I was sorry not to have any American breakfast food for you this morning. Leon said he would bring some ham and eggs when he comes, so I will do better tomorrow," she apologized.

She's really quite gorgeous, Charles thought, as he responded to the smile of her delicately molded lips by giving her his own intriguing, half-dimpled grin. Changed her hairstyle, too, he noticed. Yesterday she looked like a teenager, today she's a charming woman.

"No problem, Christine. The croissant and coffee combination was great, thank you." As he entered he could see that she had neatly tidied the room, but his suitcase sat exactly as he'd left it, a jarring incongruity by the sofa bed.

"It was kind of you to take us to dinner last night. I hope you enjoyed the piano."

"I liked it so well I'm planning a repeat tonight. Could you and Leon stand an encore?"

"No, merci. I promised I would go with Leon to a lecture he must attend at the university tonight," she said, "but why don't you try a different place this evening? The Petit Journal on Boulevard St. Michel is supposed to have Clark Terry, a very fine trumpet man, and they also serve an adequate dinner."

"I have some Clark Terry records made when he played with Count Basie. Couldn't have hoped to catch him here in Paris. What does Leon do that he's forced to give up that great trumpet for the sake of a lecture?"

"I'm not exactly sure," she evaded. "I believe it is something to do with the government."

She's a rotten liar, Charles thought, as her eyes avoided his. She doesn't want to say, or else she hasn't been in this relationship long enough to know.

"You'll manage very well without us, I am sure. How is your article on Marie Curie coming, Mr. Harmon?" The change of subject was abrupt. "It must suddenly be a popular subject with you Americans. Late this afternoon, just as I was leaving the institute, an American lady was asking about the Marie Curie journals." This time her clear brown eyes held no deception.

"Did you happen to catch her name?"

"No, I'm sorry. Actually, she spoke very good French with Dr. Remy, but it sounded as if she may have been asking about you."

"About me?" Charles no longer camouflaged his deep interest in Christine's story with casual tones.

"Well, not necessarily about you, I suppose. I heard her ask Dr. Remy if any Americans had been in the archives this past week reading the Curie journals."

"Did she use any names?" Now he openly pressed for details.

"You sound upset, Mr. Harmon. Is this lady perhaps someone you know?"

"No, maybe you don't know about American writers, how they try to scoop your story. Are you sure she didn't mention any names?"

"You are right, je ne comprendes pas 'scoop.' There was a name mentioned, I recall. Something like Gorman, maybe."

"Could it have been Griman, a Mr. Frank Griman?" Charles persisted.

"It could have been. Pourquoi? Tell me, after all these years, why the sudden interest in Marie Curie's somewhat, how do you say, ancient experiments?"

"I'm sorry, Christine, I should have explained. My editor told me that several magazines are doing stories on the heavy transuranium elements. *World Science magazine* picked up the idea from a series in the *New York Times* science section, and so did some other publications. This Mr. Griman writes for the competition, and now apparently there's a woman also after the same stuff."

"How about that Mr. Black you asked about? I thought he was doing a biography. You must admit, all this furor is a bit strange—" She moved to answer the buzzer.

As Leon entered the room, Charles was thankful for the interruption. The bullshit was getting a bit deep. It's fairly obvious she doesn't know any more about Black, but it's also pretty clear that Karen Bright has arrived in Paris.

* * *

It was after eight when Charles descended the steps from the street level to enter the Petit Journal. Last night Leon had deftly managed to get them seated directly in front of the bandstand, but now the maitre d' indicated a booth near the entrance, and Charles could see the instruments set up at the rear of the low-ceilinged, long, narrow room.

"Puis je avoir une table piano la plus proche, s'il vous plait?" Charles asked, slowly.

"Pardon, monsieur, je ne comprendes pas." The man in the spotless white jacket looked puzzled, and his narrow mustache tweaked as he suppressed a grin.

"I blew it again. I'll just have to give up on this damned book," moaned Charles as he thrust his "French for Tourists" guidebook back into his coat pocket and pointed in the direction of the bandstand. The headwaiter stubbornly now pointed in the opposite direction.

Karen observed the dialogue from her solitary spot in a booth near the center of the room.

"Perhaps I can help," she beckoned to the waiter and addressed him in her fluent French. He turned, suddenly affable and accommodating, with many hand gestures to the front, then to the rear of the room.

She turned to speak directly to Charles. "He says there are no dining tables available near the piano now, but when the music starts, in about forty-five minutes, he'll get you a chair at a small table near the musicians."

Karen took a good look at this American male for the first time, this attractive lone Yankee with the winsome smile. "I wanted to be close, too, and they told me the same thing," Karen grinned. For a moment she thought of offering to share her booth, but rejected the notion as he turned to follow the headwaiter.

"Many thanks for your help," Charles called over his shoulder as he moved down the narrow aisle between the booths and tables.

The room was crowded, and most of the diners had been served. He could see each enticing plate as he walked by and realized he was really hungry again. With a little boy smile and hand gestures he won the help of his waiter, who suggested poulet saute aux fines herbes, haricot verts et salade. When it arrived, Charles laughed to himself, "Call it what you will, fried chicken will take care of a man's hunger any way you say it!" He found himself beginning to enjoy the little cups of strong coffee and was just ordering a finishing after dinner brandy when a waiter arrived to escort him to the vicinity of the bandstand.

The musicians were in the process of setting up, the drummer in place and electronic guitarist fiddling with the amplifying system. Looked like a tenor saxophone on the floor by the other empty chair, but Charles saw no signs of a trumpet.

"Will Clark Terry be playing tonight?" he asked his white jacketed escort.

"No, monsieur, his engagement ended last night." This fellow spoke excellent English, to Charles' surprise. "But you will enjoy this group very much, I think. The pianist is of one of Paris' best, 'le roi du boogie,' Jean-paul Amoureau."

Charles was shown to a group of tiny tables set up no more than ten feet from the musicians, an arrangement very similar to the one last night. You'd think the musicians would get claustrophobic, he thought, as he squeezed through the narrow slot between the tables and tried to find a space for his long legs. To his surprise, he discovered he was playing kneesies with his lovely translator helper.

"Hi, I see they took care of you," she smiled.

"Sorry, I hope I'm not overcrowding you." Charles wriggled in his chair and placed his brandy glass on the little space next to her wine glass. What was it about this lady that made him feel as gauche as a high school freshman at his first dance?

Before she could frame her answer, the pianist hit a solid chord, the spotlight overhead concentrated all attention on the intense artists, and a hypnotizing blend of sounds from guitar and tenor sax took over all thought. The pianist soloed with something that sounded almost familiar, but was obviously French, his flying fingers finally settling into a boogie beat that left both Karen and Charles breathless.

"Wow," they said simultaneously as the number finally ended.

A very large black woman, swathed in layers of shiny black satin, pushed through the maze of tables to take her place at the piano, and Karen and Charles grinned in mutual enjoyment. The singer's vibrato brought golden tones to life as she sang in English:

My story is much too sad to be told,
The only exception I know is the case
When I'm out on a quiet street
Fighting the old ennui
And I suddenly turn and see
Your fabulous face . . .

They looked at each other and said in chorus, "I get no kick from champagne . . ." Smoothly, the vocalist picked up the lyrics in rhythm, and they continued to look shyly into each other's eyes.

As the house lights came on at the end of the first set, and people rose to stretch, reality came back to Karen. She watched some of the crowd move toward the entrance. I'd better not forget I'm in a strange city, she thought, with no Old William for security. I should grab a cab and get back to my hotel while there are still lots of people around.

Regretfully, she collected her purse and stood up. "Excuse me," she murmured to Charles, and followed the pencil slim French girl in black leather pants who was leaving the table next to them.

Charles carefully saved her chair and waited for her to return from the powder room. But the second set started, and his delightful companion did not come back.

CHAPTER 12

Le Havre, France

Saturday, June 13

The pension in Le Havre was, in Frank Griman's estimation, what a Bed & Breakfast in the United States tried to be, but seldom was. He felt a certain homey comfort in this strange abode where English was neither spoken nor understood. His failure to communicate with the inn-keeper and her family served to strengthen his position as an honored guest. They did their best to please without question. All particularly helpful at this time when he needed anonymity so desperately.

Now, however, as he sat eating his third croissant in the cheery breakfast room, watching the bright morning sun dancing on the shiny green leaves in the little enclosed garden, he was brought sharply back to reality when the inn's big calico cat dragged a dead bird across the stone path that bisected the grassy square.

Seeking out the plump, always moving owner, he spoke slowly, "Madame, puis-je utiliser votre telephone?" indicating the credit card in his hand. She nodded her approval, and Frank picked up the phone on the little table by the wall.

After dialing the many digits necessary for an overseas credit card call, he checked the time with the Delft-like clock on the wall, a blue and white windmill with two little Dutch girls' arms designating hours and minutes. I don't care if I wake the bastard, Frank thought, I have to get him before he heads for the golf course. Hard to believe it was just a week ago Bill Higginbotham and I were in Herman Butler's office. Who would have believed so much could go wrong in that little time?

The fourth ring brought forth an answering machine response, "You've reached the Bill Higginbotham residence. Please leave your name and number."

Listening to the interminably long series of beeps, Frank felt dismay hit him like a fist in his belly. Without the attorney's help his New York arrival with Lisa's body would be very messy. Besides, he'd hoped to lay his troubles on Bill's shoulders. Where was that half-assed cousin of his when Frank really needed him?

Paris

Saturday Morning, June 13

Charles' credit card call reached Herman Butler at his home in New York early Saturday morning.

"Bringing you up to date, Herman. The passenger list confirms our hunch. Karen Bright and Frank Griman are both listed. There's also a Henry Black, but I have no way of knowing yet if he's our guy."

"So far, so good, Charles. Now all you have to do is get on the ship, find out which one of them has the superconductor stuff, make whatever kind of deal you have to make, and bring our prize home. If Griman's playing cute, remind him of our contract, tell him we'll sue his ass off. If it's one of the others, you can negotiate beyond the half mil if you need to . . ." Herman paused, awaiting affirmation.

"There may be other problems, Herman."

"What other problems can there be?"

"Well, honestly, I really don't know who got Madame Curie's little treasure in that Quai de Bethune action, but some Slavic character was ahead of me in the Euro-American office, also asking for a passenger list. He may be the Norman Teal who seems to be after me, but we can't know who his friends are." Herman may as well know this is no simple Parisian vacation.

"Charles, your thinking's getting cloudy. Remember, our boy has to be someone who has read the letter, someone who is aware of the very existence our little conundrum. No matter what else is going on, it has to be Griman, Bright, or someone working with them." Herman now sounded like a priest pointing out that God is in his heaven, so just be a good boy and do right.

"I have learned that Karen Bright made it to Paris, and has been to the Institut du Radium asking if Griman has been there."

"So why haven't you made contact with her at the Intercontinental?"

"That's next on my agenda."

"Then why are we wasting time? With your winning smile and notorious bachelor talents, with those crazy eyes of yours, you should be able to charm this lady into instant cooperation." Herman was back to biting sarcasm.

"I'm trying to tell you, Herman, it's a cloudy picture here. We're dealing with too many unknowns. I just don't see some academic broad who speaks a lot of languages going out to hire a killer who likes to cut people's throats while she's on public view at a big conference. And your Mr. Griman's approach doesn't make sense. Why would he make a deal with you in the first place if he was shopping for the high bidder?"

"Charles, it serves no purpose for us to be speculating on an overseas phone call. You're the one with the snooping talent, and you're being well paid to get the job done, so don't bother me with details. Do what you have to do, but bring me the superconductor." And Charles, call me again before you sail."

Butler rang off with his usual abruptness, but Charles heard an extra click before he hung up. Funny, he thought, there's no other extension in this tiny flat. Must have something to do with the satellite connection.

So get a move on, you corporate investigator, Charles told himself, there's only one day left before the ship sails. As he prepared to leave Christine's place, he wondered at his unusual inability to get organized. Finally, foot on the top step, he concluded, it's that girl, that girl from last night. I've really thought about nothing else for hours. Why didn't I get her name?

By the time he'd made his way to Rue du Rivoli, fought for a space on the sidewalk among the Saturday morning shoppers, and found his way to the bus Christine had assured him would take him directly to the area of the Intercontinental hotel, his thoughts were clear. Okay, so he had to see her again. He'd go back to the Petit Journal tonight. If it was real chemistry running in both directions, she'd be there. If not, he had a ship to catch. Herman was right, his thinking had been cloudy, but not in the way Herman thought!

* * *

Karen awakened early, her mind whirling with alternatives. One day in Paris to do whatever she pleased, but one day only. The prospect was overwhelming. Up and out of bed, she parted the heavy draperies to peer out her window at Rue Castiglione below. On the far side of the street was the cliche image of Paris in the early morning, a man on a bicycle carrying a baguette of bread under his arm. He narrowly missed two young girls in very short skirts earnestly absorbed in hand-to-hand conversation. They don't have to make every precious minute count, thought Karen with a bit of jealousy.

Sorting through her options as she dressed for comfort and freedom of movement in her red summer dress and matching jacket, with its patch pockets big enough to hold both map and guide books, she decided the visit to Galeries Lafayette would definitely be her first stop after breakfast. Then she would indulge in a full examination of the tantalizing windows of all the couturiers on Fauberg St Honore. After that maybe she could even manage to spend some of the afternoon at the new Musee d'Orsay. As she slid her feet into low heeled red shoes, she remembered her mother's words: "Feet never get tired in red shoes." They'd better not, I don't have time to cope with that problem, Karen thought, and grabbing her purse and key, she hurried to the elevator.

On her way down she found herself standing next to a big Russian-looking man with an unkempt grayish beard and rumpled woolen suit. I never finished Dr. Dromensky's translation, she remembered, and suddenly she felt an uncomfortable chill as she recalled Berlin, the funny man following her, and those TV spy cameras. Was Dr. Dromensky somehow connected with all that? Thank God there's been no sign of anyone following me here, but I'm not sorry I remembered to check my room for any signs of those spying bugs last night, tired as I was, Karen thought.

In the busy coffee shop, tucked into a corner facing the rapidly filling tables in the center of the room, she savored the strong coffee and flaky croissant, but her mind spun like a roulette wheel, the ball bouncing from one space to another until it finally settled in a slot marked "lonesome." I don't really want anyone to interfere with my plans today, but by evening things will be different. Old William was really a sweet guy, and so comfortable to be with. Where did Philip Brown say he was staying, maybe I should make an effort to contact him. God, he's such an ass, why would I bother, she argued with herself.

Just then a tall, obviously American business man, fresh and ready for the new day, followed the hostess past her table and Karen caught a vague fragrance that brought last night into sharp focus, her music sharing companion vividly remembered. Strangely at ease now, she relaxed as she realized the handsome stranger had really been the underlying reason for her discontent, and she firmly decided she'd go back to the Petit Journal tonight. He'll be there, she told herself confidently, as she gathered her things and prepared to pay her check.

* * *

Charles Holden and Ivan Denkov were both in the Intercontinental Hotel. Each was told by the switchboard operator that Karen Bright's room did not answer, the operator's voice showing a touch of impatience at the second request following so close to the first. Their actions took a divergent path when Charles moved to the writing area in the small sitting space around the corner from the concierge and reception desks. He took one of the hotel memo pads conveniently placed next to the waiting pen, and hastily wrote out a message to leave for Karen.

Denkov turned away from the phone, muttering a few Russian words under his breath and deep in thought. He nearly bumped into Charles, who was by now on his way to the front desk. The two men uttered brief excuses, and Ivan moved back to pick up a phone once again. "Miss Karen Bright's room please, I believe she's in 307." Ivan had used this ploy before; he hoped he would not get the same operator he'd talked to earlier.

"Ne quittez pas, s'il vous plait. Hold the line please. Sir, Miss Bright is not in chambre 307, she is in 415. I will ring her now." Denkov smiled complacently, at the same time feeling in his pocket for his small case of lock picks.

"Sorry, monsieur, that room does not answer. You may leave a message for your party at the front desk."

At the front desk Charles held out his note and asked the uniformed attendant, "Would you kindly leave this message for Miss Karen Bright?"

"Oui, monsieur."

Charles was watching carefully as the white gloved hand carefully slipped the folded paper into the key box compartment faced with the white embossed number 415. He'd make connections with her before the day was over, he told himself.

As he passed a couch on his way to the street entrance, a discarded copy of the Paris edition of the *Herald Tribune* caught his eye. He swerved to focus on it better, to see if the world had blown up since he last paid attention to the news, and the word "superconductor" jumped at him from a small article near the bottom of the page. At full attention now, he picked up the paper and read the story describing a special exhibit at the Science museum, a demonstration of some new "SQUID" equipment, employing the latest high temperature superconductor "YIBCO". That's the stuff Joe Saunders made me read about. Maybe I should go to the museum while I'm waiting for this gal to finish running around Paris. Metro, here I come again, he groaned to himself. He took out his much folded subway map, and started searching for the address given in the paper, near the Porte de Portin, in the 19th arrondisement.

* * *

When Leon arrived at the Palais de Justice office Saturday morning, Inspector Bodine was deep in conversation with two men who looked strangely out of place in the inner offices of the Criminal Division.

"You two are my best operatives," Bodine was saying, "and I am asking one of you to appear to be nothing but a typical French tourist on a holiday to New York City. The *Royale* is a large ship, and you must be very flexible. Your duty will be to keep track of this Charles Holden, also known as Cecil Harmon, at all times, but we must also learn everything about those people who associate with him. As I told you, we have reason to believe that he, or by now one of his cohorts, is in possession of an extremely valuable chemical which is French property. And do not underestimate him, or them. They are very vicious. One of them is responsible for this savage throat slashing." He held out a photograph of the bloodied body of the building manager of 36 Quai de Bethune for their inspection. "Talk it over, decide which one of you will take the job." He turned to give his attention to the waiting Leon.

"It took longer to get the photographs developed than I expected." Leon was always a little uncomfortable in the presence of his superior.

"These show the complete contents of Holden's brief case?" Bodine shuffled through several pictures taken of each separate piece of paper in Charles' case. He came to Butler's notations describing the key facts in Marie Curie's letter, and stopped to read it meticulously, even though Leon had told him about it on the phone.

"My hunch was correct. Doctor Remy will be most interested in this. Imagine, Marie Curie's room temperature superconductor buried in that place in Quai de Bethune all these years!"

"I must tell you, Inspector, this girl Christine is a delightful person. She has not only been cooperative in every way, but she has been charming. Doctor Remy's assistant is certainly first rate." Leon concluded.

"And I hope mine is, too," Bodine interjected. "Remember, you were not assigned to have an affair with this girl." Softening, he smiled and added, "You also have done a fine job. Did you find Holden's tickets for his passage on the *Royale*?"

"No, but I think he was on his way to the EuroAmerican lines to pick them up when he fortunately decided to leave his brief case in Christine's apartment." Reaching into his jacket pocket, he continued, "Would you like to hear a tape of Holden's conversation with a Mr. Butler in New York this morning?"

"Of course," and accepting the offered tape, Bodine hurried to place it in a small tape player he took from his desk drawer.

CHAPTER 13

Karen was finally in the right section of Galleries La Fayette, after making the mistake of entering the mens' store first, and then riding the wrong escalators up four floors until she finally found the glassed-in bridge spanning the two stores. She wandered around in a bewildering maze of china, crafts from countries the world over, a seemingly endless display of children's miniature automobiles, trains and all their components, and then, miraculously, she found women's articles. At the top of another set of escalators she found a directory indicating the way to lingerie.

Now the choices were tantalizing. The negligees displayed on the mannequins caught her admiration for their delicate workmanship and the fluid draping of tissue fine silk, but they were only a minor distraction. Her real interest lay in the many tables displaying the bras she was seeking, lace and net bits of nothing, but ingeniously designed for comfort as well as beauty. Some were exported to the United States, but usually they carried a price tag far beyond her reach.

Now, before the mirror in the tiny dressing room, as she studied the smooth round contours of her firm breasts supported by the film of black lace, she caught herself thinking again of her companion at Petit Journal. Blushing, she hurried to change. But she also decided she'd buy the bra in two colors, black and nude, three of each along with matching panties.

The salesgirl who'd shown her the way to the dressing room told Karen she would have to take her sales slip to the cashier to complete the sale. Mumbling about how much time she'd already used of her precious allotment, she fumbled her way around strange corners one more time. Her good humor was restored by the smiling woman at the desk who offered to charge her purchases directly to Karen's account at Saks Fifth Avenue in New York City. With a bit of money left in my wallet I'll have more fun window shopping on Fauberg St. Honore, Karen thought, as she clutched her packages close and headed for the DOWN escalator.

* * *

Charles really felt victorious as he emerged from the Metro station and saw direction signs indicating that he had, at last, arrived at the location of the Musee des Sciences et Techniques, 30 Avenue Corentin Carjou. The last few minutes on the train he'd wondered if he really was heading the right direction. The people jamming the cars looked more like commuting workers than museum visitors, and as far as he could tell, all of them lived somewhere nearby. Also, the trip had taken twice as long as he'd expected.

Once inside the impressive new building, he discovered he had to wait in line to purchase two sets of tickets before he would be allowed to ascend the escalator rising from the center of the main hall to the Special Exhibits Hall, where SQUID demonstrations were scheduled at thirty minute intervals.

In the little amphitheater, which was now filling rapidly, earphones were on the back of each seat, on each armrest was a multiple language switch. Charles found the "English" location and sat back to watch the stage. The scene reminded him of a Frankenstein movie set transplanted to Seaworld, highlighted by a large cumbersome machine poised beside a chair resembling those in dentists' offices.

As he watched, a man in a white laboratory technician's coat escorted a young, voluptuous blonde to the chair, then adjusted a white tube sticking out of the big machine until he had it pointed directly behind the girl's left ear, close, but not touching, because not a hair of her impeccable coiffure moved. Reminded Charles of having his teeth x-rayed.

The earphones stopped playing music and a deep male French accented voice said, "Good afternoon, ladies and gentlemen, you are about to witness the operation of a SQUID." He continued, "The SQUID is an application of Josephson junctions, and the letters stand for "Superconducting Quantum Interference Device." A Josephson junction, named for its inventor, Brian Josephson, in 1962, is made up of a very thin electrically insulating film between two pieces of YIBCO, the new high temperature superconducting substance.

"We will demonstrate to you that this machine, a magnetoencephalograph, is so sensitive that it is able to detect extremely tiny magnetic fields of the brain. When the junction is charged with a high frequency signal, a low voltage response is generated. But this response is diminished dramatically when a magnetic field approaches the superconductor, so that these very small magnetic fields inside the brain representing actual thoughts become externally visible when a voltage drop is noted. These thin film devices probably represent one of the earliest practical uses for the newest high temperature superconductors."

The voice continued, "You were given an information sheet when you purchased your ticket. If you will consult this, you will see that you have been given a more detailed explanation of the working of this device."

Charles looked at the green paper in his hand, written totally in French.

"Thanks to new high temperature superconductors, the SQUID can now be used without the need for liquid helium cooling, which would prevent us from placing this tube so close to this young lady's brain. The machine you see here uses liquid nitrogen."

What's it all about, Charles wondered. Are they going to do a brain scan on this cutie, or a hair dye job?

"This device, then, is extraordinarily sensitive to changes in electromagnetic fields." The accented voice leaped to a pace Charles strained to follow. "And the thoughts people have are actually faint magnetic signals associated with electrical activity in the brain. We are close enough with our machine now to pick up only the strong signals, which you will see displayed on the monitor to your left."

"Aha," Charles said to himself, "I've caught on. With a room temperature superconductor the coils could touch the scalp. Son-of-a-bitch, I'm looking at a crude mind-reading machine."

As if reading Charles' mind, the explanation went on, "Some day room temperature superconductors will enable us to read thoughts. Today we are merely showing you the possibilities. We will ask our lovely volunteer some questions, and her thoughts will be converted into simple yes and no responses displayed on our screen by computer enhancement of the voltage signals."

I could develop some voltage just looking at her legs, thought Charles, fascinated now.

"I will now ask the young lady, is she comfortable?"

The monitor screen projected two columnar graphs, YES and NO columns. As they watched, bouncing shadows turned into firm dark shading on the YES column.

Scary damned stuff, thought Charles, adjusting his earphone.

Now the white coated technician held a sheet of red paper before the girl's eyes. "Is this paper red?" Once again the YES column darkened. "Or is it black?" This time the NO column shaded as the other returned to normal.

"I've seen enough," Charles said to himself, rising to go. "The poor girl is lucky they didn't ask any personal questions. Talk about a lie detector! The whole thing really reinforces the importance of this mission of mine. Where the hell is that Bright girl?" Looking at his watch, he decided he'd head for Christine's, and hope Karen would call in answer to his note. She'd have to return to the Intercontinental Hotel sometime soon.

Paris

A Small Hotel

Flacon 216 presented certain problems of transportation. The reason for taking it by ship was to avoid the x-ray inspection being done for extra security by the airlines these days. So far, on passenger liners, only passengers and their carry-on bags were being inspected when boarding. Just have to trust that large suitcases were still being handled in mass quantity by the porters, piled high to be hauled to the various staterooms from the central point.

Once aboard, however, the safe thing to do was to keep it close at all times. You just don't go leaving a couple of million dollars worth of stuff hanging around a ship's stateroom. So, the answer seemed to be a good plastic container, secure and not too big. The test kit from Colorado had recommended plastic. In fact the forceps furnished with it were plastic, suitable for handling both the rare earth magnet and the superconductor itself.

The apothecary by the hotel had the perfect answer. A little white plastic box containing a first aid kit, complete with bright red cross on its lid. Bigger than a pack of cigarettes, and smaller than a passport folder, it would fit in a breast pocket. And look like a real first aid kit if any searching of luggage ever took place.

Now to dump out the assorted bandages, cotton swabs, and salves—whatever happened to iodine? The slick black powder poured smoothly into a waterproof oil skin pouch purchased in a sporting goods store, double bagged with another one, and into your pretty new home, baby, safe traveling!

* * *

Karen took care to choose the right escalator when she left the lingerie department. She'd already spent more than enough time in the men's section. At the street level, the combined fragrances of French perfume filled the whole cosmetic section. Skillfully placed overhead lights reflected hypnotizing twinkles from the beckoning crystal vials. If I stop to look at one, I'll be hooked, she thought, and she hastily pushed her way to the exit doors.

On the street, she was quickly absorbed by the swirling crowd flowing around the massive stone Opera House, and she let herself move forward with the flow. Stopped finally by the traffic signals, Karen found herself on the Boulevard des Capuchines. Perfect. She smiled to herself. If I do this correctly, I'll end up on Boulevard de la Madeleine, and once I see that old Cathedral, I'll be on my way to fantasy land.

She tried to move along quickly, but the charm of her surroundings slowed her pace every few feet, first a fabric store with swags of silk prints like giant butterfly wings, then the charming little flower shop with nosegays of multicolored blossoms, each arranged in a different shaped basket. She almost stopped to stare when she was passed by the tall young woman whose face was often seen on the pages of *Vogue* magazine, now casually strolling along with her string shopping bag.

Finally arriving at the rear of the Cathedral of the Madeleine, she found her way around to the front of the rugged brown stone building to the Place du Madeleine, down Rue Royal, and there was her target, Fauberg St. Honore! And I can't go a step farther until I find a place to sit down, she realized.

Looking for any source of relief, she spotted a small name plate swinging from the corner of what seemed to be an alley a few doors up the street. That must be a restaurant, and if it's in this area, it has to be good, she decided, and gathered enough energy to investigate.

Not only was the restaurant convenient to her needs, so far the place was charming. Outdoor tables, but set back under a slight roof overhang to provide some shelter and protection. Hanging baskets of flowers and pink tablecloths added enough color to make you forget that you were indeed, in an alley between two very dark and ugly high walls. The menu was extensive, but Karen settled for a salade Nicoise with a glass of white wine, using her fluent French to give her order. As he left her, Karen heard the young waiter say to his bus boy helper, "That last American was so difficult, it's a pleasure to help a beautiful French woman."

As she waited for her order, Karen idly picked up the French newspaper provided for the benefit of the regular luncheon clientele. She let her eyes scan the front page, testing her French skill more than reading the news. She was jerked to attention by the headline, "Police Baffled by Murder in Marie Curie Quai de Bethune Residence."

A deep shudder racked her whole body, and the details of that damned letter assailed her. It all had to tie together. Someone had figured it out from Marie Curie's journal, and the superconductor had been hidden in the apartment on Quai de Bethune. Hence the murdered building manager.

Taking a very unladylike gulp of the wine that had been placed close to her hand, Karen told herself to use a little reason. She'd done the translating job for Frank Griman, and she knew he had someone he was selling the letter to. Who else would be involved? The people at the Institute had mentioned two people ahead of her, asking for the journal. What were their names?

Somehow she managed to consume most of the warm bread from its linen wrapping in the basket, but her waiter, ignored as he hovered near by, told his bus boy, "She may be pretty, but what a grouch!"

"Harmon and Black." The words uttered out loud startled Karen back to reality. As she remembered the names of the other Institute visitors, she said to herself, "Old Albatross, you've won. I can't carry this load by myself one more day. Even though it is Saturday, there must be someone at the American Embassy I can dump this on."

Barely glancing at "l'addition" on the little tray, she left some of the oversized colorful French bills and drew her Paris map from its nesting place in her jacket pocket. That's what I thought, she reassured herself, it's nearly just around the corner.

It didn't take her long to find the Embassy at 2 Avenue Gabriel. The large American flag flew high and bold over the cobblestone courtyard entrance. One door for public use was open, but no officials were available on Saturday afternoon.

The bored looking woman at the front desk, surprisingly, a French employee, seemed to respond to Karen's obvious urgent need.

"Mr. Clayton, the assistant consulate, will check in about 5:00 p.m. If you wish, you can probably speak with him then."

"May I leave my name, or a message?"

"That won't be necessary. Just be here at five promptly." She turned her back to resume her paper filing.

In other words, thought Karen, Get the hell out!

* * *

It was late afternoon by the time Charles climbed the stairs to Christine's apartment. He was surprised to have Leon answer his knock. Charles sensed something not quite normal about the relationship between Christine and Leon, but maybe it was just his investigating antenna working overtime.

"Did you have a good day in our beautiful city, Monsieur?"

"Just fine, Leon, thank you. Do you know if anyone called here for me?"

"Not that I know of. Christine's in the shower; she may have taken a call. Looks like you've done some shopping. Getting ready for shipboard evenings on the *Royale*?"

"Just a tie I picked up from one of those salesmen in the Metro while I was waiting for my connection at Chatelet." I don't remember mentioning to either of them that I was going home by ship. I did tell them I'd be leaving tomorrow. Charles frowned at his suspicions.

"Did you visit the Louvre?" Leon seemed to sense Charles' distraction.

"No, actually, I went out to the Museum of Science and Technology. Very good place to do your homework when you're writing for a science magazine." Charles wished Christine would come out, he really wanted to know if Karen had called.

"That's very true. Did you happen to see the demonstration of the SQUID they're doing this week? Interest in superconductors is getting very strong in Europe these days." Leon added.

Charles stared at Leon a few moments before answering. What was behind that impassive face? Sounds like a loaded question to me. Oh hell, maybe I'm just reading way too much into a few off-hand remarks, he concluded. He walked into the room to sit on one of Christine's lumpy easy chairs and answered, "That's going on in the U.S. too, Leon."

Christine suddenly appeared in a terrycloth robe, her arms raised to hold the pink towel wrapped around her wet hair. The top button of the robe was loose, and most of one breast surged its way through the opening. Leon's face growing redder by the second was interesting to Charles. Not quite what would have been expected of someone merely reviewing familiar territory, he observed.

"Did anyone telephone me here, Christine?" Charles asked, trying to avert his eyes from Leon's target.

"Not since I've been home, Mr. Harmon, but that's only been a couple of hours." Christine discovered the gap and now pulled the robe tightly together at the neck. "Were you expecting an important call? I have an answering machine, but it hasn't been working right lately, so I disconnected it. Sorry."

Charles shrugged and Christine continued, "Is it more jazz for you tonight, Mr. Harmon?"

"Oui, mademoiselle, oui. You were certainly correct about the Petit Journal, the music was as good there as the Petit Opportune."

"Perhaps tonight you would like to try another. The Caveau de la Huchette, not far from the Petit Journal, also has very fine music."

Leon picked up the conversation as Christine headed for the bedroom. "Yes, let us take you there tonight, it is our turn to treat. I know a place on the Boul Mich nearby where we could have something to eat before we go to hear the music."

"That's very kind of you, Leon, but this time I'm afraid it's my turn to decline with regrets. I have an errand to do, and then I want to return to the Petit Journal." Charles noticed that Christine had closed the bedroom door behind her. "You see, there was this girl last night . . ."

"Ah, l'amour," Leon interrupted, "you have a liaison?"

"Well, sort of, I guess. Anyway, I have to get organized. I leave for Le Havre tomorrow." Charles thought to himself, why am I telling all this to Leon, particularly since I don't even like the guy?

"Je regrette, monsieur. I am going to drive north tomorrow to see my brother in Caen, so why not let me drive you to Le Havre? It's practically on my way," Leon prodded.

"No, thank you, that's really not necessary. I can easily take the train."

"I insist, Mr. Harmon. If you won't let us repay your dinner invitation, you must allow me to drive you. I won't take no for an answer."

* * *

As soon as Karen was out of the Embassy courtyard she realized that her mood for dreaming and fantasy was gone. So much for window shopping on Fauberg St. Honore. Her watch told her it would be about two hours before she'd want to be back here to try again.

With a determined straightening of her shoulders, she decided a soothing interlude with some of her favorite art was just what her faltering spirit needed. The Musee d'Orsay was much too far away, but l'Orangerie was just across the Place de la Concorde on the edge of the Tuileries, and some of the most soothing works of the impressionists were housed there.

On with it! she told herself, remember this is your only day in Paris!

She blinked in surprise as she entered the Place de la Concorde. Tall walls serving as reconstruction barricades ringed the half circle by the Crillon Hotel, and they were brightly painted in garish primary colors, a comic facade to keep one in good humor during construction inconvenience, Karen surmised. I guess I needed that, she told herself, as she threaded her way over planks and piles of dirt. She finally gained access to the pedestrian lane that would keep her safe from the speeding cars careening around the traffic circle.

The Renoirs and Cezannes in the perfect little gem of an art museum did not disappoint her. She was thrilled when she wound her way down to the lower level and found herself in a soothing gray carpeted oval room completely surrounded by Monet's "Water Lilies." As she absorbed the beauty of the peaceful floating illusions, all soft blues, lavenders and aquamarines, the tension slowly left her spine. Another viewer with a heavy footstep finally broke the spell, and Karen, still clutching the now wrinkled and tattered bag from Galeries LaFayette, climbed the stone steps back to the entrance, and headed for the embassy.

She needn't have hurried, she found. She presented herself to a young, bouncy, pony-tailed American girl replacing the earlier dragon.

"I'm Dr. Bright. I was told I could speak with Mr. Clayton if I were here exactly at five o'clock."

"I'm sorry, Dr. Bright. Mr. Clayton phoned in about an hour ago to say that he'd been detained at a luncheon in Versailles. I don't think he'll be in until Monday morning." The girl looked down at her book, "I don't see your name on the appointment list. May I schedule you for Monday morning?"

"No, I'm sailing on the *Royale* tomorrow. Isn't there someone in authority I can contact?" Karen's obvious annoyance registered, even though she knew this young girl had nothing to do with her troubles.

"The problem is, there just isn't anyone around now. The officials usually on duty were all invited to this big do in Versailles. It's market week, you know. Is it a matter of urgency, do you need help with the police or anything like that? I do have an emergency phone number." The girl pulled open a drawer and pulled out a card on which a few large phone numbers were written in pencil.

Karen debated her answer. She had to be believable, and she had to share this load somehow. "My business is not so much personal as it is important to the United States Government. I don't mean to sound cryptic, but what I have to say must be told to someone with authority to act. And the information must be kept secret." Karen hoped she would be taken seriously, but she was afraid of telling too much.

The receptionist stood up and walked over to Karen, who by now looked as if she were just about to burst into tears. "Hey, are you okay? I guess you want me to call one of the emergency numbers. Please just come over here and sit down. I'll bring you some coffee and then we'll see what I can do about getting hold of one of our guys." She ushered Karen into a plush seat and soon returned with a styrofoam cup in her hand.

"Is black all right? We really don't seem to have anything around here on Saturday afternoon."

"Black is fine; you're very kind." Karen was pulling herself back together, ashamed of letting her emotions take over.

After a long five minutes, the receptionist came back to ask Karen where she was staying in Paris. She returned a second time to ask what time she would be checking out tomorrow. Finally she told Karen that she had located the Duty Officer, a Mr. Norton. He would telephone Karen's room at the hotel at 8:30 tomorrow morning, and would be of every possible assistance. Yes, he understood it was important government business, but he was on his way to the airport to meet an arriving diplomat who would occupy the rest of his evening.

The interview ended with the receptionist helping Karen into a taxi and giving instructions in beautiful French to have the driver take Karen directly to the Intercontinental. A grateful Karen settled back on the cushions, realizing she was ready to let someone else take over, even a Paris taxi driver, who would even if you didn't want him to, she grinned wryly.

Afternoon crowds were gathering in the public rooms of the hotel, noisy tourists returning to home base for a regrouping before the next activity, determined men heading for the cocktail lounge, many women with many packages bringing their trophies home. It seemed to Karen she'd never get her turn at the front desk to retrieve her key. They put those enormous weights on them so you can't make a mistake and carry them away, but they really aren't in any hurry to give them back to you, she moaned to herself.

"Madame, you also have a message." The clerk had to break his impassive formality and even raise his voice a tone, Karen had been so quick to turn to leave.

"Oh, I'm sorry. Thank you," Karen apologized, and accepted the folded paper.

The elevator was so crowded Karen had to keep her hands close to her body, clutching her very bedraggled paper sack and holding her purse firmly to her side. No way to read the message here, she told herself, but her curiosity was strong, and her anxiety level rose as she tried to figure out who knew she was here. Don't let it be bad news from home, she prayed. Finally, as she fiddled with the cumbersome key, she thought of Philip, he knew she was in Paris. But wasn't I careful not to tell him where I was staying?

In the room, she dropped her purse and sack on the desk and opened the note.

"Please call me as soon as possible. We need to talk about the Curie letter . . ." After the telephone number was the bold signature, "C. Harmon."

"Dear Lord, what do I so now?" mouthed Karen as her trembling fingers dropped the frightening piece of paper. The mysterious Mr. Harmon, and Mr. Black is probably right there with him. Is there no escape? First that awful knife attack on Old William, then the spy cameras, and now this! She looked wildly around the room for signs of intrusion, fear supplying the energy for furious searching. Did I leave that folder of papers out of my suitcase?

Exhausted, satisfied she had left no corner unexamined, Karen decided a soak in that giant tub, complete with bubbles, couldn't hurt, and it would certainly help her aching body. As she lay there trying to calm down, she went over her choices of action. She could try to run, find another hotel, but what about that call from the embassy tomorrow morning? Besides, whoever is after me seems to be all-seeing. Finally, she decided, why not just act natural? I'll follow my plan, go find that sexy guy at the Petit Journal and to hell with them!

CHAPTER 14

Paris

Saturday Night, June 13

Charles sat at a table for two in the Petit Journal, facing the entrance in order to inspect every arriving patron. He sipped slowly from his martini, hoping he'd have company before the glass was empty, too stimulated by expectancy to need the added kicker of quickly consumed alcohol.

As he waited, he reviewed his actions of the past hour. The now weary desk clerk at the Intercontinental Hotel had assured him Miss Bright had been given her message, and the operator had obligingly rung room 415 many times, with no answer. Then, after some cooing persuasion by Charles, she had begrudgingly checked again with the front desk to be sure there had been no mistake in the room number. All blank and zero. A telephone call back to Christine's had yielded no response. To hell with it! I don't know this damned city well enough to begin the kind of investigation needed for a girl who doesn't want to be found, Charles lamented. At least she'll be confined to a limited area once she's aboard the *Royale*, and we've moved out to sea.

Charles decided he'd have to pin his hopes on the future. He sat back to relax when his eyes opened wide, and he jerked to his feet involuntarily, nearly spilling his drink and knocking over his chair.

"You're not too late. I have a place for you right here." Charles moved to extend his hand to the petite blonde with the flawless skin, exquisite in her simple black dress.

Karen nodded to the maitre d', acknowledging her acceptance of Charles' invitation, and slid smoothly into the offered chair. "How did you know I'd be here tonight?" she said softly as Charles took her in, inch by inch.

"I really don't know, but I'm glad you are."

"I think I'm glad I am, too. You're quite a mind reader," she said, suddenly shy.

"This time I'm better than a SQUID." Charles certainly approved of what she did for that black dress, and his winning smile confirmed it.

"I beg your pardon?"

"Oh, sorry. I'm not talking about a baby octopus," he added, "SQUID means . . ."

". . . Superconductor Quantum Interference Device," she interrupted.

"How do you know that?" Charles beckoned a waiter and set his menu aside while a surprisingly agile elderly man, with a toupee bad enough to match his teeth, approached for Karen's order.

"Beefeater martini on the rocks for me," Karen said, forgetting what it would cost.

"The same," Charles added.

"We'll order later," she instructed the waiter, in expert French as usual.

Charles returned to his shocked inquiry. "You know about SQUIDs because you've been to the Science Museum; that must be it."

"Excuse me?"

"Wasn't that a humbling, frightening experience, though?"

"What experience?" It suddenly dawned on Karen that they were conversing as if they'd been friends for years. Or maybe more than friends.

"The mind reading show. What else?"

"I went to l'Orangerie, not the Science Museum, and I didn't know SQUIDs were used for mind reading. I thought they were just a fancy adaptation of a Josephson junction."

"You must be some kind of Physics Ph.D. I can't believe Josephson junctions have joined our martini time, but I don't have to be a mind reader to recognize a beautiful genius when I see one." Charles hoped he didn't sound like a clod. "But, if I were a mind reader, I'd know your name, which I don't and wish I did, because how could I have found you if you hadn't shown up tonight?"

"It's Karen." They leaned together, beginning to enjoy each other. "Now it's my turn to SQUID you —"

"Right here and now?" he teased impishly.

"Why not?"

"First, Karen, the answer to my question. Are you a scientist?"

"Heavens no. I did get a Ph.D., but in language study. I know about SQUIDS because I just came in from Berlin where I was working as a translator for an international conference on superconductors. SQUIDs were the subject of a paper I translated."

Charles' face went paper white. Beads of moisture popped out on his forehead. Drops of martini sloshed onto the white linen cloth.

Astonished at this sort of reaction to such a mundane matter, Karen said quickly, "What's the matter? Are you okay?"

"Yeah. My SQUID's working so well it's spooky." He went on before she could say anything, "Your name is Bright, Karen Bright. You work for Translators International in New

York. You translated a very important letter for a Mr. Frank Griman before you left for Berlin, where you stayed at the Bristol Hotel Kempinski. When you arrived in Paris you went over to the Institut du Radium after you had checked into room 415 at the Intercontinental, and why the hell when someone leaves you an urgent message don't you respond?" Charles finished by taking a big gulp of the remaining martini.

"You son of a bitch, Mr. Cecil Harmon." Now it was Karen's turn to go pale. "Where the hell do you get off searching my hotel rooms and planting those obscene TV cameras. I suppose you know what color underwear I have on. To think that last night I almost thought it was that super, sticky, really naive love at first sight, and all the time it was just pure and simple instinctive hate!" Karen almost choked on her drink.

"Wait one damn little minute, Dr. Bright. I don't know anything at all about your hotel rooms being searched. Mostly, I think you should know you may be in real danger—and not from me. Believe me, and, for crissakes, hear me out!" He wanted to pick her up and shake her, then hug the hell out of her.

"Your note said . . ." Karen took the crumpled memo from her purse. She spread it on the table, smoothing it out as the waiter replaced the empty glasses with new drinks in response to Charles' urgent hand signal.

"I know what it said. Just because I mentioned the Curie letter, don't jump to the conclusion that I've been searching your rooms. You've just confirmed my suspicions that someone is probably after you. I'm with Consolidated Electronics, and Mr. Griman has a contract with us. He sold us a stake in the recovery of the Curie material, but there has been a leak. Someone got to the stuff before we did. What color is it?"

"So, he did sell it, just as he'd hoped. What color is what?"

"Your underwear." He studied the olive looking up at him from its icy bath.

"None of your damn business. It's black." Pulling her brows together, Karen reasoned, "You know what, I think I may know who has Flacon 216." She took a sip of her new cocktail and winced. Two of these liquid demons might be beyond her capacity. Could she trust this guy? He'd certainly done something to her senses, be it love or hate.

"That's why I wanted you to call me. Believe me, I'm not dancing you around. I gave it to you straight. Except that my real name is Charles Holden. What's the third item down?" He picked up the menu and held it for her inspection.

"Veal with lemon. Don't you want to know who has Griman's superconductor?"

"You, I thought."

"Don't be an ass. The knowledge of this whole potential has been killing me." With a crazy sigh of relief, she felt compelled to tell him everything. She signaled to the waiter, and when she took care of the order for both of them, she launched into her story. Before their meals arrived, the details of the last few days bubbled out of her non-stop, even the part about Old William. Purged, she sat back and drew a breath.

"Tell me more about this Dr. Dromensky." Charles tipped his glass and looked at her questioningly.

"No more for me. Just a glass of Evian, please. Not much to tell, except I'm pretty sure he couldn't have been the guy following me in Berlin. I only caught a quick glimpse of him, but Dromensky didn't have the same body build, although I really do think that translation job he wanted me to do was a phony." She paused while the waiter stopped all conversation with fragrant bowls of some kind of hearty soup and a basket of warm bread.

"Seriously, I think your Mr. Griman must be playing games with you. When I went to the Institute, two people had been there before me. One was Cecil Harmon; I guess that was you—rather obvious alias if you ask me—and a Mr. Black, probably a Frank Griman alias. He must have been the one who broke into the Curie apartment."

"You're right about the Cecil Harmon bit, Karen. I agree it was a lousy alias." Charles couldn't keep from trusting this woman, although it was certainly a different feeling for the guy who'd been such an independent bachelor. "But Griman couldn't be the mysterious Mr. Black."

"How do you know that?" Karen wondered at herself, knowing she'd believe whatever he told her.

"Because, I know Griman was in a different city when the murder at Quai de Bethune took place. By the way, how do you know about that? Did Dr. Remy tell you?"

"No, I read it in a newspaper this afternoon. That's when I decided to tell the whole story of the Curie letter to the people at the American Embassy here."

"Oh, shit!" Charles reddened at the unrestrained expletive. "Sorry, but are you saying you've told the Embassy the whole story?"

"Not yet. Seems no one in authority hangs around the place on Saturday to help loyal U.S. citizens with a problem like mine. They promised that a duty officer named Norton would call me tomorrow morning before I sail for the States," she muttered shyly, wondering what response it would provoke.

"I'm glad to hear that you are sailing, Karen, because I am, too," Charles smiled, then said almost harshly, "Listen to me, sweet lady, do not say one solitary word about that Curie letter to anyone, least of all the officials at the Embassy."

"But why?"

"It'll get you involved in an international situation, maybe even murder, and you'll find yourself up to your mysterious black underwear in enough red tape to cancel any plans for a slow boat, that's for sure. Besides, don't you professional translators have a code of ethics about client confidentiality?"

"The man's done his homework, I see."

"I hope so."

"In this case that code of ethics turned into a rotten egg that hatched into a three ton albatross hanging on my neck. I find it difficult to justify keeping such a serious secret from my own country to protect a sleaze like Frank Griman!"

"What you say is true, Karen, but now we can work together to see that the secret makes its way safely to the States, and together we'll dump your albatross without snagging you in a net of murder charges in a foreign country—no matter how well you speak the language. Can you believe me?"

Karen nodded, wondering at what must certainly look like submission. How could I put such trust in a man I barely know, she thought. "How do you mean, work together? I'm in this thing up to my, my whatevers, might as well jump in up to my neck."

"And a neck well worth saving, I'd say."

"Thanks a lot. Now, back to my question. How are we supposed to work together? I'm leaving on the *Royale* for New York tomorrow."

"Of course you are. I have the passenger list right here." Charles removed the computer printout from his breast pocket. Unfolding it, his eyes quickly moved to find the red checks in the "B's." "Here you are, Karen Bright, Stateroom P-142 on the Provence Deck."

"I have to admire your thoroughness. Are you sure you didn't know I have on black underwear, Mr. Detective?"

"Yeah, sure, but I have given that subject some thought. Anyhow, I'm almost positive the Curie compound is going to New York on the *Royale*."

"How so?" Karen interrupted.

"Because, and you should know this, it can't be transported by air when every passenger goes through a metal detector, as does all the luggage these days on overseas flights. A room temperature superconductor would set off all the alarms; also, the material itself may be altered so that Consolidated Electronics Laboratories can't analyze it for duplication."

"Yup, you are a pretty smart detective, Mr. Holden-alias-Harmon. You know, I really don't like the name 'Cecil.' I'm awfully glad you're a Charles, Charles. So, now it's clear. You are going on the ship because you have an idea that a Mr. Black has Madame Curie's Flacon 216 room temperature superconductor. Our elusive Mr. Black will be on the *Royale* taking it to the States, and you must have some idea of how you're going to find him, and I'm supposed to help you. Is that about it?"

"I'm sure lucky to hook up with a Ph.D. You're so damned smart, even your name is Bright. Very descriptive, indeed."

"What's next, Charles?"

"Let's go up to the bandstand and listen to the music we came for. We can worry about our mystery tomorrow. I'll do my best to protect you from now on." Charles was confident and determined he could, and would, do exactly that.

When Charles delivered Karen back to the Intercontinental Hotel, the city that never sleeps was at least napping. It had been difficult to find a cab that late at night, and the streets looked deserted. He had suggested they go to the ship together in the morning, but Karen protested that she'd already paid for the bus ride. Besides, she wanted to leave early to avoid the call from the Embassy. In the end, they agreed to meet on the ship. It was just as well since Charles absolutely burned to get into bed with this lady, and yet he knew this would not be the time for it.

CHAPTER 15

Bristol Hotel, Paris

Late Saturday Night

Dr. Chernov Dromensky was disappointed. Until this afternoon he'd really believed he'd be allowed to stay with this superconductor business and take the cruise ship to New York. After all, he told himself, wasn't he the person the Grimans had contacted in the first place? Moscow wouldn't even know anything about the Curie letter if he, Dromensky, the expert on electronic sciences, hadn't been alert enough to recognize that letter's real significance. Now he was called home to evaluate some American "Star Wars" document just received from an agent in Washington.

As he began to collect his belongings from where he had strewn them all over the spacious area of the suite, Dromensky retrieved his silk robe from behind the bathroom door. He stroked its satin lapels regretfully, and wondered if he should give it to Ivan to take on the ship? Hell no, he decided, that GRU jerk might just have trumped up some deal with the head of the surveillance division of the Seventh Directorate to get me out of the picture. Does he think all those gimmicks, his TV cameras and two-way mirrors, are better than a little ordinary scientific reasoning?

At that moment the door opened, and Denkov slid in noiselessly. Startled, but damned if he'd show it, Dromensky stroked his beard and said casually, "Has the great hunter located his prey? Do you have the Curie stuff safely in your pocket?"

Choosing to ignore the sarcasm, Ivan replied, "It will be necessary to continue the search on the ship. I will find it necessary to leave very early tomorrow morning for Le Havre. Will you still be here, or shall we talk now about settling our bill and making arrangements to check out early? I know you will have many room service charges to account for. I am aware that you have offered hospitality to some of the ladies of Paris."

"Comrade, I am the one who made these hotel arrangements. Moscow put me in charge of this expedition, and I shall be the one who completes the business." Dromensky walked into the bedroom and closed the door firmly.

Le Havre, France

Sunday Morning, June 14

Frank Griman watched the bow of the *Royale* grow in height as the world's newest transatlantic vessel approached the pier. Before her bow the skirt of velvety green water parted its pleats smoothly in a welcoming gesture as the majestic floating city came slowly into position. As the ship's bowthrusters churned white heaps of foam on the starboard side, unseen hands from high above hurled huge coils of creosoted lines to the feet of waiting dock hands, those husky men in blue shirts who twirled the heavy lines onto the concrete stanchions with grace as seemingly effortless as a ballet dancer's.

Within minutes of the ship's arrival, vendors with flowers and small French flags appeared to set up booths in the center of the long concrete walkway leading to the metal sided two-story embarkation building, and welcoming banners were strung where the gangplank would soon connect the ship to solid ground. A small military marching band, wearing cobalt blue uniforms prominently displaying the stylized "R" logo of the *Royale*, emerged from the wide opening on the building's second level, the musicians already testing their instruments with tentative toots and beeps.

The flurry of activity that accompanied the regal appearance of the *Royale* eased Frank's gloom and irritation at needing to comply with one more bit of red tape. He still had to pay an extra transfer fee required for loading a casket on Sunday. Sounded like a big rip-off to him. If the ship only loads on Sunday, why in the hell would they charge extra? He knocked on the office door and muttered, "C'mon you Frenchies, open up."

A small girl with black curls breaking loose from the red beret which matched her red pinafore tugged at Frank's sleeve. "Pardon, are you Monsieur Griman?"

Startled, Frank looked down with suspicion at the girl who couldn't be any older than ten. "How do you know my name, little one?"

"I speak English quite well, n'est pas?"

"So you do! What can I do for you?"

"My grandfather, he would like to speak with you. He told me you would be here. He does not understand English, and he asked me to bring you to him, please."

"I'm sorry, I have to wait here for this office to open. Why don't you go get your grandfather and bring him over here to me, okay?" Frank didn't know what her name was, or who had sent her, but he figured he'd be safe right here in the middle of all this busy action.

Now Little Red Riding Hood looked doubtful. "I will try, Mr. Griman." She turned abruptly and ran toward the parking area.

The indifferent freight clerk was indicating the last place which needed signing and Frank was ready to dig into his wallet for the final amount specified, when the small hand nudged again. This time her other hand was held by a dignified but nervous old gentleman who stood quietly, awaiting Frank's attention.

"My grandfather says, please, you must have an autopsy on your wife's body when you arrive in New York City."

Now that's a sure attention grabber, Frank gasped to himself. "What's that again, please?"

"My grandfather is the mortician who did not embalm your wife's body." The little girl seemed troubled by her words, but determined to carry on. The old man was nodding his head and speaking, pointing at Frank, urging her to continue.

"Go on," Frank was now at full attention.

"He says there were some things about the body—he does not think your wife died of a heart attack." The old man was still talking as she continued translating.

"Please tell your grandfather to slow down. Tell him I will listen to what he wants me to know." Frank bent closer to be sure she understood.

"He says he has seen such signs once before from a poisonous snake bite. My father's friend was a zoo keeper who would have died if he had not had a bad cough when he was bit. It was the coughing that saved him."

Frank had visions of the Russians at the railway station with a bag of poisonous snakes—much too preposterous!

"My grandfather did not tell the authorities about this condition. He understood you had made all the arrangements to leave with the ship for New York. But he wants you to know that he can inform the police if you would like him to, if you suspect some trouble about your wife's death. Otherwise he will say nothing." The man was now looking directly at Frank, awaiting his response.

"Please, thank him very much—he certainly did the right thing—and thank him for the information. I will consult my attorney in New York, and if we need any further information, he will contact you. Does your grandfather have a business card?"

The girl explained in French. The old man reached for a card from his well-worn wallet and offered it, saying, "En vous priant d'accepter nos sinceres condoleances, monsieur."

Frank tried to offer the gentleman a hundred franc note, but the old man raised his hand in objection. "Bon voyage, sans danger."

The two walked away and quickly melted into the rapidly forming crowd of embarking passengers.

Enroute to Le Havre

Sunday Morning

Charles roused from his semi-dozing day dreams and reminiscences of last night with Karen as Leon wheeled the little green Renault around a sharp blind corner, narrowly missing an oncoming heavily loaded, lumbering lorry. Charles could see the needle of the speedometer from where he was sitting, and it had climbed past 140 kilometers.

"Jesus, Leon, take it easy! The ship doesn't sail until 5:30, and I'd like to be alive long enough to board her!"

Without changing speed, Leon charged the lethal missile onto a strip of highway bounded by vision obscuring high bushes on each side, saying, "I have heard that you Americans have put some arbitrary limit on the speed you control your automobiles. Why do you not drive your vehicles the way they are designed?"

"We choose to exercise a bit of prudence when caution is called for, Leon, and I'm not kidding—slow down, or I'll pull those damned keys right out of the ignition."

Realizing that Charles was not bluffing, Leon hit the brakes too firmly, and the little car swerved as it slowed.

"Seriously, Leon," Charles continued, "you haven't had enough sleep for great coordination. I'm sorry you and Christine felt it necessary to wait up for me last night. I told Christine not to worry about me, I would be saying farewell to Paris." Paris, hell, thought Charles, Leon couldn't imagine how hard it had been to leave Karen after helping her check for intruders in her hotel room. Admirably, she'd been stubborn about staying alone and sticking with her plan to take the excursion bus to the ship this morning. Hope she got away before that guy from the embassy called.

As they approached the outer fringes of Le Havre, Leon was forced by the increased traffic to pay attention to his driving, and they finally arrived at the Pier 18 passenger terminal without need for continued conversation. Leon maneuvered the Renault into position near the gathered porters. As he stepped out to help open the trunk and remove Charles' suitcase, he tipped his hat to the bald man in the pinstriped suit standing by the porter's rack, who flipped a finger in response.

"Well, thanks for the buggy ride, Leon, I hope you and your toy rocket make it back to Paris in one piece!"

"Sorry it got a little rough, I hope you have a smooth trip home. Au revoir, Mr. Holden."

A blue shirted porter with a many pocketed apron moved to pick up the suitcase Charles offered, then chattered rapidly in a French not heard in any American high school class. Impatient, since each delayed moment meant money lost, the porter finally managed to convey the message that Charles' bag could not be handled until properly tagged with a stateroom number. Some competent travel agent should have supplied the tag to be made out in advance, but none had been given to Charles with his hurriedly purchased ticket. Charles and the porter had almost arrived at an impasse of international misunderstanding, when a blue-haired grandmother emerged from the rapidly gathering, murmuring mass behind them and triumphantly restored communication. The ticket properly displayed, the porter laboriously scribbled on a spare tag fished from the depths of one of his copious pockets, and Charles was free at last to proceed to the pre-boarding area and a long table set up with hospitality trays, some filled with bits of cheese and crackers, and others loaded with previously poured glasses of champagne.

He sipped from the plastic substitute for a glass, registering the details of the action before him. The area was a warehouse, blocked off with ribbon draped standards and strips of canvas to indicate walkways. A ship's photographer and his smiling helper, part of the cruise staff, no doubt, were poised to take each passenger's picture as tickets were checked at the desk at the far end.

A few folding chairs were set up in front of the Passport Control desk, but traffic there was moving smoothly and the chairs found no waiting takers. Before the exit door at the end was a rudimentary metal detector arch manned by a uniformed sailor. He doesn't look alert enough to recognize his own mother, but maybe that's a pose, thought Charles.

He shifted his briefcase and tossed the empty plastic glass into the waiting basket. He decided he might as well board. He'd been stalling, hoping Karen would appear. He moved forward and suddenly thought, did that bird Leon refer to me as Holden? Funny how sounds come back to you in your memory, but I must be mistaken; God knows the commotion and noise level around the car was at a maximum top level.

"It's very exciting, getting on such a beautiful ship, don't you think?"

"I beg your pardon?" Charles turned to find the little bald fellow in the pinstriped suit waiting behind him in line for the security check.

"I merely said, it's a thrill to be boarding. Isn't she beautiful?"

"Yes, doctor, I agree. A very handsome ship she is."

"I am not a doctor, merely a French tourist looking forward to visiting the United States. You are an American, I presume?"

"Yes, of course. We don't seem able to hide our identity. I thought you were a doctor because of the MD initials on your brief case. Sorry about that."

"The MD?," Pinstriped Suit seemed puzzled, then he laughed, "Oh, Marcel Dubois, that is I! I had forgotten that I, too, am carrying a label, with my initials on my case. I expect we will get to know each other better when we are sailing, n'cest pas?"

"No doubt," said Charles, hoping his indifference didn't sound rude.

* * *

The Euro-American lines offered a very efficient bus transport from Paris to the pier where the *Royale* was waiting in Le Havre, and Karen caught its first available bus Sunday morning. After a very short night, the chamber maid fortunately answered her early call for coffee very quickly. Happy to see a warm, fresh baked brioche also on the little tray, Karen stuffed quick bites of flaky goodness into her mouth as she hurriedly repacked. After all of Charles' warnings the night before about the consequences of discussing the Curie letter with the American embassy, she knew she wouldn't be able to handle that 8:30 call from old what's his name.

Even with all her rushing, Karen heard the telephone ringing in the room as she pulled the door shut behind her. He will chalk it up to some dumb excitable female, Karen assured herself.

If Karen was early, Ivan Denkov was earlier still. Resorting to his favorite disguise, a daily newspaper which could hide his face when necessary, but still could be peered around, he was slouched in the very last row of seats in the bus, waiting patiently. If the Bright woman didn't board this bus, he'd make some excuse to get off and wait for the next one, and try again.

Karen Bright stepped into the bus, searching for an empty seat. She was looking fresh and perky, dressed in her pink knit travel suit, this time with a print silk blouse, collar open at the throat, and a single strand of freshwater pearls her only jewelry. Ivan admired the effect, and chuckled for the first time in several days as he visualized his wife, Lena, in such an outfit. She would, of course, require a much larger skirt for her ample rump, and the flimsy blouse would be at great risk trying to cover her generous bosom. Denkov, the agent who could kill without a qualm, now felt a twinge of guilt as he recalled Karen's naked curves and pink nipples on his video tapes. Still, she was not to be forgiven for making a fool of him with Dromensky!

Finding a window seat about midway down the aisle, Karen settled in for the four hour ride. She had a new whodunit in her purse, packed in New York and as yet untouched, but she also put into her lap a map, folded to the route through which they would be driving, and a green Michelin guide that listed details of each town and village on the way. A motherly American woman, with salt and pepper hair and a broad, uncomplicated smile, took the seat beside her.

"Hi! I'm Betty Lou. I just love to see tourists making the most of their travel, dearie. That's my business, travel agent, you see, and it's wonderful to be with happy travelers—guess that's why the companies send us on these free FAM trips-that's fam for familiarization, you know. My friend Mary was supposed to be with me, but she got delayed somewhere in Paris. Guess I'll have to make connections with her on the ship."

As the woman finally paused to take a breath, Karen thought she could sympathize with Mary. Wonder how many days they've been together on the road? At that, I could have done worse, Karen told herself, as she caught a good look at the man occupying the seat across the aisle. From the first quick look, it's easy to see he's a thoroughly unappetizing person. Dour expression, wrinkled clothes, dusty shoes. Probably smells, too. Ugh! Thank you for sitting here, Betty Lou, Karen said to herself. Chatter on, and I'll read!

Denkov wondered why Karen didn't have a male companion. Wasn't Charles Holden supposed to be with her? Dromensky had been so sure they were working together. Just another example of Dromensky's inept reasoning. Maybe the connection would be made aboard ship. I can wait, he thought.

* * *

Philip Brown was delighted by his luxurious stateroom aboard the *Royale*. If he had to pay a premium to indulge his horrendous fear of flying, at least this time it was worth going over his budget. The only ship he'd been on before was a tired old converted ferry boat, dirty as a third-rate motel, posing as "Your Happy, Fun in the Sun ticket to Paradise in the Caribbean!" That disaster had not prepared him for the quiet elegance of this room, with it's wide window of one-way glass overlooking the Promenade Deck, curtained with an understated print the colors of the sea, all swirling blues, grays and greens. A love seat and lounge chair stood under the window, the far wall was a bank of closets and built-in drawers near the door leading to the bathroom. On the other wall was a long counter, writing desk at one end, and at the other end a small refrigerator on the bottom, above it a glass-doored cupboard which stored glasses and even a dish of pretzels and peanuts. And the bed! Booked as a double room, he'd prepared for the usual twin bed arrangement, little expecting to see them made up as a giant king, resplendent under a quilted spread proudly centered with the stylized *Royale* logo. That'll give a man ideas!

On the desk was his room key, which was actually a small computer-punched card, and a printed card listing his table number in the dining room. Also, a copy of the ship's daily program, entitled "The Royale World." A brief reading told Philip he'd have no excuse to be bored. Activities were planned for every hour, even this first day. Tonight's dinner would be casual, but after dinner in the Grande Lounge an orientation program was scheduled. Maybe that would be a good chance to see if he could locate Karen Bright, Philip thought. She's supposed to be on board somewhere. Funny, he hadn't given her much thought until he'd seen that huge bed, even though she'd probably been thinking of him.

With Karen fully in mind now, Philip carefully surveyed his clothing choices as he stowed his personal possessions in the many available drawers, and on the hooks and hangers. Maybe tonight was the perfect time to break out his Paris purchase, the striped shirt with the purple and green polka dot tie. Nothing but the best for Karen, he smiled.

* * *

Charles contemplated the irony of travel planning. He knew people who stewed over the details of space bookings and reservations, sometimes as long as six months in advance, and here he was, resplendent in a veranda suite on the *Royale's* Versailles Deck, all arranged at the last minute. Thank you, Herman Butler, you don't know what you accomplished!

As he looked over his generous space, the cozy many-pillowed couch and easy chair facing the television set, sliding glass doors which opened to a balcony with a table and pair of lounge chairs, a separate alcove for the king-sized bed, lighted dressing table and wall of mirrored closets, he firmly resolved to have Karen ensconced here at the earliest opportunity. The bar, with champagne chilling in its bucket of ice and two glasses waiting on the silver tray, reinforced the idea.

Quickly finding spaces for his sparse wardrobe, Charles reviewed the challenge of that elusive Curie superconductor. With everything locked into place, the cast of people limited to those on board with no way to escape, the job should be a piece of cake for an experienced investigator. For beginners, he told himself, he could happily write Karen off any list of suspects. She had to be telling the truth about all that harassment in Berlin, and that had taken place at the same time the elusive Mr. Black visited the Institut du Radium. And her total disdain of Frank Griman could not be faked; any consideration of a conspiracy between them was out of the question. For that matter, Griman had also been in Berlin when the murder took place in the Curie apartment, so the problem really comes back to "who is Black?"

The phone on the desk suddenly buzzed with its penetrating European signal, repeated three times while Charles found his way around the bunched quilted fabric corners of the bedspread to pick up the receiver.

"Well, you handsome investigator, are you coming to join me so we can learn together how a ship sails from Le Havre?"

"Karen, I've just been waiting for your call. I didn't realize your bus had arrived. How was the trip?"

"We jolted our way through some lovely territory, thank you. How was yours?"

"Let's just say I whizzed through the same space!"

"We deserve a gala bon voyage, then, Charles. Let's hit the deck and see the action."

"Sounds good to me, Karen. My steward told me I must report to the head maitre d' for a dining table assignment. Do you have yours?"

There's a card here on my desk listing a table number, but if you don't have your number yet, let's see if we can change mine and sit together—or am I being a bit presumptive?"

"What kind of talk is that? I thought we understood each other last night."

"Right. So why don't we hurry up to the bar on the Lido Deck and wave fond farewell to France."

"The Lido bar it is, soon as possible!"

As Charles headed for the stateroom door, he paused briefly to place the champagne bottle into his little bar refrigerator. "Your time will come, soon, I hope, buddy."

CHAPTER 16

Chernov Dromensky had arranged for Ivan Denkov's stateroom to be on the Lafayette Deck, down the hall and across from Frank Griman. It was an outside single, and Denkov was delighted with the privacy and space all for himself. His porthole was close to the water's level, and he could watch the play of the waves if he stood close and looked down. The television set, mounted on the wall so it could be viewed from the bed, was turned on, and currently displayed the view from the bridge as seen by the ship's captain. If he could finish his work quickly, Denkov told himself, he might even have some time to enjoy himself on this luxury cruise!

Dromensky had given him Karen's room number, but Ivan, not familiar with the ways of luxury liners, wasn't sure he could find his way around the ship. A cutaway diagram of all the decks, picturing the public rooms and listing room numbers for each deck, was mounted at the head of the wide center stairs on each landing. Denkov figured this would be a good time to study the chart without being obvious. So many of the new passengers were milling around getting settled, he'd just be one of the mob. While he was at it, he could check the location of his table in the dining room. Fortunately, there would be only a single sitting, so he would be able to keep track of his quarry at meal times.

When he opened his door to the passageway, a strong odor of chlorine made him catch his breath. Looking for the reason, he noticed for the first time signs with arrows pointing toward mid-ship, indicating SPA and SWIMMING POOL. Something else to enjoy later. In the other direction, toward the stern and just beyond the rear stairs, a lighted sign read HOSPITAL. Frank Griman's room, 813, was just a few feet down from his, but across the hall. Must be an inside view, Denkov noted, feeling superior. He made sure he had his little plastic key safely in his pocket and set off on his tour.

* * *

The ship's departure was something of an anticlimax. Charles had located Karen easily at the Lido bar, one deck up from the swimming pool overlooking the stern, where they could see through the windows the activity on the docks of Le Havre as they sailed. But the *Royale* was spanking new, outfitted with all the sophisticated equipment available, and she had such efficient maneuverability she didn't require the services of those merry little tug boats that churn up the water and murmur and hum, and make a big production of getting under way.

Karen and Charles had barely raised their glasses to toast "bon voyage," when the ship slipped silently from the pier, moving so effortlessly the motion was imperceptible. Ten minutes later the shores of France faded in the distance.

"So much for that." Charles removed his sunglasses and restored them to his breast pocket. "May the rest of the trip be as smooth, including my job. Speaking of duties, we'd better hurry down to the dining room and get those table assignments."

"I'll trust you to do that for us," Karen said, "but I really have to ask you about your wonderful two-colored eyes. Does every person who sees you in the bright sunlight ask you if you've lost a contact lens?"

"Some people have known me a long time before they notice them, Karen. It's just that I have two brown eyed parents who each had a blue eyed parent, and I guess the recessive gene was fighting for its survival but didn't quite make it. One doctor warned me to always wear sunglasses to protect the light eye, because the dark one would keep me from feeling uncomfortable."

"That's interesting, Charles. I have brown eyes, but my mother has blue ones. Guess I carry the recessive gene, too." She picked up her purse and stood up. "I didn't really take time to get settled, and I'd feel better if I were organized. Why don't you come to my stateroom and pick me up when it's time to go to dinner? Remember, I'm on the Provence Deck, P 142. That's just one deck below the Promenade level. Didn't I read in the program that dinner starts at 7:30?"

"Yes, and yes again. I'll get the best table I can, and although I'm sure there's a bit of flexibility about the time we have to be in the dining room, maybe the first night we should try to be prompt. Besides, I seem to have missed lunch somewhere along the way."

They moved to the door at the side of the bar, where a passageway would lead them to the large center stairwell. People were already entrenched in all the available spaces at the cocktail tables there. So many faces, thought Charles as he walked past. Which one belongs to Black?

Karen left him after they had descended two flights of the seashell patterned stairs, the carpet so new footprints still left marks in the heavy pile.

"Don't get too well entrenched," Charles cautioned softly, not knowing if she heard him.

Another flight down and he knew he'd arrived at the right place. Just inside a pair of half opened etched glass doors, so beautiful they could have been Lalique, a uniformed officer was seated at a dining table, pencil in hand and table sized chart spread out before him. His face was expressionless and mask-like, the set of his body firm, and waiting before him was a long line of petitioners, each looking determined.

Most of the people in line were men, Charles noted, as he took his place among them. Patience, he told himself, this guy is going to go with the whole nit-picking routine, so just relax!

The restaurant manager looked expectantly at the unassuming little Frenchman in the pinstriped suit who stood before him, first in line.

"How may I help you?" he asked. "Do you wish to change your table arrangement?"

Before speaking, the passenger extended a small leather case containing an impressive metal badge with engraved name plate, offering it for examination.

"I see, Inspector Dubois, how may I be of service?"

"To begin, you will forget my title. For this trip I shall be just a passenger, referred to as M. Dubois, but I require some help from you in order to carry out my mission. I am here to observe a certain American, Charles Holden, whom we suspect is carrying a substance of vital concern to France. It is my duty to see that he does not succeed in transporting it to the United States. I shall endeavor to keep track of his movements, and it would be of great help if I could be seated near him in the dining room. Do you have him listed there, on your chart?"

"He is on my list of late bookings whose tables have not as yet been assigned. I expect I shall see him shortly after the ship is under way."

"May I then suggest that I be assigned a seat at the same table with him? Perhaps a table with several more people, so that my interest in the gentleman would not be so obvious?"

"Yes, M. Dubois, I think I can very easily seat both of you at a table for six that I have available. It is in fact, a very nice table, right next to a starboard window and not too close to the bus boy's station. We usually reserve one fine large table for adjustment purposes.

"That will be very satisfactory. I appreciate your help, sir, and I hope I will not have to bother you any further." M. Dubois carefully tucked into his pocket the numbered seating card offered him, and scurried silently to the rear exit.

* * *

Karen and Charles thought they were early, but the spacious gold and blue dining room was already buzzing with activity, white coated waiters with loaded trays carried high on their shoulders moving with practiced nimble feet through the slow lines of new passengers, who were taking their own leisurely time, getting used to the new atmosphere, looking for their table numbers, and locating friends.

"The odd numbers are on this side, even on the opposite, and we're looking for 47, so we must be getting close. Next time let's enter this room from the aft stairs," said Karen.

"It would just be the same difference," Charles said, "I had a harder time threading my way through the casual amblers on the Normandie Deck when I crossed over from the flat end where my stateroom is to the pointed end where you are. People stop right in the middle of the passageway without caring if they block someone behind them. Isn't that our table over there by the window?"

Three people were already seated at the large round table, a couple, who remained seated, and a short, dark, balding gentleman who jumped up quickly to acknowledge Karen's arrival. Charles gave a start of recognition, saying, "You're the

M.D. who's not a doctor! We met on the pier, but, I'm sorry, I don't remember your name."

"Dubois," he said, with a slight duck of his head, "How nice to have dinner companions who are not total strangers. I am Marcel Dubois, from Paris."

Charles completed the introductions of himself and Karen, then the three turned to the seated twosome. Tweed suited, they looked like a matched pair, long faces with drab salt and pepper hair, and since she wore no visible make-up, even their ruddy skin tones were the same. The man stood up, and up and up. Must be six foot five, thought Charles, and she sits fairly tall in that chair. "We are June and Mel Hopkins, and we are from Stanford University in California, returning to the United States after attending a conference in Berlin and spending a few days sightseeing in France."

Karen was about to explore the area of common interest, but before she could speak, their waiter approached with menus and simultaneously, from the other side, arrived a breathless aging blonde, curls springing all directions like independent spirits, diamond eardrops dangling from large lobed ears onto narrow shoulders sloped forward by the weight of her generous bosoms escaping from the control of red silk.

"Hi! I'm Jane McKenzie from Baltimore, I fancy you're all going to be my tablemates for this trip."

"As Samuel Johnson said in 1774," the little Frenchman muttered under his breath, "we may take Fancy for a companion, but must follow Reason as our guide . . ."

"Sam had something there, didn't he Marcel?" said Karen, who was close enough to overhear the remark. If that's what McKenzie wears when the program calls for casual dress, Karen thought to herself, then I can hardly wait to see her in formal garb for the Captain's dinner!

* * *

Immediately after dinner, everyone headed for the evening's program in the Grand Lounge, where the Cruise Director, professional smile firmly fixed and mellow voice purring into the gracefully held microphone, introduced his staff, the several musical soloists and the professional dance team who would be the featured performers during the voyage. When all were lined up on the raised platform, the stage musicians joined in an enthusiastic fanfare. Professional smiles stimulated favorable responses from the audience as the young energetic drummer raised his sticks high over the glittering transparent instrument before him.

The ship's captain strode on stage, a tall Nordic Viking guaranteed to inspire the confidence of all the passengers whose well-being was in his hands. He welcomed all his new guests with practiced ease, and finally, he turned to introduce what many of the experienced cruisers were anticipating, his young handsome junior officers who would become sought after dance partners for the many single women aboard.

Charles and Karen had managed to find places to sit at the rear of the Grande Salon, off to the side of the elaborate control bank for the stage lighting system, and with his convenient long arms Charles had swooped drinks from the loaded trays of the harried waiters.

"You know, Karen, this is getting to be a drag. Are they going to say everything in English and then repeat it in French every time they announce something for five long days?"

"Probably only for the welcoming instructions, when they want to be sure everyone understands the basics. If you listen carefully, you might pick up a bit of French."

"I don't have to learn a little French, I brought my own interpreter."

"Let's say you found your interpreter."

"And just in time, too. She's soon to be obsolete . . ."

"Do you mean she's only going to last for the duration of the journey?"

"Hell no, I figure she's in for the long haul, but Madame Curie's superconductor could make her profession obsolete. When I was doing my homework on superconductors, I read that Carnegie Mellon University is already working on a project called SPHINX which will make it possible to speak English into a telephone, and French will come out the other end of the line. And when we supply the Curie stuff, that project could be completed right away."

"Speaking of the superconductor, after our Stanford physicist recovered from the McKenzie shock, we shared some interesting chatter about the Berlin conference. Until his professional erudition started going over my head, that is. He said something about not being able to understand the new materials by deducing macroscopic behavior from microscopic assumptions. Is there a chance he could be the mysterious Mr. Black you're looking for, Mr. Super Sleuth?"

"I think that would be unlikely, Karen. Remember, Black was busy cutting that poor Frenchman's throat at the time the Hopkins were supposedly at the Berlin conference." He drained the last of his drink, and very serious now, the magnetic smile turned almost grim. "That brings me to reality, Karen. I don't want you to have to stand in line for one of those handsome young gigolos, and I don't want you to miss all the fun on this cruise—you planned and worked a long time for it—but I have a job to do. Griman's the obvious one to question first. I have his room number, and I tried to phone him before dinner, with no luck, but he'll probably be heading for his room as soon as this thing is over, and I want to catch him. Sorry to cut out on you, but it's really important to our future."

"Does that 'our' mean the whole world, or you and me, Charles?" She held her glass high, and said, "Either way, I'll drink to that!" She stood, felt the motion of the ship, and rocked back, catching herself on her heels. "I just realized how very tired I am. Morning came early. Probably just as well."

"Will you two people shut up so we can hear what's happening on the stage?" The sweet-faced old lady sitting at the table next to Karen rose and shook her fist.

Mumbling brief apologies, Karen and Charles began to work their way through the close packed tables to the exit at the rear. Just then the orchestra sounded an invitational chord, and eager dancers rose immediately, shoving chairs and pushing forward boldly to find a niche on the tiny dance floor. Across the room, Philip Brown spotted Karen and tried to cross over to her, but his clumsy attempts to work his way through the determined dancers failed with the first shove from the Big Mama in the plastic shoes.

Ivan Denkov kept his eyes glued to Karen as he slid smoothly toward the exit from his standing position on the back wall. That must be the mysterious Charles Holden with her, he decided, and added to himself, maybe our beautiful lady will distract Mr. Holden, make him a little careless. It would make my job easier. He opened the heavy door to the Promenade Deck a discreet minute after it had closed behind the couple leaving arm in arm. No question about it, he smiled, as he carefully stopped to hide in the shadow of a lifeboat hanging from its davit above the Promenade Deck. He watched as the easy moving brown haired man and the slender young blonde at the ship's rail embraced hungrily, oblivious of any audience, lips touching tenderly at first, then suddenly with crushing intensity.

"Yes," Denkov said to himself, "I can safely deal with Griman first."

* * *

Frank Griman grabbed his robe and hastily tied the sash across his round little belly as he heard the firm knock on his stateroom door, but the sound of a key card being pushed into the lock came immediately. Prickles of apprehension made the russet hairs on his arms stand erect as he watched the door open silently.

"Good evening, sir. I am Helga, and I will be serving you on this voyage." Helga was a Norwegian blonde in her early twenties, her round cheeks rosy pink, and her eyes a bright clear aquamarine blue. With a saucy pony tail braided to one side of her head, she looked like a souvenir doll in a carnival prize booth.

Frank sat down abruptly on the little chair by the desk and grunted with relief.

"Are you feeling okay? I do not think you have gone to dinner?" she asked, as she leaned over to remove the heavy bedspread from the low berth on the wall opposite the desk. Frank was now comfortable enough to admire her splendid long legs, and wonder idly why no panty line showed under that tight short skirt.

"Thank you for asking, Helga. I just wasn't up to meeting all those strangers. You see, I have just lost my wife. She had a heart attack while we were in Paris, and I'm taking her body back to New York."

"Oh, how awful it must be for you." Helga seemed truly upset. "How can I make this trip easier?"

"It's nice of you to be concerned, Helga. You know, it's the little things. I have this tension in the spot in the middle of my back, and my wife would just sort of knead out the muscles right here." Frank pointed to a spot right beneath his shoulder blades.

"Perhaps I could help you on this sad journey home," said Helga, and she moved to stand behind him. Frank noticed the flash of bare legs, and then her strong fingers were on his shoulders, massaging firmly and moving down his spine.

"You have a marvelous touch. That certainly helps." Frank reached back and his hand darted under the crisp white skirt.

The telephone on the bedside table buzzed with determined persistence, but the noise subsided after six unanswered rings.

* * *

Ivan Denkov was becoming familiar with the small touches taken for granted in the Western world of decadence. He knew by now he must be patient enough for completion of the ritual of the turned down beds and candy left on pillows. As he made his way down the passage to his stateroom, he could see through an open door that the stewardess had progressed no farther than the center of the line of staterooms opposite his.

His own quarters were invitingly ready for retiring: his bed folded back to reveal crisp white sheets, the predictable piece of chocolate awaiting, reading lamp by the bed turned on to a soft low glow, and through the bathroom door, stacks of fresh towels replacing the ones he'd left on the floor wet and rumpled.

No wonder she's slow, he told himself, she's doing quite a thorough job. And Griman's room will be the last in line, too. Well, nevermind, I can use the time to get ready.

Ivan reached down under the bed to wrestle out the battered suitcase he'd stowed there, then he dragged his desk chair to a dim corner where he could sight a line through the crack of the barely open door. Placing the suitcase on his lap with the lid open to hide the movements of his hands from any accidental glance of a person happening to walk down the corridor, he worked inside the opened case, carefully assembling a spring loaded needle and a miniature ampoule into a tiny tube the size and shape of a fountain pen. A quick button release would cause a deadly neurotoxin to eject through the shiny bit of steel, and then the problem of Griman would be finished.

He almost missed the quiet footsteps of the floor stewardess as she moved swiftly to the last door. The gleam of the corridor lights reflected from her bouncing pony tail white skirt as Griman's door closed behind her.

As he watched, a slim bare arm extended through a tiny crack and fumbled into place a "DO NOT DISTURB" sign onto the heavy handle of Griman's door.

CHAPTER 17

Monday Morning, June 15

After three rings the telephone was answered with a grunt followed by a muffled thump.

"Karen, are you there?" said a startled Charles.

"Oh, good morning, sorry about all that," returned Karen, "The phone's on the wrong side of the bed, and I got tangled up in the sheets."

"I should have been there to help with the untangling. We'll take care of that later, but now it's time for you to rise and shine."

"Anything to oblige. How much should I shine?" giggled Karen, her voice still rough from sleep.

"The proverbial bright-eyed—no pun intended, Ms. Bright—and you can leave off the bushy tail. Seriously, I really need your eyes. I managed to make contact early this morning with Frank Griman, and he's promised to meet me here on the Lido Deck where they serve the early morning coffee and Continental breakfast at eight o'clock. You know the man, and I want to be sure I'm meeting the right guy. Think you can make it?"

"What time is it now? They left a note on my bed last night to change my watch an hour, so are you new and early?" Karen was fully awake now, and alert.

"I'm on ship's clock time; I hope you realize by now I'm always up-to-date. That gives you a half hour. Sweat suits seem to be the costume of the day here, with Nike and Reebok shoes. If the early birds haven't made their rounds of the deck for their early morning constitutional, at least they look as if they had. The breakfast layout is really quite complete. Waiters keep refilling the trays of fresh fruit, cereal is available, and the different kinds of rolls are unbelievable."

"Go ahead and indulge, Charles. After that big dinner we ate last night, I'm a coffee only person today, but I'll hustle my buns and join you."

"Griman made a funny comment when I called him, Karen. I introduced myself by name, and his answer was something like, 'Glad to know you're safe.' I'll puzzle about that remark while I wait for you."

Karen hurried to the bathroom, and just as she had the water running in the sink and her mouth full of toothpaste, a man's booming voice from the bedroom said, "Good morning." Before she could even begin to wipe the smear of foam from under her nose where she'd jabbed her toothbrush in dismay, the message was repeated in French. Laughing with relief, Karen moved into the bedroom to listen more carefully to the announcement coming through the little speaker on the desk.

"This is your Captain speaking. May I remind all passengers that a mandatory life boat drill will be conducted this morning at 10:15. This drill is required by Maritime Law, and everyone must assemble at his proper station, where the ship's personnel will give you further information. The ship's horn will sound one long blast followed by three short blasts. At that time you must follow the instructions posted in your cabin, put on your life jacket and proceed directly to the life boat station number assigned to you. We assure you this drill will be completed by 10:45. We thank you for your cooperation."

Well, thought Karen, my leisurely cruise is getting busier by the minute. I guess it's just as well Charles woke me when he did. Hurry seems to be the order of the day. She debated taking her life jacket with her so she wouldn't have to return for it. She found it on the top shelf of the closet and tried putting it on, but she decided she'd never be able to cope with the bulk of the jacket in the public rooms, especially the Lido lounge. Running up and down the stairs will be my exercise for the day, since the morning promenade is over by now, she told herself. She looked at her watch and decided the time to begin running was now.

The morning sunshine shone brightly through the full length windows of the lounge, occasional flashes of brilliance reflecting from the moving surface of the blue water outside. Breakfast items were displayed along one side of the room, and smiling waiters at the table in the corner filled coffee cups and drew hot water from the steaming silver canister for those ordering tea. A shiny white grand piano, with cushioned bar stools around its perimeter, stood silently awaiting its master and the cheerful passengers who would gather for cocktails and music before lunch. A few early imbibers were already in place at the bar, most of them silently studying the contents of the glass in hand.

Charles had selected a corner table in the lounge where he could observe the doors leading from the area outside on the deck where the chairs and tables were arranged to overlook the swimming pool. He could also see the people entering from the starboard side where bridge players were already locked in concentration. One lone passenger at the far end of the room carefully selected pieces for the jigsaw puzzle laid out before him.

Karen entered from the interior, and Charles' dimpled grin spread wide the moment she emerged. She hurried to his welcome embrace, a restrained nuzzle, and patted her chest with an exaggerated gesture of breathlessness. Before they could exchange words, a rumpled little man opened the door from the deck. His eyes searched the room tentatively.

"That's Griman, for sure," Karen whispered, and moved aside so Charles could intercept Frank.

Griman had made an effort to make himself look like a typical cruise ship passenger. He'd managed to dig out of his suitcase one of the sport shirts Lisa always nagged him to wear, and his rubber soled shoes looked appropriate. He recognized Karen instantly, but showed some surprise at finding her with Holden.

"Nice to see you again, Miss Bright," he said, nodding to her, and extending his hand to Charles, "I am certainly relieved to find you, Mr. Holden."

Puzzled at this reaction, Charles covered smoothly, saying, "May I get you some coffee, Mr. Griman, before we talk?" Karen sipped the coffee Charles had waiting for her. She watched closely as Charles went into action, oozing charm, exposing a new facet of this fascinating man.

"To be honest, Mr. Holden, I see the bar is open, and what I'd really like is a Bloody Mary."

"Please call me Charles, and I think we can take care of that easy enough. I see a waiter heading this way. I'm sorry your wife couldn't join us. Where is she, by the way?"

"My wife? Did I mention my wife?" Griman didn't hide his surprise, but he paused to gratefully receive the waiter's offering, a rosy drink, tall and frosty, with a crisp celery stalk rising high from its center.

"You may as well know, Mr. Griman, Mr. Butler of Consolidated Electronics was keeping tabs on you and Mrs. Griman when you left Berlin."

"He was in Berlin?" interrupted Karen, "Charles, you didn't tell me."

"Later, Karen."

"What's the deal here? How did Miss Bright get into this act? She told me all her work was private and confidential. Consolidated told me that you, Mr. Holden, would be on this job. In fact they told me you were the best in the business and we'd be lucky if you were available, but how did my translator get involved?" Griman was disturbed enough to become bold. Fear had submerged his thoughts of money, but they bobbed to the surface rapidly as he recalled his dealings with Butler. Now he was once more maneuvering to protect his position.

"Miss Bright's presence here is my personal concern, Mr. Griman, but she has become involved with your business in spite of herself. Since her translation of the Curie letter, she has been followed, searched and very definitely frightened." Firmly forcing Griman to look him directly in the eye, Charles said, "My question to you is, have you sold out to a higher bidder?"

"Yeah, well not exactly, it's a complicated story." Frank squirmed, "But first I need to know, and I hope to god you have the right answer, Mr. Holden." He was sweating now and his Bloody Mary glass was drained to the tomato stained ice. Lowering his voice, he whispered softly, "Do you have the Curie superconductor?"

Karen and Charles inhaled simultaneously with quick gasps, not realizing they had been hoping breathlessly that Griman's words would provide some answers. Charles rocked back in his chair, and signalled the waiter to come for an order as Karen took her cup to the coffee station for a refill. Minutes later when they were settled, Charles bore down, "I think we'd better have the whole story, Griman, and I think you know better than to leave anything out."

Griman began his scenario gingerly at first, blaming Lisa for their actions. He told of the chain of events leading to her murder, and, as he emphasized the word "murder," his emotions began to surface. The role of Dr. Dromensky was revealed, and his raw fear of the Russians was evident. Twice Karen tried to ask questions, but Charles waved them off, letting Griman's story flow.

"I tell you, Charles, I know they're after me. They want to kill me. You've got to do something. They'll kill you too. Funny thing is, though, they haven't got the Curie superconductor, because they think you've got it, and I thought they were right."

"Mr. Griman, Frank, that is, " Karen finally managed to ask, "Did you tell this Dr. Dromensky that I had translated the letter?"

"No, Miss Bright, I did not. But they're a canny bunch. I must tell you, even when we opened that suitcase and saw the one million in cash with our own eyes, I knew we were making a bad move, but Lisa, God rest her soul, didn't see it that way. So what the Russkies got was a copy of the Curie letter, a copy of my contract with Consolidated, and Mr. Holden's name and the name of his hotel—which I had learned from Butler. That's it, that was the million dollar deal, nothing more."

"I'd say that was more than enough. That does explain the Norman Teal bit," said Charles.

"I've never heard that name—" said Griman.

"The name doesn't matter," explained Charles. "Someone using that name tried to chase me down in Paris. And someone beat me to the Euro-American lines office and got the ship's passenger list before I did. That had to be either Dromensky or one of his cohorts."

"That still doesn't explain how he got my name," insisted Karen.

"I swear your name never came into any of our conversations, Miss Bright, and I'm really sorry you've been frightened. But I tell you, I'm shook up by all this, and scared as hell. I know one of those Russians is after me. I saw one on my way up here. I'm sure I'm being followed. I peek around corners, change directions as I walk, check mirrors to see if anyone suspicious is behind me. I'm so jittery I'm seeing things. I even thought I saw my cousin Bill on the deck this morning. That bum, I really need him to help me with the arrangements getting Lisa's body to New Jersey, and I can't find him. He should have stayed in the Marines, then the family could have found a decent lawyer."

"Calm down, Frank," soothed Charles, "I don't think they're after you. It's me they really want."

"Or me," shuddered Karen. "Why don't you check that passenger list of yours, Charles, and see if Dromensky's on it?"

"He's too smart for that. No way he'd use his own name, whatever it is. I've checked for Teal, and he's not listed. We still go back to the question, who the hell is Mr. Black?"

"I don't much like this checker game you fellows got me into," said Karen, putting her coffee cup aside and standing up. "We're in trouble either way, if not the Reds then from Black."

"Very cute, my dear, but not funny." Charles stood also, and turned to Griman. "Frank, just stand by, and if I need you, you'll hear from me. When I find Mr. Black, we might be able to talk Butler into giving you some of that half million you blew when you and your wife got greedy."

"Now we have to hurry to get our life jackets, because that clock above the bar says five minutes to ten," said Karen. "Do we go to the same place, Charles? My station's 16."

"No, mine's eight."

"So if she goes down, we aren't going to be in the same boat," Karen teased.

"Only if we start from the same bed."

"Then we better not go down. Shall we meet for lunch at the Lido pool? I understand they have a buffet service there when the weather is nice, and it sure is beautiful right now."

"Perfect. I'll make some phone calls after the drill and get there as soon as I can."

Even though it was expected, the sudden blast from the ship's horn startled them, its urgency intense, and all three hurried off to retrieve life jackets for the drill.

* * *

With a little help, Karen struggled through the tedious life jacket procedure. She caught on to the technique of criss-crossing the long woven straps dangling from the back of the bulky orange vest, bringing them forward to tie around her middle, and the ship's officer in charge of her boat was only too glad to assist her in finding the little signal whistle which had escaped its pocket and was hiding on a long string somewhere between her breast and her armpit. The group of people assigned to her station stood in a cluster, eyes squinting in the sun and their hair ruffled by the breeze. They listened semi-attentively, reminding Karen of the kids in grade school who shuffled their feet and poked their friends during fire drills. To his surprise, everyone on his list answered when roll was called, and the officer dismissed them all readily, glad his job was over.

After the All Clear, Karen was heading for the nearest door when she heard, "Hey Karen, wait up!" Turning around, Karen gaped in surprise. There, swinging his life jacket, boisterous as a teenager on his way to the local hangout, was Philip Brown.

"Where did you come from, Philip?"

"I spotted you last night in the lounge, but I couldn't catch up with you. So how was Berlin? How did you get along with those superconductor experts? Did you try to reach me in Paris?" He had to pause to catch his breath.

"The conference went fine, and I didn't call you in Paris."

"Well, the important thing is, we've found each other now. Certainly going to make the trip better. Why don't we go have one of those renowned morning Bloody Marys?" Philip hoped he sounded as suave as one of the characters from those old Fred Astaire movies.

"Actually, Philip, I have an appointment. Maybe we can get together later. I'll call you. What's your cabin number?"

"I'm in 32 on the Promenade Deck." Philip hoped she'd be impressed, she was probably in an inside single somewhere way down. "That sounds good, Karen. Don't forget to call me!"

"See you later, I have to run," Karen hurried to catch the open elevator.

* * *

It was just before noon when Karen changed to a beach outfit purchased just for this trip, a smooth contoured azure one piece swim suit covered by a matching short coat with terrycloth lining. Shiny sequin dotted sandals on her feet were the only frivolous touch. She hurried, hoping she hadn't wasted too much time in her stateroom.

She was dismayed to find double lines of people stretching from inside the Grand Lounge to the door to Lido Deck. Most of them were in swim suits, over which the cover-ups ranged from flimsy robes, revealing more than concealing, to tee-shirts with graphic designs which boasted of other travels. Some eager passengers had plates in their hands already, although they'd still have to make their way through the doorway to the long buffet set up on the deck outside. Then they could begin to choose from the gross abundance of shrimp, fresh crab, fried chicken, cold turkey, salads, fruits, and every kind of bread and roll a chef had ever seen. And then they'd arrive at the desserts. Karen could visualize the mounds of food they would pile high.

Detouring quickly around the front of the now empty stage, she crossed the floor to the starboard side, and there stood Charles, watching her progress.

"Another point in common, I see," he grinned, "Your recoil from waiting in a food line was beautiful, and, incidentally, so are you."

"Thank you, kind sir, glad you approve of my actions and my looks. I'm in my swim suit because we were going to eat at the pool, but I can't bear that line. Shall I go back and change?"

"I think if we're lucky we can find ourselves a spot on the next deck up, the Sun Deck. There's a hamburger stand sending out tempting aromas up there next to a small jacuzzi. Care to try that?"

"That's certainly better than hitting the dining room for a formal luncheon," Karen agreed, "but you'll have to be very clever. I shall insist on some witty little quotations a la Monsieur Dubois if you are depriving me of his company."

"I'll try to match Dubois' wit if you'll match McKenzie's tits."

"That's not very nice, Mr. Holden," Karen reddened.

"Sorry, but I'm sure she thinks they are very nice, or she wouldn't keep bouncing them."

"Enough! Lead me to the hamburger, and for that you might have to supply a drink, also."

Charles pointed to the outside stairway toward the stern, just beyond the ping pong table sheltered in the corner, and they headed up to the sunshine. As the light caught the golden luster in her hair and her brown eyes glistened, Charles warned himself, you'd better not let this lovely thing get away from you.

"Looks as though we're not the only people who know about this place," said Karen as they surveyed the crowded tables ringed about the jacuzzi on the sunny deck. "Want to try somewhere else, maybe?"

"By now the burger bug has bitten me. I think the folks at this table right here look like they're leaving. You stand by to grab it, and I'll get in line for the grill."

"Don't forget the grilled onions."

"Onions? What'll that do at the kissing hour, which might be at any time now?"

"I thought you were going to be busy chasing suspects? You get the burgers, I'll leave my purse and glasses to hold the table and go over to the end of the counter to pick up the iced tea." Karen smiled at the old man in the deck chair who was thoroughly enjoying her bare legs. She moved before his imagination could proceed past the short cover-up.

"That may actually have been the best hamburger I've ever eaten," Karen purred later, stretching in the sun, "or was it just the sea air? I could join those bare fat tummies over by the pool and nap on one of the chaises. How about you?"

"I still have to track down one more name. Maybe later," Charles replied.

"I should have asked you sooner. What kind of luck did you have after the life boat drill?"

"One name really turned out to be a dud. Mr. Noire on Lafayette Deck is a shaky octogenarian traveling with a wife who is recovering from a recent stroke. I caught them both in their stateroom right after the drill. They were very nice people, only too happy to talk, but they're going round trip, didn't even disembark in port yesterday. I made a date with Henry Black, gave him a story, and he'll meet me just before tea this afternoon. Said his wife was demanding he take her to lunch immediately. But I couldn't get any answer from Gerard P. Brown in Promenade cabin 32."

"Did you say 32? That's the same number Philip Brown gave me just now." Karen interrupted.

"Just now?"

"Of course not, Charles, but right after that life boat drill."

"Would you like to tell me who he is?"

"He's a jerk from my office at Translator's International."

"That's who I thought he'd be. You're telling me he's on this ship? So make that 'P' for Philip, and your 'guy from home' could just turn out to be a fuckin' murderer, not to mention a thief and one big pain you know where!"

"Now wait just one damn minute, Mr. Investigator, how do you get the 'my guy' business? And what's this 'that's what I thought' insinuation? Seems to me you left something out of our so-called honest sharing of information!" Karen's skin whitened in anger. The tiny band of freckles across her nose stood out like a warning signal. "How do you know about someone from my office?"

"Hush a minute, Karen, calm down and listen to the words of the snooper who's crazy about you. This is serious. We're talking about a throat cutting murderer, remember? As soon as I realized that the Curie letter was no longer a secret, naturally I reported back to Butler, and we started tracing the possibility of a leak. Didn't take Butler long to discover that 'your' Brown was missing from the office, ostensibly traveling in France. And naturally Butler inquired if Brown and you had any ties. You, after all, were the one who translated the damn letter." He paused to see if she was showing any signs of understanding.

"And I suppose you all decided Philip and I had really cooked up a super superconductor plan at dinner that Saturday night."

"Come off it, Karen, we were just wondering if he ever had a chance to see the letter when it was in your office."

Karen wrinkled her nose and seemed to be deep in thought. Finally, she admitted, "Well, he was in the office that morning before Griman came for my translation. I guess, if he'd wanted to, he could have sneaked a peak while I was in the john."

"Sometimes a quick sneak is all it takes, especially with today's fancy copy machines."

"We've got a brand new Xerox in the next room. But I really don't think he's bright enough to realize that the letter would be worth anything."

"That may be true, but he could be playing dumb like a fox. It wouldn't take much to realize that any number of people, or companies, for that matter, would pay top dollar for a copy. Witness Lisa Griman's sellout to the Russians."

"So you really think Philip might be your Mr. Black, a murderer?" Karen reflected, "Of course, he thought the room temperature superconductor was hidden at 36 Quai de Bethune, that's what he found out at the Institute. The pieces are beginning to fall in place. But why would he wreck the place if Marie Curie's journal told where the stuff was? According to the Paris newspaper, the apartment was almost demolished." She paused to sip the dregs of her iced tea. "I guess the manager got in his way, but didn't you say that the man killed was a friend of yours? How would you know the building manager?"

"You're asking an awful lot of questions. Let me get you a refill."

"Come on, Charles, don't change the subject. Let's have some answers to these questions that beget questions that you're being cute about."

"I'm not trying to be cute, as you say, it's just that the jigsaw puzzle is not quite complete. The Curie journal was rather cryptic. Madame Curie must have sensed that someday Flacon 216 would be very important, because she didn't reveal its whereabouts directly. She dreamed up a little riddle, involving a contemporary French poet named Valery and his symbolist poem about columns."

"Fascinating," Karen interrupted. "So you figure Philip copied the letter, went to the Institute where he posed as Mr. Black, found the journal, got hold of the poem and then went to Ile St. Louis where the manager caught him smashing open columns."

"Hold on, Karen, there are a few glaringly inconsistent facts."

"Such as?"

"Such as, the American who bought the Valery book couldn't speak French."

"Trust a professional investigator to remember that. But what about your friend the building manager?"

"Not my friend. There was another throat slit in New York City. It belonged to my friend who was busy following somebody, who in turn was following—guess who?"

"Frank Griman?"

"Wrong, he was following one Dr. Karen Bright."

"Oh shit!"

"Watch your language with me, Miss Translator!" He grinned at her quick blush.

"Geez, I'm getting more and more confused. What should we do then? About Philip, I mean? I just told him I'd call so I could get rid of him."

"If you really want to help, I think you should make a date with him, see if you could learn anything from him. And while you keep him busy, I can search his room. If he has the stuff, I doubt if he'd leave it in his room, but I may get some kind of lead."

"Well, I suppose that can be done. I was thinking of fixing him up with Miss Boobs McKenzie, but for you, I guess I could suffer through anything. Maybe I can lure him to lunch tomorrow."

"That's a nice snooper's helper. Now how about a stroll around the deck before my tea date? Don't forget, that will be followed by a red hot Bingo game!"

CHAPTER 18

Monday Afternoon

Marcel Dubois picked up the handset of the beeping bedside phone and learned a call was coming in from Paris. The tiny stateroom didn't provide any lounging space at the telephone, so he carefully moved his glass of white wine to make room for a writing pad, then sat uncomfortably erect on the edge of the bed.

"Yes, this is Dubois speaking."

"Glad to hear you speaking English like a tourist, Dubois. Have you found Holden's little prize package yet?" Chief Inspector Bodine wasted no time with unnecessary amenities.

"Sir, there has hardly been time for me to locate anything. However, I have managed to get seated at his dining table. He and the translator girl, that Miss Bright, seem quite close. I think it's more pleasure than business, though."

"What about Mr. Black? Is Holden meeting with anyone?"

"He has already met with Mr. Griman this morning—but I couldn't get close enough to hear what they were talking about. I've yet to find anyone fitting the artist's drawing from Dr. Remy's description of Black. There is a Henry Black on the passenger list whom I plan to check out."

"Did you search Holden's room?"

"Yes, when he was at lifeboat drill. I didn't have much time, but, if the superconductor stuff is there, it's well hidden. I used the portable magnetometer as you directed, and the red light did not go on. Does that Meissner Effect work from a distance?"

"How the hell do I know? I'm no scientist. What I do know is that Holden's probably waiting to make his contact. So, stay with it, Dubois, and let me know the minute you find something."

"You can count on me, sir."

Bodine said a curt good-bye in both French and English.

* * *

Henry Black, a plump, fiftyish dentist from Rock Springs, Wyoming, wearing a velour warmup suit and Reeboks, made his way into the crowded King Louis Lounge, the luxurious observation area of the *Royale* perched forty feet above the ship's bow. The room was quiet and housed deep cushioned easy chairs under tinted and sloped floor-to-ceiling windows. These chairs, offering 180 degree views of the Atlantic, were the favorite landing place for the more sedentary voyagers, those who were too old or too bored for the active social schedule relentlessly promoted by the cruise director. The passengers lucky enough to find empty chairs seldom moved for hours, alternately napping conversing with their neighbors.

Charles sat at the bar since a few stools were still available to newcomers who could enjoy the view reflected from the full mirror behind the many colorful bottles on the back bar. He watched Black cross the slightly elevated threshold and raised a hand.

Black circled behind him to read the green script logo of the Gotham Tennis Club on Charles' sleeve. "You must be the Charles Holden I'm supposed to meet here."

"That's right, and thank you for coming Mr. Black."

"Actually, it's Dr. Black, Mr. Holden. I'm a dentist. So, what do you have for me?"

"It's more crowded here than I expected. Would you mind if we moved? I believe there's a small, empty card room down the passageway—unless you'd prefer a drink here." Charles turned on his charm and dimpled smile.

"No, I don't want a drink now. What's the reason for all this mystery, Mr. Holden?" Black had become openly reluctant. So much for the charm.

"I'll tell you in a minute," said Charles as he held the heavy door open for Black to precede him. As they walked, Charles studied Black's muscular torso, a strange contradiction to the flabby midsection and spindly legs. The thinning salt-and-pepper hair was carefully combed to cover a round bald spot, and the scent of aftershave was strong. Not your typical thief, much less a slasher. But, then, they never are typical, Charles mused silently.

"I was in the Cafe de la Paix a few days ago," Charles began after the two seated themselves at the felt covered card table. They faced each other, their faces reflecting a faint greenish glow from the carefully positioned card lamp.

"So? Really, Mr. Holden, I'm not interested in where you were or what you were doing. You said you had something belonging to me. My wife's expecting me to go buy her bingo cards, and I don't intend to disappoint her. So, let's dispense with all this mystery. What do you have?"

"As I left the cafe, I found this book just outside on the sidewalk." Charles extended his copy of Valery's poems." He watched Black's eye movements as he took the book and examined it by flipping through the pages.

"It's in French," Black mumbled, handing it back. "It's not mine, Mr. Holden. What made you think it might be?

Charles produced an advertising flyer he'd picked up at the Euro-American Lines office, an ad for this sailing of the *Royale*. On the paper was lightly penciled the name, "Henry Black." He handed the paper to the disgruntled dentist and explained, "This was in the front of the book. So, since I, too, was scheduled for this sailing . . ."

"I can understand, Mr. Holden, but I haven't the foggiest idea why the ad has my name on it. I've never seen it, or your book of poems."

"Oh, you know it's poetry?"

"Of course. Don't you read French, Mr. Holden? I don't see why you're making such a fuss over this; I could have told you over the phone it's not my book. We weren't anywhere near the Cafe de la Paix on this trip. Now, you really must excuse me..."

"Then you don't know what I found on page 108 by the poem "Cantique des Colonnes"? Now, Charles thought, if he's my man there will be a flicker of recognition.

"So, what was that?" said Black casually, poised to leave.

"This hundred dollar bill was marking the page." Charles produced a bill. "I had to be careful about asking a stranger if he'd lost money, but I wanted to do the right thing. I suppose now I can keep it with a clear conscience." He rose and offered his hand to Henry Black, smiling again. "Thanks for all your trouble, Dr. Black. I hope I haven't made you late."

"No trouble." Black seemed satisfied. "You have a nice smile, young man. You ought to spend that hundred having the little chip on your incisor repaired. Also, do you realize you've lost a contact lens?"

Charles watched him leave and was vaguely surprised that a man so apparently intelligent would buy such a juvenile scenario. Or had he?

* * *

Frank Griman woke from his afternoon nap with a start. For a moment he didn't know where he was. Then, as he lay on the bed, savoring the slight, soothing motion of the ship, he encountered a zest for living he hadn't known since college. He simultaneously felt the erosion of his body and spirit which had taken place over recent years. If he was going to lead a different life, why not start today? The health spa, just down the corridor from his room, would be open for the afternoon session. A brief workout, a quick swim, then a turn around the deck before dinner, would be a good beginning.

Wriggling into his bathing trunks, probably tossed in by mistake during that frenzied packing, he thought about the last time he'd worn them. It was the swimming party at the Holmes'. The very day Lisa concocted her fatal plan for the hurry-up trip to Berlin. Why didn't he mourn her now? A searching introspection, something in which he rarely indulged, dredged a myriad of acrid feelings he had forcefully submerged while Lisa was alive. Clearly, she had robbed him of his self respect so stealthily he had barely noticed its evaporation. The intense encounter with Helga had given him a promise of renewal. If he could still retrieve something of his deal with Butler, he'd be in a position to build a new life, perhaps with someone comparable to that Scandinavian bombshell.

His time in the spa was even more pleasant than he anticipated. When he left, still dripping from the pool, Frank was more concerned with catching a glimpse of Helga than he was in paying attention to his surroundings. He ignored the bearded passenger who followed him out of the gym, until the clumsy oaf bumped into him out in the corridor.

Frank turned to encounter Ivan Ilych Denkov.

"I am so sorry, sir," Denkov said politely.

A surprising, intensely sharp pain made Frank grab his right shoulder. The cold reality of terror and instant death hit him full force.

"Now? Dear God, not now..." The mortician's daughter at the pier, 'Little Red Riding Hood,' what was it she said? The walls inwardly collapsing, the hard floor turning to Jello, flickering images barely visible. "If it hadn't been for his coughing, the neurotoxin surely would have killed him." The friendly old mortician and the little girl leaving him at the pier—leaving him now as he fought to stay conscious—cough, you son-of-a-bitch—cough, Frank, keep coughing, coughing, coughing . . .

Helga did appear after all, as Denkov disappeared down the hall, startled to see Frank coughing violently, falling against the metal wall panels, grabbing at his shoulder, slipping and coughing until the spasms became involuntary, obviously helpless.

Moving quickly, the young woman used her sturdy strength to support the nearly inert man, still hiccupping, until she had propelled him the short distance to the hospital quarters.

"Just a few more steps, Mr. Griman."

The ex-navy nurse on duty at the front desk took a quick look at Frank's blue lips, rang the emergency bell for the doctor, and raced to prepare an injection. She quickly emptied the syringe into Frank's arm, then helped Helga carry Frank to the tiny, but well equipped operating room. He continued coughing, but so weakly he barely took a breath as Helga mopped his brow.

"Good Lord, the man's dying!" the navy nurse cried as the ship's physician, not even fully dressed, raced into the room. "Do you think we can save him, Doctor?"

"We can sure as hell try!" replied the elderly surgeon whose nose with its network of broken capillaries betrayed a lifetime of alcohol. Totally sober or not, he was all business now, almost remembering how it had been once — once when he had been pretty damned good at saving lives.

Monday Night

At the dinner table Mel Hopkins finished his professorial explanations of superconductivity in response to polite prodding by Marcel Dubois. With a practiced wave of his hand, obviously a summing-up gesture from the classroom, he concluded, "Science has taken on a distasteful nationalistic flavor lately. One must always bear in mind that nationalistic is not the same as patriotic. This is why the recent Berlin conference was so necessary." He looked to his table companions for affirmation.

"Well Professor Hopkins," observed M. Dubois, "I believe it was Anton Chekhov who said, 'There is no national science, just as there is no national multiplication table. What is national is no longer science.'" He lifted his pristine white napkin to gently touch his lips.

"I like that, M. Dubois," Karen chimed in, fork poised with its load of calories in the form of multilayered chocolate cream.

"Sounds good to me," chirped Jane McKenzie, in bright green satin this time, with matching emerald earrings twinkling and dangling their ode to nouveau riche. All this super-whatever doodah was fine, but she had something important in mind. "Is anyone going to go international with me after dinner and take in some of that marvelous Latin American music for dancing?" She looked pointedly at Charles.

As if deliberately staged, the maitre d' leaned over Charles' shoulder at that moment and said softly, "If you please, sir, your presence is desired in the offices of the ship's hospital."

Charles nodded, offered his excuses to the table and rose to go. Karen immediately jumped up and took his arm. "Not so fast, my boy; we're in this together. No secrets, remember?"

They left the dining room through the beautifully etched glass doors now standing wide open, and Charles paused on the wide landing to check the ship's diagram displayed at the head of the stairwell. Pinpointing the location of the hospital, he turned to Karen and said, "Really, Karen, I don't know what this is all about. Wouldn't you rather listen to Jane's musicians?"

"You really are determined to protect me, aren't you? I promise, if I'm out of place being with you, I'll be a good little girl and go to my room."

"What's with this sexist crap?"

"Precisely."

"I got your point, Dr. Bright."

"I'm proud of you, Mr. Holden."

"I'm not too keen on your roaming around by yourself, anyway. Let's take the stairs; it'll be faster than the elevator."

"Glaciers are faster than this elevator."

"Maybe the stairs will work off some of that chocolate."

"Amen to that."

* * *

One thing Colonel Ivan Ilych Denkov had learned from his many years of GRU service was patience. If there was anything a foreign operative had to have, it was patience. But even Denkov had his limits.

He'd watched the action at the infirmary, his stateroom door barely open a crack, but he found it impossible to figure out what was going on. The ship's doctor had been in and out several times, as had the nurse, but no ship official had come near, as far as he could determine. and certainly they would, had he been successful.

Was Frank Griman dead or not? He would have to think up some excuse to go see for himself soon, before that Viking bitch started her evening bed turn-down rounds. It's bad enough I had to miss dinner, he thought, I should have been in position to watch Holden with that little Frenchman at his table. The more I think about it, the more it seems logical that the little guy must be the link to the transfer of the super stuff either way, back or forth.

Deciding to take some action, Denkov rose from his chair, rubbing the back of his neck and his shoulders, and began to ease out into the hallway. But he jumped back, startled by Charles and Karen's arrival at the infirmary door. As he watched, the weary physician greeted them. Straining to catch the sounds, Ivan felt a chill as he overheard. "Sorry to disturb you, but Mr. Griman keeps asking for you. . . "

"You big, fat prick, Dromensky," Denkov very quietly moaned aloud as he closed the cabin door. "Always fatal neurotoxin, my ass." He smashed his fist on the door frame in frustration. Stalking into his bathroom, Ivan rummaged rapidly through his jumbled bag of toiletries. "That Griman got a damned good look at me, and that Yankee pig can identify me. Dromensky, I hate you. My wife hates you. For her I grew the beard." He grabbed a pair of scissors and snipped at his short, pointed beard, leaving a jagged gap in the groomed symmetry.

* * *

The *Royale's* fully equipped hospital was small, but efficient. It offered round-the-clock service, and was staffed by three nurses, a medical rating assistant and a physician qualified in surgery. A nurse sat at an appointment desk in a small entrance office, tucked in among filing cabinets and shelves filled with reference books. Behind her two doors led to the hospital proper, one providing direct entry to an examining room which in turn led to a complete operating room. The other door led to a miniature hospital ward: six beds in a long row along a cramped corridor, each surrounded by curtained partitions for privacy.

The doctor, now wearing a white laboratory coat, but still not in uniform, escorted Karen and Charles into the curtained cubicle where Frank Griman lay on the narrow bed. His eyes were open. He lay motionless and waxy white, except for faint spots of rosy flush on each cheek.

"He's had a hard time, poor fellow," the doctor explained, "but he should rest, and we can't seem to settle him down. He insists it's urgent he speak with you, Mr. Holden."

Frank slowly but continually gained strength with every passing minute, although his shoulder obviously caused him considerable pain. The sight of Charles made him very anxious, and he cried, "The rotten bastard who did this to me has to be the one who did in Lisa!"

"Careful, Frank, take it easy," warned Charles, leaning closer to Frank's head. "I believe you, and I want to help, but you have to think about your own survival right now."

"I'm okay. The worst is over. Look, I gotta tell you . . ."

"I want to hear it all, don't worry, but are you sure you should talk?"

"I'll get better a helluva lot faster if you'll promise to take care of the sonofabitch!"

"Consider it done, so give me the facts. But the doctor will stop us if you show signs of overdoing it."

Charles drew the doctor close, and Karen edged up, her finely tuned translator's ears catching the underlying fear in Frank's voice.

They listened with horror as Griman narrated the encounter with the bearded man in the corridor. Then he went on to tell of the mortician's warning in Le Havre and the story of the person who survived poison by coughing.

"By George," interjected the doctor, "that's what it looked like to me, exactly as if you'd been struck by a cobra. That coughing did save your life, Mr. Griman. The involuntary spasms prevented complete paralysis of the heart muscle." He couldn't keep from adding proudly, "Of course, you're fortunate I still had the antivenin I'd brought with me from my days sailing with Grace Lines. We used to have some deadly centipedes on those banana boats. When the nurse told me about your grabbing your shoulder, it looked like a poisonous bite. Thank God the stuff worked."

When Griman described his assailant in detail, it was Karen's turn to interrupt. "Charles, that sounds exactly like that person who followed me in Berlin!"

"Seems as if our GRU man is right on the job."

"What's a 'GRU'?" asked the doctor.

"Most people mistakenly call it KGB. KGB is domestic, except when accompanying Soviets visiting abroad, a civilian secret police similar to the FBI in the states. GRU,—nominally part of the army, is foreign espionage, like the CIA. Believe me, I wish it were the KGB; those people are a stroll in the park compared to the guy we've got on our hands. For everyone's safety we'd better find him fast."

Turning to the doctor, Charles continued, "If this was an attempted liquidation, and I have no doubt of that whatsoever, it would be best to keep Mr. Griman here until we can be sure he's all right."

"Well, the effects of the neurotoxin don't last long, and Mr. Griman is out of danger now. I really must share this information with the ship's command."

The doctor obviously did not want to be responsible for protecting someone from a murderer. He picked up the telephone and asked to speak to the Captain. He waited as the operator dialed the Captain's quarters first, then the bridge. At last the Captain came on the line. The doctor spoke carefully, explaining the situation in few words.

"I see. Of course. Yes, sir. Very good, sir." Turning to Charles, the doctor reported, "The Captain is very busy. Seems we're trying to outrun a storm. He says there is an agent of the French police aboard, and he will send him to take charge. Mr. Holden and his companion are free to go."

"Dr. Bright," Karen threw in.

"Of course. Mr. Holden and Ms. Bright."

"Close enough."

"Please leave matters to me at this juncture. I will keep Mr. Griman here, at least until the French agent has interviewed him. I'm sure you two do not need further involvement. Thank you for coming, and we'll call you if we need you." He practically pushed the two out of the door. Karen started to protest, but Charles cut her off.

"Thank you, doctor. We'll talk to Mr. Griman when he's feeling better. Come on, Karen, we have a date, remember?"

* * *

Marcel Dubois had placed a folding chair in a shadowy curtained corner of the hospital ward room, trying to ignore the heavy antiseptic odors while he listened to the regular breathing and occasional snorts of the sole hospital occupant, the now sedated Frank Griman. It was not the sort of police duty he relished, but once the facts of the assault on Griman had been reported to him, he was certain the assailant would return to finish his bungled job.

As he sat, silent and motionless in the darkened room, his mind raced to answer the questions about Griman's presence on the ship. Why was he here, and not in New York? The copies of Holden's papers that Chief Inspector Bodine had shown him had included a contract with that outfit Consolidated Electronics, and he seemed to remember that Holden had been the designated courier, with Griman specifically prohibited from participating in the recovery of Curie's superconductor. So, why and how had Griman gotten into the act? Now someone else had interfered with this pleasure cruise, but who? "Que vuet dire ceci!" Dubois certainly intended to find out!

He had asked the nurse at the front desk to take frequent coffee breaks, leaving the front door open and unattended. But now it was nearly 2:00 a.m., and Dubois longed for either action or sleep. Why hadn't the attacker accepted his invitation?

Ivan Denkov began to feel the increased motion of the ship. He didn't know if it was just a reaction to the long hours of sitting in a fixed position behind that stupid crack in the door, or if the sea was really kicking up. The moon that shone through his porthole had disappeared a couple of hours ago, and when he'd sneaked a peek on his way back from a bathroom stop a few minutes ago, even the action of the waves became obscured by inky blackness. Whatever, it was time to make a move.

No one had come near the hospital door since that little Frenchman entered three hours ago. Was he after something, or was he just nosing around? But he's been there too long; they either put him to bed, or I missed seeing him leave when I went to the toilet. The nurse has left her desk again—she seems to leave for fifteen minutes every hour, plenty of time to get the job done, and done right this time.

As he fingered the slim, shiny blade of his trusted knife—never should have played with that idiot gadget of Dromensky's—he laughed to himself. I can always tell them I came for seasick pills if I've miscalculated.

He moved so stealthily and silently the Frenchman almost missed it. Ivan had the blade poised over the sleeping man before Dubois shouted, "Don't move! You are under arrest! A startled Denkov turned to face a snub nose revolver pointed directly at his head as it emerged from the curtained darkness.

"Drop the knife right there!"

As the knife clattered to the floor, the little Frenchman, revolver still aimed steadily at the intruder's skull, ordered, "Turn around and move toward the door."

The Soviet agent ducked down, and with lightning speed in that narrow, confined space, he whirled in a circle, plucked another knife from its leg sheath and slashed upward across the chest and throat of the Frenchman. At the same instant the trigger finger squeezed.

Its noise magnified by the confined space, the single shot threw bits of flesh and shattered bone through the opening to rain on the nurse as she entered the office door. She screamed, then fell silent.

When the doctor and medical attendant arrived, they saw Dubois sitting in the midst of the human debris. Conscious but unable to speak, the French cop slumped over the virtually headless Soviet.

Griman slept on, smiling a dream of being with Lisa in Hawaii, watching a volcano erupt with an enormous bang.

CHAPTER 19

Late Monday

"Enough!" cried Karen, freeing herself from Charles' firm grasp of her elbow. "Running up three flights of stairs is more action than I need after that big dinner. What's the big rush?"

"Sorry, but the trip will do you good. Seriously, Karen, I wanted to duck the official traffic sure to be heading back the way we came. The Captain has called for our resident gendarme, and the less involved I get with him, the more free I am to do my job. I have no intention of sharing the details of our story with any Frenchman. If I do, they'll claim full title to the Curie stuff if it's found onboard. Don't forget, we're sailing under a French flag."

"Does anything about the attack give you a better idea of where to look?" Karen recovered her breath and started deducing things again.

"Not really. It doesn't change the picture much. Just tells me the Russians are still desperate to get their hands on the superconductor, and they wanted Griman out of the way. It does remind me of how dangerous they are, and warns me to take no chances." Taking her arm again, gently this time, he said, "How about a change of scene? Let's waltz on out to the Promenade Deck right there and get some fresh air. Whaddaya say?"

"Sounds like a welcome change. Think it'll be cold?"

"I think I can manage to keep you warm."

"Promise?"

The full moon cut a silver path over the jet black Atlantic and highlighted the white caps, bigger now, with heavy tops curling over to fall back with rhythmic swishing sounds. An airliner traced a path above them, flickering lights marking its trail. Karen sighed and said, "Would you believe I'd almost rather be up there?"

"What? After working so hard to achieve this glorious cruise in the lap of luxury?" he teased.

"This lap of luxury, as you call it, is full of thorns, some of which just may be fatal."

"I think I have just the thing to alter your mood, my dear."

"Such as?"

"Such as a nice cold bottle of champagne waiting to be shared." Holding her close to his side, he guided her to the entrance obscured by the shadow of the lifeboat suspended above them.

"Wow," Karen gasped as Charles ushered her into his suite, already prepared by the steward for bedtime. A lamp turned low cast its beams over the many cushioned couch. Music played softly, and a basket heaped with a variety of fresh fruit waited on the desk top next to the freshly filled bucket of ice and tray of glasses. "I see what you meant by lap of luxury, Mr. Holden. How can you stand mingling with us peons?"

"Mingling is what I do best, as I hope you will come to know. Sometimes, when I'm on a job, I get some very nice fringe benefits. Not always, but this happens to be one of those times. My last assignment had me flying to the Orient in a coach seat on what I would charitably call a shabby airplane, a trying experience with these long legs, to say the least."

Charles had the champagne out of the refrigerator and now worked on loosening the cork. It came out with a loud POP.

"Not supposed to do that," he muttered. "If I were really practiced and skilled, I could have eased that out instead of firing a broadside to starboard."

"Either way, it looks festive and tempting." Karen selected a tulip stemmed glass from the tray and held it out for filling. She took a sip, then carried her glass to the couch, kicking off her shoes and curling her feet under her. Charles filled his glass and joined her on the couch, setting the napkin-wrapped bottle on the coffee table.

"Mmmm, this is nice. I think you had a very good mood altering idea."

"I'm glad you do," replied Charles. He held her close and spoke firmly, "because it was place altering, too. I have no intention of letting you out of my sight with that sneaky Russian still on the loose."

Karen suddenly giggled. "When you look all fierce and serious like that, the brown eye gets darker and the green one greener. Is that how I tell you really mean what you're saying?"

"That way, or I can show you . . ." He gathered her in his arms, tipping her head to meet her waiting mouth. Tongues flicked, tentatively at first, then thrusting urgently. Two champagne glasses tinkled to the carpet as trembling hands searched and caressed.

When they broke apart, Charles looked down at her now very rumpled silk dress as his fingers nervously loosened the buttons. "Yep, a very good buy."

"What are you talking about?"

"I said you made a very good buy."

"I always do, but what is it this time?"

"Your black French lingerie. Most effective, but unnecessary." He exposed her breasts and kissed the erect nipples.

"Perfection needs no adorning, and, besides, you have too many clothes on."

"Not at the rate you're removing them."

"Shall we retire to the other part of the suite, my dear?"

"Whatever for?" she replied coquettishly, covering her bosom in mock modesty.

Charles wiggled his eyebrows and took her hand. Karen allowed herself to be led to the bedroom alcove where the waiting king-size bed was already turned back. The *Royale's* blue logo on the crisp white sheets looked like an engraved invitation.

He slid his hands gently down her sleek hips, taking off her panties in the process. He flung the last of the Galaries Lafayette lingerie across the room, and Karen sighed, "Hell, it's just underwear, but at two hundred francs, it deserves better treatment."

"Honey, you deserve the better treatment, not the lingerie." His trousers dropped to the floor, and they fell across the bed together.

It was close to three in the morning when Charles carefully untangled himself from Karen's arms and legs and rose to secure a flapping curtain on the partly open sliding door to the suite's private veranda. He stepped outside, and a fierce blast of wind pushed him back. Tumbling billows of clouds raced across the moon, letting occasional paths of light pinpoint hissing waves rising high and breaking fast, their white caps spraying wildly.

He returned to the warm bed, curling up to Karen. Kissing her on the neck, he said, "I think we're moving into some weather. We may have to stay here all day."

"That's okay with me," she answered sleepily, then mumbled something in French, not a word of which Charles understood, yet he thought he knew exactly what she meant.

Tuesday Morning, June 16

"Good morning, ladies and gentlemen, this is your Captain speaking."

Karen lifted her head from the pile of pillows and searched sleepily for the switch to the loudspeaker. Disoriented, she was keenly aware she was now in Charles' suite, but damned if she could remember the details of the bedroom itself. What was the Captain saying? She pulled the top sheet off the bed to wrap herself in and stumbled into the other room where the speaker was mounted on the wall behind the desk.

"The outer decks are very wet and slippery. We are advising passengers to stay inside while we pass through this minor squall. We don't expect it to last too long. Meanwhile, your cruise staff is ready to supply items for your amusement. We want you to remember, the *Royale* is your home at sea. I do hope you all have a pleasant day. Thank you."

Charles peeked around the corner from the bathroom door, razor in hand and cheeks half covered with shaving cream. "Good morning, beautiful lady. I must say I admire your costume."

"Oh, Charles," said Karen in dismay, "I hope everyone does what the Captain said, and stays in his room."

"What's the big deal?"

"Well, I don't exactly relish having an audience when I go back to my room looking like a lady of last evening."

"Together we can face anything, I'm sure, and, being a true gentleman, I'm prepared to offer a raincoat, just right for the storm at sea." He covered her with soapy kisses and inquired, "How's your tummy? Does the ship's rolling bother you?"

"Luckily, I've never had a problem with seasickness. Just rugged, I guess. How about you?"

"I feel so wonderful that I'm starved. Do you realize it's almost noon? They won't be serving lunch on the deck today, so I think we should go to our regular table in the dining room. Feel up to it?"

"If we can go to my cabin first."

"While I finish dressing, why don't you call the infirmary and check on Frank Griman's condition."

"I'd almost forgotten that terrible part of last night."

"Just don't forget about the good part."

"I'll call right now." She went to the bedside table, picking up strewn clothing on the way. By the time Charles emerged from the dressing room, Karen had discarded the sheet and was fully clad, if rumpled, in the blue silk gown and satin shoes. She'd found her evening purse, managed to apply a dab of lipstick, and her lustrous blonde cap of curls needed only a quick touch of a comb to fall into groomed symmetry.

"How did you manage to get dressed so fast?" Charles asked, obviously pleased.

"One, I didn't have to pick out what to wear, and, two, nobody in the infirmary would talk to me. Said they had such a bad night, and so many calls today, I'd better just come down later this afternoon."

"I wonder why their night was so bad. Hope the doctor didn't hit the bottle again. I'll check after lunch, but first things first. Ready to make your public appearance?"

"I'd follow you anywhere," she winked as she skipped out the door.

A half hour later in the dining room with Charles, Karen looked well-groomed and sedate in her tailored slacks and blazer. She scanned the room, more than half empty now, with no fully occupied table. Even a couple of the waiters appeared a bit green and shaky. She noticed one singularly unattractive fellow at the table in the corner eating his soup with enthusiasm. At least he has a good stomach, even if he does have a bad complexion, she silently told herself.

Turning to Charles, who was doing his own good job with a bowl of minestrone, she asked, "Do you suppose our tablemates are sick."

"One can only hope. You're not feeling sick, are you?"

"No, but I think our waiter is, and judging from the scarcity of diners, a lot of people must be."

"Yes, I've been noticing—oops, there goes the fruit plate, better catch those apples. I think it's fun rolling around like this, don't you?"

"Oh, hell yes, until we slide into the Atlantic. I wonder if they've got the stabilizer flaps out. I don't really know how they're supposed to work. Do you?"

Charles began to show with flattened palms the function of the stabilizer fins, and was about to get into an explanation of the gyros, when he winced against a sudden flash of light.

"Sorry!"

When the green blotch in front of his eyes faded, Charles saw June Hopkins holding her polaroid camera.

"I didn't mean to startle you, but Mel's holed up in our stateroom, so this seemed a good time to get some pictures of the ship's interior for our travel memories book. Let me—whoops!" June almost dropped her camera, grabbing a chair for support as the *Royale* dipped rather sharply. "Let me get a proper one of you two while I can still stand up." She ripped off the developing picture and prepared for another one. "Now, smile!"

She took her place at the table and placed the two processing pieces of film on the tablecloth, carefully avoiding the several wet spots from the sloshing water glasses. When the images were clearly visible, she said, "Here you are, the two lovebirds riding the stormy Atlantic."

Not rising to the bait, Karen took the offered photo and studied it, remarking, "It's rather good of you, Charles," and, smiling sweetly at June, she said simply, "Thank you. That will be nice to have."

After lunch, watching June walk away from them with the wide stance and slightly bent knees of an experienced cruiser, Charles lamented, "With everyone secure in their quarters, so to speak, I don't think I'll have much luck pursuing my search."

"I'm really fascinated by the storm. I'd like to watch the sea from that front observation lounge," remarked Karen. "Care to join me?"

"Maybe later. For now, I think I ought to check on Griman."

"In that case, maybe I'll drop by the library, find a book to take with me. Don't I just have to go up one deck?"

"It may be a good idea to escort you, see you safely ensconced on one of those big comfy chairs, hopefully with a protective octogenarian on either side of you, before I head for the infirmary."

"Isn't that slightly overdoing the knight-in-shining-armor bit? Don't get me wrong, I love your company, protective or otherwise, but . . ."

"Can't you see I'm suffering?" His grin was meant to be reassuring, but her brow creased with worry lines.

She decided to play along, though, and said, "Then I'll race you up the stairs!" She laughed as a sudden roll of the ship caught her off guard.

Charles caught her arm, "Settle for a slow walk?"

A few hardy passengers crowded into the tiny wood paneled room, actually little more than a corner nook. Two walls of bookshelves apparently justified its being called a library. The selection of books was eclectic. Aside from a very basic collection of reference works, Bibles, volumes of

Shakespeare and an assortment of Maupassant, Proust and Dumas (probably in French), the hardback volumes were few.

Karen reminded herself the ship was only on its third voyage, and it was plain to see the books would accumulate as passengers contributed those they carried aboard and donated as they left. Three dog-eared copies of the latest bestseller and a Victorian romance occupied the paperback section, along with a few westerns and several of the recent spy stories.

Spy stories were about the last thing she needed. She had enough intrigue of her own to worry about. Finally, she settled for an old copy of Errol Flynn's *My Wicked, Wicked Ways.*

"This should be distracting enough." Clutching the chosen book, she went over to the corner where Charles was studying the sign-up sheets laid out in a row on the long table.

"Here you go, Karen. See all the various activities they've dreamed up for your enjoyment? How would you like to join the class in napkin folding or maybe you'd prefer joining the group making crepe paper costumes for the masquerade evening?" He drew her near to read with him.

"I suppose I should go to exercise class, but it starts too early in the morning. And I should take advantage of 'Bridge for Beginners.' Here's one that I'd really like to do: they're offering a tour of the ship's bridge, not the playing cards, the navigation one. It's scheduled for 10:30 Thursday morning. Want to sign up with me and learn the secrets of sailing this vessel?" She picked up the attached pencil and added her name to the list.

"Maybe later, but don't write me down until I know more. Let's see if we can find that napping chair for you."

"If we can't, my stateroom will do. A nap and a nice hot shower are definitely on the agenda."

"Now that's an activity I intend to share! But you can start without me." His long arm went around her shoulders as they left the room.

CHAPTER 20

Wednesday, June 17

The waiter at their assigned table was learning, but very slowly.

"Please, not regular, no 'cafe normal' for me," Charles explained once again, "But I would like some decaffeinated." Karen never had to repeat. There seemed to be a certain magical communication system between her and the French speaking waiter. She never even had to ask about the menu, or even finish a sentence. She just had to say a phrase or two in French, smile a bit at the waiter, and voila! She was served exactly what she wanted. Charles wondered absently if there was a French "SQUID" between them.

Karen was seated next to Charles, but Jane McKenzie took the place at his left. Jane had awakened without a trace of yesterday's seasickness, and today's calm sea had restored her breakfast appetite. Sitting next to that gorgeous hunk of man made the meal more exciting, Jane thought, especially when he looked at her straight on and she could study those fascinating eyes. Too bad he was wasting his time on the simple little gal next to him. Hopefully, before the end of the trip she'd get a chance to show him what a real woman is, the dumb ass didn't know what he was missing.

"I made the date with Philip," Karen explained quietly to Charles, "I'm meeting him for lunch on the Lido Deck at one. Remember, he's in N-32."

"I know where he is, sweet girl," Charles responded rather testily. "You'll have to be very skillful in pumping him for information, and don't get too chummy with him, if you know what I mean."

"Do I detect a trace of jealousy?" Karen blushed as the mental picture of last night's love making flashed through her mind without warning. Charles did not answer.

"Where do you suppose the Hopkins and that cute little Frenchman are?" Jane McKenzie asked, surveying the bewildering heaps of croissants, Danish pastries, raisin toast, and English muffins, as she lifted the white napkin from the silver tray in front of her.

"Probably had breakfast in their staterooms," Charles offered. "I noticed the companionways on the way here this morning were full of trays."

"But no strays," Jane pouted, "Are you going to the investments lecture this morning?" she threw in hopefully.

"Sorry, I have to go visit a friend in the hospital," Charles explained.

"I know a nice fellow on the ship you might like to meet, Jane," Karen immediately regretted the remark.

"I'm really not quite that desperate, dear. If I don't find someone by rutting-season, I'll let you know."

* * *

Philip Brown opened the wardrobe door in his suite. The easy rhythmic sway of the *Royale* was a pleasant change from the bucking bronco action of last night. The slight motion gave the jackets and assorted trousers a jaunty bounce on the closet rod.

"My mother told me to choose this one," Philip muttered. His finger rested on a linen madras sport coat. He then selected mauve slacks and a lime green three-button sports shirt.

"On second thought, for her, better a tie," remembering how Karen always stared at his ties in awed admiration. He went to the closet drawers where he selected a white dress shirt and a snappy red silk tie blotched with bright yellow hour-glasses. "C'est important," he mumbled. "Clothes make the man, so the man can make the woman," he hoped he wasn't overdressed, but then, Karen deserved the best.

It was precisely one o'clock when Karen found a table under an umbrella on the wide balcony overlooking the large swimming pool on the Lido deck. When she made the date to meet Philip, she decided the crowds of people at the buffet lunch outside would be a welcome diversion, and they would discourage any misguided attempts at intimacy on Philip's part.

She gave a tug at the elastic waistband of her cotton skirt, definitely tighter now than when she packed it. Her plan to ask Philip to go through the line, pick up the food for both of them, wouldn't hurt, it might do her figure some good. The elastic tension definitely told her that another of yesterday's hamburgers was a no-no.

Karen noticed many heads were turning toward the man approaching her table. My god! Where does he find that stuff? The tie was probably purchased in one of those Halloween spook alley basement stores.

"Good to see you Philip, you look great," Karen exclaimed, hoping she wouldn't get nauseous in the company of the Madras and hour-glasses. "I managed to get this table, but I don't think we dare leave it, the people with loaded trays will grab it instantly."

"I didn't realize so many people came out here for lunch," Philip said, "I've been eating in the dining room."

"I guess the vacationers want to spend as much time as possible near the pool before they have to go back to work." Karen tried to sound pleasant. "Why don't you leave your jacket here on the chair and go to the food line for us, and I'll catch the waiter's eye and order a couple of Bloody Marys. All I want is a little bit of shrimp salad and a piece of fruit. Think you can manage?"

"Right on, Karen. Sounds good to me, back in a jiffy." Removing his jacket, Philip was pleased that Karen was obviously impressed by his twenty dollar necktie.

* * *

Charles carefully laid his stateroom key, a plastic rectangular card perforated by computerized punches, over a Polaroid film sheet he'd stripped from a newly purchased film cartridge. He traced the edges of the card so that the polaroid could be trimmed to exactly the same size as the key-card. Then, he used a tiny bit of adhesive tape he'd extracted from a BandAid, doubled over on itself, to stick the trimmed Polaroid film to a playing card, a joker he'd removed from the game room. Now, using his manicure scissors, he cut the sandwiched piece along the lines. Checking the assembly for size against his own key-card, Charles was satisfied with the job.

When he got to Philip Brown's stateroom, he glanced up and down the wide center hallway. No one was in sight. Now Charles hastily peeled the developer layer from the key card film strip and deftly inserted his manufactured assembly into the door slot for 32. When he removed the card a few moments later a faint pattern of light spots appeared on the now blackened film. Using the point of his ball-tip pen,

Charles punched through each spot, trimming the hole edges on the back of the card with the manicure scissors, and finally he punched the spots out again from the other side. Then he trimmed and smoothed one more time. Satisfied that the hole pattern was complete and ready for use, he once again inserted the key-card into the door slot. Charles heaved a sigh of relief as the doorknob turned in his hand.

He vowed to cover methodically every inch of Philip's stateroom. He started with the bathroom, sorting through the toilet kit, then the shelves and drawers. Moving on to the closets, he inspected every pocket in every shirt, jacket and trousers. He removed the ventilator cover using (appropriately, he thought) a Phillips-head screwdriver. If Philip Brown had the superconductor in his room, Charles couldn't detect it. He had been using a small key chain compass as a sort of Geiger Counter. Joe had explained that a compass needle would spin if it were close to a superconductor.

Charles was about to give up, concluding that if Philip had it, he had stashed it elsewhere or he carried it on his person. He decided to have a closer look at the contents of the nightstand's drawers. Removing an elasticized packet of papers, he riffled through the folded sheets, and four folded pages stapled together slid out of the bundle.

"Hello! What have we here?" Charles muttered aloud. "Looks like pay dirt at last." Charles sat down on the bed to read for the first time Karen's complete translation of Madame Marie Curie's letter to Georges Colbert. Finally he replaced the letter, carefully reinserting it in its original location. The same drawer held a packet of condoms and Charles swore as he thought of the son-of-a-bitch now having lunch with Karen.

Charles left Philip's room virtually undisturbed. He debated with himself over his gut feeling that no matter what evidence pointed to Philip Brown, he just didn't fit the picture of Mr. Black.

Karen and Charles had agreed to meet in the small card-room at 2:30, the same room in which Dr. Black, the dentist, told Charles to get his front tooth fixed. Arriving first, Charles sat at one of the three green felt tables in the now empty room, pensively running his finger over the offending tooth. Guess I'd better follow the Wyoming expert's advice, if I ever get the time.

He was deep in thought when Karen arrived, but he answered her wide smile with, "Now there's a gorgeous set of choppers!"

"I beg your pardon? Have I missed something?"

"Just admiring your teeth. You don't look like you need any dental work."

"Mind your manners there, fellow." Karen said sharply, "you're not buying a horse, you know."

"I hope you minded yours with old Brownie boy. How was lunch; I never got any myself."

"Well, the food was okay, but Philip's so darn much fun to be with I could hardly stand it."

"I could guess that after inspecting his entire wardrobe. You should see some of those ties."

"I have, lucky me. Don't forget we work in the same office. What about the superconductor? Your state of no excitement tells me you came home empty-handed, right?"

"Not entirely. Seems as if he sho-nuff found Missie Karen's translation."

"Really, Charles?"

"Yep, all four pages."

"But no Flacon 216. Charles, I still can't believe that Philip is your Mr. Black."

"I don't know, Karen. My instinct is to agree with you. On the other hand, he gets a copy of that letter, talks to you about superconductivity at the River Cafe and . . ."

"Riviera," Karen corrected.

"Okay, Riviera. Anyhow, then he gives you some phony reason for going to Paris, tells you he's going to fly there, then says he's afraid to fly. Now he's on this ship."

"What about the lady in the bookstore telling you Mr. Black couldn't speak French? I know Philip. He's a bore, even an ass, but he speaks fluent French. And I don't think he's clever enough to pretend he can't speak French just to throw someone off the track."

"Maybe he's more clever than we think. Perhaps, if you could get him to drink some of those French 75's they've promised to serve at the Captain's Gala tonight, you could cozy it up enough so he'd tell you why he copied your translation."

"That's interesting."

"So you'll do it?"

"Do what?"

"For gosh sakes, Karen didn't you just agree it's an interesting plan?"

"I was noticing that the greenish light in here makes both your eyes look brown, that's what's interesting. As for Philip, no way I'm about to cozy up to that creep! Those sneaky hands have been after my behind for a long time. Not even for you, my love, are they going to land there."

"Forget I asked. We'll work it out another way. Now let's go see if we can talk to Griman."

When Charles and Karen arrived at the infirmary, a small group of ship's officers were gathered in the doorway talking to the doctor, who looked as if he'd had one rough night. The lines in his aging face all pointed downward, the ravages of gallons of booze showing as the light illuminated his weary countenance.

"Hello, Doctor, do you remember us from yesterday?" Charles squeezed Karen into the center of the group. The three officers opened ranks to include the pretty girl, and Charles quickly followed.

"We're Frank Griman's friends, Ms. Bright and Charles Holden. We came to find out how he's getting along, and if there's a chance you'll be letting him out of there," pointing to the infirmary.

Wordlessly, the officers dispersed, the one with the clipboard back into the hospital facilities. The doctor was left to answer, "I remember you both, of course, Mr. Holden. I'm sorry, but your friend's condition is more serious than I expected. I do not want him disturbed today."

"Do you mean we can't see him? I'd really like to ask him a question."

"Perhaps later. You can't talk to him now, he has been heavily sedated. He had quite a shock to his system, you must realize." The doctor obviously wanted to end the conversation.

"Do you know if his assailant was found?" Charles persisted, "I'm asking because Frank seemed to think the man might be after me, too."

"I can see why you are concerned. My understanding is that the assailant, as you call him, will never bother anyone again. He was shot and killed."

"No kidding!" Charles' surprise was real. "How did it happen, and who was he?"

"I can't say any more. The matter is currently under investigation. It has caused a lot of work, I don't mind telling you. But if you want any more information, you must speak with the Captain. I've said too much already." He turned abruptly, walked into his office just inside the entrance of the hospital, and closed the door firmly, leaving Karen and Charles to stare at the NO ADMITTANCE sign.

"Shall we go find the Captain? Who do you think shot whom? Or is it really true?" Karen voiced her bewilderment, looking hopefully at Charles.

"Oh yes, it's true, the doctor would know if someone was shot. Let's just hope whoever it was got the right guy. As for the Captain, the less we have to do with him, the better. I'm sure he'll want to know more about our connection with Griman, if there's any further investigation. I'm surprised he hasn't sent for us by now."

"Then let's take a break, act like ordinary fun-loving cruise passengers. How about a drink on the Sun Deck? You can eat some peanuts or pretzels to make up for the lunch you missed, and we can breathe some fresh sea air, instead of this creepy atmosphere."

"Fine idea. Let's take these back stairs. They lead to the outer deck the easiest way."

"Hi, you two!" June Hopkins waved from the Sun Deck veranda as Karen and Charles began to mount the steps up from the lower deck. "Come join us for a little sunset libation. The sky is magnificent."

Karen happily accepted the offer, and led Charles to the table where Mel Hopkins was seated, tall glass filled with pale red liquid before him and clutter of papers in his lap. He stood to greet Karen and the papers slid to the deck in a heap.

"Greetings, tablemates. Glad to see you. Join us for a 'Master of the Hounds.'" Mel handed his glass to a puzzled Charles, "This is great drinking stuff, can you hold it for me a minute? I seem to have scattered my junk all over."

"What's in it?"

"Just some stuff from the Berlin conference," said Mel, gathering the papers and stuffing them into a manila folder, "first chance I've had to read all these pre-prints."

"I mean, what's in this so-called 'Master of the Hounds'?" persisted Charles.

"Something we discovered in London last year. Just whiskey with a little cherry brandy and a dash of bitters. Good insulation against these Atlantic breezes."

"I'll bet it is," Charles shuddered, turning to the waiter standing expectantly at his elbow, "but I think we'll stick to a couple of vodka martinis on the rocks, please."

Karen nodded her agreement, and resumed her travel wardrobe discussion with June.

"What I'm hoping to do," Mel continued, seeing he had regained Charles attention, "is to convince Hewlett-Packard to give some consulting fee money for a project I have in mind. I know they're talking to DuPont about collaborating on new superconductor research. Anyhow this paper from the British scares me a little, seems they have some of the same ideas. Funny, the way it is with scientific theories—they often pop up in different parts of the world at the same time."

Not always, Charles thought. Some of them popped up fifty years ago, and got lost. He diverted Mel back to a discussion of liquor combinations until Karen, girl talk exhausted, extended her empty glass and stood, excusing herself.

"Come on, Charles, let's leave these people at peace with their hounds. Another martini and I wouldn't be able to dress for dinner, and isn't tonight the Captain's Gala?"

* * *

Jane McKenzie could be heard three tables away over the muted clink of silver on china and glass. The flash of light reflecting from the dangling diamonds at her ears emphasized her words as she complained. "French 75's bullshit. In plastic glasses, to boot! Catch me standing in line again. I won't shake the Captain's hand at his farewell cocktail party if he doesn't have his waiters serve enough drinks while I wait!"

Any more drinks and you'd be flat on your face, thought Karen, almost hypnotized by the size of the diamond resting in Jane's dramatic cleavage. Karen had dressed conservatively for the formal evening, in a simple cocktail length black silk dress with pearls, and she thought Charles looked smashing in his bow tie and dark suit. Some of their fellow passengers had added more glitter, but Jane outshone them all.

"If Monsieur Dubois could have been here, he would have agreed with me about the quality of the French 75's," Jane continued.

Hoping to end the tirade, Karen asked quickly, "Why do you say 'could have been' Jane?"

"Didn't you hear?" the noisy blonde responded, "the waiter told me our friend Dubois is in the hospital."

"I hope he's not still sea sick," June Hopkins entered the conversation.

"Not on this sea, it's smooth as glass." said Mel Hopkins, "Besides, June, they don't put people in the hospital for seasickness." Speaking softly, with concern, he asked Jane, "Did the waiter say what's wrong? M. Dubois has been a pleasant companion, maybe we should see if he needs help. He was quite alone."

"Of course, it's always the pleasant lonely ones that get in all the trouble. . ."

Charles interrupted Jane's crude answer to say, "Karen and I have a friend in the hospital we are planning to visit after dinner. I'll look in on Dubois, and let you know if we can do anything for him."

The lights in the Pavilion restaurant suddenly dimmed as the ship's musicians paraded down the aisle, trumpet, trombone, saxophone, and snare drum playing a spirited march as they were followed by dining room waiters carrying above their heads giant trays bearing flaming baked Alaska, each topped with a miniature Eiffel Tower spouting colored sparklers.

"Let's sneak out of here, Karen, we don't need all those calories. . ." Charles suggested.

"You don't like French fireworks?" Karen laughed.

"I think we'll have enough fireworks of our own. I have a feeling that our nice little Frenchman just got into the problem. I'd like to have another try at talking to Griman, he may know what's going on by now."

"I hope you people will excuse us," Charles offered as he helped Karen with her chair, "we are going to avoid the temptation of that beautiful baked Alaska."

"You're not missing much," said Jane, with a mouthful, "the Eiffel tower tastes like the smell of gunpowder."

"I still think McKenzie and Philip Brown would make a good combination," murmured Karen to Charles as they left the room.

* * *

The hospital nurse on duty politely informed the duo that Mr. Griman would be released to his own stateroom sometime tomorrow, but could receive no visitors, as he had been sedated for the night.

"You have a M. Dubois in the hospital. He dines at our table. May we see him?"

"I'm very sorry, sir. Doctor's orders, no visitors. M. Dubois is still a very sick man, he lost a lot of blood." The matronly woman, salt and pepper curls covered by a crisp white cap, looked sincerely sorry to refuse the request of this charming man with the very pretty girl at his side.

"Do you know the nature of his indisposition?" said Karen, trying to sound idly curious.

"His indisposition was caused by a stab wound. He nearly bled to death saving the life of your friend Mr. Griman, I understand." The RN's cheeks grew pink with intensity.

"We're sorry, we didn't know. Please tell him we asked about him, give him our best. Thank you for your help." Charles gave her his best smile as they left.

CHAPTER 21

Thursday Morning, June 18

Karen arrived early. The scheduled Navigation Tour of the ship's bridge was supposed to begin at 10:30 this morning, not until fifteen minutes from now. Seated in one of the soft swivel chairs in the King Louis Observation Lounge where she'd come to watch the wild action of the sea during the storm, she marveled at how peaceful and innocent those same waters looked today. Twinkling glints of sunlight danced from unbroken lines of gentle swells that moved in soothing rhythm, all signs of Tuesday's storm resided only in memory. It would be more exciting to see all the sailors on the bridge function under duress, thought Karen, but then, visitors would have been a needless nuisance.

A uniformed officer, typical viking with pale yellow hair and eyebrows, round pink cheeks and definite Scandinavian accent, called names from a list on his clipboard. Karen was surprised to see how many women were in the group of 20, but she moved to join the line when she heard her name.

"I am Chief Navigator, Olaf Johanson. If you will all just follow me, please." He led them through a door labeled PRIVATE, almost hidden behind heavy velvet curtains, which opened to the outer deck. Then he headed them back toward the bow to a steep outside stairway leading up to the little area that extended over the side of the ship. Karen was happy she'd had enough sense to wear rubber soled shoes.

"Please use the hand rails when you go up the ladder," the young officer cautioned. "Our speed is only 24 knots, but it is wise to be careful."

One of the men who had been talking non-stop to his buddy, now asked, "What is a knot?"

Oh dear, thought Karen as the group was called to a halt to hear the officer's careful explanation of nautical speed versus miles per hour. "One minute of latitude is equal to one nautical mile covered in one hour . . ." I bet we're going to hear it all again in French, with a conversion to kilometers.

The line of people moved slowly into the working area of the bridge, the leader's voice never still, and Karen dropped back to be able to see, away from the pushing crowd.

Behind the wall of glass, a giant windshield, the narrow aisle was flanked on both sides by electronic devices and panels of instruments. Helpfully, each different unit was manned by a sailor eager to explain his instrument's purpose in simple terms.

"These engine speed controls are linked to eight separate diesel engines, all rotating at a modest 144 RPM, so we are able to travel at a top speed of 33 knots," proudly explained the young seaman in the center.

"Here we have the latest Krupp Atlas Radar, for precise measurements of the distance from us to any object we sight," said the next, pointing to the lighted screen in front of him. Karen watched the sweep of the dial around the pale green screen marked in concentric circles, flashing a blip at its outer edge. "A freighter in a far sea lane," the sailor agreed to her unspoken question, "too far away to see."

Farther along, the tour slowed to hear the details of the uncanny powers of a Global Satellite Computer Navigation system as it was being extolled by still another young seaman, this one sprouting an obviously new beard.

Karen studied the different flags stowed in wooden cubbyholes of the wall behind them, trying to identify each country represented. She realized she had arrived at a round gray device, about the shape and size of a washtub. "What is this thing for?" she asked the waiting sailor.

"Our magnetic gyro-compass, ma'am," He pointed to the luminous dial inside a bobbing circular dish, "used to obtain an exact directional setting for our automated—Good lord!" A sudden thrust from behind shoved Karen until her head was almost in the tub, but she could see all the iridescent arrows spinning like a roulette wheel. As she watched, they slowed and settled into a fixed position once again, swinging gently in a small arc.

"Something wrong, sailor?" asked the officer with gilded striped sleeves who had made his way to them at first sound of the sailor's oath.

"The compass was spinning like a top!"

The officer peered close. "Seems okay to me." He pointed to the visiting passengers and admonished the perturbed sailor, "Have to keep the excitement level down, fellow, better watch it."

Karen fervently hoped she hadn't touched something by mistake, and moved quickly to follow the tall man who hurried ahead of her. He must have been the one who shoved me, she thought, as they arrived at a big enclosed black box. Suddenly the ship lurched, then slowly rolled sideways, leaning nearer to the water's edge than it had at the worst of yesterday's storm. Grasping at anything, counter edges, sticking out handles, or each other, the horrified passengers watched frozen by fear as the ship slowly righted itself and calmly sailed forward.

The same officer leaped to the area, trying to gain control and calm his visitors at the same time. He had no way of knowing all the magnetic relays in the automatic pilot had momentarily lost their hold of the ship's steering mechanism.

"Please, Ladies and Gentlemen," in a reassuring voice, "do not touch any of the ship's instruments as you pass through the bridge. You may exit the door at the far side, your director, Mr. Johanson, will escort you back to the King Louis Lounge." A mask of fear covered the face of the tall man as he looked back over his shoulder before he bolted out the door.

Karen didn't know which was more welcome, the comforting smile on Charles' face, or the Bloody Mary he had waiting for her at the table by the Lido bar.

"Was that you taking a turn steering the ship when we gave that big lurch?" he teased.

"Don't laugh, my love, I haven't recovered from the flow of adrenalin yet." She took a giant swallow of her waiting drink, then captured his attention completely as she described the morning's events. She concluded, "One guy was so upset he beat the whole crowd in his rush to get out of there. . . ."

Charles leaped out of his chair, "the bastard had the superconductor on him! I've got to get that list right now, before he tosses it away. Meet you at the hamburger stand." He pushed his way past the crowded tables to hurtle up the outside stairs.

* * *

"Okay, so here we are." Charles had the list of the people who took the navigation tour placed before him, next to a plate containing one lone French fry. A tiny drop of Poupon mustard found its way from the end of his hot dog to the corner of the page he was studying so intently. "There are five couples. Let's eliminate them, so we're down to ten people right away."

"What are you mumbling about, dear boy?" Karen's eyes returned from their amused analysis of the sun worshippers draped around the pool in various unflattering poses.

"Well, Mr. Black was alone. So the people on the list, the two sets of Mr. and Mrs. names, we can forget about. That leaves us with eight men."

"You can cross off Mr. Baker. I saw him in the tour group. Remember, he's the escort we talked to, that fellow from Miami who gets a free trip if he'll mingle with the lonely ladies. He said his name is George Baker. Anyhow, if there's a Baker on your list, you can cross him off."

"Right, here he is. So now we're down to seven. Have you got a pencil in that bulging bag of yours?"

"Always. I suppose you want a piece of paper, too." She tore a deposit slip from her leather check book holder and thus added her contributions to the computer printout passenger list and the morning tour list already spread out on the table.

"Good. Now we make a new list. Seven names and seven stateroom numbers."

"What are you going to do, Mr. Investigator? Just go knocking on doors, saying, 'Are you Black?'" Regretting the double entendre, she stopped, waiting for his answer.

"No, Karen," ignoring her play on words, "I hatched another idea."

"An idea you're going to share?"

"The photographer's shop." He spoke as if his meaning were obvious. Seeing the questioning frown in response, he explained, "The photographer took a picture of every passenger as we came on board, and also of everyone who stood in line last night while waiting to shake hands with the Captain at the cocktail party. There are still a lot of those photos unclaimed in the display cases. Our man may just be there."

"Helluva good idea, Charles. I know mine must be there, but I sure wouldn't pay any money to bail it out."

"Wrong. I already bought yours. I hope it wasn't a bad investment," he teased. "It's not going to give us everything. We won't know his name, and it will still be a lot of leg work, but a picture would really help." Charles was deep in planning again. "We might each take half of the ship and start looking."

"I hope you appreciate that you're the one getting the pay, while I'm the one doing half the work." Karen couldn't help needling him.

"Never fear, we'll have one of those community property marriages and you'll have half of everything."

Karen choked on her last swallow of iced tea.

Descending the wide steps of the center staircase on their way to the tiny photography shop just off the main lounge, Karen spoke. "That's the first word I've heard from you about marriage. You'd better be warned, that's a serious subject with some of us girls. I'm not sure I like your capricious handling of the term."

"Kee-riminy, Karen! You know I'm not being capricious! Hang in there, we'll settle the details later. Right now, I have a job to do!"

"Well, thank you! I guess when you're ready to talk, I'll be the first to hear?"

"The very first, I promise," Charles agreed. "Now let's have a look at those photographs."

The photographer had a little desk with file box and cash register in a small anteroom between the foyer and the entrance to the main entertainment room. Photos, taken at random during the voyage, were arranged in rows on racks where passengers could view and remove a picture. Once they had a picture in hand, they had to pass by the desk, where a gum snapping young girl in a colorful brief, tight skirt was ready to collect six dollars. Extra prints were available for four more dollars.

"Bingo!" Karen yelped.

Hurrying to her side, Charles ruffled his hair until the cowlick stood like an antenna. "You really see him?"

"Yup, in all his ugliness. See here. Hello, Mr. Black!" Removing the photo from its slot in the plastic railing, she held it out for closer inspection. "Funny thing is, I've seen this guy before this morning, but darned if I know where."

"Try to remember, pretty lady, it could be a big piece of the puzzle. I'll get a duplicate so we can each have a copy to study."

"Ugh, do I have to?" She pursed her lips in a pout, but he was already at the desk.

"I don't know if I can get this for you today, sir. We close for the day in a few minutes." The girl pointed at the time on her orange Swatch watch.

"Please try, Miss," urged Charles, giving her his big smile and pushing a $20 bill into her hand.

She put the photo in a little sack, opened the register and offered him $14 in change.

"No, you keep the money. Where can I pick up the extra print?"

"Down on deck 7, the photo lab," she gave in reluctantly, "I'll phone the number in for you, and Andre should have it ready by three o'clock this afternoon. I don't need the gratuity, sir, just let me see that number on the back of the picture."

"I insist you keep the ten. You and Andre deserve it for the extra service." He pocketed his copy of the picture as she pocketed the money.

Charles' plan was simple enough. While they waited for the photographer to finish his job, they sat on a couch under the windows of the main lounge, papers spread on the table before them. The concentrated exertions of the dance class taking place on the center floor, the sounds of start and stop samba music, the instructor counting, "ready, and one, two," the voices of eager women urging reluctant partners, all guaranteed complete privacy.

"This sign-up sheet gives us seven names for our elusive Mr. Black. Two are on your deck, Karen, the Provence, one is on mine, the Versailles, and two more are on the Promenade. That's where Philip is. Suppose there's a connection? Then down on Lafayette, deck 8, there's one name, Couchman, and for some reason the computer print-out has no such listing. It might be an alias and the key to our problem, but we have to check them all, just to be sure. Are you willing to help?"

"Silly boy! Try to stop me, now that it's getting exciting."

"Okay, then, but it's a lot of work for those gorgeous legs of yours. The idea is, when we get that extra picture, we'll go to the different stewards, asking something like, 'do you know where I can find my friend, which room he's in?' Think you can handle that?" He didn't give her time to answer, saying, "You've already charmed your own steward, so that should help."

"Aye-aye, sir, let's get on with it!"

A few of the tired dancers watched with admiration as the handsome young couple left the room arm in arm, with energy and enthusiasm.

* * *

Captain Soderberg, his Scandinavian countenance deeply serious, interrupted the doctor's story, "Please, doctor, let's go over the facts once more. I must have the details straight. I intend to call in the proper authorities to meet the ship when we dock tomorrow, but we are a vessel flying a French flag, heading for a U.S. port, and I must be accurate."

He paused to light his pipe, giving the doctor a chance to think, then he bore down. "This tale sounds a bit melodramatic, don't you agree? First you tell me of an attempt to murder a man named Griman with a poison dart. Now you're telling me there has actually been a killing of another passenger, the presumed assailant of Griman?"

"It wasn't a poison dart, Captain," the weary doctor corrected, the broken blood vessels in his nose standing out in high relief with tension. "I'm not sure what kind of weapon was used to inject the neurotoxin into Mr. Griman."

"But the killing, the second attack, did not involve Mr. Griman?" the Captain probed.

"No, a man we have identified as Ivan Denker, traveling on a Dutch passport, was shot and killed by a Frenchman named Dubois, but not until he managed to cut up the Frenchman pretty bad."

"I am familiar with M. Dubois. He is a police inspector from Paris, and he was sailing with us in line of duty. He will recover, will he not?"

"I have done my best to sew him up, and I certainly hope so, but he lost a lot of blood. That man Denker managed to give him a stab wound in the throat that nicked a vocal chord, and he is unable to talk. However, he should recover full use of his voice in time." The doctor spoke more confidently now, proud of the job he'd done.

"I will, of course, notify his superiors of his condition, he has given me a letter of credentials from an Inspector Bodine, so I know whom to address. But I must also report this crime at sea as soon as possible to the law enforcement agency having jurisdiction of the waterway where we first touch land. That will be the authorities in New York. What can you tell me about the dead man?" Captain Soderberg lit his pipe for the third time.

"Afraid that's a confusing story, sir. This Griman character maintains that Denker is a Russian agent, says he's the same man who killed his wife in Paris. Incidentally, we do have the body of Mrs. Griman on board. But that story of Griman's doesn't jibe with Denker's Dutch passport. Mr. Griman has a couple of American friends aboard, they may know something."

"Very well, Doctor, thank you for your help. You take good care of those patients, and I will have my First Mate, Mr. Ingvolsted, interview Griman, see if he can learn any more. Now I must return to the bridge." Leaving an aromatic trail of tobacco smoke, he vaulted up the steps two at a time.

* * *

Karen and Charles had agreed to celebrate success with a cocktail before dinner in the Lido Lounge. Their celebration became more like a "drown your sorrows" as each admitted defeat.

"I managed to convince each steward I desperately needed help," began Karen, "and I was embarrassed by the young steward on Philip Brown's deck when I gave him some weak song and dance about meeting this man, then forgetting his name. The steward's reaction made me feel like a career woman, the career being unmentionable!"

"I tried the 'cross your palms with silver' approach, with no better luck," confessed Charles, "but I think I did get honest answers. None of my stewards gave a glimmer of recognition of the picture."

"You were right about the leg work, I must admit. I know this ship is a floating city, but until now I haven't begun to realize how big it is. All that up and down, and round and round gave me a healthy appetite. Are we going to take time to go to the dining room for our last night aboard?"

"Of course, my love, I can't bear to miss dining with Jane!"

"Oh, pooh to you." Karen made a face. "I forgot to tell you, but on my way up here I managed to introduce Magnificent McKenzie to Philip Brown. Turns out they're on the same deck, not too far from each other, and I ran into both of them in the hall. Last I saw of them, they were headed for the bar in the Observation Lounge."

"Then her trip won't be a total loss. But seriously, since it's the last night, isn't the required dress for the evening very casual? That would make life much more simple."

"That's what I read in the schedule shoved under the door this morning, and we also have to be prepared to leave our luggage out in the hall for collection by midnight tonight. All except our overnight case, that is. But right now I'd still like to take a quick shower and change, at least my shoes."

"Good idea. May I suggest, when you get your stuff together, your overnight case has a spot just waiting for it on the Versailles Deck. We can transfer it after dinner, it might make leaving the ship tomorrow a little easier."

"Anything to make life easier, that's my motto. I'm really charmed by the romantic invitation!"

"That's good, Karen," was all Charles could say.

"Would you like to walk part of the way to my humble quarters with me? I'm ready to stop playing detective long enough to try to look enticing by dinner time."

"Not too enticing. I like you just the way you are. You'll have to take me without much fancy dressing though. I'm going to give the picture one more try. We didn't locate Couchman, whoever he is, remember? He was the name without a stateroom assignment." Charles gulped the last of his martini and grabbed a handful of peanuts from the dish on the table. "I've been thinking, we didn't really check the penthouse suites, and Couchman could possibly be there. In addition to the steward, those suites have a private butler who could be very helpful."

"I've been thinking, too, trying to remember where I've seen this face before," Karen tapped the photograph in her hand, "and I'm sure he was on the bus with me from Paris to

Le Havre. But, besides that, I think I saw him in New York. It's dim, but there's something about the way his head sits on his shoulders."

"Knowing he was in Paris is a nail in his coffin, but what about New York?"

"When I was packing to leave, I looked out of my apartment window and saw a man on the street looking up, watching me."

"That was no doubt my friend Albert Winch, he was being paid to tail you. I told you about that."

"Yes, you did, but that whole experience frightened me so much it stuck in my mind, like a movie in freeze frame. I keep seeing it, and in the background there's another tall person with the same body build as the man who pushed past me on the navigation bridge this morning."

"It might just be your imagination merging two frightening situations, but if you're right, it would explain why Albert Winch and that building manager got wiped out with the same M/O. Let's give it a rest for now, okay?"

* * *

"What do you think, Doc? I'd really like to get back to my room for the last night of this trip. I feel okay, outside of this sore shoulder." Frank Griman was thinking it would be nice to see Helga again.

"You're going to be weak as a pup for a few days, and you'd better have your doctor in New York watch that shoulder. The neurotoxin used on you may cause some disintegration of the flesh. But I think you can go back to your stateroom now. I'd advise you to stay in bed and take it easy." The doctor was happy to be free of Griman. Looking after M. Dubois was enough to worry about.

"How's my hero doing over there?" Griman pointed to the adjacent cubicle as he gingerly climbed out of bed and stood shakily, wondering if he should get dressed or just pad across the passageway to flop into his own bunk.

"I'm afraid Inspector Dubois' recovery will be much longer than yours. However, he was very lucky. The knife wound that barely nicked his vocal cord could easily have severed his jugular vein. As it is, he'll probably be able to speak by tomorrow."

Frank hoped to be far away, and out of the picture when Dubois was able to talk about this miserable episode.

* * *

The last dinner aboard the *Royale* was a pleasant interlude. Mel and June Hopkins were already looking ahead to their return to California, and they hadn't attempted any brilliant table talk. Jane McKenzie did not appear at all, the food choices on the menu were inviting, and the service was smooth and quick.

Now back in the Versailles Suite after a quick stop at Karen's room to leave her tagged luggage for the porter. Karen responded to its ambience, the soft music, the low lights, the many-cushioned couch.

"What now, Sleuth, a short break?" she asked invitingly.

"No way, sweetheart, we have to keep at it. We still have to talk to the dining room manager, the casino personnel, and all the bartenders. I figure the maitre d' won't be able to give us his attention until after the last lingering diners have gone, and the casino and bars we can always hit later. How about trying to see Frank Griman in the meantime? Or do you want me to do that alone?"

"If I stop now it'll be tough to gear up again. Besides, I'm curious about old Frank. Let's go!"

Frank Griman was propped up in his bed feeling a bit stronger after a simple supper. The doctor had been correct in telling him he'd be weak. His fantasy about being with Helga again faded with the realization that he could barely walk. Now he only hoped that she would bring him some hot tea before bed time.

"The door's not locked, enter," he called in answer to the knock.

"It's Charles and Karen, Frank, may we come in?"

"Come ahead," Frank answered, chagrined. He'd almost forgotten about them. "Sorry if I sounded rude. I thought you were the waiter come to collect the dinner tray. Maybe you'd better put the tray outside, make room to sit."

"We have some questions we hope you can clear up," Charles began, drawing the desk chair near to the head of the bed. Karen dropped her purse and the photograph to the floor so she could remove the tray of dishes from the other chair. After putting the tray outside, she pulled up the chair to join the men.

"I'm glad to see you two. Gawd, it's good to be out of that ward across the hall. The smells there will kill you! So, have you heard about the Russky? Frog policeman got him, shot the bastard deader'n a doornail."

Frank Griman was certainly back among the living, but so wound up he took over the conversation, not even listening to any of Charles' questions, but launching into a detailed account of the murderous attack and Dubois' heroic rescue. Finally, he slumped back, exhausted.

"You'd better get some rest now, Frank. We'll see you tomorrow morning." Charles patted him on the shoulder.

"One thing, Holden," Frank persisted, "Is there still a chance Butler will pay me?"

"We'll talk about that later, Frank, but Karen and I are still working on it. In fact, we're going to do some work right now. Sleep well . . ."

The after dinner passengers, making their way to the Grande Lounge for a final evening of entertainment and dancing, swirled around the young couple at the head of the center staircase. Karen and Charles barely noticed the activity.

"Why don't I tackle the dining room now," decided Charles, "and maybe you can start showing the photograph to some of the dealers in the casino."

"Oh, my gosh, the picture!" Karen cried, "I don't have it. I must have left it on the floor in Griman's room. I know I was carrying it with my purse . . ."

"Never mind, I'll go get it. Wait for me on that couch over there. I'll be right back." Charles was already halfway down the stairs.

When he arrived at Griman's door, it was closed. Trying the handle, he found it was also locked. He hoped Frank hadn't already settled down to sleep. He gave a couple of soft taps. Finally a pasty faced Griman, looking more like a shipwrecked sailor than a passenger on a luxury liner, opened to the sound.

"I'm really sorry to bother you, Frank," Charles apologized, "but Karen forgot a picture we need. I think I see it on the floor over there, under the chair."

Griman silently stepped aside, allowing the investigator access. Charles picked up the picture, gave it a brief glance and was about to leave when Griman, catching a brief glance of the photo, said, "What the hell are you doing with a picture of my cousin?"

"Your cousin?"

"Yeah, my lawyer cousin Higginbotham, the fellow I've been trying to find to give me some help with Lisa's body. How did you get his picture?"

"This is your cousin the lawyer, the one who helped you with Butler's contract?"

"Of course, who else?"

"Did he, by any chance, read the Curie letter?"

"Naturally, he read it when we went over the contract." Frank was beginning to catch on, and he sat down weakly.

"See you later, Frank." Charles waved good bye and broke into a run.

He already had the computer print-out in his hand when he reached Karen. Breathless, either from running the steps or the excitement, he flopped down beside her and studied the list of names.

"We've hit pay dirt, m'gal, see? Griman recognized the man in the photo, his lawyer cousin, Bill Higginbotham. Here he is, on Provence Deck, 226, big as life! And that is the end of the Couchman mystery."

"But that's my deck, Charles. Why haven't I seen him? Besides, I showed the picture to both of the stewards."

"He's a wily bird, Karen, and it's a very big ship. Not too hard to avoid people if you want to." Charles tried to reassure her. "About your steward, we'll just have to ask him later."

"Why don't we do that right now?"

"Not we, my dear, I'm off to 226, and it could get dangerous from here on. I'll do a better job if I know you're safe in the suite."

"While you go have a wrestling contest for Flacon 216? You win, you get the stuff; you lose, you get his razor and a red necktie?"

"Don't start acting smart, Karen, this is my job, remember?"

She gave him a quick, intense kiss and cautioned, "You be careful now; I'm trusting you with the life of the man I love!"

CHAPTER 22

Thursday Evening

In his quarters, Captain Soderberg was speaking on the telephone. "That is correct, his name is Frank Griman. Right. Yes, in my quarters at 10:00 a.m., immediately after the pilot boat arrives. Well, this is the first time I've had to deal with a crime at sea, but I understand Inspector Dubois, under Article 27 of the International Law of the Sea, had the authority to use arms to prevent a criminal act. We expect him to remain in the hospital and return to France with us." The Captain paused, listened, then spoke again.

"Will the office notify the port authorities there's a chance of a delay? We can still arrive on time if the U.S. Marshall doesn't hold us up too long. I understand he has the authority to investigate, search, even arrest onboard, but I'll try to make it easy for him, have the people ready." He listened again, then answered, "Well, Griman has a couple of friends aboard, and I guess the marshall will want to question them also, so I'll have them here when he comes. Yes, sir, I'll do my best, thank you Sir." The Captain put down the telephone thoughtfully and reached for his faithful pipe.

* * *

"You're back in just three minutes and twenty-six seconds. Well done, Super Sleuth, I presume you have Higginbotham locked in the brig and the superconductor in your pocket." Karen regretted her flip remarks when she saw the grim look on Charles' face.

"Don't I wish! Will you come back with me? Higginbotham's room is not only empty, it's clean, no luggage, no signs of occupancy, as if no one was ever in there. I want you to be with me when I ring for the steward, see if he's the one who told you he didn't recognize the picture."

Charles led Karen to the empty stateroom, its door still wide open. As they waited for the steward to respond to the call button, Charles speculated aloud, "That door is held open by a strong magnetic catch . . . wonder if it worked when he had the superconductor in here? That stuff seems to raise hell with magnets."

"Did you ring for me?" A short stout man in a white jacket stared at the pair waiting on the made-up couch bed. He rubbed his nose and said accusingly, "Who are you people? Are you lost? I don't believe you belong in this room."

"You're the one lost. You seem to have lost one of your passengers." Karen was indignant. She pushed the picture at him and said, "Do you remember my asking you about this man earlier this afternoon?"

"I remember you, madame, but I told you before, I've never seen this man." The steward's eyes refused to leave the photograph. Charles had no doubt the man was lying.

Charles unfolded his long limbs, swiftly moved to look down on the sturdy runt, not much more than five feet tall. Overpowering him with size and intensity, Charles said sternly, "I'm in no mood for games. I want to know what's become of Bill Higginbotham."

The little man cringed, tried to protest, but gave in immediately to the implied physical threat. Karen watched, fascinated.

"I promised I wouldn't say anything." His voice quivered and he rubbed his nose again.

"Smart of you to know when to cooperate. Now let's have the truth. When you say he left here, where did he go? One doesn't catch a bus in the middle of the ocean. . ."

"I believe he mentioned something about the crew's quarters."

Charles moved menacingly closer, the steward raised an objecting hand. "Okay, he asked me how he could get a bunk in the crew's quarters, and I arranged for him to stay with a friend of mine. Mr. Higginbotham said he's a lawyer for the seaman's union, and he's investigating an objection about living conditions on the *Royale.*" The man's shoulders relaxed a bit as he added, "He didn't want any of the Euro-American people to know about it. You're not one of them, are you?"

"No, no worry there. I just need to find Higginbotham, and you are going to take me to him."

"Now? I'm on duty."

"Right now." Turning to Karen, Charles said, "Please go to the room. I'll meet you there after this nice gentleman takes me to Bill Higginbotham." He took a firm grip on the steward's upper arm and said, "Now, if you please."

"Yes, dear, see you in Versailles." No flip remark this time, and Karen walked quickly out the door.

When Charles and the distraught steward reached the door marked "Crew Only" at the far end of the corridor, it opened to reveal an entirely different aspect of the *Royale's* decor, a sharp contrast to the plush public rooms. If the ship's architects had meant to entice the crew into spending their time working, rather than lingering in their own quarters, Charles figured they had succeeded admirably. These narrow, dimly lit gray corridors had a distinct antiseptic smell, and open doors revealed bunk beds in cubicles reminiscent of pullman berths in old passenger trains.

They crossed through a recreation room area strewn with magazines and filled ashtrays, past a communal shower area where a blonde Nordic beauty could be seen washing her hair in naked splendor, and rounded a corner where the steward stopped to knock on a closed door.

"You there, Andy?" he called, then opened the door to reveal two sailors snoring in their bunks, another sailor in the lower bunk opposite them.

"Who the hell is it?" A peevish voice spoke from under a gray wool blanket.

"It's me, Jim. Is that lawyer guy still around?"

Charles moved in and pulled the blanket from the voice's body. The black haired, astonished sailor spun out of the bunk and stood in his skivvies with black eyes glaring, and confronted Charles, "What the fuck do you think you're doing? Who the hell are you?"

Charles' long arm reached to grab the sailor by the back of his shirt, and holding him at arm's length, with his other hand he shoved the photograph into the sailor's face, saying, "Never mind who I am, just tell me if you've seen this man?"

"Yeah, that's the fellow Jim, here, brought over. We made a deal, him and me." A crooked front tooth gave him a slight lisp.

"What kind of deal?" Charles shifted his grip to a firm hold on the sailor's upper arm.

"Okay, okay. So the deal was, he gave me some very nice stuff, said he didn't need it any more. See, in the locker over there, his suitcase with a suit, couple of nice shirts, socks and stuff . . ."

"What did he get in exchange?" The hold tightened.

"All he wanted was my shirt and pants, and he wanted to know where the Chief keeps his keys."

"Where is he now?"

"Hell, man, I haven't seen him since he got into my clothes this afternoon. He left here about two o'clock."

"What did you tell him about the keys, and what would they fit?"

"I told him I didn't know how he could get the chief's keys, that sucker never lets his control very far from his pocket. But they're just regular keys, you know, like to the maintenance shop, supply lockers, the motor launches. Stuff like that. Why don't you ask the Chief? For crissakes, let go."

The sailor was getting angry, and began to wriggle against the pressure.

"Listen good, Andy, and you, too, Jim." Charles turned to include the puzzled steward in his warning. "This union lawyer you've been helping is a killer and a thief. So far, the Captain doesn't know anything about your part in this, but if I learn you are still protecting this man, you'll never work again. Have I made myself clear?"

They both withered and said in unison, "Yes sir, anything you say, sir." The sleeping duo in the other bunks hadn't moved a muscle.

* * *

When Charles opened the door of V109, Karen was sound asleep, music still playing and all lights blazing. Her rhythmic breathing changed slightly when the door closed. He studied the face on the pillow, noticing for the first time the smooth arc of the eyebrows and the sweep of dark lashes. Almost forgotten was the white envelope he'd picked off the floor as he entered.

One of the eyelids opened and a soft voice muttered, "That's your Dear John letter. I think the jig is up. I got mine when I stopped by my room to get this sexy black nightgown which nobody's seen anyway." Karen opened the other eye and raised herself from the covers, displaying the upper part of her torso.

"I love it," he said, slitting the envelope to remove the single sheet of paper.

"Did you find Higginbotham? What? You love your letter from the Captain?" Karen wasn't fully awake.

"No, the nightgown. I haven't found Higginbotham yet, and this letter from the Captain is okay; I've been thinking about getting him to help."

"Doesn't your letter read like mine? Something like, 'Imperative you be available for a meeting in my quarters at 10:00 a.m. to meet with New York authorities before we dock.' That sounds more ominous than okay."

"Just leave things to Charlie, he won't let the big bad Captain bother the beautiful blonde in the sexy black nightgown."

"Thank you, my hero. Now, how about telling me what the hell's going on!"

* * *

Higginbotham watched from the shadows of the huge storage area directly under the kitchen, below the waterline of the ship. The wine steward's assistant struggled with a cart filled with partly consumed bottles of wine, all recorked and labeled with names, ready to be restored to their owners for consumption at lunch tomorrow, the last meal of the voyage. The slight young man was obviously taking special care of a precious cargo, but his cart was wide and the aisle was narrow.

Bracing the cart against a door and using a key fished from his apron pocket, the young man swung wide a second door to reveal an enormous wine cellar, stark white and immaculate, bottles by the thousands on the wooden racks, and also lined up in rows of wire cages.

Cradling as many bottles as he could safely carry, the assistant entered the cool compartment. Higginbotham drew close enough to see inside the area, and was surprised to find it was actually four sections connected inside by aisles, each section accessible by a separate door, and each full of bottles. The assistant placed his load on a rack at the rear of the cellar close to a desk back there, then came out for a second armful.

When the careful young man headed back into the cellar, whistling cheerfully with a second load, Higginbotham slipped inside the door and was safely hidden behind the racks in the fourth compartment before it was time for the third and last load.

CHAPTER 23

Friday Morning, June 19

Charles knew he'd have to get an early start if he wanted to search the crew's quarters before the Captain's cryptic command performance. Asking for help was a possibility, but only as a last resort. It would require far too many explanations.

When the beeping alarm jolted Karen to reality at 6:00 a.m., she found herself locked in a tangle of arms and legs and smothered with sleepy kisses. She came up for air and said accusingly, "You set the fucking alarm clock!"

"Crude, but well put, my dear," answered her determined lover, responding to the urgency of his desire and delaying his search.

Later, arms still locked behind his neck, Karen asked sleepily, "Why is Griman's cousin so vicious? Is money the key to the whole motive?"

"Karen, that's it!"

"You mean I've finally given you some help? You just thought about the motive?"

"No, lovely helper, not motive. The key word is key. Which key did he want? And did he get it from the Chief? I've got to get going!" He jumped out of bed.

"You mean you're leaving me just like that? You bum!"

"Meet you in the Captain's quarters at 10:00 if I'm not back here sooner." As he hurried into his clothes, Charles recalled the sailor's words, "just the regular keys, maintenance shop, supply lockers, motor launches . . ."

Forget the supply lockers, and the idea of hiding in the motor launches was too trite and obvious. Where the hell was the maintenance shop? That steward will have to help, Charles decided, and he set off for the Provence Deck.

The steward still felt guilty about protecting a murderer, and he led the way with no protest to the maintenance shop deep in the bowels of the ship. Finally climbing down a metal ladder, Charles and the contrite steward reached a door marked, "Authorized Personnel Only."

"You will get me in, and tell them I am a company inspector," Charles ordered.

"Yes, sir," he responded meekly. As soon as the door was opened by an elderly grease stained sailor wiping his hands on an oil soaked rag, the steward said only. "Company inspector wants to look around."

"Come in, young man, what can I do for you? I usually get advance notice of an inspection." The gray haired mechanic looked almost eager for companionship.

"Seems a new lathe was ordered for the shop here, to be installed after we dock in New York. I didn't want to worry you too soon, but the company records show the lathe to be too new for replacement."

Charles had taxed his ingenuity for naught, the maintenance shop was too compact and carefully manned for any kind of concealment. As he retraced his steps to the upper decks alone, the steward disappeared as soon as possible. Charles laughed to himself ruefully. At least they did have a brand new lathe.

* * *

Captain Soderberg cut the *Royale's* engine speed as the early light of day illuminated the distant shoreline dimly over the choppy seas. They had been favored by a strong following breeze, and the ship's latitude reading told him they would arrive too early at the pilot boat pick up point if he didn't cut back to about twelve knots. The slower speed would make the motion of the ship more noticeable, but it was too late to change the time of the scheduled docking procedures.

Bill Higginbotham was awakened from fitful sleep on the rug by the little desk in the wine cellar. His body reacted to the ship's change of speed, and he was suddenly aware that time was closing in on him. A long night alone in the dark studying his possibilities had convinced him that, if he wanted to keep his prize package, the only safe way off the ship would be to escape on the pilot boat.

That episode on the bridge had been a good warning of what would happen if he had to pass through any kind of detection device, and yesterday he heard two of the sailors talking about the new policy requiring all ship's personnel to go through security. So his original plan to leave the ship with the crew wouldn't work.

He checked for his little white plastic box and found it safely under the desk where he'd kept it hidden while he slept. Last night he just carried it in his hand, but it would have to be stowed safely today. The borrowed sailor's dungarees were so small, nothing could possibly fit in the pockets, and the shirt's breast pocket was too small, too. With care he could wedge the box into his waistband and let his shirt hang out to cover it.

Luckily, the wine cellar doors were equipped with safety locks operable from the inside, and with the studied nonchalance of an ordinary seaman, Higginbotham made his way from the wine cellar through a cargo area on D Deck to a large watertight door just above the water line directly below the bridge.

Two sailors were uncoiling a number of lines which would secure the pilot launch for its brief connection to the *Royale*, and a ladder had been placed by the hatch door. One of the sailors spied Higginbotham and called out in English, "Lend us a hand here, sailor," pointing to the large locking wheel on the heavy steel door. "Time to open up. Give it some turns, man."

Higginbotham strained at the slippery handle. By hanging onto the wheel with his full body weight he moved it a fraction, then it spun so rapidly it nearly knocked him over.

The sailor eyed Higginbotham suspiciously and said, "What happened, mate, did you get too close to the wine last night?"

"How did you know?" Bill Higginbotham retorted.

* * *

It was well after 9:00 a.m. by the time Charles made his way to the Sports Deck, the highest deck on the *Royale*, where a paddle tennis court, golf mats with clubs, buckets of balls and a hitting net, work out bars, ping pong tables, and shuffle board equipment were available to ease the tensions of athletes cooped up on a long sea voyage. From here it was possible to look down on the life boats and launches suspended from their davits above the Boat deck.

Finally out of ideas, Charles made his way around the perimeter of the deck, inspecting the tightly laced canvas coverings of all the lifeboats. The two motor launches would be easier to hide in, because they did not have canvas covers. But they were hung close to the ship, and any activity in either of them would not only be observed, but looked on as very suspicious. All seemed tightly secure and undisturbed.

A small pilot boat sturdily churning through the choppy waves toward their starboard side told Charles his time was running out. He leaned on the rail reluctantly, knowing the arrival of the pilot meant the last leg of the journey. The early rising passengers crowded the rails on the decks below, all watching with fascination as the small boat, pitching and bobbing, approached the side of the *Royale* under the door near the water line. It gaped open in readiness to welcome the specialist who would guide them safely to port.

A ladder had been suspended to receive the visitor, and, as Charles watched, not one man, but two, climbed up to the open door, swinging precariously as the ladder described a frightening arc with the sway of the ship. Hands extended to help bring in the second man with a small briefcase on his wrist.

Suddenly a skinny sailor was making his way rapidly down the ladder. Charles caught a good look at his face, and startled by instant recognition, he yelled, "Bill Higginbotham, wait one damned minute!" Higginbotham looked up, then scampered more rapidly down the rungs of the swaying ladder.

Charles' foot had been resting against a red wooden disc, part of an abandoned shuffleboard game. Instantly, not thinking, with one rapid swing of his long arm, he picked up the disc and flung it at the fleeing sailor. The heavy object narrowly missed Higginbotham's head, but it did deliver a sharp blow to his right shoulder, then glanced off his hand.

Caught in mid step, the descending foot had not yet found a secure place on the next rung, and when the hand lost its grip, the sailor-suited figure dropped into the frothy waters below.

"Man overboard!" cried the chorus of passengers at the rail, who watched horrified as the figure flailed, perilously close to being crushed between the steel hull of the *Royale* and the churning engines of the departing pilot boat.

The combined voices gave enough volume to the cry to attract the skipper's attention, and slowly the pilot boat circled back until a line could be thrown to the man bobbing below in the sloshing water.

A seaman reached over the side of the low lying vessel and grabbed Higginbotham to haul him over the rubber fender. His arms were extended up, stretched by the pulling, bearing his full weight. A little white box slipped from under his loose shirt. It fell into the choppy water, swirled around in the boat's prop wash, then sank.

"Oh shit! There it goes!" Charles had no doubt he had just watched Marie Curie's treasure slip beneath the ocean waves.

Charles curbed his initial urge to dive in. Instead he made a headlong dash for the bow and, ignoring the small wooden sign saying "No Admittance," he ran down the steps into the navigation bridge and arrived there just as the Captain and the newly arrived pilot entered from the other direction.

"Captain, you have to stop that launch. The sailor they just rescued is a murderer!" Charles was breathless and distressed.

"What the hell are you talking about, and what are you doing here?" The Captain was angry, and he and the pilot looked at Charles as if he were a lunatic.

"I'm Charles Holden, and that man they just rescued is not a sailor, he's just dressed like one. He's really a dangerous criminal. Please, signal that pilot boat to bring him back . . ." He had regained his composure, and sounded more convincing.

"If he's right, Captain, my assistant is in danger. I think you should do as he suggests. Besides, no stranger is supposed to be aboard a pilot boat."

"Are you the Holden who's supposed to be in my quarters for a meeting this morning?" the Captain persisted.

"Yes, sir, and I promise I can give you a full explanation at that time, but I beg you, act now."

"Very well." Reluctantly the Captain consulted with his officers, giving the orders to radio the little boat, and to ready the crew for receiving the man.

While the Captain talked, Charles turned to the pilot and said, "Do you know the exact coordinates of the spot where the ships meet the pilot boats?"

"Of course, we don't vary much from 40.27 north latitude and 73.55 west longitude. Why do you ask?"

"No more talking, Holden, time for you to leave. We have work to do. Now get back to your side of the chain, and I'll see you in my quarters at ten o'clock." Captain Soderberg was clearly strained to the limit.

"Yes, sir. Thank you, sir. I'm leaving right now."

* * *

Karen didn't want to admit to herself she was frightened by Charles' long absence. She had packed his toilet kit and few overnight things, although he'd been so neatly organized it only took a minute. The photo of herself, taken when she came on board, was tucked into a pocket of his shaving kit. Feeling a bit like a snoop, she couldn't resist studying it critically, and she took it from the bathroom to the couch to take a better look. She remembered the polaroid photo June Hopkins had taken of the two of them, and decided to compare them. After a frantic moment or two, rummaging in her now bulging purse, she found the photo safe in an inside zipper pocket, and put the two pictures side by side, to examine.

Charles was one handsome, photogenic man, and the blonde in June's photo was an improvement over that babe in the picture the ship's photographer took. Studying the details in June's picture, Karen suddenly shivered with fear. There, calmly eating in the background just two tables behind her chair, was Higginbotham. He was watching us all the time, knows all about Charles, she thought, and she prayed again for Charles' safety.

Not daring to leave the room to go to breakfast, she'd ordered coffee and rolls, and now, as she waited for the tray to arrive, she toweled her hair, watched the sea and wondered at her commitment to this crazy guy who spends his life running full tilt into danger.

The buzzer interrupted her thoughts, and she clutched her terrycloth robe tightly around her to open the door. Instead of the steward, there stood Charles, intercepted breakfast tray in hand.

"Room service," he smiled, leaning over to kiss her.

"Okay, you're okay . . ."

"Yeah, I'm okay, but you don't have much time for this breakfast now, we're due at the Captain's quarters in a few minutes."

"Do we really have to go to that meeting?"

"Now more than ever. Why don't I pour you some coffee while you get dressed?"

"I'll be ready on time, I promise." She shook her golden curls and dropped the robe to the floor as Charles, distracted by the view, spilled coffee all over the tray. "You haven't told me, did you find Higginwhatsis, and do you have the superconductor?"

"Get some clothes on, you're driving me crazy."

"You didn't get it, did you?" she guessed, zipping her skirt and buttoning her blouse. "I can't believe that ugly jerk of a lawyer outsmarted you, Charles. Is it over? Have you given up the long hunt?" Her brown eyes almost pleaded.

"You're right, it's over. That ugly jerk, as you called him, dropped the stuff in the ocean!"

"Oh," she said in dismay, "what an absolute bummer! I'm so sorry —"

He patted her on the fanny and headed her toward the door. "Don't worry, you and I are going to be just fine."

* * *

Frank Griman sat alone at the fine-grained rosewood oval conference table, nervous and impatient. The masculine room, in colors of the sea with many wood and brass accents, was bathed in a rosy glow of florescent light, but there were no windows, and Frank knew they should soon pass by the Statue of Liberty on their way up the Hudson River. A television set on the opposite wall displayed the view from the ship's bow, but the picture only showed a dim view of the distant city skyline.

The captain's orderly, white jacketed and crisply efficient, silently placed a cup and saucer at Frank's elbow. Holding aloft a handsome silver coffee pot, he raised his eyebrows to inquire if Frank wanted the cup filled. Silent also, Frank tapped his fingers in agreement.

The door opened, and Captain Soderberg ushered in a stocky, weatherbeaten man in khaki uniform, followed by a younger officer in *Royale's* uniform.

"Good morning, Mr. Griman. I'm happy to see you looking so well," said the Captain. "This is U.S. Marshall Monson, who has come aboard to interview you about the unfortunate attack." He waited as the two men exchanged a tentative hand shake. "And this is First Officer Mr. Ingvolsted; I believe you met him in the hospital."

Frank thought the young man looked familiar, but maybe it was just the uniform. He said nothing as they, too, shook hands.

"I must return to the bridge, but, Ingvolsted, you be sure to let me know when Holden and the Bright woman arrive."

"Will you want me to replace you on the bridge at that time, sir?" the first officer asked.

"I'll let you know." The Captain bounded up the spiral staircase at the far end of the room.

The marshall began in a deep husky voice, "Mr. Griman, as a U.S. Marshall, I am here to protect your interests as a citizen, but first I must ask, did you do anything to provoke the attack from that foreigner who was shot?"

"I resent your insinuations," Frank answered indignantly. "I had no knowledge of that fellow, so how could I have done anything to provoke him? I haven't the slightest idea why he should have tried to kill a perfect stranger."

"But Mr. Griman," the astonished young officer jumped in, "I'm certain you told me this fellow Ivan was a Soviet agent who had murdered your wife, and was now after you."

"I must have been out of my head, sir, probably because of the poison. My poor wife died of a sudden heart attack in Paris." Frank was feeling bolder now.

"Very well, Mr. Griman. Now perhaps you can tell us about these friends of yours, Charles Holden and Karen Bright. I understand you tried to warn them about this man Ivan Denker?" The marshall asked calmly, ignoring the tension between the two.

"They're just some people I know from New York City. I don't recall warning them. Like I said, the poison must have made me a bit goofy."

The marshall was extracting an official looking paper from his briefcase when the orderly answered the knock on the door. Charles and Karen came into the room and introduced themselves as the First Officer hurried to the wall telephone.

"Put Holden on the phone, Ingvolsted," the Captain demanded, loud enough to be heard across the room.

Without a word, Charles picked up the receiver. "I'm here, Captain."

"We have this fellow now, Mr. Holden. He says he knows nothing about any murders, that he was jumping on the pilot launch to win a bet with another passenger. He claims to be a lawyer and is threatening to sue the Euro-American lines for false charges."

"That's a lie, sir, and it should be easy enough to prove. Just try to find the other half of the bet. He's a lawyer, true, from New York City, where his victim was a man named Albert Winch. You must place him under arrest."

"I told you before, Holden, you don't tell me what I have to do! Are you prepared to make these charges? If you are, the U.S. Marshall can hold this man. Frankly, I don't want to be involved. I have a ship to sail; that's enough."

"I'll not only make the charges, but I'll offer to help prove them, Captain. The murdered man was my friend." Charles was determined.

"I'll have him brought down to you immediately."

"Thank you, Captain, and happy landing!" Charles' smile, as he returned to the table, was contagious.

Down the spiral steps came a deck officer, leading a tall man wrapped in a *Royale* terrycloth robe, hair still damp and tousled, and wet shoes squishing as he walked. Guarding the rear was a seaman, at least two hundred pounds of solid determination. Higginbotham was shown to a chair where he sat and faced the room in defiance.

"You dumb bastard!" snarled Frank, shaking off Charles' restraining arm, "Fine family member you are."

"You know this man?" asked the bewildered Marshall.

"Know him? The big ass is my cousin!"

Charles interrupted, "Marshall Monson, I think you'd better let me clue you in. This man, Bill Higginbotham, not only killed a man in New York City, but he is also deeply involved in some serious criminal activities in France. And since this vessel flies a French flag . . ."

The Marshall nodded his head firmly, quickly catching the drift of Holden's implications. "Go on, Mr. Holden."

"As I understand it, the injured man who was involved in the attack on Mr. Griman, a French inspector named Dubois, would prefer to remain onboard and return to France. He would let the proper authorities in Paris deal with the killing of this Mr. Denker, who is also a European."

Charles paused to gauge the response to his words, and was glad to see he had Higginbotham's full attention. He went on, "If the French authorities involve Higginbotham, a U.S. citizen, in their investigations, the legal tangle might go on for years."

"I see what you're driving at, Mr. Holden. What about the Captain?" the Marshall asked.

"He's only too ready to be rid of the whole problem and turn the investigation of Ivan Denker's death over to France."

"Let's cut the bullshit and get done with it," Bill Higginbotham said as he stood up. "Take me in, Marshall, I'm ready."

Frank Griman and Karen looked at each other, jaws open in surprise, but Holden and the Marshall had expected the quick submission of Higginbotham.

"Thank you, Mr. Holden. If you will leave me your address, I'll take it from here, with the help of this fine seaman." Marshall Monson dismissed the meeting.

CHAPTER 24

New York City

Friday, June 19

"Let's go out on deck and see if we can say hello to the Statue of Liberty," Charles urged, leading the way from the Captain's quarters to the Promenade Deck. Karen followed close, but Frank Griman also stuck right with them.

They were lucky and found an empty spot on the rail where they could join the other passengers as the *Royale* sailed past the grand old lady who held her torch high in the morning sunlight. Karen blinked away a tear, swallowed the lump in her throat, and said, "I know how lucky I feel to be coming home safe, Charles, but please explain what that was all about just now, with Higginbotham?"

"Yeah, why did the jerk give up so quick?" joined in Griman. "Didn't seem like the fighting Marine I knew him to be."

"Well," answered Charles, "it's not too hard to understand. Higginbotham is a lawyer, you know, so he knows there's no capital punishment in New York state, and as a marine, he discovered a lot about criminal justice in other countries . . ."

"But he's heading for a murder trial, Charles," objected Karen, "and he didn't have anything to do with that attack on Griman and the shooting by Dubois."

"Ah, but when he found out the French authorities were going to investigate, he knew the trail would lead back to the murder on Quai de Bethune. He's no dummy, you know. He knew this Denker, or whoever he really is, was only after Griman because of the Curie letter."

"I was afraid to open an international can of worms, myself. That's why I denied saying I thought the Russians were responsible for the attack on Lisa and me," Griman said. "If I had been thinking clearly, I wouldn't have made any of those accusations when I was in the hospital, so I guess I really didn't lie when I said the poison made me talk goofy."

"I don't suppose the French authorities will ever be able to untangle those threads leading to the Soviet interference, or to Lisa's death, for that matter, Frank," Charles reassured him.

"I want to say goodbye to M. Dubois," Karen said. "Do we have time before we dock?"

"Time, and then some, my girl. It takes ages to get this big ship safely into her berth. I understand they're even going to serve lunch. And then it seems like forever before the emigration officials clear it so passengers can disembark. Let's go to the hospital right now."

"This is where I leave you, then. I've had my fill of that place, and I've said goodbye to M. Dubois. I guess I'll be seeing you again?" Frank looked hesitant, then he continued, "Do you think there's a chance you'll keep up the search for the superconductor?"

"Afraid you're out of luck, Frank. That cousin of yours had it, but he dropped it in the ocean when he was trying to get away. He managed to drown your hopes of glory."

"Somehow, I felt it might end this way. Guess I'll have to return to reality, but not until after the funeral. Can you imagine me trying to explain this story to Lisa's family?"

Karen was surprised at her feelings of sympathy for the lonely little man as he walked away from them.

* * *

The stewardess received no answer to her knock on the door of suite 32. She tried again, seriously this time.

"Go away!" finally answered a muffled voice.

"Sir, the people with yellow tags on their luggage must report to the Grande Lounge for the emigration authorities, and you have yellow tags."

"Later . . ."

"But, sir, everyone on the ship must report before any passenger may disembark in New York."

Philip was much too busy responding to the demanding undulations of Jane McKenzie's generous hips on the bed he had earmarked for Karen Bright.

Jane had come across the hall to his room with an open bottle of champagne, dressed for shore and bored with waiting. After two glasses of champagne, she suggested, "Look, Philip, there's still time. Why don't we put a little spice into this farewell party?"

"What's this farewell business, Jane? Do you have an entanglement in New York?"

"Not really, I just thought—well, you know how these shipboard romances are."

"I guess I'm learning," he said, unbuttoning her blouse and removing his black and white checkered trousers.

"I think this is one romance that should be continued," Jane said, helping with the trousers and sliding her hands down the inside of his white thigh to fondle his urgent hardness. "Do you have a job, or are you just a playboy?" Her yellow skirt joined the checkered pants.

"I'm just a poor working boy. I went to France with a letter that could have made me rich, but then I chickened out. I need someone to . . ." Her mouth covered his, her exploring tongue ending the words.

When she finally did release him, she said, "Don't worry, Philip, I've got enough money for both of us . . ."

* * *

Marcel Dubois, still in his hospital bed, sat up when the nurse drew back the curtains of his cubicle.

"A couple of people out here would like to visit you. Do you feel well enough to see them?"

"I've been expecting them, nurse. Will you please bring a couple of chairs?" Dubois was very hoarse, but his words could be understood.

Charles approached the bed, Karen close behind him, and all three started speaking at once. Recognizing Dubois' speech difficulty, the couple subsided immediately in order to listen.

"You knew we were both after the same thing?" Dubois asked hoarsely.

"Not until just lately, Monsieur. I'm sorry you got in the way of that assassin's knife. He never was anything but a secondary character in the story. Our culprit turned out to be Frank Griman's lawyer cousin, Bill Higginbotham." Charles wasn't sure what Dubois had learned of this morning's action.

"Please, Miss Bright, will you open my briefcase here on the bottom of this nightstand?" Karen was quick to oblige. "Now, if you don't mind, will you bring me the papers in the upper left pocket?"

"Are you sure we aren't tiring you? Karen and I just stopped by to wish you a speedy recovery." Charles didn't want their visit to harm the gentleman.

"No, don't leave. Tell me, please, could this be the lawyer, alias Mr. Black?" Dubois handed Charles the artist's sketch Dr. Remy's description had produced.

"Look at this, Karen!"

"A very good likeness, I'd say," she agreed.

"So you found Mr. Black after all," mused Dubois, resting back on his pillow. "You know, my chief, Inspector Bodine, thought you were working with Black."

"Monsieur Dubois, how did you get into this situation, and how did you find out about the superconductor? Did Griman tell you?"

"No, not a word from him. We learned everything from the papers in your brief case. Leon photographed them, and even taped your conversation with Mr. Butler after Inspector Bodine did not believe your story about your interest in Madame Curie's apartment."

"Leon, of course. He was Bodine's man. And the lovely Christine. Is she also with the police?"

"No, Mr. Holden, she was just a fortunate coincidence who agreed to cooperate." He struggled up from the pillow to ask, "Did the lawyer have the superconductor? My mission was to return it to France, where it belongs, you realize!"

"It's nobody's property now, M. Dubois," Karen said softly. "Higginbotham dropped it into the sea when he tried to escape."

"Mon Dieu!" Dubois fell back exhausted, then he said in English:

"I beg your greatness not to give the law —
In other realms; but beaten, to withdraw."

"I beg your pardon?" Charles looked puzzled.

"Oh, just a quote from Dryden. I doubt if Inspector Bodine would have understood it, either. Good night, and goodbye, Mr. Holden, and charming Miss Bright. France will not give up the quest, you know. They will send a diving expedition."

"Goodbye, Monsieur Dubois, we wish you well. You have added much to our voyage." Karen brushed his forehead with her lips.

* * *

Just like going to the bank, I'm in the wrong line as usual, Karen lamented to herself, as she waited in the Grande Lounge with the other passengers holding red cards, to present her passport for clearance by the emigration officials. Two parallel lines had formed before the desk where two uniformed men sat peering at papers and wielding rubber stamps with heavy hands and stern faces. Ten people in the other line had moved forward while Karen remained fixed in one spot.

Finally her line moved, and when she reached the desk her passport was stamped so rapidly she didn't think the official even bothered to look at her picture. He waved her on impatiently, but to her surprise, he said quietly, "Welcome home."

Charles waited for her on the suite's outdoor veranda where he could watch the bustling activity on the pier. His color code, green, was the second one called, and he'd gone through the line earlier without a hitch. Then the yellow card people had waited, it seemed forever, because a couple of people from that group couldn't be located. Only then had the red group been summoned.

"Are you tempted to stay on board, give this cruising life a second chance, instead of going back to reality and facing up to Herman Butler's disappointment?" Karen tucked her arm through his and snuggled close.

"Some day we'll cruise again, Karen, but I don't have that many complaints about this trip." Charles put his arm around her shoulders. "After all, we did manage to spend most of our time together."

"Oh come on, you know what I mean." She studied his expression, "But you are looking a bit smug. Have I missed the third act while I stood in that interminable line?"

"Something like that. I managed to get into the library just before it was locked up, and I verified what I hoped was true. I can report to Butler that he does not have to be disappointed. We know where the superconductor is, and he can get it."

"We know it's down at the bottom of the ocean somewhere," Karen frowned. "We know from Dubois that France will try to claim it, say it belonged to the French people and came from French territory."

"They can try, Karen, but according to the United Nations Conference of 1982, 'Convention on the Law of the Sea,' article 77, paragraph 2, the rights of the coastal state (United States, in this case) over exploration of the continental shelf belong exclusively to said coastal state, unless said coastal state expressly gives consent for any other state to explore the continental shelf." His eyes twinkled as he read from a crumpled note in his hand and asked, "Does that explain it?"

"Yes, I understand the bit about jurisdiction, and all that, but are you sure the superconductor is on the continental shelf?"

"That's what I had to double check in the library. The pilot gave me the exact longitude and latitude, and I just had to locate it on the map. The stuff is well within the limits, and I'm sure Higginbotham packed it in waterproof wrappings. Butler can fly his trusty magnetometer over the site to pick up the exact spot. He'll probably get Uncle Sam to join in the dive, and they'll find it, you can be sure!"

"So you might say you've won, after all?"

"Yes, you might say that. I'm sorry about my friend Albert Winch, though. That's a loss I hadn't counted on." He hugged the slender girl tucked so trustingly close to his side, and said, "But my new lady love Karen, that's a gain I hadn't counted on."

"When we hear about Butler's success, I have a new, very dear friend in California named William Foester who deserves to hear the whole story. In fact, I think I told you about him, how he helped me in Berlin." She smiled, a bit embarrassed. "Oh, I forgot to tell you what I discovered in the picture . . ."

She was interrupted by a voice from the ship's intercom saying, "The ship has now been cleared. Passengers are free to disembark."

"I want to hear it all, my love, but now, let's go home!"

Watch for these titles by Seabar Publishing.

I'd Gladly Pay You Tuesday... *Election '92: Candidates and Issues.* By Richard Carlson. ISBN 1-56672-003-6 Trade Paperback First Edition. $13.95

Back To Baja, *Retracing the Erle Stanley Gardner Expeditions.* By Choral Pepper. ISBN 1-56672-002-8 Trade Paperback First Edition. $12.95

Did you enjoy *The Curie Conundrum?* Would you like to be informed of the availability of the next Charles Holden mystery by Donald & Jackie Rosenblatt? If so, send us your name, and we will send you a postcard upon the release of the next book. We maintain a database of readers who wish to be notified of the availability of our books. Indicate whether you are interested in a genre, an author, or all of our books. This does NOT obligate you to purchase the book.

Though you may order direct, you will save postage costs by purchasing our books from your local bookstore. Indicate your favorite store, and we will notify both you and the bookstore of the availability of each book.

Name: ______________________________

Address: ______________________________

City, State, Zip: ______________________________

Favorite bookstore: ______________________________

____

Interested in: ______________________________